BORDERS®

CLASSICS

WILLIAM SHAKESPEARE

Three Romantic Tragedies

BORDERS.

CLASSICS

Please direct editorial or sales inquiries to:
editorial@annarbormediagroup.com
sales@annarbormediagroup.com

This edition is published by
Borders Classics, an imprint of Borders Group, Inc.
by special arrangement with
The Ann Arbor Media Group, LLC
2500 South State Street, Ann Arbor, MI 48104

Dust jacket copy by John C. Keller, Jr.
Production team: Mae Barnard, Tina Budzinski, Alison Durham,
Lori Holland, Steven Moore, Kathie Radenbaugh, and Andrea Worthing

Printed and bound in the United States of America
by Edwards Brothers, Inc.

ISBN 1-58726-087-5

06 05 04 03   10 9 8 7 6 5 4 3 2 1

CONTENTS

ROMEO AND JULIET

Dramatis Personæ

Chorus
Escalus, Prince of Verona
Mercutio, kinsman to the Prince and friend to Romeo
Paris, a young count, kinsman to the Prince
Page to Count Paris
Montague, head of house at variance with Capulet household
Lady Montague, wife to Montague
Romeo, son to Montague
Benvolio, nephew to Montague, and friend to Romeo
Abraham, servant to Montague
Balthasar, servant to Romeo
Capulet, head of house at variance with Montague household
Lady Capulet, wife to Capulet
Juliet, daughter to Capulet
An Old Man, uncle to Capulet
Tybalt, nephew to Lady Capulet
Gregory, servant to Capulet
Sampson, servant to Capulet
Nurse to Juliet
Peter, servant to Juliet's Nurse
Friar Laurence, Franciscan
Friar John, Franciscan
An Apothecary
An Officer
Three Musicians
Citizens of Verona
Gentlemen and Gentlewomen of both houses
Maskers
Torchbearers
Pages
Guards
Watchmen
Servants and Attendants

Prologue

Enter Chorus

CHORUS
>Two households, both alike in dignity,
>>In fair Verona, where we lay our scene,
>
>From ancient grudge break to new mutiny,
>>Where civil blood makes civil hands unclean.
>
>From forth the fatal loins of these two foes
>>A pair of star-cross'd lovers take their life;
>
>Whose misadventur'd piteous overthrows
>>Doth with their death bury their parents' strife.
>
>The fearful passage of their death-mark'd love,
>>And the continuance of their parents' rage,
>
>Which, but their children's end, naught could remove,
>>Is now the two-hours' traffic of our stage;
>
>The which if you with patient ears attend,
>>What here shall miss, our toil shall strive to mend.

Exeunt

ACT I

SCENE I—Verona. A public place.
*Enter Sampson and Gregory (with swords and bucklers)
of the house of Capulet*

SAMPSON Gregory, on my word, we'll not carry coals.

GREGORY No, for then we should be colliers.

SAMPSON I mean, an we be in choler, we'll draw.

GREGORY Ay, while you live, draw your neck out of collar.

SAMPSON I strike quickly, being moved.

GREGORY But thou art not quickly moved to strike.

SAMPSON A dog of the house of Montague moves me.

GREGORY To move is to stir, and to be valiant is to tand. Therefore, if thou art moved, thou runn'st away.

SAMPSON A dog of that house shall move me to stand. I will take the wall of any man or maid of Montague's.

GREGORY That shows thee a weak slave; for the weakest goes to the wall.

SAMPSON 'Tis true; and therefore women, being the weaker vessels, are ever thrust to the wall. Therefore I will push Montague's men from the wall and thrust his maids to the wall.

GREGORY The quarrel is between our masters and us their men.

SAMPSON 'Tis all one. I will show myself a tyrant. When I have fought with the men, I will be cruel with the maids—I will cut off their heads.

GREGORY The heads of the maids?

SAMPSON Ay, the heads of the maids, or their maidenheads. Take it in what sense thou wilt.

GREGORY They must take it in sense that feel it.

SAMPSON Me they shall feel while I am able to stand; and 'tis known I am a pretty piece of flesh.

GREGORY 'Tis well thou art not fish; if thou hadst, thou hadst been Poor John. Draw thy tool! Here comes two of the house of Montagues.

Enter two other Servingmen [Abraham and Balthasar]

SAMPSON My naked weapon is out. Quarrel! I will back thee.

GREGORY How? turn thy back and run?

SAMPSON Fear me not.

GREGORY No, marry. I fear thee!

SAMPSON Let us take the law of our side; let them begin.

GREGORY I will frown as I pass by, and let them take it as they list.

SAMPSON Nay, as they dare. I will bite my thumb at them; which is disgrace to them, if they bear it.

ABRAHAM Do you bite your thumb at us, Sir?

SAMPSON I do bite my thumb, Sir.

ABRAHAM Do you bite your thumb at us, Sir?

SAMPSON *[aside to Gregory]* Is the law of our side if I say ay?

GREGORY *[aside to Sampson]* No.

SAMPSON No, Sir, I do not bite my thumb at you, Sir; but I bite my thumb, Sir.

GREGORY Do you quarrel, Sir?

ABRAHAM Quarrel, Sir? No, Sir.

SAMPSON But if you do, Sir, I am for you. I serve as good a man as you.

ABRAHAM No better.

SAMPSON Well, Sir.

Enter Benvolio

GREGORY *[aside to Sampson]* Say "better." Here comes one of my master's kinsmen.

SAMPSON Yes, better, Sir.

ABRAHAM You lie.

SAMPSON Draw, if you be men. Gregory, remember thy swashing blow.

They fight

BENVOLIO Part, fools! *[Beats down their swords]* Put up your swords. You know not what you do.

Enter Tybalt with sword drawn

TYBALT What, art thou drawn among these heartless hinds? Turn thee Benvolio! Look upon thy death.

BENVOLIO I do but keep the peace. Put up thy sword, Or manage it to part these men with me.

TYBALT What, drawn, and talk of peace? I hate the word As I hate hell, all Montagues, and thee. Have at thee, coward! *[They fight]*

Enter an officer, and three or four Citizens with clubs or partisans

OFFICER Clubs, bills, and partisans! Strike! beat them down!

CITIZENS   Down with the Capulets! Down with the Montagues!
             Enter old Capulet in his gown, and his Wife
CAPULET   What noise is this? Give me my long sword, ho!
CAPULET'S WIFE   A crutch, a crutch! Why call you for a sword?
             Enter Old Montague and his Wife
CAPULET   My sword, I say! Old Montague is come
   And flourishes his blade in spite of me.
MONTAGUE   Thou villain Capulet! —Hold me not, let me go.
MONTAGUE'S WIFE   Thou shalt not stir one foot to seek a foe.
             Enter Prince Escalus with his Train
ESCALUS   Rebellious subjects, enemies to peace,
   Profaners of this neighbour-stained steel.
   Will they not hear? What, ho! you men, you beasts,
   That quench the fire of your pernicious rage
   With purple fountains issuing from your veins!
   On pain of torture, from those bloody hands
   Throw your mistempered weapons to the ground
   And hear the sentence of your moved prince.
   Three civil brawls, bred of an airy word
   By thee, old Capulet, and Montague,
   Have thrice disturb'd the quiet of our streets
   And made Verona's ancient citizens
   Cast by their grave-beseeming ornaments
   To wield old partisans, in hands as old,
   Cank'red with peace, to part your cank'red hate.
   If ever you disturb our streets again,
   Your lives shall pay the forfeit of the peace.
   For this time all the rest depart away.
   You, Capulet, shall go along with me;
   And, Montague, come you this afternoon,
   To know our farther pleasure in this case,
   To old Freetown, our common judgment-place.
   Once more, on pain of death, all men depart.
          Exit all but Montague, his Wife, and Benvolio
MONTAGUE   Who set this ancient quarrel new abroach?
   Speak, nephew, were you by when it began?
BENVOLIO   Here were the servants of your adversary
   And yours, close fighting ere I did approach.
   I drew to part them. In the instant came
   The fiery Tybalt, with his sword prepar'd;

Which, as he breath'd defiance to my ears,
He swung about his head and cut the winds,
Who, nothing hurt withal, hiss'd him in scorn.
While we were interchanging thrusts and blows,
Came more and more, and fought on part and part,
Till the Prince came, who parted either part.

MONTAGUE'S WIFE   O where is Romeo? Saw you him today?
Right glad I am he was not at this fray.

BENVOLIO   Madam, an hour before the worshipp'd sun
Peer'd forth the golden window of the East,
A troubled mind drive me to walk abroad;
Where, underneath the grove of sycamore
That westward rooteth from the city's side,
So early walking did I see your son.
Towards him I made; but he was ware of me
And stole into the covert of the wood.
I, measuring his affections by my own,
Which then most sought where most might not be found,
Being one too many by my weary self,
Pursu'd my humour, not pursuing his,
And gladly shunn'd who gladly fled from me.

MONTAGUE   Many a morning hath he there been seen,
With tears augmenting the fresh morning's dew,
Adding to clouds more clouds with his deep sighs;
But all so soon as the all-cheering sun
Should in the farthest East begin to draw
The shady curtains from Aurora's bed,
Away from light steals home my heavy son
And private in his chamber pens himself,
Shuts up his windows, locks fair daylight out,
And makes himself an artificial night.
Black and portentous must this humour prove
Unless good counsel may the cause remove.

BENVOLIO   My noble uncle, do you know the cause?

MONTAGUE   I neither know it nor can learn of him

BENVOLIO   Have you importun'd him by any means?

MONTAGUE   Both by myself and many other friends;
But he, his own affections' counsellor,
Is to himself—I will not say how true—
But to himself so secret and so close,

So far from sounding and discovery,
As is the bud bit with an envious worm
Ere he can spread his sweet leaves to the air
Or dedicate his beauty to the sun.
Could we but learn from whence his sorrows grow,
We would as willingly give cure as know.

Enter Romeo

BENVOLIO   See, where he comes. So please you step aside,
I'll know his grievance, or be much denied.
MONTAGUE   I would thou wert so happy by thy stay
To hear true shrift. Come, madam, let's away.

Exit Montague and Wife

BENVOLIO   Good morrow, cousin.
ROMEO   Is the day so young?
BENVOLIO   But new struck nine.
ROMEO   Ay me! sad hours seem long.
Was that my father that went hence so fast?
BENVOLIO   It was. What sadness lengthens Romeo's hours?
ROMEO   Not having that which having makes them short.
BENVOLIO   In love?
ROMEO   Out—
BENVOLIO   Of love?
ROMEO   Out of her favour where I am in love.
BENVOLIO   Alas that love, so gentle in his view,
Should be so tyrannous and rough in proof!
ROMEO   Alas that love, whose view is muffled still,
Should without eyes see pathways to his will!
Where shall we dine? O me! What fray was here?
Yet tell me not, for I have heard it all.
Here's much to do with hate, but more with love.
Why then, O brawling love! O loving hate!
O anything, of nothing first create!
O heavy lightness! serious vanity!
Misshapen chaos of well-seeming forms!
Feather of lead, bright smoke, cold fire, sick health!
Still-waking sleep, that is not what it is!
This love feel I, that feel no love in this.
Dost thou not laugh?
BENVOLIO   No, coz, I rather weep.
ROMEO   Good heart, at what?

BENVOLIO   At thy good heart's oppression.

ROMEO   Why, such is love's transgression.
  Griefs of mine own lie heavy in my breast,
  Which thou wilt propagate, to have it prest
  With more of thine. This love that thou hast shown
  Doth add more grief to too much of mine own.
  Love is a smoke rais'd with the fume of sighs;
  Being purg'd, a fire sparkling in lovers' eyes;
  Being vex'd, a sea nourish'd with lovers' tears.
  What is it else? A madness most discreet,
  A choking gall, and a preserving sweet.
  Farewell, my coz.

BENVOLIO   Soft! I will go along,
  And if you leave me so, you do me wrong.

ROMEO   Tut! I have lost myself; I am not here.
  This is not Romeo, he's some other where.

BENVOLIO   Tell me in sadness, who is that you love?

ROMEO   What, shall I groan and tell thee?

BENVOLIO   Groan? Why, no; but sadly tell me who.

ROMEO   Bid a sick man in sadness make his will.
  A word ill urg'd to one that is so ill!
  In sadness, cousin, I do love a woman.

BENVOLIO   I aim'd so near when I suppos'd you lov'd.

ROMEO   A right good markman! And she's fair I love.

BENVOLIO   A right fair mark, fair coz, is soonest hit.

ROMEO   Well, in that hit you miss. She'll not be hit
  With Cupid's arrow. She hath Dian's wit,
  And, in strong proof of chastity well arm'd,
  From Love's weak childish bow she lives unharm'd.
  She will not stay the siege of loving terms,
  Nor bide th' encounter of assailing eyes,
  Nor ope her lap to saint-seducing gold.
  O, she is rich in beauty; only poor
  That, when she dies, with beauty dies her store.

BENVOLIO   Then she hath sworn that she will still live chaste?

ROMEO   She hath, and in that sparing makes huge waste;
  For beauty, starv'd with her severity,
  Cuts beauty off from all posterity.
  She is too fair, too wise, wisely too fair,
  To merit bliss by making me despair.

She hath forsworn to love, and in that vow
Do I live dead that live to tell it now.

BENVOLIO Be rul'd by me; forget to think of her.

ROMEO O, teach me how I should forget to think!

BENVOLIO By giving liberty unto thine eyes.
Examine other beauties.

ROMEO   'Tis the way
To call hers exquisite, in question more.
These happy masks that kiss fair ladies' brows,
Being black puts us in mind they hide the fair.
He that is strucken blind cannot forget
The precious treasure of his eyesight lost.
Show me a mistress that is passing fair,
What doth her beauty serve but as a note
Where I may read who pass'd that passing fair?
Farewell. Thou canst not teach me to forget.

BENVOLIO I'll pay that doctrine, or else die in debt.

Exeunt

SCENE II—A Street.
Enter Capulet, County Paris, and the Clown [Peter]

CAPULET But Montague is bound as well as I,
In penalty alike; and 'tis not hard, I think,
For men so old as we to keep the peace.

PARIS Of honourable reckoning are you both,
And pity 'tis you liv'd at odds so long.
But now, my lord, what say you to my suit?

CAPULET But saying o'er what I have said before;
My child is yet a stranger in the world,
She hath not seen the change of fourteen years;
Let two more summers wither in their pride
Ere we may think her ripe to be a bride.

PARIS Younger than she are happy mothers made.

CAPULET And too soon marr'd are those so early made.
The earth hath swallowed all my hopes but she;
She is the hopeful lady of my earth.
But woo her, gentle Paris, get her heart;
My will to her consent is but a part.
An she agree, within her scope of choice
Lies my consent and fair-according voice.

This night I hold an old accustom'd feast,
Whereto I have invited many a guest,
Such as I love; and you among the store,
One more, most welcome, makes my number more.
At my poor house look to behold this night
Earth-treading stars that make dark heaven light.
Such comfort as do lusty young men feel
When well-apparell'd April on the heel
Of limping Winter treads, even such delight
Among fresh female buds shall you this night
Inherit at my house. Hear all, all see,
And like her most whose merit most shall be;
Which, on more view of many, mine, being one,
May stand in number, though in reck'ning none.
Come, go with me. [*Giving Peter a paper*] Go, sirrah, trudge about
Through fair Verona; find those persons out
Whose names are written there, and to them say,
My house and welcome on their pleasure stay.

                                        Exit Capulet and Paris

SERVANT   Find them out whose names are written here? It is written
that the shoemaker should meddle with his yard and the tailor
with his last, the fisher with his pencil and the painter with his
nets; but I am sent to find those persons whose names are here
writ, and can never find what names the writing person hath here
writ. I must to the learned. In good time!

                        Enter Benvolio and Romeo

BENVOLIO   Tut, man, one fire burns out another's burning;
        One pain is lessoned by another's anguish;
        Turn giddy, and be holp by backward turning;
        One desperate grief cures with another's languish.
        Take thou some new infection to thy eye,
        And the rank poison of the old will die.
ROMEO   Your plantain leaf is excellent for that.
BENVOLIO   For what, I pray thee?
ROMEO   For your broken shin.
BENVOLIO   Why, Romeo, art thou mad?
ROMEO   Not mad, but bound more than a madman is;
        Shut up in prison, kept without my food,
        Whipp'd and tormented and—Good e'en, good fellow.
SERVANT   God gi' good e'en. I pray, Sir, can you read?

ROMEO   Ay, mine own fortune in my misery.

SERVANT   Perhaps you have learned it without book. But I pray, can
    you read anything you see?

ROMEO   Ay, If I know the letters and the language.

SERVANT   Ye say honestly. Rest you merry!

ROMEO   Stay, fellow; I can read. [*He reads*]
    "Signior Martino and his wife and daughters;
    County Anselmo and his beauteous sisters;
    The lady widow of Vitruvio;
    Signior Placentio and his lovely nieces;
    Mercutio and his brother Valentine;
    Mine uncle Capulet, his wife, and daughters;
    My fair niece Rosaline and Livia;
    Signior Valentio and his cousin Tybalt;
    Lucio and the lively Helena." [*Gives back the paper*]
    A fair assembly. Whither should they come?

SERVANT   Up.

ROMEO   Whither? To supper?

SERVANT   To our house.

ROMEO   Whose house?

SERVANT   My master's.

ROMEO   Indeed I should have ask'd thee that before.

SERVANT   Now I'll tell you without asking. My master is the great rich
    Capulet; and if you be not of the house of Montagues, I pray
    come and crush a cup of wine. Rest you merry!

Exit Servant

BENVOLIO   At this same ancient feast of Capulet's
    Sups the fair Rosaline whom thou so lov'st;
    With all the admired beauties of Verona.
    Go thither, and with unattainted eye
    Compare her face with some that I shall show,
    And I will make thee think thy swan a crow.

ROMEO   When the devout religion of mine eye
    Maintains such falsehood, then turn tears to fires;
    And these, who, often drown'd, could never die,
    Transparent heretics, be burnt for liars!
    One fairer than my love? The all-seeing sun
    Ne'er saw her match since first the world begun.

BENVOLIO   Tut! you saw her fair, none else being by,
    Herself pois'd with herself in either eye;

But in that crystal scales let there be weigh'd
Your lady's love against some other maid
That I will show you shining at this feast,
And she shall scant show well that now seems best.
ROMEO   I'll go along, no such sight to be shown,
But to rejoice in splendour of mine own.

Exeunt

SCENE III—Capulet's house.
Enter Capulet's Wife, and Nurse
WIFE   Nurse, where's my daughter? Call her forth to me.
NURSE   Now, by my maidenhead at twelve year old,
I bade her come. What, lamb! what ladybird!
God forbid! Where's this girl? What, Juliet!
Enter Juliet
JULIET   How now? Who calls?
NURSE   Your mother.
JULIET   Madam, I am here. What is your will?
WIFE   This is the matter—Nurse, give leave awhile,
We must talk in secret. Nurse, come back again;
I have rememb'red me, thou's hear our counsel.
Thou knowest my daughter's of a pretty age.
NURSE   Faith, I can tell her age unto an hour.
WIFE   She's not fourteen.
NURSE   I'll lay fourteen of my teeth—
And yet, to my teeth be it spoken, I have but four—
She is not fourteen. How long is it now
To Lammastide?
WIFE   A fortnight and odd days.
NURSE   Even or odd, of all days in the year,
Come Lammas Eve at night shall she be fourteen.
Susan and she (God rest all Christian souls!)
Were of an age. Well, Susan is with God;
She was too good for me. But, as I said,
On Lammas Eve at night shall she be fourteen;
That shall she, marry; I remember it well.
'Tis since the earthquake now eleven years;
And she was wean'd (I never shall forget it),
Of all the days of the year, upon that day;
For I had then laid wormwood to my dug,

Sitting in the sun under the dovehouse wall.
My lord and you were then at Mantua.
Nay, I do bear a brain. But, as I said,
When it did taste the wormwood on the nipple
Of my dug and felt it bitter, pretty fool,
To see it tetchy and fall out with the dug!
Shake, quoth the dovehouse! 'Twas no need, I trow,
To bid me trudge.
And since that time it is eleven years,
For then she could stand high-lone; nay, by th' rood,
She could have run and waddled all about;
For even the day before, she broke her brow;
And then my husband (God be with his soul!
A was a merry man) took up the child.
"Yea," quoth he, "dost thou fall upon thy face?
Thou wilt fall backward when thou hast more wit;
Wilt thou not, Jule?" and, by my holidam,
The pretty wretch left crying, and said "Ay."
To see now how a jest shall come about!
I warrant, an I should live a thousand yeas,
I never should forget it. "Wilt thou not, Jule?" quoth he,
And, pretty fool, it stinted, and said "Ay."

WIFE   Enough of this. I pray thee hold thy peace.

NURSE   Yes, madam. Yet I cannot choose but laugh
To think it should leave crying and say "Ay."
And yet, I warrant, it bad upon it brow
A bump as big as a young cock'rel's stone;
A perilous knock; and it cried bitterly.
"Yea," quoth my husband, "fall'st upon thy face?
Thou wilt fall backward when thou comest to age;
Wilt thou not, Jule?" It stinted, and said "Ay."

JULIET   And stint thou too, I pray thee, Nurse, say I.

NURSE   Peace, I have done. God mark thee to his grace!
Thou wast the prettiest babe that e'er I nurs'd.
An I might live to see thee married once,
I have my wish.

WIFE   Marry, that "marry" is the very theme
I came to talk of. Tell me, daughter Juliet,
How stands your disposition to be married?

JULIET   It is an honour that I dream not of.
NURSE   An honour? Were not I thine only Nurse,
    I would say thou hadst suck'd wisdom from thy teat.
WIFE   Well, think of marriage now. Younger than you,
    Here in Verona, ladies of esteem,
    Are made already mothers. By my count,
    I was your mother much upon these years
    That you are now a maid. Thus then in brief;
    The valiant Paris seeks you for his love.
NURSE   A man, young lady! lady, such a man
    As all the world—why he's a man of wax.
WIFE   Verona's summer hath not such a flower.
NURSE   Nay, he's a flower, in faith—a very flower.
WIFE   What say you? Can you love the gentleman?
    This night you shall behold him at our feast.
    Read o'er the volume of young Paris' face,
    And find delight writ there with beauty's pen;
    Examine every married lineament,
    And see how one another lends content;
    And what obscur'd in this fair volume lies
    Find written in the margent of his eyes,
    This precious book of love, this unbound lover,
    To beautify him only lacks a cover.
    The fish lives in the sea, and 'tis much pride
    For fair without the fair within to hide.
    That book in many's eyes doth share the glory,
    That in gold clasps locks in the golden story;
    So shall you share all that he doth possess,
    By having him making yourself no less.
NURSE   No less? Nay, bigger! Women grow by men.
WIFE   Speak briefly, can you like of Paris' love?
JULIET   I'll look to like, if looking liking move;
    But no more deep will I endart mine eye
    Than your consent gives strength to make it fly.

Enter Servingman

SERVANT   Madam, the guests are come, supper serv'd up, you call'd,
    my young lady ask'd for, the Nurse curs'd in the pantry, and ev-
    erything in extremity. I must hence to wait. I beseech you follow
    straight.

WIFE   We follow thee. [*Exit Servingman*] Juliet, the County stays.
NURSE   Go, girl, seek happy nights to happy days.

Exeunt

SCENE IV—A street.
Enter Romeo, Mercutio, Benvolio, with five or six other Maskers
ROMEO   What, shall this speech be spoke for our excuse?
   Or shall we on without apology?
BENVOLIO   The date is out of such prolixity.
   We'll have no Cupid hoodwink'd with a scarf,
   Bearing a Tartar's painted bow of lath,
   Scaring the ladies like a crowkeeper;
   Nor no without-book prologue, faintly spoke
   After the prompter, for our entrance;
   But, let them measure us by what they will,
   We'll measure them a measure, and be gone.
ROMEO   Give me a torch. I am not for this ambling.
   Being but heavy, I will bear the light.
MERCUTIO   Nay, gentle Romeo, we must have you dance.
ROMEO   Not I, believe me. You have dancing shoes
   With nimble soles; I have a soul of lead
   So stakes me to the ground I cannot move.
MERCUTIO   You are a lover. Borrow Cupid's wings
   And soar with them above a common bound.
ROMEO   I am too sore enpierced with his shaft
   To soar with his light feathers; and so bound
   I cannot bound a pitch above dull woe.
   Under love's heavy burthen do I sink.
MERCUTIO   And, to sink in it, should you burthen love—
   Too great oppression for a tender thing.
ROMEO   Is love a tender thing? It is too rough,
   Too rude, too boist'rous, and it pricks like thorn.
MERCUTIO   If love be rough with you, be rough with love.
   Prick love for pricking, and you beat love down.
   Give me a case to put my visage in. [*He puts on a mask*]
   A visor for a visor! What care I
   What curious eye doth quote deformity?
   Here are the beetle brows shall blush for me.
BENVOLIO   Come, knock and enter; and no sooner in
   But every man betake him to his legs.

ROMEO   A torch for me! Let wantons light of heart
 Tickle the senseless rushes with their heels;
 For I am proverb'd with a grandsire phrase,
 I'll be a candle-holder and look on;
 The game was ne'er so fair, and I am done.
MERCUTIO   Tut! dun's the mouse, the constable's own word!
 If thou art Dun, we'll draw thee from the mire
 Of this sir-reverence love, wherein thou stick'st
 Up to the ears. Come, we burn daylight, ho!
ROMEO   Nay, that's not so.
MERCUTIO   I mean, Sir, in delay
 We waste our lights in vain, like lamps by day.
 Take our good meaning, for our judgment sits
 Five times in that ere once in our five wits.
ROMEO   And we mean well, in going to this masque;
 But 'tis no wit to go.
MERCUTIO   Why, may one ask?
ROMEO   I dreamt a dream tonight.
MERCUTIO   And so did I.
ROMEO   Well, what was yours?
MERCUTIO   That dreamers often lie.
ROMEO   In bed asleep, while they do dream things true.
MERCUTIO   O, then I see Queen Mab hath been with you.
BENVOLIO   Queen Mab, what's she?
MERCUTIO   She is the fairies' midwife, and she comes
 In shape no bigger than an agate stone
 On the forefinger of an alderman,
 Drawn with a team of little atomi
 Athwart men's noses as they lie asleep;
 Her chariot is an empty hazelnut.
 Made by the joiner squirrel or old grub,
 Time out o' mind the fairies' coachmakers.
 Her wagon spokes made of long spinners' legs;
 The cover, of the wings of grasshoppers;
 Her traces, of the smallest spider's web;
 Her collars, of the moonshine's wat'ry beams;
 Her whip, of cricket's bone; the lash, of film;
 Her wagoner, a small grey-coated gnat,
 Not half so big as a round little worm
 Prick'd from the lazy finger of a maid.

And in this state she gallops night by night
Through lovers' brains, and then they dream of love;
O'er courtiers' knees, that dream on cursies straight;
O'er lawyers' fingers, who straight dream on fees;
O'er ladies' lips, who straight on kisses dream,
Which oft the angry Mab with blisters plagues,
Because their breaths with sweetmeats tainted are.
Sometime she gallops o'er a courtier's nose,
And then dreams he of smelling out a suit;
And sometime comes she with a tithe-pig's tail
Tickling a parson's nose as a lies asleep,
Then dreams he of another benefice.
Sometimes she driveth o'er a soldier's neck,
And then dreams he of cutting foreign throats,
Of breaches, ambuscadoes, Spanish blades,
Of healths five fathom deep; and then anon
Drums in his ear, at which he starts and wakes,
And being thus frighted, swears a prayer or two
And sleeps again. This is that very Mab
That plaits the manes of horses in the night
And bakes the elf-locks in foul sluttish hairs,
Which once untangled much misfortune bodes.
This is the hag, when maids lie on their backs,
That presses them and learns them first to bear,
Making them women of good carriage.
This is she—

ROMEO   Peace, peace, Mercutio, peace!
          Thou talk'st of nothing.

MERCUTIO   True, I talk of dreams;
          Which are the children of an idle brain,
          Begot of nothing but vain fantasy;
          Which is as thin of substance as the air,
          And more inconstant than the wind, who woos
          Even now the frozen bosom of the North
          And, being anger'd, puffs away from thence,
          Turning his face to the dew-dropping South.

BENVOLIO   This wind you talk of blows us from ourselves.
          Supper is done, and we shall come too late.

ROMEO   I fear, too early; for my mind misgives
          Some consequence, yet hanging in the stars,

Shall bitterly begin his fearful date
With this night's revels and expire the term
Of a despised life, clos'd in my breast,
By some vile forfeit of untimely death.
But He that hath the steerage of my course
Direct my sail! On, lusty gentlemen!

BENVOLIO   Strike, drum. [*They march about the stage*]

Exeunt

SCENE V—Capulet's house.
Servingmen come forth with napkins

FIRST SERVANT [*Peter*]   Where's Potpan, that he helps not to take away?
He shift a trencher! He scrape a trencher!

SECOND SERVANT   When good manners shall lie all in one or two
men's hands, and they unwash'd too, 'tis a foul thing.

FIRST SERVANT   Away with the joint stools, remove the court-cupboard,
look to the plate. Good thou, save me a piece of marzipan and, as
thou loves me, let the porter let in Susan Grindstone and
Nell. [*Exit Second Servingman*] Anthony, and Potpan!

[*Enter two more Servingmen*]

THIRD SERVANT   Ay, boy, ready.

FIRST SERVANT   You are look'd for and call'd for, ask'd for and sought
for, in the great chamber.

FOURTH SERVANT   We cannot be here and there too. Cheerly, boys!
Be brisk awhile, and the longer liver take all.

Exit Servingmen

*Enter the Maskers. Enter [with Servants] Capulet, his Wife,
Juliet, Tybalt, and all the Guests and Gentlewomen*

CAPULET   [*to Maskers*] Welcome, gentlemen! Ladies that have their toes
Unplagu'd with corns will have a bout with you.
Ah ha, my mistresses! Which of you all
Will now deny to dance? She that makes dainty,
She I'll swear hath corns. Am I come near ye now?
Welcome, gentlemen! I have seen the day
That I have worn a visor and could tell
A whispering tale in a fair lady's ear,
Such as would please. 'Tis gone, 'tis gone, 'tis gone!
You are welcome, gentlemen! Come, musicians, play.
A hall, a hall! Give room, and foot it, girls.

Music plays, and they dance. To Servingmen:
More light, you knaves! and turn the tables up,
And quench the fire, the room is grown too hot.
[*To his cousin*] Ah, sirrah, this unlook'd for sport comes well.
Nay, sit, nay, sit, good cousin Capulet,
For you and I are past our dancing days.
How long is't now since last yourself and I
Were in a mask?
COUSIN CAPULET   By'r Lady, thirty years.
CAPULET   What, man? 'Tis not so much, 'tis not so much!
'Tis since the nuptial of Lucentio,
Come Pentecost as quickly as it will,
Some five-and-twenty years, and then we mask'd.
COUSIN CAPULET   'Tis more, 'tis more! His son is elder, Sir;
His son is thirty.
CAPULET   Will you tell me that?
His son was but a ward two years ago.
ROMEO   [*to a Servingman*] What lady's that, which doth enrich the hand
Of yonder knight?
SERVANT   I know not, Sir.
ROMEO   O, she doth teach the torches to burn bright!
It seems she hangs upon the cheek of night
As a rich jewel in an Ethiope's ear—
Beauty too rich for use, for earth too dear!
So shows a snowy dove trooping with crows
As yonder lady o'er her fellows shows.
The measure done, I'll watch her place of stand
And, touching hers, make blessed my rude hand.
Did my heart love till now? Forswear it, sight!
For I ne'er saw true beauty till this night.
TYBALT   This, by his voice, should be a Montague.
[*To a page*] Fetch me my rapier, boy. What, dares the slave
Come hither, cover'd with an antic face,
To fleer and scorn at our solemnity?
Now, by the stock and honour of my kin,
To strike him dead I hold it not a sin.
CAPULET   Why, how now, kinsman? Wherefore storm you so?
TYBALT   Uncle, this is a Montague, our foe;
A villain, that is hither come in spite
To scorn at our solemnity this night.

CAPULET   Young Romeo is it?
TYBALT   'Tis he, that villain Romeo.
CAPULET   Content thee, gentle coz, let him alone.
    A bears him like a portly gentleman,
    And, to say truth, Verona brags of him
    To be a virtuous and well-govern'd youth.
    I would not for the wealth of all this town
    Here in my house do him disparagement.
    Therefore be patient, take no note of him.
    It is my will; the which if thou respect,
    Show a fair presence and put off these frowns,
    An ill-beseeming semblance for a feast.
TYBALT   It fits when such a villain is a guest.
    I'll not endure him.
CAPULET   He shall be endur'd.
    What, goodman boy? I say he shall. Go to!
    Am I the master here, or you? Go to!
    You'll not endure him? God shall mend my soul!
    You'll make a mutiny among my guests!
    You will set cock-a-hoop! You'll be the man!
TYBALT   Why, uncle, 'tis a shame.
CAPULET   Go to, go to!
    You are a saucy boy. Is't so, indeed?
    This trick may chance to scathe you. I know what.
    You must contrary me! Marry, 'tis time—[to guests]
    Well said, my hearts! You are a princox—go!
    Be quiet, or—More light, More light!—For shame!
    I'll make you quiet; what!—Cheerly, my hearts!
TYBALT   Patience perforce with wilful choler meeting
    Makes my flesh tremble in their different greeting.
    I will withdraw; but this intrusion shall,
    Now seeming sweet, convert to bitt'rest gall.

                                        Exit Tybalt

ROMEO   [to Juliet] If I profane with my unworthiest hand
    This holy shrine, the gentle fine is this;
    My lips, two blushing pilgrims, ready stand
    To smooth that rough touch with a tender kiss.
JULIET   Good pilgrim, you do wrong your hand too much,
    Which mannerly devotion shows in this;
    For saints have hands that pilgrims' hands do touch,

And palm to palm is holy palmers' kiss.

ROMEO   Have not saints lips, and holy palmers too?

JULIET   Ay, pilgrim, lips that they must use in prayer.

ROMEO   O, then, dear saint, let lips do what hands do!
   They pray; grant thou, lest faith turn to despair.

JULIET   Saints do not move, though grant for prayers' sake.

ROMEO   Then move not while my prayer's effect I take. [*He kisses her*]
   Thus from my lips, by thine my sin is purg'd.

JULIET   Then have my lips the sin that they have took.

ROMEO   Sin from my lips? O trespass sweetly urg'd!
   Give me my sin again. [*He kisses her*]

JULIET   You kiss by th' book.

NURSE   [*approching*] Madam, your mother craves a word with you.
                        Juliet retires

ROMEO   What is her mother?

NURSE   Marry, bachelor,
   Her mother is the lady of the house.
   And a good lady, and a wise and virtuous.
   I nurs'd her daughter that you talk'd withal.
   I tell you, he that can lay hold of her
   Shall have the chinks.

ROMEO   [*aside*]   Is she a Capulet?
   O dear account! my life is my foe's debt.

BENVOLIO   [*approaching*] Away, be gone; the sport is at the best.

ROMEO   Ay, so I fear; the more is my unrest.
                        The Maskers prepare to leave

CAPULET   Nay, gentlemen, prepare not to be gone;
   We have a trifling foolish banquet towards.
                        One whispers in his ear
   Is it e'en so? Why then, I thank you all.
   I thank you, honest gentlemen. Good night.
   More torches here! [*Exit Maskers*] Come on then, let's to bed.
   [*To his cousin*] Ah, sirrah, by my fay, it waxes late;
   I'll to my rest.
                        [*Exit all but Juliet and Nurse*]

JULIET   Come hither, Nurse. What is yon gentleman?

NURSE   The son and heir of old Tiberio.

JULIET   What's he that now is going out of door?

NURSE   Marry, that, I think, be young Petruchio.

JULIET   What's he that follows there, that would not dance?

NURSE   I know not.

JULIET   Go ask his name. [*Nurse goes*] If he be married,
         My grave is like to be my wedding bed.

NURSE   [*returning*] His name is Romeo, and a Montague,
         The only son of your great enemy.

JULIET   My only love, sprung from my only hate!
         Too early seen unknown, and known too late!
         Prodigious birth of love it is to me
         That I must love a loathed enemy.

NURSE   What's this? what's this?

JULIET   A rhyme I learnt even now
         Of one I danc'd withal. [*One calls within, "Juliet"*]

NURSE   Anon, anon!
         Come, let's away; the strangers all are gone.

                                                      Exeunt

                          Enter Chorus

CHORUS
         Now old desire doth in his deathbed lie,
            And young affection gapes to be his heir;
         That fair for which love groan'd for and would die,
            With tender Juliet match'd, is now not fair.
         Now Romeo is belov'd, and loves again,
            Alike bewitched by the charm of looks;
         But to his foe suppos'd he must complain,
            And she steal love's sweet bait from fearful hooks.
         Being held a foe, he may not have access
            To breathe such vows as lovers use to swear,
         And she as much in love, her means much less
            To meet her new beloved anywhere;
         But passion lends them power, time means, to meet,
            Temp'ring extremities with extreme sweet.

                                                      Exeunt

ACT II

Scene I—A lane by the wall of Capulet's orchard.

Enter Romeo alone

ROMEO   Can I go forward when my heart is here?
    Turn back, dull earth, and find thy centre out. [*Romeo retires*]
        Enter Benvolio with Mercutio

BENVOLIO   Romeo! my cousin Romeo! Romeo!

MERCUTIO   He is wise, and, on my life, hath stol'n him home to bed.

BENVOLIO   He ran this way, and leapt this orchard wall.
    Call, good Mercutio.

MERCUTIO   Nay, I'll conjure too.
    Romeo! Humours! Madman! Passion! Lover!
    Appear thou in the likeness of a sigh;
    Speak but one rhyme, and I am satisfied!
    Cry but "Ay me!" pronounce but "love" and "dove";
    Speak to my gossip Venus one fair word,
    One nickname for her purblind son and heir,
    Young Adam Cupid, he that shot so trim
    When King Cophetua lov'd the beggar maid!
    He heareth not, he stirreth not, he moveth not;
    The ape is dead, and I must conjure him.
    I conjure thee by Rosaline's bright eyes.
    By her high forehead and her scarlet lip,
    By her fine foot, straight leg, and quivering thigh,
    And the demesnes that there adjacent lie,
    That in thy likeness thou appear to us!

BENVOLIO   An if he hear thee, thou wilt anger him.

MERCUTIO   This cannot anger him. 'Twould anger him
    To raise a spirit in his mistress' circle
    Of some strange nature, letting it there stand
    Till she had laid it and conjur'd it down.
    That were some spite; my invocation

Is fair and honest: in his mistress' name,
I conjure only but to raise up him.

BENVOLIO   Come, he hath hid himself among these trees
To be consorted with the humorous night.
Blind is his love and best befits the dark.

MERCUTIO   If love be blind, love cannot hit the mark.
Now will he sit under a medlar tree
And wish his mistress were that kind of fruit
As maids call medlars when they laugh alone.
O, Romeo, that she were, O that she were
An open-arse, thou a pop'rin pear!
Romeo, good night. I'll to my truckle-bed;
This field-bed is too cold for me to sleep.
Come, shall we go?

BENVOLIO   Go then, for 'tis in vain
To seek him here that means not to be found.

Exeunt

SCENE II—Capulet's orchard.
Enter Romeo

ROMEO   He jests at scars that never felt a wound.
Enter Juliet above at a window
But soft! What light through yonder window breaks?
It is the East, and Juliet is the sun!
Arise, fair sun, and kill the envious moon,
Who is already sick and pale with grief
That thou her maid art far more fair than she.
Be not her maid, since she is envious.
Her vestal livery is but sick and green,
And none but fools do wear it. Cast it off.
It is my lady— O, it is my love!
O that she knew she were!
She speaks, yet she says nothing. What of that?
Her eye discourses; I will answer it.
I am too bold; 'tis not to me she speaks.
Two of the fairest stars in all the heaven,
Having some business, do entreat her eyes
To twinkle in their spheres till they return.
What if her eyes were there, they in her head?
The brightness of her cheek would shame those stars

As daylight doth a lamp; her eyes in heaven
Would through the airy region stream so bright
That birds would sing and think it were not night.
See how she leans her cheek upon her hand!
O that I were a glove upon that hand,
That I might touch that cheek!

JULIET   Ay me!

ROMEO   She speaks.
O, speak again, bright angel! for thou art
As glorious to this night, being o'er my head,
As is a winged messenger of heaven
Unto the white-upturned wond'ring eyes
Of mortals that fall back to gaze on him
When he bestrides the lazy-pacing clouds
And sails upon the bosom of the air.

JULIET   [to herself] O Romeo, Romeo!
Wherefore art thou Romeo?
Deny thy father and refuse thy name!
Or, if thou wilt not, be but sworn my love,
And I'll no longer be a Capulet.

ROMEO   [aside] Shall I hear more, or shall I speak at this?

JULIET   'Tis but thy name that is my enemy.
Thou art thyself, though not a Montague.
What's Montague? It is not hand, nor foot,
Nor arm, nor face, nor any other part
Belonging to a man. O, be some other name!
What's in a name? That which we call a rose
By any other name would smell as sweet.
So Romeo would, were he not Romeo call'd,
Retain that dear perfection which he owes
Without that title. Romeo, doff thy name;
And for that name, which is no part of thee,
Take all myself.

ROMEO   I take thee at thy word.
Call me but love, and I'll be new baptiz'd;
Henceforth I never will be Romeo.

JULIET   What man art thou that, thus bescreen'd in night,
So stumblest on my counsel?

ROMEO   By a name
I know not how to tell thee who I am.

My name, dear saint, is hateful to myself,
Because it is an enemy to thee.
Had I it written, I would tear the word.

JULIET   My ears have yet not drunk a hundred words
Of that tongue's utterance, yet I know the sound.
Art thou not Romeo, and a Montague?

ROMEO   Neither, fair saint, if either thee dislike.

JULIET   How cam'st thou hither, tell me, and wherefore?
The orchard walls are high and hard to climb,
And the place death, considering who thou art,
If any of my kinsmen find thee here.

ROMEO   With love's light wings did I o'erperch these walls;
For stony limits cannot hold love out,
And what love can do, that dares love attempt.
Therefore thy kinsmen are no let to me.

JULIET   If they do see thee, they will murder thee.

ROMEO   Alack, there lies more peril in thine eye
Than twenty of their swords! Look thou but sweet,
And I am proof against their enmity.

JULIET   I would not for the world they saw thee here.

ROMEO   I have night's cloak to hide me from their sight;
And but thou love me, let them find me here.
My life were better ended by their hate
Than death prorogued, wanting of thy love.

JULIET   By whose direction found'st thou out this place?

ROMEO   By love, that first did prompt me to enquire.
He lent me counsel, and I lent him eyes.
I am no pilot; yet, wert thou as far
As that vast shore wash'd with the farthest sea,
I would adventure for such merchandise.

JULIET   Thou knowest the mask of night is on my face;
Else would a maiden blush bepaint my cheek
For that which thou hast heard me speak tonight.
Fain would I dwell on form—fain, fain deny
What I have spoke; but farewell compliment!
Dost thou love me? I know thou wilt say "Ay";
And I will take thy word. Yet, if thou swear'st,
Thou mayst prove false. At lovers' perjuries,
They say Jove laughs. O gentle Romeo,
If thou dost love, pronounce it faithfully.

Or if thou thinkest I am too quickly won,
I'll frown, and be perverse, and say thee nay,
So thou wilt woo; but else, not for the world.
In truth, fair Montague, I am too fond,
And therefore thou mayst think my haviour light;
But trust me, gentleman, I'll prove more true
Than those that have more cunning to be strange.
I should have been more strange, I must confess,
But that thou overheard'st, ere I was ware,
My true-love passion. Therefore pardon me,
And not impute this yielding to light love,
Which the dark night hath so discovered.

ROMEO   Lady, by yonder blessed moon I swear,
That tips with silver all these fruit-tree tops—

JULIET   O, swear not by the moon, th' inconstant moon,
That monthly changes in her circled orb,
Lest that thy love prove likewise variable.

ROMEO   What shall I swear by?

JULIET   Do not swear at all;
Or if thou wilt, swear by thy gracious self,
Which is the god of my idolatry,
And I'll believe thee.

ROMEO   If my heart's dear love—

JULIET   Well, do not swear. Although I joy in thee,
I have no joy of this contract tonight.
It is too rash, too unadvis'd, too sudden;
Too like the lightning, which doth cease to be
Ere one can say "It lightens." Sweet, good night!
This bud of love, by summer's ripening breath,
May prove a beauteous flow'r when next we meet.
Good night, good night! As sweet repose and rest
Come to thy heart as that within my breast!

ROMEO   O, wilt thou leave me so unsatisfied?

JULIET   What satisfaction canst thou have tonight?

ROMEO   Th' exchange of thy love's faithful vow for mine.

JULIET   I gave thee mine before thou didst request it;
And yet I would it were to give again.

ROMEO   Would'st thou withdraw it? For what purpose, love?

JULIET   But to be frank and give it thee again.
And yet I wish but for the thing I have.

My bounty is as boundless as the sea,
My love as deep; the more I give to thee,
The more I have, for both are infinite. [*Nurse calls within*]
I hear some noise within. Dear love, adieu.
Anon, good Nurse! Sweet Montague, be true.
Stay but a little, I will come again.

Exit Juliet above

ROMEO   O blessed, blessed night! I am afeard,
Being in night, all this is but a dream,
Too flattering-sweet to be substantial.

Enter Juliet above

JULIET   Three words, dear Romeo, and good night indeed.
If that thy bent of love be honourable,
Thy purpose marriage, send me word tomorrow,
By one that I'll procure to come to thee,
Where and what time thou wilt perform the rite;
And all my fortunes at thy foot I'll lay
And follow thee my lord throughout the world.
NURSE   [*within*] Madam!
JULIET   I come, anon. —But if thou meanest not well,
I do beseech thee—
NURSE   [*within*] Madam!
JULIET   By-and-by I come.
To cease thy suit and leave me to my grief.
Tomorrow will I send.
ROMEO   So thrive my soul—
JULIET   A thousand times good night!

Exit Juliet above

ROMEO   A thousand times the worse, to want thy light!
Love goes toward love as schoolboys from their books;
But love from love, towards school with heavy looks.

Enter Juliet [above] again

JULIET   Hist! Romeo, hist! O for a falconer's voice,
To lure this tassel-gentle back again!
Bondage is hoarse and may not speak aloud;
Else would I tear the cave where Echo lies,
And make her airy tongue more hoarse than mine
With repetition of my Romeo's name. Romeo!
ROMEO   It is my soul that calls upon my name.
How silver-sweet sound lovers' tongues by night,

Like softest music to attending ears!
JULIET   Romeo!
ROMEO   My nyas?
JULIET   At what o'clock tomorrow
   Shall I send to thee?
ROMEO   By the hour of nine.
JULIET   I will not fail. 'Tis twenty years till then.—
   I have forgot why I did call thee back.
ROMEO   Let me stand here till thou remember it.
JULIET   I shall forget, to have thee still stand there,
   Rememb'ring how I love thy company.
ROMEO   And I'll still stay, to have thee still forget,
   Forgetting any other home but this.
JULIET   'Tis almost morning. I would have thee gone—
   And yet no farther than a wanton's bird,
   That lets it hop a little from her hand,
   Like a poor prisoner in his twisted gyves,
   And with a silk thread plucks it back again,
   So loving-jealous of his liberty.
ROMEO   I would I were thy bird.
JULIET   Sweet, so would I.
   Yet I should kill thee with much cherishing.
   Good night, good night! Parting is such sweet sorrow
   That I shall say good night till it be morrow.

Exit Juliet

ROMEO   Sleep dwell upon thine eyes, peace in thy breast!
   Would I were sleep and peace, so sweet to rest!
   Hence will I to my ghostly father's cell, his
   Help to crave and my dear hap to tell.

Exit

SCENE III—Friar Laurence's cell.
Enter Friar Laurence alone, with a basket
FRIAR   The grey-ey'd morn smiles on the frowning night,
   Check'ring the Eastern clouds with streaks of light;
   And flecked darkness like a drunkard reels
   From forth day's path and Titan's fiery wheels.
   Non, ere the sun advance his burning eye
   The day to cheer and night's dank dew to dry,
   I must up-fill this osier cage of ours

With baleful weeds and precious-juiced flowers.
The earth that's nature's mother is her tomb.
What is her burying grave, that is her womb;
And from her womb children of divers kind
We sucking on her natural bosom find;
Many for many virtues excellent,
None but for some, and yet all different.
O, mickle is the powerful grace that lies
In plants, herbs, stones, and their true qualities;
For naught so vile that on the earth doth live
But to the earth some special good doth give;
Nor aught so good but, strain'd from that fair use,
Revolts from true birth, stumbling on abuse.
Virtue itself turns vice, being misapplied,
And vice sometime's by action dignified. [*Enter Romeo*]
Within the infant rind of this small flower
Poison hath residence, and medicine power;
For this, being smelt, with that part cheers each part;
Being tasted, slays all senses with the heart.
Two such opposed kings encamp them still
In man as well as herbs—grace and rude will;
And where the worser is predominant,
Full soon the canker death eats up that plant.

ROMEO   Good morrow, father.
FRIAR   *Benedicite!*
What early tongue so sweet saluteth me?
Young son, it argues a distempered head
So soon to bid good morrow to thy bed.
Care keeps his watch in every old man's eye,
And where care lodges sleep will never lie;
But where unbruised youth with unstuff'd brain
Doth couch his limbs, there golden sleep doth reign.
Therefore thy earliness doth me assure
Thou art uprous'd with some distemp'rature;
Or if not so, then here I hit it right—
Our Romeo hath not been in bed tonight.

ROMEO   That last is true—the sweeter rest was mine.
FRIAR   God pardon sin! Wast thou with Rosaline?
ROMEO   With Rosaline, my ghostly father? No.
I have forgot that name, and that name's woe.

FRIAR   That's my good son! But where hast thou been then?

ROMEO   I'll tell thee ere thou ask it me again.
   I have been feasting with mine enemy,
   Where on a sudden one hath wounded me
   That's by me wounded. Both our remedies
   Within thy help and holy physic lies.
   I bear no hatred, blessed man, for, lo,
   My intercession likewise steads my foe.

FRIAR   Be plain, good son, and homely in thy drift
   Riddling confession finds but riddling shrift.

ROMEO   Then plainly know my heart's dear love is set
   On the fair daughter of rich Capulet;
   As mine on hers, so hers is set on mine,
   And all combin'd, save what thou must combine
   By holy marriage. When, and where, and how
   We met, we woo'd, and made exchange of vow,
   I'll tell thee as we pass; but this I pray,
   That thou consent to marry us today.

FRIAR   Holy Saint Francis! What a change is here!
   Is Rosaline, that thou didst love so dear,
   So soon forsaken? Young men's love then lies
   Not truly in their hearts, but in their eyes.
   Jesu Maria! What a deal of brine
   Hath wash'd thy sallow cheeks for Rosaline!
   How much salt water thrown away in waste,
   To season love, that of it doth not taste!
   The sun not yet thy sighs from heaven clears,
   Thy old groans ring yet in mine ancient ears.
   Lo, here upon thy cheek the stain doth sit
   Of an old tear that is not wash'd off yet.
   If e'er thou wast thyself, and these woes thine,
   Thou and these woes were all for Rosaline.
   And art thou chang'd? Pronounce this sentence then:
   Women may fall when there's no strength in men.

ROMEO   Thou chid'st me oft for loving Rosaline.

FRIAR   For doting, not for loving, pupil mine.

ROMEO   And bad'st me bury love.

FRIAR   Not in a grave
   To lay one in, another out to have.

ROMEO   I pray thee chide me not. Her I love now

Doth grace for grace and love for love allow.
The other did not so.

FRIAR   O, she knew well
Thy love did read by rote, that could not spell.
But come, young waverer, come go with me.
In one respect I'll thy assistant be;
For this alliance may so happy prove
To turn your households' rancour to pure love.

ROMEO   O, let us hence! I stand on sudden haste.

FRIAR   Wisely, and slow. They stumble that run fast.

                                   Exeunt

SCENE IV—A street.
Enter Benvolio and Mercutio

MERCUTIO   Where the devil should this Romeo be? Came he not home tonight?

BENVOLIO   Not to his father's. I spoke with his man.

MERCUTIO   Why, that same pale hard-hearted wench, that Rosaline, Torments him so that he will sure run mad.

BENVOLIO   Tybalt, the kinsman to old Capulet,
Hath sent a letter to his father's house.

MERCUTIO   A challenge, on my life.

BENVOLIO   Romeo will answer it.

MERCUTIO   Any man that can write may answer a letter.

BENVOLIO   Nay, he will answer the letter's master, how he dares, being dared.

MERCUTIO   Alas, poor Romeo, he is already dead! stabb'd with a white wench's black eye; shot through the ear with a love song; the very pin of his heart cleft with the blind bow-boy's butt-shaft; and is he a man to encounter Tybalt?

BENVOLIO   Why, what is Tybalt?

MERCUTIO   More than Prince of Cats. O, he's the courageous captain of compliments. He fights as you sing pricksong, keeps time, distance, and proportion; rests me his minim rest, one, two, and the third in your bosom! The very butcher of a silk button, a duellist, a duellist! a gentleman of the very first house, of the first and second cause. Ah, the immortal *passado*! The *punto reverso*! The *hai*.

BENVOLIO   The what?

MERCUTIO   The pox of such antic, lisping, affecting fantasticoes—these new tuners of accent! "By Jesu, a very good blade! a very tall man!

a very good whore!" Why, is not this a lamentable thing, grandsir,
that we should be thus afflicted with these strange flies, these
fashion-mongers, these pardona-mi's, who stand so much on the
new form that they cannot sit at ease on the old bench? O, their
bones, their bones!

Enter Romeo

BENVOLIO   Here comes Romeo! Here comes Romeo!

MERCUTIO   Without his roe, like a dried herring. O flesh, flesh, how
art thou fishified! Now is he for the numbers that Petrarch flowed
in. Laura, to his lady, was but a kitchen wench (marry, she had a
better love to berhyme her), Dido a dowdy, Cleopatra a gypsy,
Helen and Hero hildings and harlots, Thisbe a gray eye or so, but
not to the purpose. Signior Romeo, *bon jour*! There's a French
salutation to your French slop. You gave us the counterfeit fairly
last night.

ROMEO   Good morrow to you both. What counterfeit did I give you?

MERCUTIO   The slip, Sir, the slip. Can you not conceive?

ROMEO   Pardon, good Mercutio. My business was great, and in such
a case as mine a man may strain courtesy.

MERCUTIO   That's as much as to say, such a case as yours constrains a
man to bow in the hams.

ROMEO   Meaning, to curtsy.

MERCUTIO   Thou hast most kindly hit it.

ROMEO   A most courteous exposition.

MERCUTIO   Nay, I am the very pink of courtesy.

ROMEO   Pink for flower.

MERCUTIO   Right.

ROMEO   Why, then is my pump well-flower'd.

MERCUTIO   Well said! Follow me this jest now till thou hast worn out
thy pump, that, when the single sole of it is worn, the jest may
remain, after the wearing, solely singular.

ROMEO   O single-soled jest, solely singular for the singleness!

MERCUTIO   Come between us, good Benvolio! My wits faint.

ROMEO   Switch and spurs, switch and spurs! or I'll cry a match.

MERCUTIO   Nay, if our wits run the wild-goose chase, I am done; for
thou hast more of the wild goose in one of thy wits than I am sure
I have in my whole five. Was I with you there for the goose?

ROMEO   Thou wast never with me for anything when thou wast not
there for the goose.

MERCUTIO   I will bite thee by the ear for that jest.

ROMEO   Nay, good goose, bite not!

MERCUTIO   Thy wit is very bitter sweeting; it is a most sharp sauce.

ROMEO   And is it not, then, well serv'd in to a sweet goose?

MERCUTIO   O, here's a wit of cheveril, that stretches from an inch narrow to an ell broad!

ROMEO   I stretch it out for that word "broad," which, added to the goose, proves thee far and wide a broad goose.

MERCUTIO   Why, is not this better now than groaning for love? Now art thou sociable, now art thou Romeo; now art thou what thou art, by art as well as by nature. For this drivelling love is like a great natural that runs lolling up and down to hide his bauble in a hole.

BENVOLIO   Stop there, stop there!

MERCUTIO   Thou desirest me to stop in my tale against the hair.

BENVOLIO   Thou wouldst else have made thy tale large.

MERCUTIO   O, thou art deceiv'd! I would have made it short; for I was come to the whole depth of my tale, and meant indeed to occupy the argument no longer.

ROMEO   Here's goodly gear!

Enter Nurse and her man [Peter]

MERCUTIO   A sail, a sail!

BENVOLIO   Two, two! a shirt and a smock.

NURSE   Peter!

PETER   Anon!

NURSE   My fan, Peter.

MERCUTIO   Good Peter, to hide her face; for her fan's the fairer face of the two.

NURSE   God gi' good morrow, gentlemen.

MERCUTIO   God gi' good e'en, fair gentlewoman.

NURSE   Is it good e'en?

MERCUTIO   'Tis no less, I tell ye; for the bawdy hand of the dial is now upon the prick of noon.

NURSE   Out upon you! What a man are you!

ROMEO   One, gentlewoman, that God hath made for himself to mar.

NURSE   By my troth, it is well said. "For himself to mar," quoth a? Gentlemen, can any of you tell me where I may find the young Romeo?

ROMEO   I can tell you; but young Romeo will be older when you have found him than he was when you sought him. I am the youngest of that name, for fault of a worse.

NURSE   You say well.

MERCUTIO   Yea, is the worst well? Very well took, i' faith! wisely, wisely.

NURSE   If you be he, Sir, I desire some confidence with you.

BENVOLIO   She will endite him to some supper.

MERCUTIO   A bawd, a bawd, a bawd! So ho!

ROMEO   What hast thou found?

MERCUTIO   No hare, Sir; unless a hare, Sir, in a lenten pie, that is something stale and hoar ere it be spent. He walks by them and sings [*He sings*]

> An old hare hoar,
> And an old hare hoar,
>   Is very good meat in Lent;
> But a hare that is hoar
> Is too much for a score
>   When it hoars ere it be spent.

Romeo, will you come to your father's? We'll to dinner thither.

ROMEO   I will follow you.

MERCUTIO   Farewell, ancient lady. Farewell, [*singing*] "Lady, lady, lady."

Exit Mercutio, Benvolio

NURSE   Marry, farewell! I Pray you, Sir, what saucy merchant was this that was so full of his ropery?

ROMEO   A gentleman, Nurse, that loves to hear himself talk and will speak more in a minute than he will stand to in a month.

NURSE   An a speak anything against me, I'll take him down, an a were lustier than he is, and twenty such jacks; and if I cannot, I'll find those that shall. Scurvy knave! I am none of his flirt-gills; I am none of his skains-mates. [*to Peter*] And thou must stand by too, and suffer every knave to use me at his pleasure!

PETER   I saw no man use you at his pleasure. If I had, my weapon should quickly have been out, I warrant you. I dare draw as soon as another man, if I see occasion in a good quarrel, and the law on my side.

NURSE   Now, afore God, I am so vexed that every part about me quivers. Scurvy knave! Pray you, Sir, a word; and, as I told you, my young lady bid me enquire you out. What she bid me say, I will keep to myself; but first let me tell ye, if ye should lead her into a fool's paradise, as they say, it were a very gross kind of behaviour, as they say; for the gentlewoman is young; and therefore, if you should deal double with her, truly it were an ill thing to be off'red to any gentlewoman, and very weak dealing.

ROMEO   Nurse, commend me to thy lady and mistress. I protest unto thee—

NURSE   Good heart, and I faith I will tell her as much. Lord, Lord! she will be a joyful woman.

ROMEO   What wilt thou tell her, Nurse? Thou dost not mark me.

NURSE   I will tell her, Sir, that you do protest, which, as I take it, is a gentlemanlike offer.

ROMEO   Bid her devise
Some means to come to shrift this afternoon;
And there she shall at Friar Laurence' cell
Be shriv'd and married. Here is for thy pains.

NURSE   No, truly, Sir; not a penny.

ROMEO   Go to! I say you shall.

NURSE   This afternoon, Sir? Well, she shall be there.

ROMEO   And stay, good Nurse, behind the abbey wall.
Within this hour my man shall be with thee
And bring thee cords made like a tackled stair,
Which to the high topgallant of my joy
Must be my convoy in the secret night.
Farewell. Be trusty, and I'll quit thy pains.
Farewell. Commend me to thy mistress. [*Romeo starts to leave*]

NURSE   Now God in heaven bless thee! Hark you, Sir.

ROMEO   What say'st thou, my dear Nurse?

NURSE   Is your man secret? Did you ne'er hear say,
Two may keep counsel, putting one away?

ROMEO   I warrant thee my man's as true as steel.

NURSE   Well, Sir, my mistress is the sweetest lady. Lord, Lord! when 'twas a little prating thing—O, there is a noble man in town, one Paris, that would fain lay knife aboard; but she, good soul, had as lieve see a toad, a very toad, as see him. I anger her sometimes, and tell her that Paris is the properer man; but I'll warrant you, when I say so, she looks as pale as any clout in the versal world. Doth not rosemary and Romeo begin both with a letter?

ROMEO   Ay, Nurse; what of that? Both with an R.

NURSE   Ah, mocker! that's the dog's name. R is for the—No; I know it begins with some other letter; and she hath the prettiest sententious of it, of you and rosemary, that it would do you good to hear it.

ROMEO   Commend me to thy lady.
NURSE   Ay, a thousand times. [*Exit Romeo*] Peter!
PETER   Anon!
NURSE   Peter, take my fan, and go before, and apace.

Exeunt

SCENE V—Capulet's orchard.
Enter Juliet

JULIET   The clock struck nine when I did send the Nurse;
         In half an hour she promis'd to return.
         Perchance she cannot meet him. That's not so.
         O, she is lame! Love's heralds should be thoughts,
         Which ten times faster glide than the sun's beams
         Driving back shadows over low'ring hills.
         Therefore do nimble-pinion'd doves draw Love,
         And therefore hath the wind-swift Cupid wings.
         Now is the sun upon the highmost hill
         Of this day's journey, and from nine till twelve
         Is three long hours; yet she is not come.
         Had she affections and warm youthful blood,
         She would be as swift in motion as a ball;
         My words would bandy her to my sweet love,
         And his to me.
         But old folks, many feign as they were dead—
         Unwieldy, slow, heavy and pale as lead.
                    Enter Nurse and Peter

JULIET   O God, she comes! O honey Nurse, what news?
         Hast thou met with him? Send thy man away.
NURSE   Peter, stay at the gate.   [*Exit Peter*]
JULIET   Now, good sweet Nurse—O Lord, why look'st thou sad?
         Though news be sad, yet tell them merrily;
         If good, thou shamest the music of sweet news
         By playing it to me with so sour a face.
NURSE   I am aweary, give me leave awhile.
         Fie, how my bones ache! What a jaunce have I had!
JULIET   I would thou hadst my bones, and I thy news.
         Nay, come, I pray thee speak. Good, good Nurse, speak.
NURSE   Jesu, what haste! Can you not stay awhile?
         Do you not see that I am out of breath?
JULIET   How art thou out of breath when thou hast breath

To say to me that thou art out of breath?
The excuse that thou dost make in this delay
Is longer than the tale thou dost excuse.
Is thy news good or bad? Answer to that.
Say either, and I'll stay the circumstance.
Let me be satisfied, is't good or bad?

NURSE   Well, you have made a simple choice; you know not how to choose a man. Romeo? No, not he. Though his face be better than any man's, yet his leg excels all men's; and for a hand and a foot, and a body, though they be not to be talk'd on, yet they are past compare. He is not the flower of courtesy, but, I'll warrant him, as gentle as a lamb. Go thy ways, wench; serve God. What, have you din'd at home?

JULIET   No, no. But all this did I know before.
What says he of our marriage? What of that?

NURSE   Lord, how my head aches! What a head have I!
It beats as it would fall in twenty pieces.
My back o' t' other side, —ah, my back, my back!
Beshrew your heart for sending me about
To catch my death with jauncing up and down!

JULIET   I' faith, I am sorry that thou art not well.
Sweet, sweet, sweet Nurse, tell me, what says my love?

NURSE   Your love says, like an honest gentleman,
And a courteous, and a kind, and a handsome;
And, I warrant, a virtuous—where is your mother?

JULIET   Where is my mother? Why, she is within.
Where should she be? How oddly thou repliest!
"Your love says, like an honest gentleman,
'Where is your mother?'"

NURSE   O God's Lady dear!
Are you so hot? Marry come up, I trow.
Is this the poultice for my aching bones?
Henceforward do your messages yourself.

JULIET   Here's such a coil! Come, what says Romeo?

NURSE   Have you got leave to go to shrift today?

JULIET   I have.

NURSE   Then hie you hence to Friar Laurence' cell;
There stays a husband to make you a wife.
Now comes the wanton blood up in your cheeks;
They'll be in scarlet straight at any news.

Hie you to church; I must another way,
To fetch a ladder, by the which your love
Must climb a bird's nest soon when it is dark.
I am the drudge, and toil in your delight;
But you shall bear the burthen soon at night.
Go; I'll to dinner; hie you to the cell.

JULIET   Hie to high fortune! Honest Nurse, farewell.

Exeunt separately

SCENE VI—Friar Laurence's cell.
Enter Friar Laurence and Romeo

FRIAR   So smile the heavens upon this holy act
That after-hours with sorrow chide us not!

ROMEO   Amen, amen! But come what sorrow can,
It cannot countervail the exchange of joy
That one short minute gives me in her sight.
Do thou but close our hands with holy words,
Then love-devouring death do what he dare—
It is enough I may but call her mine.

FRIAR   These violent delights have violent ends,
And in their triumph die, like fire and powder,
Which, as they kiss, consume. The sweetest honey
Is loathsome in his own deliciousness
And in the taste confounds the appetite.
Therefore love moderately: long love doth so;
Too swift arrives as tardy as too slow.

Enter Juliet

ROMEO   Here comes the lady. O, so light a foot
Will ne'er wear out the everlasting flint.
A lover may bestride the gossamer
That idles in the wanton summer air,
And yet not fall; so light is vanity.

JULIET   Good even to my ghostly confessor.

FRIAR   Romeo shall thank thee, daughter, for us both.

JULIET   As much to him, else is his thanks too much.

ROMEO   Ah, Juliet, if the measure of thy joy
Be heap'd like mine, and that thy skill be more
To blazon it, then sweeten with thy breath
This neighbour air, and let rich music's tongue
Unfold the imagin'd happiness that both

Receive in either by this dear encounter.

JULIET   Conceit, more rich in matter than in words,
Brags of his substance, not of ornament.
They are but beggars that can count their worth;
But my true love is grown to such excess
I cannot sum up sum of half my wealth.

FRIAR   Come, come with me, and we will make short work;
For, by your leaves, you shall not stay alone
Till Holy Church incorporate two in one.

Exeunt

ACT III

SCENE I—A public place.
Enter Mercutio, Benvolio, and Men

BENVOLIO   I pray thee, good Mercutio, let's retire.
The day is hot, the Capulets abroad.
And if we meet, we shall not scape a brawl,
For now, these hot days, is the mad blood stirring.

MERCUTIO   Thou art like one of these fellows that, when he enters the confines of a tavern, claps me his sword upon the table and says "God send me no need of thee!" and by the operation of the second cup draws him on the drawer, when indeed there is no need.

BENVOLIO   Am I like such a fellow?

MERCUTIO   Come, come, thou art as hot a jack in thy mood as any in Italy; and as soon moved to be moody, and as soon moody to be moved.

BENVOLIO   And what to?

MERCUTIO   Nay, an there were two such, we should have none shortly, for one would kill the other. Thou! why, thou wilt quarrel with a man that hath a hair more or a hair less in his beard than thou hast. Thou wilt quarrel with a man for cracking nuts, having no other reason but because thou hast hazel eyes. What eye but such an eye would spy out such a quarrel? Thy head is as full of quarrels as an egg is full of meat; and yet thy head hath been beaten as addle as an egg for quarrelling. Thou hast quarrell'd with a man for coughing in the street, because he hath wakened thy dog that hath lain asleep in the sun. Didst thou not fall out with a tailor for wearing his new doublet before Easter, with another for tying his new shoes with an old riband? And yet thou wilt tutor me from quarrelling!

BENVOLIO   An I were so apt to quarrel as thou art, any man should buy the fee simple of my life for an hour and a quarter.

MERCUTIO   The fee simple? O simple!

Enter Tybalt and others

BENVOLIO   By my head, here come the Capulets.

MERCUTIO   By my heel, I care not.

TYBALT   [*to his companions*] Follow me close, for I will speak to them.
Gentlemen, good e'en. A word with one of you.

MERCUTIO   And but one word with one of us? Couple it with something; make it a word and a blow.

TYBALT   You shall find me apt enough to that, Sir, an you will give me
occasion.

MERCUTIO   Could you not take some occasion without giving?

TYBALT   Mercutio, thou consortest with Romeo.

MERCUTIO   Consort? What, dost thou make us minstrels? An thou
make minstrels of us, look to hear nothing but discords. Here's
my fiddle-stick; here's that shall make you dance. Zounds, consort!

BENVOLIO   We talk here in the public haunt of men.
Either withdraw unto some private place
Or reason coldly of your grievances,
Or else depart; here all eyes gaze on us.

MERCUTIO   Men's eyes were made to look, and let them gaze.
I will not budge for no man's pleasure, I.

Enter Romeo

TYBALT   Well, peace be with you, Sir. Here comes my man.

MERCUTIO   But I'll be hang'd, Sir, if he wear your livery.
Marry, go before to field, he'll be your follower!
Your worship in that sense may call him man.

TYBALT   Romeo, the love I bear thee can afford
No better term than this: thou art a villain.

ROMEO   Tybalt, the reason that I have to love thee
Doth much excuse the appertaining rage
To such a greeting. Villain am I none.
Therefore farewell. I see thou knowest me not.

TYBALT   Boy, this shall not excuse the injuries
That thou hast done me; therefore turn and draw.

ROMEO   I do protest: I never injur'd thee,
But love thee better than thou canst devise
Till thou shalt know the reason of my love;
And so good Capulet, which name I tender
As dearly as mine own, be satisfied.

MERCUTIO   O calm, dishonourable, vile submission!
Alla stoccado carries it away. [*He draws*]

Tybalt, you ratcatcher, will you walk?

TYBALT   What wouldst thou have with me?

MERCUTIO   Good King of Cats, nothing but one of your nine lives.
That I mean to make bold withal, and, as you shall use me hereafter, dry-beat the rest of the eight. Will you pluck your sword out of
his pitcher by the ears? Make haste, lest mine be about your ears
ere it be out.

TYBALT   I am for you. [*He draws*]

ROMEO   Gentle Mercutio, put thy rapier up.

MERCUTIO   Come, Sir, your *passado*! [*They fight*]

ROMEO   Draw, Benvolio; beat down their weapons.
Gentlemen, for shame! forbear this outrage!
Tybalt, Mercutio, the Prince expressly hath
Forbid this bandying in Verona streets.
Hold, Tybalt! Good Mercutio!
            Tybalt [*under Romeo's arm*] *thrusts into Mercutio*

PETRUCHIO   Away, Tybalt!   [*Exit Tybalt and his followers*]

MERCUTIO   I am hurt.
A plague o' both your houses! I am sped.
Is he gone and hath nothing?

BENVOLIO   What, art thou hurt?

MERCUTIO   Ay, ay, a scratch, a scratch; marry, 'tis enough.
Where is my page? Go, villain, fetch a surgeon.   [*Exit Page*]

ROMEO   Courage, man. The hurt cannot be much.

MERCUTIO   No, 'tis not so deep as a well, nor so wide as a church
door; but 'tis enough, 'twill serve. Ask for me tomorrow, and you
shall find me a grave man. I am peppered, I warrant, for this world.
A plague o' both your houses! Zounds, a dog, a rat, a mouse, a cat,
to scratch a man to death! A braggart, a rogue, a villain, that fights
by the book of arithmetic! Why the devil came you between us? I
was hurt under your arm.

ROMEO   I thought all for the best.

MERCUTIO   Help me into some house, Benvolio,
Or I shall faint. A plague o' both your houses!
They have made worms' meat of me. I have it,
And soundly too. Your houses!
                        Exit supported by Benvolio

ROMEO   This gentleman, the Prince's near ally,
My very friend, hath got this mortal hurt
In my behalf; my reputation stain'd

With Tybalt's slander—Tybalt, that an hour
Hath been my kinsman. O sweet Juliet,
Tthy beauty hath made me effeminate
And in my temper soft'ned valour's steel.

Enter Benvolio

BENVOLIO   O Romeo, Romeo, brave Mercutio's dead!
That gallant spirit hath aspir'd the clouds,
Which too untimely here did scorn the earth.

ROMEO   This day's black fate on more days doth depend;
This but begins the woe others must end.

Enter Tybalt

BENVOLIO   Here comes the furious Tybalt back again.

ROMEO   He gad in triumph, and Mercutio slain?
Away to heaven, respective lenity,'
And fire-ey'd fury be my conduct now!
Now, Tybalt, take the "villain" back again
That late thou gavest me; for Mercutio's soul
Is but a little way above our heads,
Staying for thine to keep him company.
Either thou or I, or both, must go with him.

TYBALT   Thou, wretched boy, that didst consort him here;
Shalt with him hence.

ROMEO   This shall determine that.

They fight. Tybalt falls [and dies]

BENVOLIO   Romeo, away, be gone!
The citizens are up, and Tybalt slain.
Stand not amaz'd. The Prince will doom thee death
If thou art taken. Hence, be gone, away!

ROMEO   O, I am fortune's fool!

BENVOLIO   Why dost thou stay?

Exit Romeo

Enter Citizens

FIRST CITIZEN   Which way ran he that kill'd Mercutio?
Tybalt, that murderer, which way ran he?

BENVOLIO   There lies that Tybalt.

FIRST CITIZEN   Up, Sir, go with me.
I charge thee in the Prince's name obey.

*Enter Prince [attended], Old Montague, Capulet,
their Wives, and all*

PRINCE   Where are the vile beginners of this fray?

BENVOLIO   O noble Prince. I can discover all
    The unlucky manage of this fatal brawl.
    There lies the man, slain by young Romeo,
    That slew thy kinsman, brave Mercutio.
CAPULET'S WIFE   Tybalt, my cousin! O my brother's child!
    O Prince! O husband! O, the blood is spill'd
    Of my dear kinsman! Prince, as thou art true,
    For blood of ours shed blood of Montague.
    O cousin, cousin!
PRINCE   Benvolio, who began this bloody fray?
BENVOLIO   Tybalt, here slain, whom Romeo's hand did slay.
    Romeo, that spoke him fair, bid him bethink
    How nice the quarrel was, and urg'd withal
    Your high displeasure. All this—utterèd
    With gentle breath, calm look, knees humbly bow'd—
    Could not take truce with the unruly spleen
    Of Tybalt deaf to peace, but that he tilts
    With piercing steel at bold Mercutio's breast;
    Who, all as hot, turns deadly point to point,
    And, with a martial scorn, with one hand beats
    Cold death aside and with the other sends
    It back to Tybalt, whose dexterity
    Retorts it. Romeo he cries aloud,
    "Hold, friends! Friends, part!" and swifter than his tongue,
    His agile arm beats down their fatal points,
    And 'twixt them rushes; underneath whose arm
    An envious thrust from Tybalt hit the life
    Of stout Mercutio, and then Tybalt fled;
    But by-and-by comes back to Romeo,
    Who had but newly entertain'd revenge,
    And to't they go like lightning; for, ere I
    Could draw to part them, was stout Tybalt slain;
    And, as he fell, did Romeo turn and fly.
    This is the truth, or let Benvolio die.
CAPULET'S WIFE   He is a kinsman to the Montague;
    Affection makes him false, he speaks not true.
    Some twenty of them fought in this black strife,
    And all those twenty could but kill one life.
    I beg for justice, which thou, Prince, must give.
    Romeo slew Tybalt; Romeo must not live.

PRINCE   Romeo slew him; he slew Mercutio.
    Who now the price of his dear blood doth owe?
MONTAGUE   Not Romeo, Prince; he was Mercutio's friend;
    His fault concludes but what the law should end,
    The life of Tybalt.
PRINCE   And for that offence
    Immediately we do exile him hence.
    I have an interest in your hate's proceeding,
    My blood for your rude brawls doth lie a-bleeding;
    But I'll amerce you with so strong a fine
    That you shall all repent the loss of mine.
    I will be deaf to pleading and excuses;
    Nor tears nor prayers shall purchase out abuses.
    Therefore use none. Let Romeo hence in haste,
    Else, when he is found, that hour is his last.
    Bear hence this body, and attend our will.
    Mercy but murders, pardoning those that kill.

Exeunt

SCENE II—Capulet's orchard.
Enter Juliet alone

JULIET   Gallop apace, you fiery-footed steeds,
    Towards Phoebus' lodging! Such a wagoner
    As Phaeton would whip you to the West
    And bring in cloudy night immediately.
    Spread thy close curtain, love-performing night,
    That runaways' eyes may wink, and Romeo
    Leap to these arms untalk'd of and unseen.
    Lovers can see to do their amorous rites
    By their own beauties; or, if love be blind,
    It best agrees with night. Come, civil night,
    Thou sober-suited matron, all in black,
    And learn me how to lose a winning match,
    Play'd for a pair of stainless maidenhoods.
    Hood my unmann'd blood, bating in my cheeks,
    With thy black mantle till strange love, grown bold,
    Think true love acted simple modesty.
    Come, night; come, Romeo; come, thou day in night;
    For thou wilt lie upon the wings of night
    Whiter than new snow upon a raven's back.

Come, gentle night; come, loving, black-brow'd night;
Give me my Romeo; and, when he shall die,
Take him and cut him out in little stars,
And he will make the face of heaven so fine
That all the world will be in love with night
And pay no worship to the garish sun.
O, I have bought the mansion of a love,
But not possess'd it; and though I am sold,
Not yet enjoy'd. So tedious is this day
As is the night before some festival
To an impatient child that hath new robes
And may not wear them. O, here comes my Nurse,
          Enter Nurse, with the ladder of cords in her lap
And she brings news; and every tongue that speaks
But Romeo's name speaks heavenly eloquence.
Now, Nurse, what news? What hast thou there?
The cords that Romeo bid thee fetch?

NURSE   Ay, ay, the cords.
                    Throws them down
JULIET   Ay me! what news? Why dost thou wring thy hands
NURSE   Ah, welladay! he's dead, he's dead, he's dead!
    We are undone, lady, we are undone!
    Alack the day! he's gone, he's kill'd, he's dead!
JULIET   Can heaven be so envious?
NURSE   Romeo can,
    Though heaven cannot. O Romeo, Romeo!
    Who ever would have thought it Romeo?
JULIET   What devil art thou that dost torment me thus?
    This torture should be roar'd in dismal hell.
    Hath Romeo slain himself? Say thou but "Ay,"
    And that bare vowel "Ay" shall poison more
    Than the death-darting eye of cockatrice.
    I am not I, if there be such an "Ay";
    Or those eyes shut that make thee answer "Ay."
    If be be slain, say "Ay"; or if not, "no."
    Brief sounds determine of my weal or woe.
NURSE   I saw the wound, I saw it with mine eyes—
    God save the mark! —here on his manly breast.
    A piteous corpse, a bloody piteous corpse;
    Pale, pale as ashes, all bedaub'd in blood,

All in gore-blood. I swoonèd at the sight.

JULIET   O, break, my heart! Poor bankrupt, break at once!
To prison, eyes; ne'er look on liberty!
Vile earth, to earth resign; end motion here,
And thou and Romeo press one heavy bier!

NURSE   O Tybalt, Tybalt, the best friend I had!
O courteous Tybalt! honest gentleman
That ever I should live to see thee dead!

JULIET   What storm is this that blows so contrary?
Is Romeo slaught'red, and is Tybalt dead?
My dear-lov'd cousin, and my dearer lord?
Then, dreadful trumpet, sound the general doom!
For who is living, if those two are gone?

NURSE   Tybalt is gone, and Romeo banished;
Romeo that kill'd him, he is banished.

JULIET   O God! Did Romeo's hand shed Tybalt's blood?

NURSE   It did, it did! alas the day, it did!

JULIET   O serpent heart, hid with a flow'ring face!
Did ever dragon keep so fair a cave?
Beautiful tyrant! fiend angelical!
Dove-feather'd raven! wolvish-ravening lamb!
Despised substance of divinest show!
Just opposite to what thou justly seem'st—
A damned saint, an honourable villain!
O nature, what hadst thou to do in hell
When thou didst bower the spirit of a fiend
In mortal paradise of such sweet flesh?
Was ever book containing such vile matter
So fairly bound? O, that deceit should dwell
In such a gorgeous palace!

NURSE   There's no trust,
No faith, no honesty in men; all perjur'd, all forsworn,
All naught, all dissemblers.
Ah, where's my man? Give me some aqua vitae.
These griefs, these woes, these sorrows make me old.
Shame come to Romeo!

JULIET   Blister'd be thy tongue
For such a wish! He was not born to shame.
Upon his brow shame is asham'd to sit;
For 'tis a throne where honour may be crown'd

Sole monarch of the universal earth.

. O, what a beast was I to chide at him!

NURSE   Will you speak well of him that kill'd your cousin?

JULIET   Shall I speak ill of him that is my husband?

Ah, poor my lord, what tongue shall smooth thy name

When I, thy three-hours wife, have mangled it?

But wherefore, villain, didst thou kill my cousin?

That villain cousin would have kill'd my husband.

Back, foolish tears, back to your native spring!

Your tributary drops belong to woe,

Which you, mistaking, offer up to joy.

My husband lives, that Tybalt would have slain;

And Tybalt's dead, that would have slain my husband.

All this is comfort; wherefore weep I then?

Some word there was, worser than Tybalt's death,

That murd'red me. I would forget it fain;

But O, it presses to my memory

Like damned guilty deeds to sinners' minds!

"Tybalt is dead, and Romeo—banished."

That "banished," that one word "banished,"

Hath slain ten thousand Tybalts. Tybalt's death

Was woe enough, if it had ended there;

Or, if sour woe delights in fellowship

And needly will be rank'd with other griefs,

Why followed not, when she said "Tybalt's dead,"

Thy father, or thy mother, nay, or both,

Which modern lamentation might have mov'd?

But with a rearward following Tybalt's death,

"Romeo is banished"—to speak that word

Is father, mother, Tybalt, Romeo, Juliet,

All slain, all dead. "Romeo is banished"—

There is no end, no limit, measure, bound,

In that word's death; no words can that woe sound.

Where is my father and my mother, Nurse?

NURSE   Weeping and wailing over Tybalt's corpse.

Will you go to them? I will bring you thither.

JULIET   Wash they his wounds with tears? Mine shall be spent,

When theirs are dry, for Romeo's banishment.

Take up those cords. Poor ropes, you are beguil'd,

Both you and I, for Romeo is exil'd.
He made you for a highway to my bed;
But I, a maid, die maiden-widowed.
Come, cords; come, Nurse. I'll to my wedding bed;
And death, not Romeo, take my maidenhead!

NURSE   Hie to your chamber. [*taking up the cords*] I'll find Romeo
To comfort you. I wot well where he is.
Hark ye, your Romeo will be here at night.
I'll to him; he is hid at Laurence' cell.

JULIET   O, find him! give this ring to my true knight [*giving a ring*]
And bid him come to take his last farewell.

Exeunt separately

SCENE III—Friar Laurence's cell.
Enter Friar Laurence

FRIAR   Romeo, come forth; come forth, thou fearful man.
Affliction is enamour'd of thy parts,
And thou art wedded to calamity.

Enter Romeo

ROMEO   Father, what news? What is the Prince's doom?
What sorrow craves acquaintance at my hand
That I yet know not?

FRIAR   Too familiar
Is my dear son with such sour company.
I bring thee tidings of the Prince's doom.

ROMEO   What less than doomsday is the Prince's doom?

FRIAR   A gentler judgment vanish'd from his lips—
Not body's death, but body's banishment.

ROMEO   Ha, banishment? Be merciful, say "death";
For exile hath more terror in his look,
Much more than death. Do not say "banishment."

FRIAR   Hence from Verona art thou banished.
Be patient, for the world is broad and wide.

ROMEO   There is no world without Verona walls,
But purgatory, torture, hell itself.
Hence banished is banish'd from the world,
And world's exile is death. Then "banishment"
Is death misterm'd. Calling death "banishment,"
Thou cut'st my head off with a golden axe

And smilest upon the stroke that murders me.
FRIAR   O deadly sin! O rude unthankfulness!
    Thy fault our law calls death; but the kind Prince,
    Taking thy part, hath rush'd aside the law,
    And turn'd that black word death to banishment.
    This is dear mercy, and thou seest it not.
ROMEO   'Tis torture, and not mercy. Heaven is here,
    Where Juliet lives; and every cat and dog
    And little mouse, every unworthy thing,
    Live here in heaven and may look on her;
    But Romeo may not. More validity,
    More honourable state, more courtship lives
    In carrion flies than Romeo. They may seize
    On the white wonder of dear Juliet's hand
    And steal immortal blessing from her lips,
    Who, even in pure and vestal modesty,
    Still blush, as thinking their own kisses sin;
    But Romeo may not—he is banished.
    This may flies do, when I from this must fly;
    They are free men, but I am banished.
    And sayest thou yet that exile is not death?
    Hadst thou no poison mix'd, no sharp-ground knife,
    No sudden mean of death, though ne'er so mean,
    But "banished" to kill me—"banished"?
    O friar, the damned use that word in hell;
    Howling attends it! How hast thou the heart,
    Being a divine, a ghostly confessor,
    A sin absolver, and my friend profess'd,
    To mangle me with that word "banished"?
FRIAR   Thou fond mad man, hear me a little speak.
ROMEO   O, thou wilt speak again of banishment.
FRIAR   I'll give thee armour to keep off that word;
    Adversity's sweet milk, philosophy,
    To comfort thee, though thou art banished.
ROMEO   Yet "banished"? Hang up philosophy!
    Unless philosophy can make a Juliet,
    Displant a town, reverse a prince's doom,
    It helps not, it prevails not. Talk no more.
FRIAR   O, then I see that madmen have no ears.
ROMEO   How should they, when that wise men have no eyes?

FRIAR   Let me dispute with thee of thy estate.
ROMEO   Thou canst not speak of that thou dost not feel.
  Wert thou as young as I, Juliet thy love,
  An hour but married, Tybalt murdered,
  Doting like me, and like me banished,
  Then mightst thou speak, then mightst thou tear thy hair,
  And fall upon the ground, as I do now, [*He falls upon the ground*]
  Taking the measure of an unmade grave. [*Knock within*]
FRIAR   Arise; one knocks. Good Romeo, hide thyself.
ROMEO   Not I; unless the breath of heartsick groans,
  Mistlike infold me from the search of eyes. [*Knock*]
FRIAR   Hark, how they knock! Who's there? Romeo, arise;
  Thou wilt be taken. Stay awhile! Stand up; [*Knock*]
  Run to my study. By-and-by! God's will,
  What simpleness is this. I come, I come! [*Knock*]
  Who knocks so hard? Whence come you? What's your will?
NURSE   [*within*] Let me come in, and you shall know my errand.
  I come from Lady Juliet.
FRIAR   Welcome then. [*He opens the door*]
                         Enter Nurse
NURSE   O holy friar, O, tell me, holy friar
  Where is my lady's lord; where's Romeo?
FRIAR   There on the ground, with his own tears made drunk.
NURSE   O, he is even in my mistress' case,
  Just in her case! O woeful sympathy!
  Piteous predicament! Even so lies she,
  Blubb'ring and weeping, weeping and blubbering.
  Stand up, stand up! Stand, an you be a man.
  For Juliet's sake, for her sake, rise and stand!
  Why should you fall into so deep an O?
ROMEO   [*rises*] Nurse!
NURSE   Ah Sir! ah Sir! Death's the end of all.
ROMEO   Spakest thou of Juliet? How is it with her?
  Doth not she think me an old murderer,
  Now I have stain'd the childhood of our joy
  With blood remov'd but little from her own?
  Where is she? and how doth she! and what says
  My conceal'd lady to our cancell'd love?
NURSE   O, she says nothing, Sir, but weeps and weeps;
  And now falls on her bed, and then starts up,

And "Tybalt" calls; and then on Romeo cries,
And then down falls again.

ROMEO   As if that name,
Shot from the deadly level of a gun,
Did murder her; as that name's cursed hand
Murder'd her kinsman. O, tell me, friar, tell me,
In what vile part of this anatomy
Doth my name lodge? Tell me, that I may sack
The hateful mansion. [*He draws his dagger*]

FRIAR   Hold thy desperate hand.
Art thou a man? Thy form cries out thou art;
Thy tears are womanish, thy wild acts denote
The unreasonable fury of a beast.
Unseemly woman in a seeming man!
Or ill-beseeming beast in seeming both!
Thou hast amaz'd me. By my holy order,
I thought thy disposition better temper'd.
Hast thou slain Tybalt? Wilt thou slay thyself?
And slay thy lady that in thy life lives,
By doing damned hate upon thyself?
Why railest thou on thy birth, the heaven, and earth?
Since birth and heaven and earth, all three do meet
In thee at once; which thou at once wouldst lose.
Fie, fie, thou shamest thy shape, thy love, thy wit,
Which, like a usurer, abound'st in all,
And usest none in that true use indeed
Which should bedeck thy shape, thy love, thy wit.
Thy noble shape is but a form of wax
Digressing from the valour of a man;
Thy dear love sworn but hollow perjury,
Killing that love which thou hast vow'd to cherish;
Thy wit, that ornament to shape and love,
Misshapen in the conduct of them both,
Like powder in a skilless soldier's flask,
Is set afire by thine own ignorance,
And thou dismemb'red with thine own defence.
What, rouse thee, man! Thy Juliet is alive,
For whose dear sake thou wast but lately dead.
There art thou happy. Tybalt would kill thee,

But thou slewest Tybalt. There art thou happy too.
The law, that threat'ned death, becomes thy friend
And turns it to exile. There art thou happy.
A pack of blessings light upon thy back;
Happiness courts thee in her best array;
But, like a mishavèd and sullen wench,
Thou pout'st upon thy fortune and thy love.
Take heed, take heed, for such die miserable.
Go get thee to thy love, as was decreed,
Ascend her chamber, hence and comfort her.
But look thou stay not till the watch be set,
For then thou canst not pass to Mantua,
Where thou shalt live till we can find a time
To blaze your marriage, reconcile your friends,
Beg pardon of the Prince, and call thee back
With twenty hundred thousand times more joy
Than thou went'st forth in lamentation.
Go before, Nurse. Commend me to thy lady,
And bid her hasten all the house to bed,
Which heavy sorrow makes them apt unto.
Romeo is coming.
NURSE   O Lord, I could have stay'd here all the night
To hear good counsel. O, what learning is!
My lord, I'll tell my lady you will come.
ROMEO   Do so, and bid my sweet prepare to chide.
NURSE   Here is a ring she bid me give you, Sir.
Hie you, make haste, for it grows very late.

Exit

ROMEO   How well my comfort is reviv'd by this!
FRIAR   Go hence; good night; and here stands all your state:
Either be gone before the watch be set,
Or by the break of day disguis'd from hence.
Sojourn in Mantua. I'll find out your man,
And he shall signify from time to time
Every good hap to you that chances here.
Give me thy hand. 'Tis late. Farewell; good night.
ROMEO   But that a joy past joy calls out on me,
It were a grief so brief to part with thee.
Farewell.

Exeunt separately

Scene IV—Capulet's house
Enter Old Capulet, his Wife, and Paris

CAPULET   Things have fall'n out, Sir, so unluckily
That we have had no time to move our daughter.
Look you, she lov'd her kinsman Tybalt dearly,
And so did I. Well, we were born to die.
'Tis very late; she'll not come down tonight.
I promise you, but for your company,
I would have been abed an hour ago.

PARIS   These times of woe afford no tune to woo.
Madam, good night. Commend me to your daughter.

CAPULET'S WIFE   I will, and know her mind early tomorrow;
Tonight she's mew'd up to her heaviness.

CAPULET   Sir Paris, I will make a desperate tender
Of my child's love. I think she will be rul'd
In all respects by me; nay more, I doubt it not.
Wife, go you to her ere you go to bed;
Acquaint her here of my son Paris' love
And bid her (mark you me?) on Wednesday next—
But, soft! What day is this?

PARIS   Monday, my lord.

CAPULET   Monday! ha, ha! Well, Wednesday is too soon.
Thursday let it be. O' Thursday, tell her
She shall be married to this noble earl.
Will you be ready? Do you like this haste?
We'll keep no great ado—a friend or two;
For hark you, Tybalt being slain so late,
It may be thought we held him carelessly,
Being our kinsman, if we revel much.
Therefore we'll have some half a dozen friends,
And there an end. But what say you to Thursday?

PARIS   My lord, I would that Thursday were tomorrow.

CAPULET   Well, get you gone. O' Thursday be it then.
[*To his wife*] Go you to Juliet ere you go to bed;
Prepare her, wife, against this wedding day.
Farewell, my lord.—Light to my chamber, ho!
Afore me, it is so very late that we
May call it early by-and-by. Good night.

Exeunt

SCENE V—Capulet's orchard.

Enter Romeo and Juliet aloft, at the window

JULIET   Wilt thou be gone? It is not yet near day.
It was the nightingale, and not the lark,
That pierc'd the fearful hollow of thine ear.
Nightly she sings on yon pomegranate tree.
Believe me, love, it was the nightingale.

ROMEO   It was the lark, the herald of the morn;
No nightingale. Look, love, what envious streaks
Do lace the severing clouds in yonder East.
Night's candles are burnt out, and jocund day
Stands tiptoe on the misty mountain tops.
I must be gone and live, or stay and die.

JULIET   Yon light is not daylight; I know it, I.
It is some meteor that the sun exhaled
To be to thee this night a torchbearer
And light thee on the way to Mantua.
Therefore stay yet; thou need'st not to be gone.

ROMEO   Let me be ta'en, let me be put to death.
I am content, so thou wilt have it so.
I'll say yon grey is not the morning's eye,
'Tis but the pale reflex of Cynthia's brow;
Nor that is not the lark whose notes do beat
The vaulty heaven so high above our heads.
I have more care to stay than will to go.
Come, death, and welcome! Juliet wills it so.
How is't, my soul? Let's talk; it is not day.

JULIET   It is, it is! Hie hence, be gone, away!
It is the lark that sings so out of tune,
Straining harsh discords and unpleasing sharps.
Some say the lark makes sweet division;
This doth not so, for she divideth us.
Some say the lark and loathed toad chang'd eyes;
O, now I would they had chang'd voices too,
Since arm from arm that voice doth us affray,
Hunting thee hence with hunt's—up to the day!
O, now be gone! More light and light it grows.

ROMEO   More light and light—more dark and dark our woes!

Enter Nurse

NURSE   Madam!

JULIET   Nurse?

NURSE   Your lady mother is coming to your chamber.
   The day is broke; be wary, look about.

                                              Exit Nurse

JULIET   Then, window, let day in, and let life out.

ROMEO   Farewell, farewell! One kiss, and I'll descend.
               They kiss. He climbs down from the window

JULIET   Art thou gone so, love, lord, my husband, friend?
   I must hear from thee every day in the hour,
   For in a minute there are many days.
   O, by this count I shall be much in years
   Ere I again behold my Romeo!

ROMEO   [*from below her window*]   Farewell!
   I will omit no opportunity
   That may convey my greetings, love, to thee.

JULIET   O, think'st thou we shall ever meet again?

ROMEO   I doubt it not; and all these woes shall serve
   For sweet discourses in our time to come.

JULIET   O God, I have an ill-divining soul!
   Methinks I see thee, now thou art below,
   As one dead in the bottom of a tomb.
   Either my eyesight fails, or thou look'st pale.

ROMEO   And trust me, love, in my eye so do you.
   Dry sorrow drinks our blood. Adieu, adieu!

                                             Exit Romeo

JULIET   O Fortune, Fortune! all men call thee fickle.
   If thou art fickle, what dost thou with him
   That is renown'd for faith? Be fickle, Fortune,
   For then I hope thou wilt not keep him long
   But send him back.

                   Enter Mother [Capulet's Wife]

CAPULET'S WIFE   Ho, daughter! are you up?

JULIET   Who is't that calls? It is my lady mother.
   Is she not down so late, or up so early? [*withdraws from window*]
   What unaccustom'd cause procures her hither?

CAPULET'S WIFE   Why, how now, Juliet?

JULIET   Madam, I am not well.

CAPULET'S WIFE   Evermore weeping for your cousin's death?
   What, wilt thou wash him from his grave with tears?
   An if thou couldst, thou couldst not make him live.

Therefore have done. Some grief shows much of love;
But much of grief shows still some want of wit.

JULIET   Yet let me weep for such a feeling loss.

CAPULET'S WIFE   So shall you feel the loss, but not the friend
    Which you weep for.

JULIET   Feeling so the loss,
    I cannot choose but ever weep the friend.

CAPULET'S WIFE   Well, girl, thou weep'st not so much for his death
    As that the villain lives which slaughter'd him.

JULIET   What villain, madam?

CAPULET'S WIFE   That same villain Romeo.

JULIET   [aside] Villain and he be many miles asunder.
    [To her mother] God pardon him! I do, with all my heart;
    And yet no man like he doth grieve my heart.

CAPULET'S WIFE   That is because the traitor murderer lives.

JULIET   Ay, madam, from the reach of these my hands.
    Would none but I might venge my cousin's death!

CAPULET'S WIFE   We will have vengeance for it, fear thou not.
    Then weep no more. I'll send to one in Mantua,
    Where that same banish'd runagate doth live,
    Shall give him such an unaccustom'd dram
    That he shall soon keep Tybalt company;
    And then I hope thou wilt be satisfied.

JULIET   Indeed I never shall be satisfied
    With Romeo till I behold him—dead—
    Is my poor heart so for a kinsman vex'd.
    Madam, if you could find out but a man
    To bear a poison, I would temper it;
    That Romeo should, upon receipt thereof,
    Soon sleep in quiet. O, how my heart abhors
    To hear him nam'd and cannot come to him,
    To wreak the love I bore my cousin
    Upon his body that hath slaughter'd him!

CAPULET'S WIFE   Find thou the means, and I'll find such a man.
    But now I'll tell thee joyful tidings, girl.

JULIET   And joy comes well in such a needy time.
    What are they, I beseech your ladyship?

CAPULET'S WIFE   Well, well, thou hast a careful father, child;
    One who, to put thee from thy heaviness,
    Hath sorted out a sudden day of joy

That thou expects not, nor I look'd not for.

JULIET Madam, in happy time! What day is that?

CAPULET'S WIFE Marry, my child, early next Thursday morn
The gallant, young, and noble gentleman,
The County Paris, at Saint Peter's Church,
Shall happily make thee there a joyful bride.

JULIET Now by Saint Peter's Church, and Peter too,
He shall not make me there a joyful bride!
I wonder at this haste, that I must wed
Ere he that should be husband comes to woo.
I pray you tell my lord and father, madam,
I will not marry yet; and when I do, I swear
It shall be Romeo, whom you know I hate,
Rather than Paris. These are news indeed!

CAPULET'S WIFE Here comes your father. Tell him so yourself,
And see how he will take it at your hands.

Enter Capulet and Nurse

CAPULET When the sun sets the air doth drizzle dew,
But for the sunset of my brother's son
It rains downright.
How now? a conduit, girl? What, still in tears?
Evermore show'ring? In one little body
Thou counterfeit'st a bark, a sea, a wind:
For still thy eyes, which I may call the sea,
Do ebb and flow with tears; the bark thy body is,
Sailing in this salt flood; the winds, thy sighs,
Who, raging with thy tears and they with them,
Without a sudden calm will overset
Thy tempest-tossed body. How now, wife?
Have you delivered to her our decree?

CAPULET'S WIFE Ay, Sir; but she will none, she gives you thanks.
I would the fool were married to her grave!

CAPULET Soft! take me with you, take me with you, wife.
How? Will she none? Doth she not give us thanks?
Is she not proud? Doth she not count her blest,
Unworthy as she is, that we have wrought
So worthy a gentleman to be her bridegroom?

JULIET Not proud you have, but thankful that you have.
Proud can I never be of what I hate,
But thankful even for hate that is meant love.

CAPULET   How, how, how, how, chop-logic? What is this?
  "Proud" and "I thank you" and "I thank you not"
  And yet "not proud"? Mistress minion you,
  Thank me no thankings, nor proud me no prouds,
  But fettle your fine joints 'gainst Thursday next
  To go with Paris to Saint Peter's Church,
  Or I will drag thee on a hurdle thither.
  Out, you green-sickness carrion! Out, you baggage!
CAPULET'S WIFE   Fie, fie! what, are you mad?
JULIET   Good father, I beseech you on my knees,
  Hear me with patience but to speak a word.
CAPULET   Hang thee, young baggage! disobedient wretch!
  I tell thee what, get thee to church o' Thursday
  Or never after look me in the face.
  Speak not, reply not, do not answer me!
  My fingers itch. Wife, we scarce thought us blest
  That God had lent us but this only child;
  But now I see this one is one too much,
  And that we have a curse in having her.
  Out on her, hilding!
NURSE   God in heaven bless her!
  You are to blame, my lord, to rate her so.
CAPULET   And why, my Lady Wisdom? Hold your tongue,
  Good Prudence. Smatter with your gossips, go!
NURSE   I speak no treason.
CAPULET   O, God-i'-good-e'en!
NURSE   May not one speak?
CAPULET   Peace, you mumbling fool!
  Utter your gravity o'er a gossip's bowl,
  For here we need it not.
CAPULET'S WIFE   You are too hot.
CAPULET   God's bread, it makes me mad!
  Day, night, hour, tide, time, work, play,
  Alone, in company, waking or sleeping, still my care hath been
  To have her match'd; and having now provided
  A gentleman of princely parentage,
  Of fair demesnes, youthful, and nobly lined,
  Stuff'd, as they say, with honourable parts,
  Proportion'd as one's thought would wish a man—
  And then to have a wretched puling fool,

A whining mammet, in her fortune's tender,
To answer "I'll not wed, I cannot love;
I am too young, I pray you pardon me"!
But, an you will not wed, I'll pardon you.
Graze where you will, you shall not house with me.
Look to't, think on't; I do not use to jest.
Thursday is near; lay hand on heart, advise:
An you be mine, I'll give you to my friend;
An you be not, hang, beg, starve, die in the streets,
For, by my soul, I'll ne'er acknowledge thee,
Nor what is mine shall never do thee good.
Trust to't. Bethink you. I'll not be forsworn.

Exit Capulet

JULIET   Is there no pity sitting in the clouds
That sees into the bottom of my grief?
O sweet my mother, cast me not away!
Delay this marriage for a month, a week;
Or if you do not, make the bridal bed
In that dim monument where Tybalt lies.
CAPULET'S WIFE   Talk not to me, for I'll not speak a word.
Do as thou wilt, for I have done with thee.

Exit Capulet's Wife

JULIET   O God! O Nurse, how shall this be prevented?
My husband is on earth, my faith in heaven.
How shall that faith return again to earth
Unless that husband send it me from heaven
By leaving earth? Comfort me, counsel me.
Alack, alack, that heaven should practise stratagems
Upon so soft a subject as myself!
What say'st thou? Hast thou not a word of joy?
Some comfort, Nurse.
NURSE   Faith, here it is.
Romeo is banish'd; and all the world to nothing
That he dares ne'er come back to challenge you;
Or if he do, it needs must be by stealth.
Then, since the case so stands as now it doth,
I think it best you married with the County.
O, he's a lovely gentleman!
Romeo's a dishclout to him. An eagle, madam,
Hath not so green, so quick, so fair an eye

As Paris hath. Beshrew my very heart,
I think you are happy in this second match,
For it excels your first; or if it did not,
Your first is dead—or 'twere as good he were
As living here and you no use of him.

JULIET Speak'st thou this from thy heart?

NURSE And from my soul too; else beshrew them both.

JULIET Amen!

NURSE What?

JULIET Well, thou hast comforted me marvellous much.
Go in; and tell my lady I am gone,
Having displeas'd my father, to Laurence' cell,
To make confession and to be absolv'd.

NURSE Marry, I will; and this is wisely done.

Exit Nurse

JULIET Ancient damnation! O most wicked fiend!
Is it more sin to wish me thus forsworn,
Or to dispraise my lord with that same tongue
Which she hath prais'd him with above compare
So many thousand times? Go, counsellor!
Thou and my bosom henceforth shall be twain.
I'll to the friar to know his remedy.
If all else fail, myself have power to die.

Exit

ACT IV

SCENE I. Friar Laurence's cell.

Enter Friar Laurence and County Paris

FRIAR On Thursday, Sir? The time is very short.

PARIS My father Capulet will have it so,
And I am nothing slow to slack his haste.

FRIAR You say you do not know the lady's mind.
Uneven is the course; I like it not.

PARIS Immoderately she weeps for Tybalt's death,
And therefore have I little talk'd of love;
For Venus smiles not in a house of tears.
Now, Sir, her father counts it dangerous
That she do give her sorrow so much sway,
And in his wisdom hastes our marriage
To stop the inundation of her tears,
Which, too much minded by herself alone,
May be put from her by society.
Now do you know the reason of this haste.

FRIAR [*aside*] I would I knew not why it should be slow'd.
Look, Sir, here comes the lady toward my cell.

Enter Juliet

PARIS Happily met, my lady and my wife!

JULIET That may be, Sir, when I may be a wife.

PARIS That may be must be, love, on Thursday next.

JULIET What must be shall be.

FRIAR   That's a certain text.

PARIS Come you to make confession to this father?

JULIET To answer that, I should confess to you.

PARIS Do not deny to him that you love me.

JULIET I will confess to you that I love him.

PARIS So will ye, I am sure, that you love me.

JULIET If I do so, it will be of more price,

Being spoke behind your back, than to your face.
PARIS   Poor soul, thy face is much abus'd with tears.
JULIET   The tears have got small victory by that,
  For it was bad enough before their spite.
PARIS   Thou wrong'st it more than tears with that report.
JULIET   That is no slander, Sir, which is a truth;
  And what I spake, I spake it to my face.
PARIS   Thy face is mine, and thou hast sland'red it.
JULIET   It may be so, for it is not mine own.—
  Are you at leisure, holy father, now,
  Or shall I come to you at evening mass?
FRIAR   My leisure serves me, pensive daughter, now.
  My lord, we must entreat the time alone.
PARIS   God shield I should disturb devotion!
  Juliet, on Thursday early will I rouse ye.
  Till then, adieu, and keep this holy kiss.

Exit Paris

JULIET   O, shut the door! and when thou hast done so,
  Come weep with me—past hope, past cure, past help!
FRIAR   Ah, Juliet, I already know thy grief;
  It strains me past the compass of my wits.
  I hear thou must, and nothing may prorogue it,
  On Thursday next be married to this County.
JULIET   Tell me not, Friar, that thou hear'st of this,
  Unless thou tell me how I may prevent it.
  If in thy wisdom thou canst give no help,
  Do thou but call my resolution wise [*She shows a knife*]
  And with this knife I'll help it presently.
  God join'd my heart and Romeo's, thou our hands;
  And ere this hand, by thee to Romeo's seal'd,
  Shall be the label to another deed,
  Or my true heart with treacherous revolt
  Turn to another, this shall slay them both.
  Therefore, out of thy long-experienc'd time,
  Give me some present counsel; or, behold,
  'Twixt my extremes and me this bloody knife
  Shall play the empire, arbitrating that
  Which the commission of thy years and art
  Could to no issue of true honour bring.
  Be not so long to speak. I long to die

If what thou speak'st speak not of remedy.

FRIAR   Hold, daughter. I do spy a kind of hope,
    Which craves as desperate an execution
    As that is desperate which we would prevent.
    If, rather than to marry County Paris
    Thou hast the strength of will to slay thyself,
    Then is it likely thou wilt undertake
    A thing like death to chide away this shame,
    That cop'st with death himself to scape from it;
    And, if thou dar'st, I'll give thee remedy.

JULIET   O, bid me leap, rather than marry Paris,
    From off the battlements of yonder tower,
    Or walk in thievish ways, or bid me lurk
    Where serpents are; chain me with roaring bears,
    Or shut me nightly in a charnel house,
    O'ercover'd quite with dead men's rattling bones,
    With reeky shanks and yellow chapless skulls;
    Or bid me go into a new-made grave
    And hide me with a dead man in his tomb—
    Things that, to hear them told, have made me tremble—
    And I will do it without fear or doubt,
    To live an unstain'd wife to my sweet love.

FRIAR   Hold, then. Go home, be merry, give consent
    To marry Paris. Wednesday is tomorrow.
    Tomorrow night look that thou lie alone;
    Let not the Nurse lie with thee in thy chamber.
    Take thou this vial, being then in bed,
    And this distilled liquor drink thou off;
    When presently through all thy veins shall run
    A cold and drowsy humour; for no pulse
    Shall keep his native progress, but surcease;
    No warmth, no breath, shall testify thou livest;
    The roses in thy lips and cheeks shall fade
    To pale ashes, thy eyes' windows fall
    Like death when he shuts up the day of life;
    Each part, depriv'd of supple government,
    Shall, stiff and stark and cold, appear like death;
    And in this borrowed likeness of shrunk death
    Thou shalt continue two-and-forty hours,
    And then awake as from a pleasant sleep.

Now, when the bridegroom in the morning comes
To rouse thee from thy bed, there art thou dead.
Then, as the manner of our country is,
In thy best robes uncovered on the bier
Thou shalt be borne to that same ancient vault
Where all the kindred of the Capulets lie.
In the meantime, against thou shalt awake,
Shall Romeo by my letters know our drift;
And hither shall he come; and he and I
Will watch thy waking, and that very night
Shall Romeo bear thee hence to Mantua.
And this shall free thee from this present shame,
If no inconstant toy nor womanish fear
Abate thy valour in the acting it.

JULIET   Give me, give me! O, tell not me of fear!

FRIAR   Hold! Get you gone, be strong and prosperous
In this resolve. I'll send a friar with speed
To Mantua, with my letters to thy lord.

JULIET   Love give me strength! and strength shall help afford.
Farewell, dear father.

Exeunt separately

SCENE II—Capulet's house.
Enter Father Capulet, Mother, Nurse, and two or three Servingmen

CAPULET   So many guests invite as here are writ. [*Exit a Servingman*]
Sirrah, go hire me twenty cunning cooks.

SERVANT   You shall have none ill, Sir; for I'll try if they can lick their
fingers.

CAPULET   How canst thou try them so?

SERVANT   Marry, Sir, 'tis an ill cook that cannot lick his own fingers.
Therefore he that cannot lick his fingers goes not with me.

CAPULET   Go, begone.   [*Exit Servingman*]
We shall be much unfurnish'd for this time.
What, is my daughter gone to Friar Laurence?

NURSE   Ay, forsooth.

CAPULET   Well, he may chance to do some good on her.
A peevish self-will'd harlotry it is.

Enter Juliet

NURSE   See where she comes from shrift with merry look.

CAPULET   How now, my headstrong? Where have you been gadding?

JULIET   Where I have learnt me to repent the sin
    Of disobedient opposition
    To you and your behests, and am enjoin'd
    By holy Laurence to fall prostrate here
    To beg your pardon. Pardon, I beseech you!
    Henceforward I am ever rul'd by you.
CAPULET   Send for the County. Go tell him of this.
    I'll have this knot knit up tomorrow morning.
JULIET   I met the youthful lord at Laurence' cell
    And gave him what becoming love I might,
    Not stepping o'er the bounds of modesty.
CAPULET   Why, I am glad on't. This is well. Stand up.
    This is as't should be. Let me see the County.
    [*To Nurse*] Ay, marry, go, I say, and fetch him hither.
    Now, afore God, this reverend holy friar,
    All our whole city is much bound to him.
JULIET   Nurse, will you go with me into my closet
    To help me sort such needful ornaments
    As you think fit to furnish me tomorrow?
CAPULET'S WIFE   No, not till Thursday. There is time enough.
CAPULET   Go, Nurse, go with her. We'll to church tomorrow.

Exit Juliet and Nurse

CAPULET'S WIFE   We shall be short in our provision.
    'Tis now near night.
CAPULET   Tush, I will stir about,
    And all things shall be well, I warrant thee, wife.
    Go thou to Juliet, help to deck up her.
    I'll not to bed tonight; let me alone.
    I'll play the housewife for this once. What, ho!
    They are all forth; well, I will walk myself
    To County Paris, to prepare him up
    Against tomorrow. My heart is wondrous light,
    Since this same wayward girl is so reclaim'd.

Exeunt

SCENE III—Juliet's chamber.
Enter Juliet and Nurse

JULIET   Ay, those attires are best; but, gentle Nurse,
    I pray thee leave me to myself tonight;
    For I have need of many orisons

To move the heavens to smile upon my state,
Which, well thou knowest, is cross and full of sin.

Enter Capulet's Wife

CAPULET'S WIFE   What, are you busy, ho? Need you my help?
JULIET   No, madam; we have cull'd such necessaries
As are behoveful for our state tomorrow.
So please you, let me now be left alone,
And let the Nurse this night sit up with you;
For I am sure you have your hands full all
In this so sudden business.
CAPULET'S WIFE   Good night.
Get thee to bed, and rest; for thou hast need.

Exit Capulet's Wife and Nurse

JULIET   Farewell! God knows when we shall meet again.
I have a faint cold fear thrills through my veins
that almost freezes up the heat of life.
I'll call them back again to comfort me.
Nurse! What should she do here?
My dismal scene I needs must act alone.
Come, vial. What if this mixture do not work at all?
Shall I be married then tomorrow morning?
No, No! This shall forbid it. Lie thou there. [*She lays down a dagger*]
What if it be a poison which the friar
Subtilly hath minist'red to have me dead,
Lest in this marriage he should be dishonour'd
Because he married me before to Romeo?
I fear it is; and yet methinks it should not,
For he hath still been tried a holy man.
I will not entertain so bad a thought.
How if, when I am laid into the tomb,
I wake before the time that Romeo
Come to redeem me? There's a fearful point!
Shall I not then be stifled in the vault,
To whose foul mouth no healthsome air breathes in,
And there die strangled ere my Romeo comes?
Or, if I live, is it not very like
The horrible conceit of death and night,
Together with the terror of the place—
As in a vault, an ancient receptacle
Where for this many hundred years the bones

Of all my buried ancestors are pack'd;
Where bloody Tybalt, yet but green in earth,
Lies fest'ring in his shroud; where, as they say,
At some hours in the night spirits resort—
Alack, alack, is it not like that I,
So early waking—what with loathsome smells,
And shrieks like mandrakes torn out of the earth,
That living mortals, hearing them, run mad—
O, if I wake, shall I not be distraught,
Environed with all these hideous fears,
And madly play with my forefathers' joints,
And pluck the mangled Tybalt from his shroud.
And, in this rage, with some great kinsman's bone
As with a club dash out my desp'rate brains?
O, look! methinks I see my cousin's ghost
Seeking out Romeo, that did spit his body
Upon a rapier's point. Stay, Tybalt, stay!
Romeo, Romeo, Romeo! Here's drink. I drink to thee.
She drinks and falls upon her bed within the curtains

SCENE IV—Capulet's house.
Enter Capulet's Wife and Nurse

CAPULET'S WIFE   Hold, take these keys and fetch more spices, Nurse.
NURSE   They call for dates and quinces in the pastry.
Enter Old Capulet
CAPULET   Come, stir, stir, stir! The second cock hath crow'd,
The curfew bell hath rung, 'tis three o'clock.
Look to the bak'd meats, good Angelica;
Spare not for cost.
NURSE   Go, you cotquean, go,
Get you to bed! Faith, you'll be sick tomorrow
For this night's watching.
CAPULET   No, not a whit. What, I have watch'd ere now
All night for lesser cause, and ne'er been sick.
CAPULET'S WIFE   Ay, you have been a mouse-hunt in your time;
But I will watch you from such watching now.
Exit Capulet's Wife and Nurse
CAPULET   A jealous hood, a jealous hood!
Enter three or four Fellows, with spits and logs and baskets

What is there? Now, fellow,
FIRST SERVANT   Things for the cook, Sir; but I know not what.
CAPULET   Make haste, make haste.   [*Exit First Servant*]
                         Sirrah, fetch drier logs.
Call Peter; he will show thee where they are.
SECOND SERVANT   I have a head, Sir, that will find out logs
And never trouble Peter for the matter.
CAPULET   Mass, and well said; a merry whoreson, ha!
Thou shalt be loggerhead. [*Exit Second Servant*] Good faith, 'tis day.
The County will be here with music straight,
For so he said he would. [*Play music, within*] I hear him near.
Nurse! Wife! What, ho! What, Nurse, I say!
                     Enter Nurse
Go waken Juliet; go and trim her up.
I'll go and chat with Paris. Hie, make haste,
Make haste! The bridegroom he is come already.
Make haste, I say.
                                         Exeunt

                 SCENE V—Juliet's chamber.
                     Enter Nurse
NURSE   Mistress! what, mistress! Juliet! Fast, I warrant her, she.
Why, lamb! why, lady! Fie, you slugabed!
Why, love, I say! madam! sweetheart! Why, bride!
What, not a word? You take your pennyworths now!
Sleep for a week; for the next night, I warrant,
The County Paris hath set up his rest
That you shall rest but little. God forgive me!
Marry, and amen. How sound is she asleep!
I must needs wake her. Madam, madam, madam!
Ay, let the County take you in your bed!
He'll fright you up, i' faith. Will it not be? [*She draws the bedcurtains*]
What, dress'd, and in your clothes, and down again?
I must needs wake you. Lady! lady! lady!
Alas, alas! Help, help! My lady's dead!
O welladay that ever I was born!
Some aqua vitae, ho! My lord! my lady!
                 Enter Capulet's Wife
CAPULET'S WIFE   What noise is here?
NURSE   O lamentable day!

CAPULET'S WIFE   What is the matter?

NURSE   Look, look! O heavy day!

CAPULET'S WIFE   O me, O me! My child, my only life!
   Revive, look up, or I will die with thee!
   Help, help! Call help.

Enter Capulet

CAPULET   For shame, bring Juliet forth; her lord is come.

NURSE   She's dead, deceas'd; she's dead! Alack the day!

CAPULET'S WIFE   Alack the day, she's dead, she's dead, she's dead!

CAPULET   Ha! let me see her. Out alas! she's cold.
   Her blood is settled, and her joints are stiff;
   Life and these lips have long been separated.
   Death lies on her like an untimely frost
   Upon the sweetest flower of all the field.

NURSE   O lamentable day!

CAPULET'S WIFE   O woeful time!

CAPULET   Death, that hath ta'en her hence to make me wail,
   Ties up my tongue and will not let me speak.

Enter Friar Laurence and the County Paris, with Musicians

FRIAR   Come, is the bride ready to go to church?

CAPULET   Ready to go, but never to return.
   O son, the night before thy wedding day
   Hath Death lain with thy wife. There she lies,
   Flower as she was, deflowered by him.
   Death is my son-in-law, Death is my heir;
   My daughter he hath wedded. I will die
   And leave him all; life, living, all is Death's.

PARIS   Have I thought long to see this morning's face,
   And doth it give me such a sight as this?

CAPULET'S WIFE   Accurs'd, unhappy, wretched, hateful day!
   Most miserable hour that e'er time saw
   In lasting labour of his pilgrimage!
   But one, poor one, one poor and loving child,
   But one thing to rejoice and solace in,
   And cruel Death hath catch'd it from my sight!

NURSE   O woe! O woeful, woeful, woeful day!
   Most lamentable day, most woeful day
   That ever ever I did yet behold!
   O day! O day! O day! O hateful day!
   Never was seen so black a day as this.

O woeful day! O woeful day!
PARIS   Beguil'd, divorced, wronged, spited, slain!
    Most detestable Death, by thee beguil'd,
    By cruel cruel thee quite overthrown!
    O love! O life! not life, but love in death!
CAPULET   Despis'd, distressed, hated, martyr'd, kill'd!
    Uncomfortable time, why cam'st thou now
    To murder, murder our solemnity?
    O child! O child! my soul, and not my child!
    Dead art thou, dead! alack, my child is dead,
    And with my child my joys are buried!
FRIAR   Peace, ho, for shame! Confusion's cure lives not
    In these confusions. Heaven and yourself
    Had part in this fair maid! Now heaven hath all,
    And all the better is it for the maid.
    Your part in her you could not keep from death,
    But heaven keeps his part in eternal life.
    The most you sought was her promotion,
    For 'twas your heaven she should be advanc'd;
    And weep ye now, seeing she is advanc'd
    Above the clouds, as high as heaven itself?
    O, in this love, you love your child so ill
    That you run mad, seeing that she is well.
    She's not well married that lives married long,
    But she's best married that dies married young.
    Dry up your tears and stick your rosemary
    On this fair corse, and, as the custom is,
    And in her best array bear her to church;
    For though fond nature bids us all lament,
    Yet nature's tears are reason's merriment.
CAPULET   All things that we ordained festival
    Turn from their office to black funeral—
    Our instruments to melancholy bells,
    Our wedding cheer to a sad burial feast;
    Our solemn hymns to sullen dirges change;
    Our bridal flowers serve for a buried corse;
    And all things change them to the contrary.
FRIAR   Sir, go you in; and, madam, go with him;
    And go, Sir Paris. Every one prepare
    To follow this fair corpse unto her grave.

The heavens do low'r upon you for some ill;
Move them no more by crossing their high will.

Exeunt. Manent Nurse with Musicians

FIRST MUSICIAN   Faith, we may put up our pipes and be gone.

NURSE   Honest good fellows, ah, put up, put up!
    For well you know this is a pitiful case.

Exit Nurse

FIRST MUSICIAN   Ay, by my troth, the case may be amended.

Enter Peter

PETER   Musicians, O, musicians, "Heart's ease," "Heart's ease"! O,
    an you will have me live, play "Heart's ease."

FIRST MUSICIAN   Why "Heart's ease"?

PETER   O, musicians, because my heart itself plays "My heart is full of
    woe." O, play me some merry dump to comfort me.

FIRST MUSICIAN   Not a dump we! 'Tis no time to play now.

PETER   You will not then?

FIRST MUSICIAN   No.

PETER   I will then give it you soundly.

FIRST MUSICIAN   What will you give us?

PETER   No money, on my faith, but the gleek. I will give you the minstrel.

FIRST MUSICIAN   Then will I give you the serving-creature.

PETER   Then will I lay the serving-creature's dagger on your pate. I
    will carry no crotchets. I'll re you, I'll fa you. Do you note me?

FIRST MUSICIAN   An you re us and fa us, you note us.

SECOND MUSICIAN   Pray you put up your dagger, and put out your wit.

PETER   Then have at you with my wit! I will dry-beat you with an iron
    wit, and put up my iron dagger. Answer me like men. [*Sings*]

> When griping grief the heart doth wound,
> And doleful dumps the mind oppress,
> Then music with her silver sound—

Why "silver sound"? Why "music with her silver sound"? What
say you, Simon Catling?

FIRST MUSICIAN   Marry, Sir, because silver hath a sweet sound.

PETER   Pretty! What say you, Hugh Rebeck?

SECOND MUSICIAN   I say "silver sound" because musicians sound for
    silver.

PETER   Pretty too! What say you, James Soundpost?

THIRD MUSICIAN   Faith, I know not what to say.

PETER　O, I cry you mercy! You are the singer. I will say for you. It is "music with her silver sound" because musicians have no gold for sounding. [*Sings*]

> Then music with her silver sound
> with speedy help doth lend redress.

Exit Peter

FIRST MUSICIAN　What a pestilent knave is this same?
SECOND MUSICIAN　Hang him, Jack! Come, we'll in here, tarry for the mourners, and stay dinner.

Exeunt

ACT V

SCENE I—Mantua. A street.

Enter Romeo

ROMEO   If I may trust the flattering truth of sleep
My dreams presage some joyful news at hand.
My bosom's lord sits lightly in his throne,
And all this day an unaccustom'd spirit
Lifts me above the ground with cheerful thoughts.
I dreamt my lady came and found me dead—
Strange dream that gives a dead man leave to think!—
And breath'd such life with kisses in my lips
That I reviv'd and was an emperor.
Ah me! how sweet is love itself possess'd,
When but love's shadows are so rich in joy!

Enter Romeo's Man Balthasar, booted

News from Verona! How now, Balthasar?
Dost thou not bring me letters from the friar?
How doth my lady? Is my father well?
How fares my Juliet? That I ask again,
For nothing can be ill if she be well.

BALTHASAR   Then she is well, and nothing can be ill.
Her body sleeps in Capel's monument,
And her immortal part with angels lives.
I saw her laid low in her kindred's vault
And presently took post to tell it you.
O, pardon me for bringing these ill news,
Since you did leave it for my office, Sir.

ROMEO   Is it e'en so? Then I defy you, stars!
Thou knowest my lodging. Get me ink and paper,
And hire posthorses. I will hence tonight.

BALTHASAR   I do beseech you, Sir, have patience.
Your looks are pale and wild and do import

Some misadventure.

ROMEO   Tush, thou art deceiv'd.
Leave me and do the thing I bid thee do.
Hast thou no letters to me from the friar?

BALTHASAR   No, my good lord.

ROMEO   No matter. Get thee gone
And hire those horses. I'll be with thee straight.

Exit Balthasar

Well, Juliet, I will lie with thee tonight.
Let's see for means. O mischief, thou art swift
To enter in the thoughts of desperate men!
I do remember an apothecary,
And hereabouts a dwells, which late I noted
In tatt'red weeds, with overwhelming brows,
Culling of simples. Meagre were his looks,
Sharp misery had worn him to the bones;
And in his needy shop a tortoise hung,
An alligator stuff'd, and other skins
Of ill-shaped fishes; and about his shelves
A beggarly account of empty boxes,
Green earthen pots, bladders, and musty seeds,
Remnants of packthread, and old cakes of roses
Were thinly scattered, to make up a show.
Noting this penury, to myself I said,
"An if a man did need a poison now
Whose sale is present death in Mantua,
Here lives a caitiff wretch would sell it him."
O, this same thought did but forerun my need,
And this same needy man must sell it me.
As I remember, this should be the house.
Being holiday, the beggar's shop is shut.
What, ho! apothecary!

Enter Apothecary

APOTHECARY   Who calls so loud?

ROMEO   Come hither, man. I see that thou art poor.
Hold, there is forty ducats. Let me have
A dram of poison, such soon-speeding gear
As will disperse itself through all the veins
That the life-weary taker mall fall dead,
And that the trunk may be discharg'd of breath

As violently as hasty powder fir'd
Doth hurry from the fatal cannon's womb.

APOTHECARY   Such mortal drugs I have; but Mantua's law
Is death to any he that utters them.

ROMEO   Art thou so bare and full of wretchedness
And fearest to die? Famine is in thy cheeks,
Need and oppression starveth in thine eyes,
Contempt and beggary hangs upon thy back:
The world is not thy friend, nor the world's law;
The world affords no law to make thee rich;
Then be not poor, but break it and take this.

APOTHECARY   My poverty but not my will consents.

ROMEO   I pay thy poverty and not thy will.

APOTHECARY   [*giving poison*] Put this in any liquid thing you will
And drink it off, and if you had the strength
Of twenty men, it would dispatch you straight.

ROMEO   [*giving gold*] There is thy gold—worse poison to men's souls,
Doing more murder in this loathsome world,
Than these poor compounds that thou mayst not sell.
I sell thee poison; thou hast sold me none.
Farewell. Buy food and get thyself in flesh.

                                   Exit Apothecary

Come, cordial and not poison, go with me
To Juliet's grave; for there must I use thee.

                                             Exit

SCENE II—Verona. Friar Laurence's cell.
Enter Friar John to Friar Laurence's

FRIAR JOHN   Holy Franciscan friar, brother, ho!
Enter Friar Laurence

FRIAR LAURENCE   This same should be the voice of Friar John.
Welcome from Mantua. What says Romeo?
Or, if his mind be writ, give me his letter.

FRIAR JOHN   Going to find a barefoot brother out,
One of our order, to associate me
Here in this city visiting the sick,
And finding him, the searchers of the town,
Suspecting that we both were in a house
Where the infectious pestilence did reign,
Seal'd up the doors, and would not let us forth,

So that my speed to Mantua there was stay'd.

FRIAR LAURENCE   Who bare my letter, then, to Romeo?

FRIAR JOHN   I could not send it—here it is again—
Nor get a messenger to bring it thee,
So fearful were they of infection.

FRIAR LAURENCE   Unhappy fortune! By my brotherhood,
The letter was not nice, but full of charge,
Of dear import; and the neglecting it
May do much danger. Friar John, go hence,
Get me an iron crow and bring it straight
Unto my cell.

FRIAR JOHN   Brother, I'll go and bring it thee.

Exit Friar John

FRIAR LAURENCE   Now, must I to the monument alone.
Within this three hours will fair Juliet wake.
She will beshrew me much that Romeo
Hath had no notice of these accidents;
But I will write again to Mantua,
And keep her at my cell till Romeo come—
Poor living corse, clos'd in a dead man's tomb!

Exeunt

SCENE III—Verona. A churchyard; the Capulet's monument
Enter Paris and his Page with flowers and a torch

PARIS   Give me thy torch, boy. Hence, and stand aloof.
Yet put it out, for I would not be seen.
Under yon yew tree lay thee all along,
Holding thine ear close to the hollow ground.
So shall no foot upon the churchyard tread,
Being loose, unfirm, with digging up of graves,
But thou shalt hear it. Whistle then to me,
As signal that thou hear'st something approach.
Give me those flowers. Do as I bid thee, go.

PAGE   [*aside*] I am almost afraid to stand alone
Here in the churchyard; yet I will adventure. [*Page hides*]

Strewing flowers and perfumed water

PARIS   Sweet flower, with flowers thy bridal bed I strew—
O woe! thy canopy is dust and stones
Which with sweet water nightly I will dew;
Or, wanting that, with tears distill'd by moans.

The obsequies that I for thee will keep
Nightly shall be to strew, thy grave and weep. [*He hears a whistle*]
The boy gives warning something doth approach.
What cursed foot wanders this way tonight
To cross my obsequies and true love's rite?
What, with a torch? Muffle me, night, awhile. [*Paris hides*]
Enter Romeo, and Balthasar with a torch, a mattock, and a crow of iron
ROMEO   Give me that mattock and the wrenching iron.
Hold, take this letter. Early in the morning
See thou deliver it to my lord and father.
Give me the light. Upon thy life I charge thee,
Whate'er thou hearest or seest, stand all aloof
And do not interrupt me in my course.
Why I descend into this bed of death
Is partly to behold my lady's face,
But chiefly to take thence from her dead finger
A precious ring—a ring that I must use
In dear employment. Therefore hence, be gone.
But if thou, jealous, dost return to pry
In what I farther shall intend to do,
By heaven, I will tear thee joint by joint
And strew this hungry churchyard with thy limbs.
The time and my intents are savage-wild,
More fierce and more inexorable far
Than empty tigers or the roaring sea.
BALTHASAR   I will be gone, Sir, and not trouble you.
ROMEO   So shalt thou show me friendship. Take thou that.
He gives him money
Live, and be prosperous; and farewell, good fellow.
BALTHASAR   [*aside*] For all this same, I'll hide me hereabout.
His looks I fear, and his intents I doubt. [*He hides*]
ROMEO   Thou detestable maw, thou womb of death,
Gorg'd with the dearest morsel of the earth,
Thus I enforce thy rotten jaws to open,
And in despite I'll cram thee with more food.
Romeo prepares to open the tomb
PARIS   This is that banish'd haughty Montague
That murd'red my love's cousin—with which grief
It is supposed the fair creature died—
And here is come to do some villainous shame

To the dead bodies. I will apprehend him. [*He comes forward*]
Stop thy unhallowed toil, vile Montague!
Can vengeance be pursu'd further than death?
Condemned villain, I do apprehend thee.
Obey, and go with me; for thou must die.
ROMEO   I must indeed; and therefore came I hither.
Good gentle youth, tempt not a desp'rate man.
Fly hence and leave me. Think upon these gone;
Let them affright thee. I beseech thee, youth,
Put not another sin upon my head
By urging me to fury. O, be gone!
By heaven, I love thee better than myself,
For I come hither arm'd against myself.
Stay not, be gone. Live, and hereafter say
A madman's mercy bid thee run away.
PARIS   I do defy thy conjuration
And apprehend thee for a felon here.
ROMEO   Wilt thou provoke me? Then have at thee, boy!
PAGE   O Lord, they fight! I will go call the watch.   [*Exit*]
PARIS   O, I am slain! [*He falls*] If thou be merciful,
Open the tomb, lay me with Juliet. [*He dies*]
ROMEO   In faith, I will. Let me peruse this face.
Mercutio's kinsman, noble County Paris!
What said my man when my betossed soul
Did not attend him as we rode? I think
He told me Paris should have married Juliet.
Said he not so? or did I dream it so?
Or am I mad, hearing him talk of Juliet
To think it was so? O, give me thy hand,
One writ with me in sour misfortune's book!
I'll bury thee in a triumphant grave. [*He opens the tomb*]
A grave? O, no, a lanthorn, slaught'red youth,
For here lies Juliet, and her beauty makes
This vault a feasting presence full of light.
Death, lie thou there, by a dead man interr'd.
                    He lays Paris in the tomb
How oft when men are at the point of death
Have they been merry! Which their keepers call
A lightning before death. O, how may I
Call this a lightning? O my love! my wife!

Death, that hath suck'd the honey of thy breath,
Hath had no power yet upon thy beauty.
Thou art not conquer'd. Beauty's ensign yet
Is crimson in thy lips and in thy cheeks,
And death's pale flag is not advanced there.
Tybalt, liest thou there in thy bloody sheet?
O, what more favour can I do to thee
Than with that hand that cut thy youth in twain
To sunder his that was thine enemy?
Forgive me, cousin! Ah, dear Juliet,
Why art thou yet so fair? Shall I believe
That unsubstantial Death is amorous,
And that the lean abhorred monster keeps
Thee here in dark to be his paramour?
For fear of that I still will stay with thee
And never from this palace of dim night
Depart again. Here, here will I remain
With worms that are thy chambermaids. O, here
Will I set up my everlasting rest
And shake the yoke of inauspicious stars
From this world-wearied flesh. Eyes, look your last!
Arms, take your last embrace! and, lips, O you
The doors of breath, seal with a righteous kiss
A dateless bargain to engrossing death! [*He kisses Juliet*]
Come, bitter conduct; come, unsavoury guide!
Thou desperate pilot, now at once run on
The dashing rocks thy seasick weary bark!
Here's to my love! [*He drinks*] O true apothecary!
Thy drugs are quick. Thus with a kiss I die. [*He dies*]
    Enter Friar Laurence, with lanthorn, crow, and spade

FRIAR   Saint Francis be my speed! How oft tonight
Have my old feet stumbled at graves! Who's there?

BALTHASAR   Here's one, a friend, and one that knows you well.

FRIAR   Bliss be upon you! Tell me, good my friend,
What torch is yon that vainly lends his light
To grubs and eyeless skulls? As I discern,
It burneth in the Capulet's monument.

BALTHASAR   It doth so, holy Sir; and there's my master,
One that you love.

FRIAR   Who is it?

BALTHASAR   Romeo.

FRIAR   How long hath he been there?

BALTHASAR   Full half an hour.

FRIAR   Go with me to the vault.

BALTHASAR   I dare not, Sir.
My master knows not but I am gone hence,
And fearfully did menace me with death
If I did stay to look on his intents.

FRIAR   Stay then; I'll go alone. Fear comes upon me.
O, much I fear some ill unthrifty thing.

BALTHASAR   As I did sleep under this yew tree here,
I dreamt my master and another fought,
And that my master slew him.

FRIAR   [*advancing to the tomb*] Romeo!
Alack, alack, what blood is this which stains
The stony entrance of this sepulchre?
What mean these masterless and gory swords
To lie discolour'd by this place of peace? [*He enters the tomb*]
Romeo! O, pale! Who else? What, Paris too?
And steep'd in blood? Ah, what an unkind hour
Is guilty of this lamentable chance!
The lady stirs. [*Juliet rises*]

JULIET   O comfortable Friar! Where is my lord?
I do remember well where I should be,
And there I am. Where is my Romeo? [*A noise within*]

FRIAR   I hear some noise. Lady, come from that nest
Of death, contagion, and unnatural sleep.
A greater power than we can contradict
Hath thwarted our intents. Come, come away.
Thy husband in thy bosom there lies dead;
And Paris too. Come, I'll dispose of thee
Among a sisterhood of holy nuns.
Stay not to question, for the watch is coming.
Come, go, good Juliet. [*A noise again*] I dare no longer stay.

JULIET   Go, get thee hence, for I will not away.

                               Exit Friar Laurence

What's here? A cup, clos'd in my true love's hand?
Poison, I see, hath been his timeless end.
O churl! drunk all, and left no friendly drop
To help me after? I will kiss thy lips.

Haply some poison yet doth hang on them
To make me die with a restorative. [*She kisses him*]
Thy lips are warm!
Enter Paris's Page and First Watch at the other end of the churchyard
FIRST WATCH   Lead, boy! Which way?
JULIET   Yea, noise? Then I'll be brief. O happy dagger!
                    She takes Romeo's dagger
This is thy sheath; there rest, and let me die.
                She stabs herself and falls on Romeo's body
                Enter Paris's Page and First Watch with others
PAGE   This is the place. There, where the torch doth burn.
FIRST WATCH   The ground is bloody. Search about the churchyard.
Go, some of you; whoe'er you find attach.
                                Exit some of the Watch
Pitiful sight! Here lies the County slain;
And Juliet bleeding, warm, and newly dead,
Who here hath lain this two days buried.
Go, tell the Prince; run to the Capulet's;
Raise up the Montagues; some others search.
                                Exit others of the Watch
We see the ground whereon these woes do lie,
But the true ground of all these piteous woes
We cannot without circumstance descry.
            Enter some of the Watch with Romeo's man, Balthasar
SECOND WATCH   Here's Romeo's man. We found him in the church-
yard.
FIRST WATCH   Hold him in safety till the Prince come hither.
            Enter Friar Laurence and another Watchman, with tools
THIRD WATCH   Here is a friar that trembles, sighs, and weeps.
We took this mattock and this spade from him
As he was coming from this churchyard's side.
FIRST WATCH   A great suspicion! Stay the Friar too.
                Enter the Prince and Attendants
PRINCE   What misadventure is so early up,
That calls our person from our morning rest?
                Enter Capulet and his Wife with others
CAPULET   What should it be, that they so shrieked abroad?
CAPULET'S WIFE   O, the people in the street cry "Romeo,"
Some "Juliet," and some "Paris"; and all run
With open outcry, toward our monument.

PRINCE   What fear is this which startles in our ears?

FIRST WATCH   Sovereign, here lies the County Paris slain;
     And Romeo dead; and Juliet, dead before,
     Warm and new kill'd.

PRINCE   Search, seek, and know how this foul murder comes.

FIRST WATCH   Here is a friar, and slaughter'd Romeo's man,
     With instruments upon them fit to open
     These dead men's tombs.

CAPULET   O heavens! O wife, look how our daughter bleeds!
     This dagger hath mista'en, for, lo, his house
     Is empty on the back of Montague,
     And it mis-sheathed in my daughter's bosom!

CAPULET'S WIFE   O me! This sight of death is as a bell
     That warns my old age to a sepulchre.

Enter Montague [and others]

PRINCE   Come, Montague; for thou art early up
     To see thy son and heir more early down.

MONTAGUE   Alas, my liege, my wife is dead tonight!
     Grief of my son's exile hath stopp'd her breath.
     What further woe conspires against mine age?

PRINCE   Look, and thou shalt see.

Montague sees Romeo's body

MONTAGUE   O thou untaught! What manners is in this,
     To press before thy father to a grave?

PRINCE   Seal up the mouth of outrage for a while,
     Till we can clear these ambiguities
     And know their spring, their head, their true descent;
     And then will I be general of your woes
     And lead you even to death. Meantime forbear,
     And let mischance be slave to patience.
     Bring forth the parties of suspicion.

FRIAR   I am the greatest, able to do least,
     Yet most suspected, as the time and place
     Doth make against me, of this direful murder;
     And here I stand, both to impeach and purge
     Myself condemned and myself excus'd.

PRINCE   Then say it once what thou dost know in this.

FRIAR   I will be brief, for my short date of breath
     Is not so long as is a tedious tale.
     Romeo, there dead, was husband to that Juliet;

And she, there dead, that Romeo's faithful wife.
I married them; and their stol'n marriage day
Was Tybalt's doomsday, whose untimely death
Banish'd the new-made bridegroom from this city;
For whom, and not for Tybalt, Juliet pin'd.
You, to remove that siege of grief from her,
Betroth'd and would have married her perforce
To County Paris. Then comes she to me
And with wild looks bid me devise some mean
To rid her from this second marriage,
Or in my cell there would she kill herself.
Then gave I her (so tutored by my art)
A sleeping potion; which so took effect
As I intended, for it wrought on her
The form of death. Meantime I writ to Romeo
That he should hither come as this dire night
To help to take her from her borrowed grave,
Being the time the potion's force should cease.
But he which bore my letter, Friar John,
Was stay'd by accident, and yesternight
Return'd my letter back. Then all alone
At the prefixed hour of her waking
Came I to take her from her kindred's vault;
Meaning to keep her closely at my cell
Till I conveniently could send to Romeo.
But when I came, some minute ere the time
Of her awaking, here untimely lay
The noble Paris and true Romeo dead.
She wakes; and I entreated her come forth
And bear this work of heaven with patience.
But then a noise did scare me from the tomb,
And she, too desperate, would not go with me,
But, as it seems, did violence on herself.
All this I know, and to the marriage
Her Nurse is privy, and if aught in this
Miscarried by my fault, let my old life
Be sacrificed some hour before his time
Unto the rigor of severest law.
BALTHASAR   I brought my master new of Juliet's death;
And then in post he came from Mantua

To this same place, to this same monument.
This letter he early bid me give his father,
And threat'ned me with death, going in the vault,
If I departed not and left him there.

PRINCE   Give me the letter. I will look on it.
Where is the County's page that rais'd the watch?
Sirrah, what made your master in this place?

PAGE   He came with flowers to strew his lady's grave;
And bid me stand aloof, and so I did.
Anon comes one with light to ope the tomb;
And by-and-by my master drew on him;
And then I ran away to call the Watch.

PRINCE   This letter doth make good the Friar's words,
Their course of love, the tidings of her death;
And here he writes that he did buy a poison
Of a poor apothecary, and therewithal
Came to this vault to die, and lie with Juliet.
Where be these enemies? Capulet, Montague,
See what a scourge is laid upon your hate,
That heaven finds means to kill your joys with love!
And I, for winking at you, discords too,
Have lost a brace of kinsmen. All are punish'd.

CAPULET   O brother Montague, give me thy hand.
This is my daughter's jointure, for no more
Can I demand.

MONTAGUE   But I can give thee more;
For I will raise her statue in pure gold,
That whiles Verona by that name is known,
There shall no figure at such rate be set
As that of true and faithful Juliet.

CAPULET   As rich shall Romeo's by his lady's lie—
Poor sacrifices of our enmity!

PRINCE   A glooming peace this morning with it brings.
The sun for sorrow will not show his head.
Go hence, to have more talk of these sad things;
Some shall be pardon'd, and some punished;
For never was a story of more woe
Than this of Juliet and her Romeo.

Exeunt omnes

OTHELLO

The Moor of Venice

Dramatis Personae

OTHELLO, the Moor, General of the Venetian forces
IAGO, ensign to Othello
CASSIO, Lieutenant to Othello
DESDEMONA, his wife
EMILIA, Iago's wife, lady-in-waiting to Desdemona
BRABANTIO, Venetian Senator, father of Desdemona
GRATIANO, nobleman of Venice, brother of Brabantio
LODOVICO, nobleman of Venice, kinsman of Brabantio
DUKE OF VENICE
RODERIGO, rejected suitor of Desdemona
BIANCA, mistress of Cassio
MONTANO, a Cypriot official
SENATORS
GENTLEMEN
OFFICERS
ATTENDANTS
A CLOWN in service to Othello
SAILORS
MESSENGERS
MUSICIANS

ACT I

SCENE I—Venice. A street.

Enter Roderigo and Iago

RODERIGO   Tush, never tell me! I take it much unkindly
    That thou, Iago, who hast had my purse
    As if the strings were thine, shouldst know of this.

IAGO   'Sblood, but you will not hear me.
    If ever I did dream of such a matter, abhor me.

RODERIGO   Thou told'st me thou didst hold him in thy hate.

IAGO   Despise me,
    If I do not. Three great ones of the city,
    In personal suit to make me his Lieutenant,
    Off-capp'd to him; and, by the faith of man,
    I know my price, I am worth no worse a place.
    But he, as loving his own pride and purposes,
    Evades them, with a bumbast circumstance
    Horribly stuff'd with epithets of war,
    Nonsuits my mediators; for, "Certes," says he,
    "I have already chose my officer."
    And what was he?
    Forsooth, a great arithmetician,
    One Michael Cassio, a Florentine,
    A fellow almost damn'd in a fair wife,
    That never set a squadron in the field,
    Nor the division of a battle knows
    More than a spinster; unless the bookish theoric,
    Wherein the toga'd consuls can propose
    As masterly as he. Mere prattle without practice
    Is all his soldiership. But he, Sir, had the election;
    And I, of whom his eyes had seen the proof
    At Rhodes, at Cyprus, and on other grounds
    Christian and heathen, must be belee'd and calm'd

By debitor and creditor. This counter-caster,
He, in good time, must his Lieutenant be,
And I—God bless the mark!—his Moorship's ancient.

RODERIGO   By heaven, I rather would have been his hangman.

IAGO   Why, there's no remedy. 'Tis the curse of service,
Preferment goes by letter and affection,
And not by old gradation, where each second
Stood heir to the first. Now, Sir, be judge yourself
Whether I in any just term am affined
To love the Moor.

RODERIGO   I would not follow him then.

IAGO   O, Sir, content you.
I follow him to serve my turn upon him:
We cannot all be masters, nor all masters
Cannot be truly follow'd. You shall mark
Many a duteous and knee-crooking knave,
That doting on his own obsequious bondage
Wears out his time, much like his master's ass,
For nought but provender, and when he's old, cashier'd.
Whip me such honest knaves. Others there are
Who, trimm'd in forms and visages of duty,
Keep yet their hearts attending on themselves,
And throwing but shows of service on their lords
Do well thrive by them; and when they have lined their coats
Do themselves homage. These fellows have some soul,
And such a one do I profess myself. For, Sir,
It is as sure as you are Roderigo,
Were I the Moor, I would not be Iago.
In following him, I follow but myself;
Heaven is my judge, not I for love and duty,
But seeming so, for my peculiar end.
For when my outward action doth demonstrate
The native act and figure of my heart
In complement extern, 'tis not long after
But I will wear my heart upon my sleeve
For daws to peck at: I am not what I am.

RODERIGO   What a full fortune does the thick-lips owe,
If he can carry't thus!

IAGO   Call up her father,
Rouse him, make after him, poison his delight,

Proclaim him in the streets, incense her kinsmen,
And, though he in a fertile climate dwell,
Plague him with flies. Though that his joy be joy,
Yet throw such changes of vexation on't
As it may lose some color.

RODERIGO   Here is her father's house; I'll call aloud.

IAGO   Do, with like timorous accent and dire yell
As when, by night and negligence, the fire
Is spied in populous cities.

RODERIGO   What, ho, Brabantio! Signior Brabantio, ho!

IAGO   Awake! What, ho, Brabantio! Thieves! Thieves! Thieves!
Look to your house, your daughter, and your bags!
Thieves! Thieves!

Brabantio appears above, at a window.

BRABANTIO   What is the reason of this terrible summons?
What is the matter there?

RODERIGO   Signior, is all your family within?

IAGO   Are your doors lock'd?

BRABANTIO   Why? Wherefore ask you this?

IAGO   'Zounds, Sir, you're robb'd! For shame, put on your gown;
Your heart is burst, you have lost half your soul;
Even now, now, very now, an old black ram
Is tupping your white ewe. Arise, arise!
Awake the snorting citizens with the bell,
Or else the devil will make a grandsire of you.
Arise, I say!

BRABANTIO   What, have you lost your wits?

RODERIGO   Most reverend signior, do you know my voice?

BRABANTIO   Not I. What are you?

RODERIGO   My name is Roderigo.

BRABANTIO   The worser welcome.
I have charged thee not to haunt about my doors.
In honest plainness thou hast heard me say
My daughter is not for thee; and now, in madness,
Being full of supper and distempering draughts,
Upon malicious bravery, dost thou come
To start my quiet.

RODERIGO   Sir, Sir, Sir—

BRABANTIO   But thou must needs be sure
My spirit and my place have in them power

To make this bitter to thee.

RODERIGO   Patience, good Sir.

BRABANTIO   What tell'st thou me of robbing? This is Venice;
My house is not a grange.

RODERIGO   Most grave Brabantio,
In simple and pure soul I come to you.

IAGO   'Zounds, Sir, you are one of those that will not serve God, if
the devil bid you. Because we come to do you service and you
think we are ruffians, you'll have your daughter covered with a
Barbary horse; you'll have your nephews neigh to you; you'll have
coursers for cousins, and gennets for germans.

BRABANTIO   What profane wretch art thou?

IAGO   I am one, Sir, that comes to tell you your daughter and the
Moor are now making the beast with two backs.

BRABANTIO   Thou are a villain.

IAGO   You are—a senator.

BRABANTIO   This thou shalt answer; I know thee, Roderigo.

RODERIGO   Sir, I will answer anything. But, I beseech you,
If't be your pleasure and most wise consent,
As partly I find it is, that your fair daughter,
At this odd-even and dull watch o' the night,
Transported with no worse nor better guard
But with a knave of common hire, a gondolier,
To the gross clasps of a lascivious Moor—
If this be known to you, and your allowance,
We then have done you bold and saucy wrongs;
But if you know not this, my manners tell me
We have your wrong rebuke. Do not believe
That, from the sense of all civility,
I thus would play and trifle with your reverence.
Your daughter, if you have not given her leave,
I say again, hath made a gross revolt,
Tying her duty, beauty, wit, and fortunes
In an extravagant and wheeling stranger
Of here and everywhere. Straight satisfy yourself:
If she be in her chamber or your house,
Let loose on me the justice of the state
For thus deluding you.

BRABANTIO   Strike on the tinder, ho!
Give me a taper! Call up all my people!

This accident is not unlike my dream;
Belief of it oppresses me already.
Light, I say, light!

Exit above

IAGO   Farewell, for I must leave you.
It seems not meet, nor wholesome to my place
To be produced—as, if I stay, I shall—
Against the Moor; for I do know, the state,
However this may gall him with some check,
Cannot with safety cast him, for he's embark'd
With such loud reason to the Cyprus wars,
Which even now stands in act, that, for their souls,
Another of his fathom they have none
To lead their business; in which regard,
Though I do hate him as I do hell pains,
Yet for necessity of present life,
I must show out a flag and sign of love,
Which is indeed but sign. That you shall surely find him,
Lead to the Sagittary the raised search,
And there will I be with him. So farewell.

Exit Iago

Enter, below, Brabantio, in his nightgown, and Servants, with torches

BRABANTIO   It is too true an evil: gone she is,
And what's to come of my despised time
Is nought but bitterness. Now, Roderigo,
Where didst thou see her? O unhappy girl!
With the Moor, say'st thou? Who would be a father!
How didst thou know 'twas she? O, she deceives me
Past thought! What said she to you? Get more tapers.
Raise all my kindred. Are they married, think you?

RODERIGO   Truly, I think they are.

BRABANTIO   O heaven! How got she out? O treason of the blood!
Fathers, from hence trust not your daughters' minds
By what you see them act. Is there not charms
By which the property of youth and maidhood
May be abused! Have you not read, Roderigo,
Of some such thing?

RODERIGO   Yes, Sir, I have indeed.

BRABANTIO   Call up my brother. O, would you had had her!
[*To servants*] Some one way, some another. Do you know

Where we may apprehend her and the Moor?
RODERIGO   I think I can discover him, if you please
    To get good guard and go along with me.
BRABANTIO   Pray you, lead on. At every house I'll call;
    I may command at most. Get weapons, ho!
    And raise some special officers of night.
    On, good Roderigo. I will deserve your pains.

Exeunt

SCENE II—Another street.

Enter Othello, Iago, and Attendants, with torches

IAGO   Though in the trade of war I have slain men,
    Yet do I hold it very stuff o' the conscience
    To do no contrived murder. I lack iniquity
    Sometimes to do me service. Nine or ten times
    I had thought to have yerk'd him here under the ribs.
OTHELLO   'Tis better as it is.
IAGO   Nay, but he prated
    And spoke such scurvy and provoking terms
    Against your honor
    That, with the little godliness I have,
    I did full hard forbear him. But I pray you, Sir,
    Are you fast married? Be assured of this,
    That the magnifico is much beloved,
    And hath in his effect a voice potential
    As double as the Duke's. He will divorce you,
    Or put upon you what restraint and grievance
    The law, with all his might to enforce it on,
    Will give him cable.
OTHELLO   Let him do his spite.
    My services, which I have done the signiory,
    Shall out-tongue his complaints. 'Tis yet to know—
    Which, when I know that boasting is an honor,
    I shall promulgate—I fetch my life and being
    From men of royal siege, and my demerits
    May speak unbonneted to as proud a fortune
    As this that I have reach'd. For know, Iago,
    But that I love the gentle Desdemona,
    I would not my unhoused free condition
    Put into circumscription and confine

For the sea's worth. But, look! What lights come yond?

IAGO   Those are the raised father and his friends.
  You were best go in.

OTHELLO   Not I; I must be found.
  My parts, my title, and my perfect soul
  Shall manifest me rightly. Is it they?

IAGO   By Janus, I think no.

Enter Cassio and certain Officers with torches

OTHELLO   The servants of the Duke? And my Lieutenant?
  The goodness of the night upon you, friends!
  What is the news?

CASSIO   The Duke does greet you, General,
  And he requires your haste-post-haste appearance,
  Even on the instant.

OTHELLO   What is the matter, think you?

CASSIO   Something from Cyprus, as I may divine;
  It is a business of some heat. The galleys
  Have sent a dozen sequent messengers
  This very night at one another's heels;
  And many of the consuls, raised and met,
  Are at the Duke's already. You have been hotly call'd for,
  When, being not at your lodging to be found,
  The Senate hath sent about three several quests
  To search you out.

OTHELLO   'Tis well I am found by you.
  I will but spend a word here in the house
  And go with you.

Exit Othello

CASSIO   Ancient, what makes he here?

IAGO   Faith, he tonight hath boarded a land carack;
  If it prove lawful prize, he's made forever.

CASSIO   I do not understand.

IAGO   He's married.

CASSIO   To who?

Enter Othello

IAGO   Marry, to—Come, captain, will you go?

OTHELLO   Have with you.

CASSIO   Here comes another troop to seek for you.

IAGO   It is Brabantio. General, be advised,
  He comes to bad intent.

Enter Brabantio, Roderigo, and Officers, with torches and weapons

OTHELLO   Holla! Stand there!

RODERIGO   Signior, it is the Moor.

BRABANTIO   Down with him, thief!

They draw on both sides.

IAGO   You, Roderigo! Come, Sir, I am for you.

OTHELLO   Keep up your bright swords, for the dew will rust them.
    Good signior, you shall more command with years
    Than with your weapons.

BRABANTIO   O thou foul thief, where hast thou stow'd my daughter?
    Damn'd as thou art, thou hast enchanted her,
    For I'll refer me to all things of sense,
    If she in chains of magic were not bound,
    Whether a maid so tender, fair, and happy,
    So opposite to marriage that she shunn'd
    The wealthy, curled darlings of our nation,
    Would ever have, to incur a general mock,
    Run from her guardage to the sooty bosom
    Of such a thing as thou—to fear, not to delight.
    Judge me the world, if 'tis not gross in sense
    That thou hast practiced on her with foul charms,
    Abused her delicate youth with drugs or minerals
    That weaken motion. I'll have't disputed on;
    'Tis probable, and palpable to thinking.
    I therefore apprehend and do attach thee
    For an abuser of the world, a practicer
    Of arts inhibited and out of warrant.
    [*To officers*] Lay hold upon him. If he do resist,
    Subdue him at his peril.

OTHELLO   Hold your hands,
    Both you of my inclining and the rest.
    Were it my cue to fight, I should have known it
    Without a prompter. Where will you that I go
    To answer this your charge?

BRABANTIO   To prison, till fit time
    Of law and course of direct session
    Call thee to answer.

OTHELLO   What if I do obey?
    How may the Duke be therewith satisfied,
    Whose messengers are here about my side,

Upon some present business of the state
To bring me to him?
FIRST OFFICER   'Tis true, most worthy signior;
The Duke's in council, and your noble self,
I am sure, is sent for.
BRABANTIO   How? The Duke in council?
In this time of the night? Bring him away;
Mine's not an idle cause. The Duke himself,
Or any of my brothers of the state,
Cannot but feel this wrong as 'twere their own;
For if such actions may have passage free,
Bond slaves and pagans shall our statesmen be.

                                                            Exeunt

SCENE III—A council chamber.
*Enter Duke and Senators, sit at a table and read dispatches;
Officers attending.*
DUKE   There is no composition in these news
That gives them credit.
FIRST SENATOR   Indeed they are disproportion'd;
My letters say a hundred and seven galleys.
Duke   And mine, a hundred and forty.
SECOND SENATOR   And mine, two hundred.
But though they jump not on a just account—
As in these cases, where the aim reports,
'Tis oft with difference—yet do they all confirm
A Turkish fleet, and bearing up to Cyprus.
DUKE   Nay, it is possible enough to judgement.
I do not so secure me in the error,
But the main article I do approve
In fearful sense.
SAILOR   [*within*] What, ho! What, ho! What, ho!
FIRST OFFICER   A messenger from the galleys.
                              Enter Sailor
DUKE   Now, what's the business?
SAILOR   The Turkish preparation makes for Rhodes,
So was I bid report here to the state
By Signior Angelo.
DUKE   How say you by this change?
FIRST SENATOR   This cannot be,

By no assay of reason; 'tis a pageant
To keep us in false gaze. When we consider
The importancy of Cyprus to the Turk,
And let ourselves again but understand
That as it more concerns the Turk than Rhodes,
So may he with more facile question bear it,
For that it stands not in such warlike brace,
But altogether lacks the abilities
That Rhodes is dress'd in. If we make thought of this,
We must not think the Turk is so unskillful
To leave that latest which concerns him first,
Neglecting an attempt of ease and gain,
To wake and wage a danger profitless.

DUKE   Nay, in all confidence, he's not for Rhodes—

FIRST OFFICER   Here is more news.

Enter a Messenger

MESSENGER   The Ottomites, reverend and gracious,
Steering with due course toward the isle of Rhodes,
Have there injointed them with an after fleet.

FIRST SENATOR   Ay, so I thought. How many, as you guess?

MESSENGER   Of thirty sail; and now they do re-stem
Their backward course, bearing with frank appearance
Their purposes toward Cyprus. Signior Montano,
Your trusty and most valiant servitor,
With his free duty recommends you thus,
And prays you to believe him.

DUKE   'Tis certain then for Cyprus.
Marcus Luccicos, is not he in town?

FIRST SENATOR   He's now in Florence.

DUKE   Write from us to him, post-post-haste dispatch.

FIRST SENATOR   Here comes Brabantio and the valiant Moor.

Enter Brabantio, Othello, Iago, Roderigo, and Officers

DUKE   Valiant Othello, we must straight employ you
Against the General enemy Ottoman. [*to Brabantio*]
I did not see you; welcome, gentle signior;
We lack'd your counsel and your help tonight.

BRABANTIO   So did I yours. Good your Grace, pardon me:
Neither my place nor aught I heard of business
Hath raised me from my bed, nor doth the General care
Take hold on me; for my particular grief

Is of so flood-gate and o'erbearing nature
That it engluts and swallows other sorrows,
And it is still itself.

DUKE   Why, what's the matter?

BRABANTIO   My daughter! O, my daughter!

SENATORS   Dead?

BRABANTIO   Ay, to me.
She is abused, stol'n from me and corrupted
By spells and medicines bought of mountebanks;
For nature so preposterously to err,
Being not deficient, blind, or lame of sense,
Sans witchcraft could not.

DUKE   Whoe'er he be that in this foul proceeding
Hath thus beguiled your daughter of herself
And you of her, the bloody book of law
You shall yourself read in the bitter letter
After your own sense, yea, though our proper son
Stood in your action.

BRABANTIO   Humbly I thank your Grace.
Here is the man, this Moor, whom now, it seems,
Your special mandate for the state affairs
Hath hither brought.

SENATORS   We are very sorry for't.

DUKE   [to Othello] What in your own part can you say to this?

BRABANTIO   Nothing, but this is so.

OTHELLO   Most potent, grave, and reverend signiors,
My very noble and approved good masters,
That I have ta'en away this old man's daughter,
It is most true; true, I have married her;
The very head and front of my offending
Hath this extent, no more. Rude am I in my speech,
And little blest with the soft phrase of peace;
For since these arms of mine had seven years' pith,
Till now some nine moons wasted, they have used
Their dearest action in the tented field,
And little of this great world can I speak,
More than pertains to feats of broil and battle;
And therefore little shall I grace my cause
In speaking for myself. Yet, by your gracious patience,
I will a round unvarnish'd tale deliver

Of my whole course of love: what drugs, what charms,
What conjuration, and what mighty magic—
For such proceeding I am charged withal—
I won his daughter.
BRABANTIO   A maiden never bold,
Of spirit so still and quiet that her motion
Blush'd at herself; and she—in spite of nature,
Of years, of country, credit, everything—
To fall in love with what she fear'd to look on!
It is judgement maim'd and most imperfect,
That will confess perfection so could err
Against all rules of nature, and must be driven
To find out practices of cunning hell
Why this should be. I therefore vouch again
That with some mixtures powerful o'er the blood,
Or with some dram conjured to this effect,
He wrought upon her.
DUKE   To vouch this is no proof,
Without more certain and more overt test
Than these thin habits and poor likelihoods
Of modern seeming do prefer against him.
FIRST SENATOR   But, Othello, speak.
Did you by indirect and forced courses
Subdue and poison this young maid's affections?
Or came it by request, and such fair question
As soul to soul affordeth?
OTHELLO   I do beseech you,
Send for the lady to the Sagittary,
And let her speak of me before her father.
If you do find me foul in her report,
The trust, the office I do hold of you,
Not only take away, but let your sentence
Even fall upon my life.
DUKE   Fetch Desdemona hither.
OTHELLO   Ancient, conduct them; you best know the place.
And till she come, as truly as to heaven
I do confess the vices of my blood,   [Exit Iago and Attendants]
So justly to your grave ears I'll present
How I did thrive in this fair lady's love
And she in mine.

DUKE   Say it, Othello.

OTHELLO   Her father loved me, oft invited me,
    Still question'd me the story of my life
    From year to year, the battles, sieges, fortunes,
    That I have pass'd.
    I ran it through, even from my boyish days
    To the very moment that he bade me tell it:
    Wherein I spake of most disastrous chances,
    Of moving accidents by flood and field,
    Of hair-breadth scapes i' the imminent deadly breach,
    Of being taken by the insolent foe
    And sold to slavery, of my redemption thence
    And portance in my traveller's history;
    Wherein of antres vast and deserts idle,
    Rough quarries, rocks, and hills whose heads touch heaven,
    It was my hint to speak—such was the process—
    And of the cannibals that each other eat,
    The Anthropophagi, and men whose heads
    Do grow beneath their shoulders. This to hear
    Would Desdemona seriously incline;
    But still the house affairs would draw her thence,
    Which ever as she could with haste dispatch,
    She'd come again, and with a greedy ear
    Devour up my discourse; which I observing,
    Took once a pliant hour, and found good means
    To draw from her a prayer of earnest heart
    That I would all my pilgrimage dilate,
    Whereof by parcels she had something heard,
    But not intentively. I did consent,
    And often did beguile her of her tears
    When I did speak of some distressful stroke
    That my youth suffer'd. My story being done,
    She gave me for my pains a world of sighs;
    She swore, in faith, 'twas strange, 'twas passing strange;
    'Twas pitiful, 'twas wondrous pitiful.
    She wish'd she had not heard it, yet she wish'd
    That heaven had made her such a man; she thank'd me,
    And bade me, if I had a friend that loved her,
    I should but teach him how to tell my story,
    And that would woo her. Upon this hint I spake:

She loved me for the dangers I had pass'd,
And I loved her that she did pity them.
This only is the witchcraft I have used.
Here comes the lady; let her witness it.
   Enter Desdemona, Iago, and Attendants
DUKE I think this tale would win my daughter too.
Good Brabantio,
Take up this mangled matter at the best:
Men do their broken weapons rather use
Than their bare hands.
BRABANTIO   I pray you, hear her speak.
If she confess that she was half the wooer,
Destruction on my head, if my bad blame
Light on the man! Come hither, gentle mistress.
Do you perceive in all this noble company
Where most you owe obedience?
DESDEMONA My noble father,
I do perceive here a divided duty.
To you I am bound for life and education;
My life and education both do learn me
How to respect you; you are the lord of duty,
I am hitherto your daughter. But here's my husband,
And so much duty as my mother show'd
To you, preferring you before her father,
So much I challenge that I may profess
Due to the Moor, my lord.
BRABANTIO God be with you! I have done.
Please it your Grace, on to the state affairs;
I had rather to adopt a child than get it.
Come hither, Moor. [*He joins the hands of Othello and Desdemona*]
I here do give thee that with all my heart
Which, but thou hast already, with all my heart
I would keep from thee. For your sake, jewel,
I am glad at soul I have no other child;
For thy escape would teach me tyranny,
To hang clogs on them. I have done, my lord.
DUKE Let me speak like yourself, and lay a sentence
Which, as a grise or step, may help these lovers
Into your favor.
When remedies are past, the griefs are ended

By seeing the worst, which late on hopes depended.
To mourn a mischief that is past and gone
Is the next way to draw new mischief on.
What cannot be preserved when Fortune takes,
Patience her injury a mockery makes.
The robb'd that smiles steals something from the thief;
He robs himself that spends a bootless grief.

BRABANTIO   So let the Turk of Cyprus us beguile;
We lose it not so long as we can smile.
He bears the sentence well, that nothing bears
But the free comfort which from thence he hears;
But he bears both the sentence and the sorrow
That, to pay grief, must of poor patience borrow.
These sentences, to sugar or to gall,
Being strong on both sides, are equivocal.
But words are words; I never yet did hear
That the bruised heart was pierced through the ear.
I humbly beseech you, proceed to the affairs of state.

DUKE   The Turk with a most mighty preparation makes for Cyprus.
Othello, the fortitude of the place is best known to you; and though
we have there a substitute of most allowed sufficiency, yet opinion, a sovereign mistress of effects, throws a more safer voice on
you. You must therefore be content to slubber the gloss of your
new fortunes with this more stubborn and boisterous expedition.

OTHELLO   The tyrant custom, most grave senators,
Hath made the flinty and steel couch of war
My thrice-driven bed of down. I do agonize
A natural and prompt alacrity
I find in hardness and do undertake
These present wars against the Ottomites.
Most humbly therefore bending to your state,
I crave fit disposition for my wife,
Due reference of place and exhibition,
With such accommodation and besort
As levels with her breeding.

DUKE   If you please, Be't at her father's.

BRABANTIO   I'll not have it so.

OTHELLO   Nor I.

DESDEMONA   Nor I. I would not there reside
To put my father in impatient thoughts

By being in his eye. Most gracious Duke,
To my unfolding lend your prosperous ear,
And let me find a charter in your voice
To assist my simpleness.

DUKE   What would you, Desdemona?

DESDEMONA   That I did love the Moor to live with him,
My downright violence and storm of fortunes
May trumpet to the world. My heart's subdued
Even to the very quality of my lord.
I saw Othello's visage in his mind,
And to his honors and his valiant parts
Did I my soul and fortunes consecrate.
So that, dear lords, if I be left behind,
A moth of peace, and he go to the war,
The rites for which I love him are bereft me,
And I a heavy interim shall support
By his dear absence. Let me go with him.

OTHELLO   Let her have your voices.
Vouch with me, heaven, I therefore beg it not
To please the palate of my appetite,
Nor to comply with heat—the young affects
In me defunct—and proper satisfaction;
But to be free and bounteous to her mind.
And heaven defend your good souls, that you think
I will your serious and great business scant
For she is with me. No, when light-wing'd toys
Of feather'd Cupid seel with wanton dullness
My speculative and officed instruments,
That my disports corrupt and taint my business,
Let housewives make a skillet of my helm,
And all indign and base adversities
Make head against my estimation!

DUKE   Be it as you shall privately determine,
Either for her stay or going. The affair cries haste,
And speed must answer't.

SENATOR   You must away tonight.

DESDEMONA   Tonight, my lord?

DUKE   This night.

OTHELLO   With all my heart.

DUKE   At nine i' the morning here we'll meet again.
  Othello, leave some officer behind,
  And he shall our commission bring to you,
  With such things else of quality and respect
  As doth import you.
OTHELLO   So please your Grace, my ancient;
  A man he is of honesty and trust.
  To his conveyance I assign my wife,
  With what else needful your good Grace shall think
  To be sent after me.
DUKE   Let it be so.
  Good night to everyone. [*to Brabantio*] And, noble signior,
  If virtue no delighted beauty lack,
  Your son-in-law is far more fair than black.
FIRST SENATOR   Adieu, brave Moor, use Desdemona well.
BRABANTIO   Look to her, Moor, if thou hast eyes to see;
  She has deceived her father, and may thee.

Exit Duke, Brabantio, Cassio, Senators, and Officers

OTHELLO   My life upon her faith! Honest Iago,
  My Desdemona must I leave to thee.
  I prithee, let thy wife attend on her,
  And bring them after in the best advantage.
  Come, Desdemona, I have but an hour
  Of love, of worldly matters and direction,
  To spend with thee. We must obey the time.

Exit Othello and Desdemona

RODERIGO   Iago!
IAGO   What say'st thou, noble heart?
RODERIGO   What will I do, thinkest thou?
IAGO   Why, go to bed and sleep.
RODERIGO   I will incontinently drown myself.
IAGO   If thou dost, I shall never love thee after. Why, thou silly gentleman!
RODERIGO   It is silliness to live when to live is torment, and then
  have we a prescription to die when death is our physician.
IAGO   O villainous! I have looked upon the world for four times seven
  years, and since I could distinguish betwixt a benefit and an injury, I never found man that knew how to love himself. Ere I
  would say I would drown myself for the love of a guinea hen, I
  would change my humanity with a baboon.

RODERIGO   What should I do? I confess it is my shame to be so fond, but it is not in my virtue to amend it.

IAGO   Virtue? a fig! 'Tis in ourselves that we are thus or thus. Our bodies are gardens, to the which our wills are gardeners; so that if we will plant nettles or sow lettuce, set hyssop and weed up thyme, supply it with one gender of herbs or distract it with many, either to have it sterile with idleness or manured with industry, why, the power and corrigible authority of this lies in our wills. If the balance of our lives had not one scale of reason to poise another of sensuality, the blood and baseness of our natures would conduct us to most preposterous conclusions. But we have reason to cool our raging motions, our carnal stings, our unbitted lusts; whereof I take this, that you call love, to be a sect or scion.

RODERIGO   It cannot be.

IAGO   It is merely a lust of the blood and a permission of the will. Come, be a man! Drown thyself? Drown cats and blind puppies. I have professed me thy friend, and I confess me knit to thy deserving with cables of perdurable toughness; I could never better stead thee than now. Put money in thy purse; follow thou the wars; defeat thy favor with an usurped beard. I say, put money in thy purse. It cannot be that Desdemona should long continue her love to the Moor—put money in thy purse—nor he his to her. It was a violent commencement, and thou shalt see an answerable sequestration—put but money in thy purse. These Moors are changeable in their wills—fill thy purse with money. The food that to him now is as luscious as locusts, shall be to him shortly as acerb as the coloquintida. She must change for youth; when she is sated with his body, she will find the error of her choice. She must have change, she must; therefore put money in thy purse. If thou wilt needs damn thyself, do it a more delicate way than drowning. Make all the money thou canst. If sanctimony and a frail vow betwixt an erring barbarian and a supersubtle Venetian be not too hard for my wits and all the tribe of hell, thou shalt enjoy her—therefore make money. A pox of drowning thyself! It is clean out of the way. Seek thou rather to be hanged in compassing thy joy than to be drowned and go without her.

RODERIGO   Wilt thou be fast to my hopes, if I depend on the issue?

IAGO   Thou art sure of me—go, make money. I have told thee often, and I retell thee again and again, I hate the Moor. My cause is hearted; thine hath no less reason. Let us be conjunctive in our revenge against him. If thou canst cuckold him, thou dost thyself a pleasure, me a sport. There are many events in the womb of time which will be delivered. Traverse, go, provide thy money. We will have more of this tomorrow. Adieu.

RODERIGO   Where shall we meet i' the morning?

IAGO   At my lodging.

RODERIGO   I'll be with thee betimes. [*He starts to leave*]

IAGO   Go to, farewell. Do you hear, Roderigo?

RODERIGO   What say you?

IAGO   No more of drowning, do you hear?

RODERIGO   I am changed; I'll go sell all my land.

Exit Roderigo

IAGO   Thus do I ever make my fool my purse;
For I mine own gain'd knowledge should profane
If I would time expend with such a snipe
But for my sport and profit. I hate the Moor,
And it is thought abroad that 'twixt my sheets
He has done my office. I know not if't be true,
But I for mere suspicion in that kind
Will do as if for surety. He holds me well,
The better shall my purpose work on him.
Cassio's a proper man. Let me see now—
To get his place, and to plume up my will
In double knavery—How, how?—Let's see—
After some time, to abuse Othello's ear
That he is too familiar with his wife.
He hath a person and a smooth dispose
To be suspected—framed to make women false.
The Moor is of a free and open nature,
That thinks men honest that but seem to be so,
And will as tenderly be led by the nose
As asses are.
I have't. It is engender'd. Hell and night
Must bring this monstrous birth to the world's light.

Exit

ACT II

Enter Montano and two Gentlemen

MONTANO   What from the cape can you discern at sea?

FIRST GENTLEMAN   Nothing at all. It is a high-wrought flood;
I cannot, 'twixt the heaven and the main,
Descry a sail.

MONTANO   Methinks the wind hath spoke aloud at land;
A fuller blast ne'er shook our battlements.
If it hath ruffian'd so upon the sea,
What ribs of oak, when mountains melt on them,
Can hold the mortise? What shall we hear of this?

SECOND GENTLEMAN   A segregation of the Turkish fleet.
For do but stand upon the foaming shore,
The chidden billow seems to pelt the clouds;
The wind-shaked surge, with high and monstrous mane,
Seems to cast water on the burning bear,
And quench the guards of the ever-fixed pole.
I never did like molestation view
On the enchafèd flood.

MONTANO   If that the Turkish fleet
Be not enshelter'd and embay'd, they are drown'd;
It is impossible to bear it out.

Enter a third Gentleman

THIRD GENTLEMAN   News, lads! Our wars are done.
The desperate tempest hath so bang'd the Turks,
That their designment halts. A noble ship of Venice
Hath seen a grievous wreck and sufferance
On most part of their fleet.

MONTANO   How? Is this true?

THIRD GENTLEMAN   The ship is here put in,

A Veronesa. Michael Cassio,
Lieutenant to the warlike Moor, Othello,
Is come on shore; the Moor himself at sea,
And is in full commission here for Cyprus.

MONTANO   I am glad on't; 'tis a worthy governor.

THIRD GENTLEMAN   But this same Cassio, though he speak of comfort
Touching the Turkish loss, yet he looks sadly
And prays the Moor be safe; for they were parted
With foul and violent tempest.

MONTANO   Pray heavens he be,
For I have served him, and the man commands
Like a full soldier. Let's to the seaside, ho!
As well to see the vessel that's come in
As to throw out our eyes for brave Othello,
Even till we make the main and the aerial blue
An indistinct regard.

THIRD GENTLEMAN   Come, let's do so,
For every minute is expectancy
Of more arrivance.

Enter Cassio

CASSIO   Thanks, you the valiant of this warlike isle,
That so approve the Moor! O, let the heavens
Give him defense against the elements,
For I have lost him on a dangerous sea.

MONTANO   Is he well shipp'd?

CASSIO   His bark is stoutly timber'd, and his pilot
Of very expert and approved allowance;
Therefore my hopes, not surfeited to death,
Stand in bold cure.

A cry within, "A sail, a sail, a sail!"
Enter a fourth Gentleman

CASSIO   What noise?

FOURTH GENTLEMAN   The town is empty; on the brow o' the sea
Stand ranks of people, and they cry, "A sail!"

CASSIO   My hopes do shape him for the governor.

Gunshots heard

SECOND GENTLEMAN   They do discharge their shot of courtesy—
Our friends at least.

CASSIO   I pray you, Sir, go forth,
And give us truth who 'tis that is arrived.

SECOND GENTLEMAN   I shall.

Exit Second Gentleman

MONTANO   But, good Lieutenant, is your General wived?

CASSIO   Most fortunately: he hath achieved a maid
    That paragons description and wild fame,
    One that excels the quirks of blazoning pens,
    And in the essential vesture of creation
    Does tire the engineer.

                Enter Second Gentleman
                    How now! who has put in?

SECOND GENTLEMAN   'Tis one Iago, ancient to the General.

CASSIO   He has had most favorable and happy speed:
    Tempests themselves, high seas, and howling winds,
    The gutter'd rocks, and congregated sands,
    Traitors ensteep'd to clog the guiltless keel,
    As having sense of beauty, do omit
    Their mortal natures, letting go safely by
    The divine Desdemona.

MONTANO   What is she?

CASSIO   She that I spake of, our great captain's captain,
    Left in the conduct of the bold Iago,
    Whose footing here anticipates our thoughts
    A se'nnight's speed. Great Jove, Othello guard,
    And swell his sail with thine own powerful breath,
    That he may bless this bay with his tall ship,
    Make love's quick pants in Desdemona's arms,
    Give renew'd fire to our extincted spirits,
    And bring all Cyprus comfort.

        Enter Desdemona, Emilia, Iago, Roderigo, and Attendants
                        O, behold,
    The riches of the ship is come on shore!
    Ye men of Cyprus, let her have your knees.

            The Gentlemen make curtsy to Desdemona
    Hall to thee, lady! And the grace of heaven,
    Before, behind thee, and on every hand,
    Enwheel thee round!

DESDEMONA   I thank you, valiant Cassio.
    What tidings can you tell me of my lord?

CASSIO   He is not yet arrived, nor know I aught
    But that he's well and will be shortly here.

DESDEMONA   O, but I fear—How lost you company?

CASSIO   The great contention of the sea and skies
    Parted our fellowship—
        A cry within, "A sail, a sail!" [*Gunshot heard*]
              But, hark! a sail.

SECOND GENTLEMAN   They give their greeting to the citadel;
    This likewise is a friend.

CASSIO   See for the news. [*Exit Second Gentleman*]
    Good ancient, you are welcome. [*to Emilia*] Welcome, mistress.
    Let it not gall your patience, good Iago,
    That I extend my manners; 'tis my breeding
    That gives me this bold show of courtesy. [*He kisses her*]

IAGO   Sir, would she give you so much of her lips
    As of her tongue she oft bestows on me,
    You'd have enough.

DESDEMONA   Alas, she has no speech.

IAGO   In faith, too much;
    I find it still when I have list to sleep.
    Marry, before your ladyship I grant,
    She puts her tongue a little in her heart
    And chides with thinking.

EMILIA   You have little cause to say so.

IAGO   Come on, come on. You are pictures out of doors,
    Bells in your parlors, wildcats in your kitchens,
    Saints in your injuries, devils being offended,
    Players in your housewifery, and hussies in your beds.

DESDEMONA   O, fie upon thee, slanderer!

IAGO   Nay, it is true, or else I am a Turk:
    You rise to play, and go to bed to work.

EMILIA   You shall not write my praise.

IAGO   No, let me not.

DESDEMONA   What wouldst thou write of me, if thou shouldst
    praise me?

IAGO   O gentle lady, do not put me to't,
    For I am nothing if not critical.

DESDEMONA   Come on, essay—There's one gone to the harbor?

IAGO   Ay, madam.

DESDEMONA   I am not merry, but I do beguile
    The thing I am by seeming otherwise.

Come, how wouldst thou praise me?

IAGO   I am about it, but indeed my invention
   Comes from my pate as birdlime does from frieze;
   It plucks out brains and all. But my Muse labors,
   And thus she is deliver'd.
   If she be fair and wise, fairness and wit,
   The one's for use, the other useth it.

DESDEMONA   Well praised! How if she be black and witty?

IAGO   If she be black, and thereto have a wit,
   She'll find a white that shall her blackness fit.

DESDEMONA   Worse and worse.

EMILIA   How if fair and foolish?

IAGO   She never yet was foolish that was fair,
   For even her folly help'd her to an heir.

DESDEMONA   These are old fond paradoxes to make fools laugh i' the
alehouse. What miserable praise hast thou for her that's foul and
foolish?

IAGO   There's none so foul and foolish thereunto,
   But does foul pranks which fair and wise ones do.

DESDEMONA   O heavy ignorance! Thou praisest the worst best. But
what praise couldst thou bestow on a deserving woman indeed,
one that in the authority of her merit did justly put on the vouch
of very malice itself?

IAGO   She that was ever fair and never proud,
   Had tongue at will and yet was never loud,
   Never lack'd gold and yet went never gay,
   Fled from her wish and yet said, "Now I may";
   She that, being anger'd, her revenge being nigh,
   Bade her wrong stay and her displeasure fly;
   She that in wisdom never was so frail
   To change the cod's head for the salmon's tail;
   She that could think and ne'er disclose her mind,
   See suitors following and not look behind;
   She was a wight, if ever such wight were—

DESDEMONA   To do what?

IAGO   To suckle fools and chronicle small beer.

DESDEMONA   O most lame and impotent conclusion! Do not learn of
him, Emilia, though he be thy husband. How say you, Cassio? Is
he not a most profane and liberal counselor?

CASSIO   He speaks home, madam. You may relish him more in the
    soldier than in the scholar.

Cassio and Desdemona talk apart

IAGO   [*aside*] He takes her by the palm; ay, well said, whisper. With as
    little a web as this will I ensnare as great a fly as Cassio. Ay, smile
    upon her, do; I will gyve thee in thine own courtship. You say
    true; 'tis so, indeed. If such tricks as these strip you out of your
    lieutenantry, it had been better you had not kissed your three
    fingers so oft, which now again you are most apt to play the Sir in.
    Very good. Well kissed! an excellent courtesy! 'tis so, indeed. Yet
    again your fingers to your lips? Would they were clyster-pipes for
    your sake! [*Trumpet within*] The Moor! I know his trumpet.

CASSIO   'Tis truly so.

DESDEMONA   Let's meet him and receive him.

CASSIO   Lo, where he comes!

Enter Othello and Attendants

OTHELLO   O my fair warrior!

DESDEMONA   My dear Othello!

OTHELLO   It gives me wonder great as my content
    To see you here before me. O my soul's joy!
    If after every tempest come such calms,
    May the winds blow till they have waken'd death!
    And let the laboring bark climb hills of seas
    Olympus-high, and duck again as low
    As hell's from heaven! If it were now to die,
    'Twere now to be most happy; for I fear
    My soul hath her content so absolute
    That not another comfort like to this
    Succeeds in unknown fate.

DESDEMONA   The heavens forbid
    But that our loves and comforts should increase,
    Even as our days do grow!

OTHELLO   Amen to that, sweet powers!
    I cannot speak enough of this content;
    It stops me here; it is too much of joy.
    And this, and this, the greatest discords be [*They kiss*]
    That e'er our hearts shall make!

IAGO   [*aside*] O, you are well tuned now!
    But I'll set down the pegs that make this music,
    As honest as I am.

OTHELLO   Come, let us to the castle.
   News, friends: our wars are done, the Turks are drown'd.
   How does my old acquaintance of this isle?
   Honey, you shall be well desired in Cyprus;
   I have found great love amongst them. O my sweet,
   I prattle out of fashion, and I dote
   In mine own comforts. I prithee, good Iago,
   Go to the bay and disembark my coffers.
   Bring thou the master to the citadel;
   He is a good one, and his worthiness
   Does challenge much respect. Come, Desdemona,
   Once more well met at Cyprus.
                         Exit all but Iago, Attendant, and Roderigo
IAGO   [*to his Attendant*] Do thou meet me presently at the harbor.
   [*to Roderigo*] Come hither. If thou be'st valiant—as they say base
   men being in love have then a nobility in their natures more than
   is native to them—list me. The Lieutenant tonight watches on the
   court of guard. First, I must tell thee this: Desdemona is directly
   in love with him.
RODERIGO   With him? Why, 'tis not possible.
IAGO   Lay thy finger thus, and let thy soul be instructed. Mark me
   with what violence she first loved the Moor, but for bragging and
   telling her fantastical lies. And will she love him still for prating?
   Let not thy discreet heart think it. Her eye must be fed; and what
   delight shall she have to look on the devil? When the blood is
   made dull with the act of sport, there should be, again to inflame
   it and to give satiety a fresh appetite, loveliness in favor, sympathy
   in years, manners, and beauties—all which the Moor is defective
   in. Now, for want of these required conveniences, her delicate
   tenderness will find itself abused, begin to heave the gorge, disrelish
   and abhor the Moor; very nature will instruct her in it and compel her to some second choice. Now Sir, this granted—as it is a
   most pregnant and unforced position—who stands so eminently
   in the degree of this fortune as Cassio does? A knave very voluble;
   no further conscionable than in putting on the mere form of civil
   and humane seeming, for the better compass of his salt and most
   hidden loose affection? Why, none, why, none—a slipper and subtle
   knave, a finder out of occasions, that has an eye can stamp and
   counterfeit advantages, though true advantage never present it-

self—a devilish knave! Besides, the knave is handsome, young, and hath all those requisites in him that folly and green minds look after—a pestilent complete knave, and the woman hath found him already.

RODERIGO   I cannot believe that in her; she's full of most blest condition.

IAGO   Blest fig's end! The wine she drinks is made of grapes. If she had been blest, she would never have loved the Moor. Blest pudding! Didst thou not see her paddle with the palm of his hand? Didst not mark that?

RODERIGO   Yes, that I did; but that was but courtesy.

IAGO   Lechery, by this hand; an index and obscure prologue to the history of lust and foul thoughts. They met so near with their lips that their breaths embraced together. Villainous thoughts, Roderigo! When these mutualities so marshal the way, hard at hand comes the master and main exercise, the incorporate conclusion. Pish! But, Sir, be you ruled by me. I have brought you from Venice. Watch you tonight; for the command, I'll lay't upon you. Cassio knows you not. I'll not be far from you. Do you find some occasion to anger Cassio, either by speaking too loud, or tainting his discipline, or from what other course you please, which the time shall more favorably minister.

RODERIGO   Well.

IAGO   Sir, he is rash and very sudden in choler, and haply may strike at you. Provoke him, that he may; for even out of that will I cause these of Cyprus to mutiny, whose qualification shall come into no true taste again but by the displanting of Cassio. So shall you have a shorter journey to your desires by the means I shall then have to prefer them, and the impediment most profitably removed, without the which there were no expectation of our prosperity.

RODERIGO   I will do this, if I can bring it to any opportunity.

IAGO   I warrant thee. Meet me by and by at the citadel. I must fetch his necessaries ashore. Farewell.

RODERIGO   Adieu.

Exit Roderigo

IAGO   That Cassio loves her, I do well believe it;
That she loves him, 'tis apt and of great credit.
The Moor, howbeit that I endure him not,
Is of a constant, loving, noble nature,

And I dare think he'll prove to Desdemona
A most dear husband. Now, I do love her too,
Not out of absolute lust, though peradventure
I stand accountant for as great a sin,
But partly led to diet my revenge,
For that I do suspect the lusty Moor
Hath leap'd into my seat; the thought whereof
Doth like a poisonous mineral gnaw my inwards,
And nothing can or shall content my soul
Till I am even'd with him, wife for wife.
Or failing so, yet that I put the Moor
At least into a jealousy so strong
That judgement cannot cure. Which thing to do,
If this poor trash of Venice, whom I trace
For his quick hunting, stand the putting on,
I'll have our Michael Cassio on the hip,
Abuse him to the Moor in the rank garb
(For I fear Cassio with my nightcap too),
Make the Moor thank me, love me, and reward me
For making him egregiously an ass
And practicing upon his peace and quiet
Even to madness. 'Tis here, but yet confused:
Knavery's plain face is never seen till used.

Exit

SCENE II—A street.

Enter a Herald with a proclamation; people following

HERALD   It is Othello's pleasure, our noble and valiant General, that
upon certain tidings now arrived, importing the mere perdition
of the Turkish fleet, every man put himself into triumph; some to
dance, some to make bonfires, each man to what sport and revels
his addiction leads him; for besides these beneficial news, it is the
celebration of his nuptial. So much was his pleasure should be
proclaimed. All offices are open, and there is full liberty of feasting from this present hour of five till the bell have told eleven.
Heaven bless the isle of Cyprus and our noble General Othello!

Exeunt

SCENE III—A hall in the castle.
Enter Othello, Desdemona, Cassio, and Attendants

OTHELLO   Good Michael, look you to the guard tonight.
Let's teach ourselves that honorable stop,
Not to outsport discretion.

CASSIO   Iago hath direction what to do;
But notwithstanding with my personal eye
Will I look to't.

OTHELLO   Iago is most honest.
Michael, good night. Tomorrow with your earliest
Let me have speech with you. Come, my dear love,
The purchase made, the fruits are to ensue;
That profit's yet to come 'tween me and you.
Good night.

Exit Othello, Desdemona, and Attendants
Enter Iago

CASSIO   Welcome, Iago; we must to the watch.

IAGO   Not this hour, Lieutenant; 'tis not yet ten o' the clock. Our General cast us thus early for the love of his Desdemona; who let us not therefore blame. He hath not yet made wanton the night with her, and she is sport for Jove.

CASSIO   She's a most exquisite lady.

IAGO   And, I'll warrant her, full of game.

CASSIO   Indeed she's a most fresh and delicate creature.

IAGO   What an eye she has! Methinks it sounds a parley to provocation.

CASSIO   An inviting eye; and yet methinks right modest.

IAGO   And when she speaks, is it not an alarum to love?

CASSIO   She is indeed perfection.

IAGO   Well, happiness to their sheets! Come, Lieutenant, I have a stope of wine, and here without are a brace of Cyprus gallants that would fain have a measure to the health of black Othello.

CASSIO   Not tonight, good Iago—I have very poor and unhappy brains for drinking. I could well wish courtesy would invent some other custom of entertainment.

IAGO   O, they are our friends! But one cup; I'll drink for you.

CASSIO   I have drunk but one cup tonight, and that was craftily qualified too, and behold what innovation it makes here. I am unfortunate in the infirmity, and dare not task my weakness with any more.

IAGO   What, man! 'Tis a night of revels, the gallants desire it.

CASSIO   Where are they?

IAGO   Here at the door; I pray you, call them in.

CASSIO   I'll do't, but it dislikes me.

Exit Cassio

IAGO   If I can fasten but one cup upon him,
  With that which he hath drunk tonight already,
  He'll be as full of quarrel and offense
  As my young mistress' dog. Now my sick fool Roderigo,
  Whom love hath turn'd almost the wrong side out,
  To Desdemona hath tonight caroused
  Potations pottle-deep; and he's to watch.
  Three lads of Cyprus, noble swelling spirits,
  That hold their honors in a wary distance,
  The very elements of this warlike isle,
  Have I tonight fluster'd with flowing cups,
  And they watch too. Now, 'mongst this flock of drunkards,
  Am I to put our Cassio in some action
  That may offend the isle. But here they come.
  If consequence do but approve my dream,
  My boat sails freely, both with wind and stream.

Enter Cassio, Montano and Gentlemen; Servants following with wine

CASSIO   'Fore God, they have given me a rouse already.

MONTANO   Good faith, a little one; not past a pint, as I am a soldier.

IAGO   Some wine, ho! [*Sings*]

    And let me the canakin clink, clink;
    And let me the canakin clink.
     A soldier's a man;
     O, man's life's but a span;
    Why then let a soldier drink.

 Some wine, boys!

CASSIO   'Fore God, an excellent song.

IAGO   I learned it in England, where indeed they are most potent in
  potting. Your Dane, your German, and your swag-bellied Hollander—
  Drink, ho!—are nothing to your English.

CASSIO   Is your Englishman so expert in his drinking?

IAGO   Why, he drinks you with facility your Dane dead drunk; he
  sweats not to overthrow your Almain; he gives your Hollander a

vomit ere the next pottle can be filled.

CASSIO   To the health of our General!

MONTANO   I am for it, Lieutenant, and I'll do you justice.

IAGO   O sweet England! [*Sings*]

> King Stephen was and a worthy peer,
>   His breeches cost him but a crown;
> He held them sixpence all too dear,
>   With that he call'd the tailor lown.
>
> He was a wight of high renown,
>   And thou art but of low degree.
> 'Tis pride that pulls the country down;
>   Then take thine auld cloak about thee.

Some wine, ho!

CASSIO   Why, this is a more exquisite song than the other.

IAGO   Will you hear't again?

CASSIO   No, for I hold him to be unworthy of his place that does those things. Well, God's above all, and there be souls must be saved, and there be souls must not be saved.

IAGO   It's true, good Lieutenant.

CASSIO   For mine own part—no offense to the General, nor any man of quality—I hope to be saved.

IAGO   And so do I too, Lieutenant.

CASSIO   Ay, but, by your leave, not before me; the Lieutenant is to be saved before the ancient. Let's have no more of this; let's to our affairs. God forgive us our sins! Gentlemen, let's look to our business. Do not think, gentlemen, I am drunk: this is my ancient, this is my right hand, and this is my left. I am not drunk now; I can stand well enough, and I speak well enough.

ALL   Excellent well.

CASSIO   Why, very well then; you must not think then that I am drunk.

Exit Cassio

MONTANO   To the platform, masters; come, let's set the watch.

Exit Gentlemen

IAGO   You see this fellow that is gone before;
   He is a soldier fit to stand by Caesar
   And give direction. And do but see his vice;
   'Tis to his virtue a just equinox,
   The one as long as the other. 'Tis pity of him.

I fear the trust Othello puts him in
On some odd time of his infirmity
Will shake this island.
MONTANO   But is he often thus?
IAGO   'Tis evermore the prologue to his sleep.
He'll watch the horologe a double set,
If drink rock not his cradle.
MONTANO   It were well
The General were put in mind of it.
Perhaps he sees it not, or his good nature
Prizes the virtue that appears in Cassio
And looks not on his evils. Is not this true?
Enter Roderigo
IAGO   [*aside to him*] How now, Roderigo!
I pray you, after the Lieutenant; go.

Exit Roderigo

MONTANO   And 'tis great pity that the noble Moor
Should hazard such a place as his own second
With one of an ingraft infirmity.
It were an honest action to say so
To the Moor.
IAGO   Not I, for this fair island.
I do love Cassio well, and would do much
To cure him of this evil— [*A cry within, "Help, help!"*]
But, hark! What noise?
Enter Cassio, pursuing Roderigo
CASSIO   'Zounds! You rogue! You rascal!
MONTANO   What's the matter, Lieutenant?
CASSIO   A knave teach me my duty! I'll beat the knave into a twiggen
bottle.
RODERIGO   Beat me!
CASSIO   Dost thou prate, rogue? [*He strikes Roderigo*]
MONTANO   Nay, good Lieutenant; [*Restraining him*] I pray you, Sir,
hold your hand.
CASSIO   Let me go, Sir, or I'll knock you o'er the mazard.
MONTANO   Come, come, you're drunk.
CASSIO   Drunk? [*They fight*]
IAGO   [*aside to Roderigo*] Away, I say; go out and cry a mutiny.

Exit Roderigo

Nay, good Lieutenant! God's will, gentlemen!

Help, ho!—Lieutenant—Sir—Montano—Sir—
Help, masters!—Here's a goodly watch indeed! [*a bell rings*]
Who's that that rings the bell?—Diablo, ho!
The town will rise. God's will, Lieutenant, hold!
You will be shamed forever.
    Enter Othello and Attendants, with weapons
OTHELLO What is the matter here?
MONTANO   'Zounds, I bleed still;
I am hurt to the death. [*He thrusts at Cassio*]
OTHELLO   Hold, for your lives!
IAGO Hold, ho! Lieutenant—Sir—Montano—gentlemen—
Have you forgot all place of sense and duty?
Hold! the General speaks to you! Hold, hold, for shame!
OTHELLO Why, how now, ho! from whence ariseth this?
Are we turn'd Turks, and to ourselves do that
Which heaven hath forbid the Ottomites?
For Christian shame, put by this barbarous brawl.
He that stirs next to carve for his own rage
Holds his soul light; he dies upon his motion.
Silence that dreadful bell; it frights the isle
From her propriety. What is the matter, masters?
Honest Iago, that look'st dead with grieving,
Speak: who began this? On thy love, I charge thee.
IAGO I do not know. Friends all but now, even now,
In quarter, and in terms like bride and groom
Devesting them for bed; and then, but now
(As if some planet had unwitted men),
Swords out, and tilting one at other's breast,
In opposition bloody. I cannot speak
Any beginning to this peevish odds;
And would in action glorious I had lost
Those legs that brought me to a part of it!
OTHELLO How comes it, Michael, you are thus forgot?
CASSIO I pray you, pardon me; I cannot speak.
OTHELLO Worthy Montano, you were wont be civil;
The gravity and stillness of your youth
The world hath noted, and your name is great
In mouths of wisest censure. What's the matter,
That you unlace your reputation thus,
And spend your rich opinion for the name

Of a night-brawler? Give me answer to it.

MONTANO   Worthy Othello, I am hurt to danger.
Your officer, Iago, can inform you—
While I spare speech, which something now offends me—
Of all that I do know. Nor know I aught
By me that's said or done amiss this night,
Unless self-charity be sometimes a vice,
And to defend ourselves it be a sin
When violence assails us.

OTHELLO   Now, by heaven,
My blood begins my safer guides to rule,
And passion, having my best judgement collied,
Essays to lead the way. If I once stir,
Or do but lift this arm, the best of you
Shall sink in my rebuke. Give me to know
How this foul rout began, who set it on,
And he that is approved in this offense,
Though he had twinn'd with me, both at a birth,
Shall lose me. What! in a town of war,
Yet wild, the people's hearts brimful of fear,
To manage private and domestic quarrel,
In night, and on the court and guard of safety!
'Tis monstrous. Iago, who began't?

MONTANO   [to Iago] If partially affined, or leagued in office,
Thou dost deliver more or less than truth,
Thou art no soldier.

IAGO   Touch me not so near:
I had rather have this tongue cut from my mouth
Than it should do offense to Michael Cassio;
Yet, I persuade myself, to speak the truth
Shall nothing wrong him. Thus it is, General.
Montano and myself being in speech,
There comes a fellow crying out for help,
And Cassio following him with determined sword,
To execute upon him. Sir, this gentleman [indicating Montano]
Steps in to Cassio and entreats his pause.
Myself the crying fellow did pursue,
Lest by his clamor—as it so fell out—
The town might fall in fright. He, swift of foot,
Outran my purpose; and I return'd the rather

For that I heard the clink and fall of swords,
And Cassio high in oath, which till tonight
I ne'er might say before. When I came back—
For this was brief—I found them close together,
At blow and thrust, even as again they were
When you yourself did part them.
More of this matter cannot I report.
But men are men; the best sometimes forget.
Though Cassio did some little wrong to him,
As men in rage strike those that wish them best,
Yet surely Cassio, I believe, received
From him that fled some strange indignity,
Which patience could not pass.

OTHELLO   I know, Iago,
Thy honesty and love doth mince this matter,
Making it light to Cassio. Cassio, I love thee,
But never more be officer of mine.

Enter Desdemona, attended

Look, if my gentle love be not raised up!
I'll make thee an example.

DESDEMONA   What's the matter, dear?

OTHELLO   All's well now, sweeting;
Come away to bed. [*to Montano*] Sir, for your hurts,
Myself will be your surgeon. Lead him off.

Exit Montano, attended

Iago, look with care about the town,
And silence those whom this vile brawl distracted.
Come, Desdemona, 'tis the soldier's life.
To have their balmy slumbers waked with strife.

Exit all but Iago and Cassio

IAGO   What, are you hurt, Lieutenant?

CASSIO   Ay, past all surgery.

IAGO   Marry, heaven forbid!

CASSIO   Reputation, reputation, reputation! O, I have lost my reputation! I have lost the immortal part of myself, and what remains
is bestial. My reputation, Iago, my reputation!

IAGO   As I am an honest man, I thought you had received some bodily
wound; there is more sense in that than in reputation. Reputation is an idle and most false imposition; oft got without merit
and lost without deserving. You have lost no reputation at all,

unless you repute yourself such a loser. What, man! there are ways to recover the General again. You are but now cast in his mood, a punishment more in policy than in malice; even so as one would beat his offenseless dog to affright an imperious lion. Sue to him again, and he's yours.

CASSIO   I will rather sue to be despised than to deceive so good a commander with so slight, so drunken, and so indiscreet an officer. Drunk? and speak parrot? and squabble? swagger? swear? and discourse fustian with one's own shadow? O thou invisible spirit of wine, if thou hast no name to be known by, let us call thee devil!

IAGO   What was he that you followed with your sword? What had he done to you?

CASSIO   I know not.

IAGO   Is't possible?

CASSIO   I remember a mass of things, but nothing distinctly; a quarrel, but nothing wherefore. O God, that men should put an enemy in their mouths to steal away their brains! that we should, with joy, pleasance, revel, and applause, transform ourselves into beasts!

IAGO   Why, but you are now well enough. How came you thus recovered?

CASSIO   It hath pleased the devil drunkenness to give place to the devil wrath: one unperfectness shows me another, to make me frankly despise myself.

IAGO   Come, you are too severe a moraler. As the time, the place, and the condition of this country stands, I could heartily wish this had not befallen; but since it is as it is, mend it for your own good.

CASSIO   I will ask him for my place again; he shall tell me I am a drunkard! Had I as many mouths as Hydra, such an answer would stop them all. To be now a sensible man, by and by a fool, and presently a beast! O strange! Every inordinate cup is unblest, and the ingredient is a devil.

IAGO   Come, come, good wine is a good familiar creature, if it be well used. Exclaim no more against it. And, good Lieutenant, I think you think I love you.

CASSIO   I have well approved it, Sir. I drunk!

IAGO   You or any man living may be drunk at some time, man. I'll tell you what you shall do. Our general's wife is now the General.

I may say so in this respect, for that he hath devoted and given up himself to the contemplation, mark, and denotement of her parts and graces. Confess yourself freely to her; importune her help to put you in your place again. She is of so free, so kind, so apt, so blessed a disposition, she holds it a vice in her goodness not to do more than she is requested. This broken joint between you and her husband entreat her to splinter; and, my fortunes against any lay worth naming, this crack of your love shall grow stronger than it was before.

CASSIO   You advise me well.

IAGO   I protest, in the sincerity of love and honest kindness.

CASSIO   I think it freely; and betimes in the morning I will beseech the virtuous Desdemona to undertake for me. I am desperate of my fortunes if they check me here.

IAGO   You are in the right. Good night, Lieutenant, I must to the watch.

CASSIO   Good night, honest Iago.

Exit Cassio

IAGO   And what's he then that says I play the villain?
   When this advice is free I give and honest,
   Probal to thinking, and indeed the course
   To win the Moor again? For 'tis most easy
   The inclining Desdemona to subdue
   In any honest suit. She's framed as fruitful
   As the free elements. And then for her
   To win the Moor, were't to renounce his baptism,
   All seals and symbols of redeemed sin,
   His soul is so enfetter'd to her love,
   That she may make, unmake, do what she list,
   Even as her appetite shall play the god
   With his weak function. How am I then a villain
   To counsel Cassio to this parallel course,
   Directly to his good? Divinity of hell!
   When devils will the blackest sins put on,
   They do suggest at first with heavenly shows,
   As I do now. For whiles this honest fool
   Plies Desdemona to repair his fortune,
   And she for him pleads strongly to the Moor,
   I'll pour this pestilence into his ear,
   That she repeals him for her body's lust;

And by how much she strives to do him good,
She shall undo her credit with the Moor.
So will I turn her virtue into pitch,
And out of her own goodness make the net
That shall enmesh them all.

Enter Roderigo

How now, Roderigo!

RODERIGO   I do follow here in the chase, not like a hound that hunts,
but one that fills up the cry. My money is almost spent; I have
been tonight exceedingly well cudgeled; and I think the issue will
be, I shall have so much experience for my pains; and so, with no
money at all and a little more wit, return again to Venice.

IAGO   How poor are they that have not patience!
What wound did ever heal but by degrees?
Thou know'st we work by wit and not by witchcraft,
And wit depends on dilatory time.
Does't not go well? Cassio hath beaten thee,
And thou by that small hurt hast cashier'd Cassio.
Though other things grow fair against the sun,
Yet fruits that blossom first will first be ripe.
Content thyself awhile. By the mass, 'tis morning;
Pleasure and action make the hours seem short.
Retire thee; go where thou art billeted.
Away, I say. Thou shalt know more hereafter.
Nay, get thee gone.

Exit Roderigo

Two things are to be done:

My wife must move for Cassio to her mistress—
I'll set her on;
Myself the while to draw the Moor apart,
And bring him jump when he may Cassio find
Soliciting his wife. Ay, that's the way;
Dull not device by coldness and delay.

Exit

ACT III

SCENE I—Before the castle.

Enter Cassio and some Musicians

CASSIO Masters, play here, I will content your pains;
Something that's brief; and bid "Good morrow, General."

Music begins—Enter Clown

CLOWN Why, masters, have your instruments been in Naples, that they speak i' the nose thus?

FIRST MUSICIAN How, Sir, how?

CLOWN Are these, I pray you, wind instruments?

FIRST MUSICIAN Ay, marry, are they, Sir.

CLOWN O, thereby hangs a tail.

FIRST MUSICIAN Whereby hangs a tale, Sir?

CLOWN Marry, Sir, by many a wind instrument that I know. But, masters, here's money for you; and the General so likes your music, that he desires you, for love's sake, to make no more noise with it.

FIRST MUSICIAN Well, Sir, we will not.

CLOWN If you have any music that may not be heard, to't again; but, as they say, to hear music the General does not greatly care.

First Musician We have none such, Sir.

CLOWN Then put up your pipes in your bag, for I'll away. Go, vanish into air, away!

Exit Musicians

CASSIO Dost thou hear, my honest friend?

CLOWN No, I hear not your honest friend; I hear you.

CASSIO Prithee, keep up thy quillets. There's a poor piece of gold for thee. [*He gives money*] If the gentlewoman that attends the General's wife be stirring, tell her there's one Cassio entreats her a little favor of speech. Wilt thou do this?

CLOWN   She is stirring, Sir. If she will stir hither, I shall seem to no-
    tify unto her.
CASSIO   Do, good my friend.

Exit Clown

Enter Iago
In happy time, Iago.

IAGO   You have not been abed, then?
CASSIO   Why, no; the day had broke
    Before we parted. I have made bold, Iago,
    To send in to your wife. My suit to her
    Is that she will to virtuous Desdemona
    Procure me some access.
IAGO   I'll send her to you presently;
    And I'll devise a mean to draw the Moor
    Out of the way, that your converse and business
    May be more free.
CASSIO   I humbly thank you for't.

Exit Iago

I never knew
A Florentine more kind and honest.

Enter Emilia

EMILIA   Good morrow, good Lieutenant. I am sorry
    For your displeasure, but all will sure be well.
    The General and his wife are talking of it,
    And she speaks for you stoutly. The Moor replies
    That he you hurt is of great fame in Cyprus
    And great affinity and that in wholesome wisdom
    He might not but refuse you; but he protests he loves you
    And needs no other suitor but his likings
    To take the safest occasion by the front
    To bring you in again.
CASSIO   Yet, I beseech you,
    If you think fit, or that it may be done,
    Give me advantage of some brief discourse
    With Desdemona alone.
EMILIA   Pray you, come in.
    I will bestow you where you shall have time
    To speak your bosom freely.
CASSIO   I am much bound to you.

Exeunt

SCENE II—A room in the castle.
Enter Othello, Iago, and Gentlemen

OTHELLO   [*giving letters*] These letters give, Iago, to the pilot,
And by him do my duties to the Senate.
That done, I will be walking on the works;
Repair there to me.

IAGO   Well, my good lord, I'll do't.

OTHELLO   This fortification, gentlemen, shall we see't?

GENTLEMEN   We'll wait upon your lordship.

Exeunt

SCENE III—The garden of the castle.
Enter Desdemona, Cassio, and Emilia

DESDEMONA   Be thou assured, good Cassio, I will do
All my abilities in thy behalf.

EMILIA   Good madam, do. I warrant it grieves my husband
As if the cause were his.

DESDEMONA   O, that's an honest fellow. Do not doubt, Cassio,
But I will have my lord and you again
As friendly as you were.

CASSIO   Bounteous madam,
Whatever shall become of Michael Cassio,
He's never anything but your true servant.

DESDEMONA   I know't: I thank you. You do love my lord:
You have known him long; and be you well assured
He shall in strangeness stand no farther off
Than in a politic distance.

CASSIO   Ay, but, lady,
That policy may either last so long,
Or feed upon such nice and waterish diet,
Or breed itself so out of circumstances,
That I being absent and my place supplied,
My General will forget my love and service.

DESDEMONA   Do not doubt that. Before Emilia here
I give thee warrant of thy place, assure thee,
If I do vow a friendship, I'll perform it
To the last article. My lord shall never rest;
I'll watch him tame and talk him out of patience;
His bed shall seem a school, his board a shrift;
I'll intermingle everything he does

With Cassio's suit. Therefore be merry, Cassio,
For thy solicitor shall rather die
Than give thy cause away.
              Enter Othello and Iago, at a distance
EMILIA   Madam, here comes my lord.
CASSIO   Madam, I'll take my leave.
DESDEMONA   Nay, stay and hear me speak.
CASSIO   Madam, not now. I am very ill at ease,
   Unfit for mine own purposes.
DESDEMONA   Well, do your discretion.
                                 Exit Cassio

IAGO   Ha! I like not that.
OTHELLO   What dost thou say?
IAGO   Nothing, my lord; or if—I know not what.
OTHELLO   Was not that Cassio parted from my wife?
IAGO   Cassio, my lord! No, sure, I cannot think it,
   That he would steal away so guilty-like,
   Seeing you coming.
OTHELLO   I do believe 'twas he.
DESDEMONA   How now, my lord!
   I have been talking with a suitor here,
   A man that languishes in your displeasure.
OTHELLO   Who is't you mean?
DESDEMONA   Why, your Lieutenant, Cassio. Good my lord,
   If I have any grace or power to move you,
   His present reconciliation take;
   For if he be not one that truly loves you,
   That errs in ignorance and not in cunning,
   I have no judgement in an honest face.
   I prithee, call him back.
OTHELLO   Went he hence now?
DESDEMONA   Ay, sooth; so humbled
   That he hath left part of his grief with me
   To suffer with him. Good love, call him back.
OTHELLO   Not now, sweet Desdemona; some other time.
DESDEMONA   But shall't be shortly?
OTHELLO   The sooner, sweet, for you.
DESDEMONA   Shall't be tonight at supper?
OTHELLO   No, not tonight.
DESDEMONA   Tomorrow dinner then?

OTHELLO   I shall not dine at home;
    I meet the captains at the citadel.
DESDEMONA   Why then tomorrow night, or Tuesday morn,
    On Tuesday noon, or night, on Wednesday morn.
    I prithee, name the time, but let it not
    Exceed three days. In faith, he's penitent;
    And yet his trespass, in our common reason—
    Save that, they say, the wars must make example
    Out of their best—is not almost a fault
    To incur a private check. When shall he come?
    Tell me, Othello. I wonder in my soul,
    What you would ask me, that I should deny,
    Or stand so mammering on. What? Michael Cassio,
    That came awooing with you, and so many a time
    When I have spoke of you dispraisingly
    Hath ta'en your part—to have so much to do
    To bring him in! Trust me, I could do much—
OTHELLO   Prithee, no more. Let him come when he will;
    I will deny thee nothing.
DESDEMONA   Why, this is not a boon;
    'Tis as I should entreat you wear your gloves,
    Or feed on nourishing dishes, or keep you warm,
    Or sue to you to do a peculiar profit
    To your own person. Nay, when I have a suit
    Wherein I mean to touch your love indeed,
    It shall be full of poise and difficult weight,
    And fearful to be granted.
OTHELLO   I will deny thee nothing,
    Whereon, I do beseech thee, grant me this,
    To leave me but a little to myself.
DESDEMONA   Shall I deny you? No. Farewell, my lord.
OTHELLO   Farewell, my Desdemona; I'll come to thee straight.
DESDEMONA   Emilia, come. Be as your fancies teach you;
    Whate'er you be, I am obedient.

                      Exit Desdemona and Emilia

OTHELLO   Excellent wretch! Perdition catch my soul,
    But I do love thee! and when I love thee not,
    Chaos is come again.
IAGO   My noble lord—
OTHELLO   What dost thou say, Iago?

IAGO   Did Michael Cassio, when you woo'd my lady,
  Know of your love?
OTHELLO   He did, from first to last. Why dost thou ask?
IAGO   But for a satisfaction of my thought;
  No further harm.
OTHELLO   Why of thy thought, Iago?
IAGO   I did not think he had been acquainted with her.
OTHELLO   O, yes, and went between us very oft.
IAGO   Indeed!
OTHELLO   Indeed? Ay, indeed. Discern'st thou aught in that?
  Is he not honest?
IAGO   Honest, my lord?
OTHELLO   Honest? Ay, honest.
IAGO   My lord, for aught I know.
OTHELLO   What dost thou think?
IAGO   Think, my lord?
OTHELLO   "Think, my lord?" By heaven, he echoes me,
  As if there were some monster in his thought
  Too hideous to be shown. Thou dost mean something.
  I heard thee say even now, thou like'st not that,
  When Cassio left my wife. What didst not like?
  And when I told thee he was of my counsel
  In my whole course of wooing, thou criedst, "Indeed!"
  And didst contract and purse thy brow together,
  As if thou then hadst shut up in thy brain
  Some horrible conceit. If thou dost love me,
  Show me thy thought.
IAGO   My lord, you know I love you.
OTHELLO   I think thou dost;
  And for I know thou'rt full of love and honesty
  And weigh'st thy words before thou givest them breath,
  Therefore these stops of thine fright me the more;
  For such things in a false disloyal knave
  Are tricks of custom; but in a man that's just
  They're close dilations, working from the heart,
  That passion cannot rule.
IAGO   For Michael Cassio,
  I dare be sworn I think that he is honest.
OTHELLO   I think so too.

IAGO   Men should be what they seem;
   Or those that be not, would they might seem none!
OTHELLO   Certain, men should be what they seem.
IAGO   Why then I think Cassio's an honest man.
OTHELLO   Nay, yet there's more in this.
   I prithee, speak to me as to thy thinkings,
   As thou dost ruminate, and give thy worst of thoughts
   The worst of words.
IAGO   Good my lord, pardon me;
   Though I am bound to every act of duty,
   I am not bound to that all slaves are free to.
   Utter my thoughts? Why, say they are vile and false;
   As where's that palace whereinto foul things
   Sometimes intrude not? Who has a breast so pure,
   But some uncleanly apprehensions
   Keep leets and law-days, and in session sit
   With meditations lawful?
OTHELLO   Thou dost conspire against thy friend, Iago,
   If thou but think'st him wrong'd and makest his ear
   A stranger to thy thoughts.
IAGO   I do beseech you—
   Though I perchance am vicious in my guess,
   As, I confess, it is my nature's plague
   To spy into abuses, and oft my jealousy
   Shapes faults that are not—that your wisdom yet,
   From one that so imperfectly conceits,
   Would take no notice, nor build yourself a trouble
   Out of his scattering and unsure observance.
   It were not for your quiet nor your good,
   Nor for my manhood, honesty, or wisdom,
   To let you know my thoughts.
OTHELLO   What dost thou mean?
IAGO   Good name in man and woman, dear my lord,
   Is the immediate jewel of their souls.
   Who steals my purse steals trash; 'tis something, nothing;
   'Twas mine, 'tis his, and has been slave to thousands;
   But he that filches from me my good name
   Robs me of that which not enriches him
   And makes me poor indeed.
OTHELLO   By heaven, I'll know thy thoughts.

IAGO   You cannot, if my heart were in your hand;
       Nor shall not, whilst 'tis in my custody.
OTHELLO   Ha!
IAGO   O, beware, my lord, of jealousy!
       It is the green-eyed monster, which doth mock
       The meat it feeds on. That cuckold lives in bliss
       Who, certain of his fate, loves not his wronger;
       But O, what damned minutes tells he o'er
       Who dotes, yet doubts, suspects, yet strongly loves!
OTHELLO   O misery!
IAGO   Poor and content is rich, and rich enough;
       But riches fineless is as poor as winter
       To him that ever fears he shall be poor.
       Good heaven, the souls of all my tribe defend
       From jealousy!
OTHELLO   Why, why is this?
       Think'st thou I'ld make a life of jealousy,
       To follow still the changes of the moon
       With fresh suspicions? No! To be once in doubt
       Is once to be resolved. Exchange me for a goat
       When I shall turn the business of my soul
       To such exsufflicate and blown surmises,
       Matching thy inference. 'Tis not to make me jealous
       To say my wife is fair, feeds well, loves company,
       Is free of speech, sings, plays, and dances well;
       Where virtue is, these are more virtuous.
       Nor from mine own weak merits will I draw
       The smallest fear or doubt of her revolt;
       For she had eyes and chose me. No, Iago,
       I'll see before I doubt; when I doubt, prove;
       And on the proof, there is no more but this—
       Away at once with love or jealousy!
IAGO   I am glad of it, for now I shall have reason
       To show the love and duty that I bear you
       With franker spirit. Therefore, as I am bound,
       Receive it from me. I speak not yet of proof.
       Look to your wife; observe her well with Cassio;
       Wear your eye thus, not jealous nor secure.
       I would not have your free and noble nature

Out of self-bounty be abused. Look to't.
I know our country disposition well;
In Venice they do let heaven see the pranks
They dare not show their husbands; their best conscience
Is not to leave't undone, but keep't unknown.

OTHELLO   Dost thou say so?

IAGO   She did deceive her father, marrying you;
And when she seem'd to shake and fear your looks,
She loved them most.

OTHELLO   And so she did.

IAGO   Why, go to then.
She that so young could give out such a seeming,
To seal her father's eyes up close as oak—
He thought 'twas witchcraft—but I am much to blame;
I humbly do beseech you of your pardon
For too much loving you.

OTHELLO   I am bound to thee forever.

IAGO   I see this hath a little dash'd your spirits.

OTHELLO   Not a jot, not a jot.

IAGO   I'faith, I fear it has.
I hope you will consider what is spoke
Comes from my love. But I do see you're moved;
I am to pray you not to strain my speech
To grosser issues nor to larger reach
Than to suspicion.

OTHELLO   I will not.

IAGO   Should you do so, my lord,
My speech should fall into such vile success
Which my thoughts aim not at. Cassio's my worthy friend—
My lord, I see you're moved.

OTHELLO   No, not much moved.
I do not think but Desdemona's honest.

IAGO   Long live she so! and long live you to think so!

OTHELLO   And yet, how nature erring from itself—

IAGO   Ay, there's the point, as—to be bold with you—
Not to affect many proposed matches
Of her own clime, complexion, and degree,
Whereto we see in all things nature tends—
Foh, one may smell in such a will most rank,

Foul disproportion, thoughts unnatural.
But pardon me. I do not in position
Distinctly speak of her; though I may fear,
Her will, recoiling to her better judgement,
May fall to match you with her country forms,
And happily repent.

OTHELLO   Farewell, farewell.
If more thou dost perceive, let me know more;
Set on thy wife to observe. Leave me, Iago.

IAGO   [*going*] My lord, I take my leave.

OTHELLO   Why did I marry? This honest creature doubtless
Sees and knows more, much more, than he unfolds.

IAGO   [*returning*] My lord, I would I might entreat your honor
To scan this thing no further; leave it to time.
Though it be fit that Cassio have his place,
For sure he fills it up with great ability,
Yet, if you please to hold him off awhile,
You shall by that perceive him and his means.
Note if your lady strain his entertainment
With any strong or vehement importunity;
Much will be seen in that. In the meantime,
Let me be thought too busy in my fears—
As worthy cause I have to fear I am—
And hold her free, I do beseech your honor.

OTHELLO   Fear not my government.

IAGO   I once more take my leave.

                              Exit Iago

OTHELLO   This fellow's of exceeding honesty,
And knows all qualities, with a learned spirit,
Of human dealings. If I do prove her haggard,
Though that her jesses were my dear heartstrings,
I'd whistle her off and let her down the wind
To prey at fortune. Haply, for I am black
And have not those soft parts of conversation
That chamberers have, or for I am declined
Into the vale of years—yet that's not much—
She's gone. I am abused, and my relief
Must be to loathe her. O curse of marriage,
That we can call these delicate creatures ours,
And not their appetites! I had rather be a toad,

And live upon the vapor of a dungeon,
Than keep a corner in the thing I love
For others' uses. Yet, 'tis the plague of great ones:
Prerogatived are they less than the base;
'Tis destiny unshunnable, like death.
Even then this forked plague is fated to us
When we do quicken. Desdemona comes:

Enter Desdemona and Emilia

If she be false, O, then heaven mocks itself!
I'll not believe't.

DESDEMONA How now, my dear Othello!
Your dinner, and the generous islanders
By you invited, do attend your presence.

OTHELLO I am to blame.

DESDEMONA Why do you speak so faintly?
Are you not well?

OTHELLO I have a pain upon my forehead here.

DESDEMONA Faith, that's with watching; 'twill away again.

She offers her handkerchief

Let me but bind it hard, within this hour
It will be well.

OTHELLO Your napkin is too little;

He puts the handkerchief from him, and she drops it

Let it alone. Come, I'll go in with you.

DESDEMONA I am very sorry that you are not well.

Exit Othello and Desdemona
Emilia picks ups the handkerchief

EMILIA I am glad I have found this napkin;
This was her first remembrance from the Moor.
My wayward husband hath a hundred times
Woo'd me to steal it; but she so loves the token,
For he conjured her she should ever keep it,
That she reserves it evermore about her
To kiss and talk to. I'll have the work ta'en out,
And give't Iago. What he will do with it
Heaven knows, not I;
I nothing but to please his fantasy.

Enter Iago

IAGO How now, what do you here alone?

EMILIA Do not you chide; I have a thing for you.

IAGO   A thing for me? It is a common thing—
EMILIA   Ha!
IAGO   To have a foolish wife.
EMILIA   O, is that all? What will you give me now
    For that same handkerchief?
IAGO   What handkerchief?
EMILIA   What handkerchief?
    Why, that the Moor first gave to Desdemona,
    That which so often you did bid me steal.
IAGO   Hast stol'n it from her?
EMILIA   No, faith; she let it drop by negligence,
    And, to the advantage, I being here took't up.
    Look, here it is.
IAGO   A good wench! Give it me.
EMILIA   What will you do with't, that you have been so earnest
    To have me filch it?
IAGO   [snatching it]   Why, what is that to you?
EMILIA   If't be not for some purpose of import,
    Give't me again. Poor lady, she'll run mad
    When she shall lack it.
IAGO   Be not acknown on't;
    I have use for it. Go, leave me.   [Exit Emilia]
    I will in Cassio's lodging lose this napkin,
    And let him find it. Trifles light as air
    Are to the jealous confirmations strong
    As proofs of holy writ; this may do something.
    The Moor already changes with my poison:
    Dangerous conceits are in their natures poisons,
    Which at the first are scarce found to distaste,
    But with a little act upon the blood
    Burn like the mines of sulphur.
                        Enter Othello
                        I did say so.
    Look, where he comes! Not poppy, nor mandragora,
    Nor all the drowsy syrups of the world,
    Shall ever medicine thee to that sweet sleep
    Which thou ow'dst yesterday.
OTHELLO   Ha, ha, false to me?
IAGO   Why, how now, General! No more of that.

OTHELLO   Avaunt! be gone! Thou hast set me on the rack.
    I swear 'tis better to be much abused
    Than but to know't a little.
IAGO   How now, my lord?
OTHELLO   What sense had I of her stol'n hours of lust?
    I saw't not, thought it not, it harm'd not me;
    I slept the next night well, was free and merry;
    I found not Cassio's kisses on her lips.
    He that is robb'd, not wanting what is stol'n,
    Let him not know't and he's not robb'd at all.
IAGO   I am sorry to hear this.
OTHELLO   I had been happy if the general camp,
    Pioneers and all, had tasted her sweet body,
    So I had nothing known. O, now forever
    Farewell the tranquil mind! Farewell content!
    Farewell the plumed troop and the big wars
    That make ambition virtue! O, farewell,
    Farewell the neighing steed and the shrill trump,
    The spirit-stirring drum, the ear-piercing fife,
    The royal banner, and all quality,
    Pride, pomp, and circumstance of glorious war!
    And O you mortal engines, whose rude throats
    The immortal Jove's dread clamors counterfeit,
    Farewell! Othello's occupation's gone!
IAGO   Is't possible, my lord?
OTHELLO   Villain, be sure thou prove my love a whore;
    Be sure of it. Give me the ocular proof;
    Or, by the worth of man's eternal soul,
    Thou hadst been better have been born a dog
    Than answer my waked wrath!
IAGO   Is't come to this?
OTHELLO   Make me to see't; or at the least so prove it,
    That the probation bear no hinge nor loop
    To hang a doubt on; or woe upon thy life!
IAGO   My noble lord—
OTHELLO   If thou dost slander her and torture me,
    Never pray more; abandon all remorse;
    On horror's head horrors accumulate;
    Do deeds to make heaven weep, all earth amazed;

For nothing canst thou to damnation add
Greater than that.

IAGO   O grace! O heaven defend me!
Are you a man? have you a soul or sense?
God be wi' you; take mine office. O wretched fool,
That livest to make thine honesty a vice!
O monstrous world! Take note, take note, O world,
To be direct and honest is not safe.
I thank you for this profit, and from hence
I'll love no friend sith love breeds such offense.

OTHELLO   Nay, stay; thou shouldst be honest.

IAGO   I should be wise; for honesty's a fool,
And loses that it works for.

OTHELLO   By the world,
I think my wife be honest, and think she is not;
I think that thou art just, and think thou art not.
I'll have some proof. Her name, that was as fresh
As Dian's visage, is now begrimed and black
As mine own face. If there be cords or knives,
Poison or fire, or suffocating streams,
I'll not endure it. Would I were satisfied!

IAGO   I see, Sir, you are eaten up with passion;
I do repent me that I put it to you.
You would be satisfied?

OTHELLO   Would? Nay, I will.

IAGO   And may. But, how? how satisfied, my lord?
Would you, the supervisor, grossly gape on?
Behold her topp'd?

OTHELLO   Death and damnation! O!

IAGO   It were a tedious difficulty, I think,
To bring them to that prospect. Damn them then,
If ever mortal eyes do see them bolster
More than their own! What then? how then?
What shall I say? Where's satisfaction?
It is impossible you should see this
Were they as prime as goats, as hot as monkeys,
As salt as wolves in pride, and fools as gross
As ignorance made drunk. But yet, I say,
If imputation and strong circumstances,

Which lead directly to the door of truth,
Will give you satisfaction, you may have't.
OTHELLO   Give me a living reason she's disloyal.
IAGO   I do not like the office;
But sith I am enter'd in this cause so far,
Prick'd to't by foolish honesty and love,
I will go on. I lay with Cassio lately
And, being troubled with a raging tooth,
I could not sleep. There are a kind of men
So loose of soul that in their sleeps
Will mutter their affairs. One of this kind is Cassio.
In sleep I heard him say, "Sweet Desdemona,
Let us be wary, let us hide our loves";
And then, Sir, would he gripe and wring my hand,
Cry, "O sweet creature!" and then kiss me hard,
As if he pluck'd up kisses by the roots,
That grew upon my lips; then laid his leg
Over my thigh, and sigh'd and kiss'd; and then
Cried, "Cursed fate that gave thee to the Moor!"
OTHELLO   O monstrous! monstrous!
IAGO   Nay, this was but his dream.
OTHELLO   But this denoted a foregone conclusion.
'Tis a shrewd doubt, though it be but a dream.
IAGO   And this may help to thicken other proofs
That do demonstrate thinly.
OTHELLO   I'll tear her all to pieces.
IAGO   Nay, but be wise; yet we see nothing done;
She may be honest yet. Tell me but this;
Have you not sometimes seen a handkerchief
Spotted with strawberries in your wife's hand?
OTHELLO   I gave her such a one; 'twas my first gift.
IAGO   I know not that; but such a handkerchief—
I am sure it was your wife's—did I today
See Cassio wipe his beard with.
OTHELLO   If it be that—
IAGO   If it be that, or any that was hers,
It speaks against her with the other proofs.
OTHELLO   O, that the slave had forty thousand lives!
One is too poor, too weak for my revenge.

Now do I see 'tis true. Look here, Iago,
All my fond love thus do I blow to heaven. 'Tis gone.
Arise, black vengeance, from thy hollow hell!
Yield up, O love, thy crown and hearted throne
To tyrannous hate! Swell, bosom, with thy fraught,
For 'tis of aspics' tongues!

IAGO   Yet be content.

OTHELLO   O, blood, blood, blood!

IAGO   Patience, I say; your mind perhaps may change.

OTHELLO   Never, Iago. Like to the Pontic Sea,
Whose icy current and compulsive course
Ne'er feels retiring ebb, but keeps due on
To the Propontic and the Hellespont,
Even so my bloody thoughts, with violent pace,
Shall ne'er look back, ne'er ebb to humble love,
Till that a capable and wide revenge
Swallow them up. [*Kneeling*] Now, by yond marble heaven,
In the due reverence of a sacred vow
I here engage my words.

IAGO   Do not rise yet. [*He kneels*]
Witness, you ever-burning lights above,
You elements that clip us round about,
Witness that here Iago doth give up
The execution of his wit, hands, heart,
To wrong'd Othello's service! Let him command,
And to obey shall be in me remorse,
What bloody business ever. [*They rise*]

OTHELLO   I greet thy love,
Not with vain thanks, but with acceptance bounteous,
And will upon the instant put thee to't:
Within these three days let me hear thee say
That Cassio's not alive.

IAGO   My friend is dead!
'Tis done at your request. But let her live.

OTHELLO   Damn her, lewd minx! O, damn her, damn her!
Come, go with me apart; I will withdraw,
To furnish me with some swift means of death
For the fair devil. Now art thou my Lieutenant.

IAGO   I am your own forever.

                                              Exeunt

SCENE IV—Before the castle.

Enter Desdemona, Emilia, and Clown

DESDEMONA   Do you know, sirrah, where Lieutenant Cassio lies?

CLOWN   I dare not say he lies anywhere.

DESDEMONA   Why, man?

CLOWN   He's a soldier; and for one to say a soldier lies,'tis stabbing.

DESDEMONA   Go to! Where lodges he?

CLOWN   To tell you where he lodges, is to tell you where I lie.

DESDEMONA   Can anything be made of this?

CLOWN   I know not where he lodges, and for me to devise a lodging,
and say he lies here or he lies there, were to lie in mine own throat.

DESDEMONA   Can you inquire him out and be edified by report?

CLOWN   I will catechize the world for him; that is, make questions
and by them answer.

DESDEMONA   Seek him, bid him come hither. Tell him I have moved
my lord on his behalf and hope all will be well.

CLOWN   To do this is within the compass of man's wit, and therefore
I will attempt the doing it.

Exit Clown

DESDEMONA   Where should I lose that handkerchief, Emilia?

EMILIA   I know not, madam.

DESDEMONA   Believe me, I had rather have lost my purse
Full of crusadoes; and, but my noble Moor
Is true of mind and made of no such baseness
As jealous creatures are, it were enough
To put him to ill thinking.

EMILIA   Is he not jealous?

DESDEMONA   Who, he? I think the sun where he was born
Drew all such humors from him.

EMILIA   Look, where he comes.

Enter Othello

DESDEMONA   I will not leave him now till Cassio
Be call'd to him. How is't with you, my lord?

OTHELLO   Well, my good lady. [*aside*] O, hardness to dissemble!
How do you, Desdemona?

DESDEMONA   Well, my good lord.

OTHELLO   Give me your hand. [*She gives her hand*] This hand is moist,
my lady.

DESDEMONA   It yet has felt no age nor known no sorrow.

OTHELLO   This argues fruitfulness and liberal heart;

Hot, hot, and moist. This hand of yours requires
A sequester from liberty, fasting, and prayer,
Much castigation, exercise devout,
For here's a young and sweating devil here
That commonly rebels. 'Tis a good hand,
A frank one.

DESDEMONA   You may, indeed, say so;
For 'twas that hand that gave away my heart.

OTHELLO   A liberal hand. The hearts of old gave hands;
But our new heraldry is hands, not hearts.

DESDEMONA   I cannot speak of this. Come now, your promise.

OTHELLO   What promise, chuck?

DESDEMONA   I have sent to bid Cassio come speak with you.

OTHELLO   I have a salt and sorry rheum offends me;
Lend me thy handkerchief.

DESDEMONA   Here, my lord. [*She offers a handkerchief*]

OTHELLO   That which I gave you.

DESDEMONA   I have it not about me.

OTHELLO   Not?

DESDEMONA   No, faith, my lord.

OTHELLO   That's a fault. That handkerchief
Did an Egyptian to my mother give;
She was a charmer, and could almost read
The thoughts of people. She told her, while she kept it,
'Twould make her amiable and subdue my father
Entirely to her love, but if she lost it
Or made a gift of it, my father's eye
Should hold her loathed and his spirits should hunt
After new fancies. She dying gave it me,
And bid me, when my fate would have me wive,
To give it her. I did so, and take heed on't;
Make it a darling like your precious eye;
To lose't or give't away were such perdition
As nothing else could match.

DESDEMONA   Is't possible?

OTHELLO   'Tis true; there's magic in the web of it.
A sibyl, that had number'd in the world
The sun to course two hundred compasses,
In her prophetic fury sew'd the work;
The worms were hallow'd that did breed the silk,

And it was dyed in mummy which the skillful
Conserved of maiden's hearts.

DESDEMONA   Indeed! is't true?

OTHELLO   Most veritable; therefore look to't well.

DESDEMONA   Then would to God that I had never seen't!

OTHELLO   Ha! Wherefore?

DESDEMONA   Why do you speak so startingly and rash?

OTHELLO   Is't lost? is't gone? speak, is it out o' the way?

DESDEMONA   Heaven bless us!

OTHELLO   Say you?

DESDEMONA   It is not lost; but what an if it were?

OTHELLO   How?

DESDEMONA   I say, it is not lost.

OTHELLO   Fetch't, let me see it.

DESDEMONA   Why, so I can, Sir, but I will not now.
      This is a trick to put me from my suit.
      Pray you, let Cassio be received again.

OTHELLO   Fetch me the handkerchief, my mind misgives.

DESDEMONA   Come, come, You'll never meet a more sufficient man.

OTHELLO   The handkerchief!

DESDEMONA   I pray, talk me of Cassio.

OTHELLO   The handkerchief!

DESDEMONA   A man that all his time
      Hath founded his good fortunes on your love,
      Shared dangers with you—

OTHELLO   The handkerchief!

DESDEMONA   In sooth, you are to blame.

OTHELLO   'Zounds!

                                        Exit Othello

EMILIA   Is not this man jealous?

DESDEMONA   I ne'er saw this before.
      Sure there's some wonder in this handkerchief;
      I am most unhappy in the loss of it.

EMILIA   'Tis not a year or two shows us a man.
      They are all but stomachs and we all but food;
      They eat us hungerly, and when they are full
      They belch us.

                        Enter Cassio and Iago
              Look you! Cassio and my husband.

IAGO   [*to Cassio*] There is no other way; 'tis she must do't.

And, lo, the happiness! Go and importune her.

DESDEMONA   How now, good Cassio! What's the news with you?

CASSIO   Madam, my former suit: I do beseech you
　　That by your virtuous means I may again
　　Exist and be a member of his love
　　Whom I with all the office of my heart
　　Entirely honor. I would not be delay'd.
　　If my offense be of such mortal kind
　　That nor my service past nor present sorrows
　　Nor purposed merit in futurity
　　Can ransom me into his love again,
　　But to know so must be my benefit;
　　So shall I clothe me in a forced content
　　And shut myself up in some other course
　　To Fortune's alms.

DESDEMONA　　　　　　Alas, thrice-gentle Cassio!
　　My advocation is not now in tune;
　　My lord is not my lord, nor should I know him
　　Were he in favor as in humor alter'd.
　　So help me every spirit sanctified,
　　As I have spoken for you all my best
　　And stood within the blank of his displeasure
　　For my free speech! You must awhile be patient.
　　What I can do I will; and more I will
　　Than for myself I dare. Let that suffice you.

IAGO   Is my lord angry?

EMILIA　　　　　　He went hence but now,
　　And certainly in strange unquietness.

IAGO   Can he be angry? I have seen the cannon,
　　When it hath blown his ranks into the air
　　And, like the devil, from his very arm
　　Puff'd his own brother. And can he be angry?
　　Something of moment then. I will go meet him.
　　There's matter in't indeed if he be angry.

DESDEMONA   I prithee, do so.

　　　　　　　　　　　　　　　　　　　Exit Iago

　　　　　　　　Something sure of state,
　　Either from Venice or some unhatch'd practice
　　Made demonstrable here in Cyprus to him,

Hath puddled his clear spirit; and in such cases
Men's natures wrangle with inferior things,
Though great ones are their object. 'Tis even so;
For let our finger ache, and it indues
Our other healthful members even to that sense
Of pain. Nay, we must think men are not gods,
Nor of them look for such observancy
As fits the bridal. Beshrew me much, Emilia,
I was, unhandsome warrior as I am,
Arraigning his unkindness with my soul;
But now I find I had suborn'd the witness,
And he's indicted falsely.

EMILIA   Pray heaven it be
State matters, as you think, and no conception
Nor no jealous toy concerning you.

DESDEMONA   Alas the day, I never gave him cause!

EMILIA   But jealous souls will not be answer'd so;
They are not ever jealous for the cause,
But jealous for they are jealous. 'Tis a monster
Begot upon itself, born on itself.

DESDEMONA   Heaven keep that monster from Othello's mind!

EMILIA   Lady, amen.

DESDEMONA   I will go seek him. Cassio, walk hereabout.
If I do find him fit, I'll move your suit,
And seek to effect it to my uttermost.

CASSIO   I humbly thank your ladyship.

Exit Desdemona and Emilia
Enter Bianca

BIANCA   Save you, friend Cassio!

CASSIO   What make you from home?
How is it with you, my most fair Bianca?
I'faith, sweet love, I was coming to your house.

BIANCA   And I was going to your lodging, Cassio.
What, keep a week away? seven days and nights?
Eight score eight hours? and lovers' absent hours,
More tedious than the dial eight score times?
O weary reckoning!

CASSIO   Pardon me, Bianca.
I have this while with leaden thoughts been press'd;
But I shall in a more continuate time

Strike off this score of absence. Sweet Bianca,
>   [*giving her Desdemona's handkerchief*]
Take me this work out.
BIANCA   O Cassio, whence came this?
This is some token from a newer friend.
To the felt absence now I feel a cause.
Is't come to this? Well, well.
CASSIO   Go to, woman!
Throw your vile guesses in the devil's teeth,
From whence you have them. You are jealous now
That this is from some mistress, some remembrance.
No, by my faith, Bianca.
BIANCA   Why, whose is it?
CASSIO I know not, sweet. I found it in my chamber.
I like the work well. Ere it be demanded—
As like enough it will—I'ld have it copied.
Take it, and do't; and leave me for this time.
BIANCA Leave you! wherefore?
CASSIO I do attend here on the General;
And think it no addition, nor my wish,
To have him see me woman'd.
BIANCA   Why, I pray you?
CASSIO Not that I love you not.
BIANCA   But that you do not love me.
I pray you, bring me on the way a little,
And say if I shall see you soon at night.
CASSIO 'Tis but a little way that I can bring you,
For I attend here, but I'll see you soon.
BIANCA 'Tis very good; I must be circumstanced.
>   *Exeunt*

ACT IV

SCENE I—Cyprus. Before the castle.
Enter Othello and Iago

IAGO   Will you think so?

OTHELLO   Think so, Iago?

IAGO   What, to kiss in private?

OTHELLO   An unauthorized kiss.

IAGO   Or to be naked with her friend in bed
    An hour or more, not meaning any harm?

OTHELLO   Naked in bed, Iago, and not mean harm!
    It is hypocrisy against the devil.
    They that mean virtuously and yet do so,
    The devil their virtue tempts and they tempt heaven.

IAGO   So they do nothing, 'tis a venial slip.
    But if I give my wife a handkerchief—

OTHELLO   What then?

IAGO   Why, then, 'tis hers, my lord, and being hers,
    She may, I think, bestow't on any man.

OTHELLO   She is protectress of her honor too.
    May she give that?

IAGO   Her honor is an essence that's not seen;
    They have it very oft that have it not.
    But for the handkerchief—

OTHELLO   By heaven, I would most gladly have forgot it.
    Thou said'st—O, it comes o'er my memory,
    As doth the raven o'er the infected house,
    Boding to all—he had my handkerchief.

IAGO   Ay, what of that?

OTHELLO   That's not so good now.

IAGO   What, if I had said I had seen him do you wrong?
    Or heard him say—as knaves be such abroad,
    Who having, by their own importunate suit,

Or voluntary dotage of some mistress,
Convinced or supplied them, cannot choose
But they must blab—

OTHELLO   Hath he said anything?

IAGO   He hath, my lord; but be you well assured,
No more than he'll unswear.

OTHELLO   What hath he said?

IAGO   Faith, that he did—I know not what he did.

OTHELLO   What? what?

IAGO   Lie—

OTHELLO   With her?

IAGO   With her, on her, what you will.

OTHELLO   Lie with her! Lie on her! We say lie on her, when they belie
her. Lie with her! 'Zounds, that's fulsome! Handkerchief—confes-
sions—handkerchief! To confess and be hanged for his labor—first,
to be hanged, and then to confess. I tremble at it. Nature would
not invest herself in such shadowing passion without some instruction. It is not words that shakes me thus. Pish! Noses, ears,
and lips. Is't possible? Confess? Handkerchief? O devil!

He falls down in a trance

IAGO   Work on, my medicine, work! Thus credulous fools are caught,
And many worthy and chaste dames even thus,
All guiltless, meet reproach. What, ho! My lord!
My lord, I say! Othello!

Enter Cassio

How now, Cassio!

CASSIO   What's the matter?

IAGO   My lord is fall'n into an epilepsy.
This is his second fit; he had one yesterday.

CASSIO   Rub him about the temples.

IAGO   No, forbear;
The lethargy must have his quiet course.
If not, he foams at mouth, and by and by
Breaks out to savage madness. Look, he stirs.
Do you withdraw yourself a little while,
He will recover straight. When he is gone,
I would on great occasion speak with you.

Exit Cassio

How is it, General? Have you not hurt your head?

OTHELLO   Dost thou mock me?

IAGO   I mock you? No, by heaven.
    Would you would bear your fortune like a man!
OTHELLO   A horned man's a monster and a beast.
IAGO   There's many a beast then in a populous city,
    And many a civil monster.
OTHELLO   Did he confess it?
IAGO   Good Sir, be a man;
    Think every bearded fellow that's but yoked
    May draw with you. There's millions now alive
    That nightly lie in those unproper beds
    Which they dare swear peculiar. Your case is better.
    O, 'tis the spite of hell, the fiend's arch-mock,
    To lip a wanton in a secure couch,
    And to suppose her chaste! No, let me know,
    And knowing what I am, I know what she shall be.
OTHELLO   O, thou art wise; 'tis certain.
IAGO   Stand you awhile apart,
    Confine yourself but in a patient list.
    Whilst you were here o'erwhelmed with your grief—
    A passion most unsuiting such a man—
    Cassio came hither. I shifted him away,
    And laid good 'scuse upon your ecstasy;
    Bade him anon return and here speak with me
    The which he promised. Do but encave yourself
    And mark the fleers, the gibes, and notable scorns,
    That dwell in every region of his face;
    For I will make him tell the tale anew,
    Where, how, how oft, how long ago, and when
    He hath and is again to cope your wife.
    I say, but mark his gesture. Marry, patience,
    Or I shall say you are all in all in spleen,
    And nothing of a man.
OTHELLO   Dost thou hear, Iago?
    I will be found most cunning in my patience;
    But—dost thou hear?—most bloody.
IAGO   That's not amiss;
    But yet keep time in all. Will you withdraw? [*Othello retires*]
    Now will I question Cassio of Bianca,
    A hussy that by selling her desires
    Buys herself bread and clothes. It is a creature

That dotes on Cassio, as 'tis the strumpet's plague
To beguile many and be beguiled by one.
He, when he hears of her, cannot refrain
From the excess of laughter. Here he comes.

                    Enter Cassio

As he shall smile, Othello shall go mad;
And his unbookish jealousy must construe
Poor Cassio's smiles, gestures, and light behavior
Quite in the wrong. How do you now, Lieutenant?

CASSIO   The worser that you give me the addition
Whose want even kills me.

IAGO   Ply Desdemona well, and you are sure on't.
Now, if this suit lay in Bianco's power,
How quickly should you speed!

CASSIO   [*laughing*] Alas, poor caitiff!

OTHELLO   [*aside*] Look, how he laughs already!

IAGO   I never knew a woman love man so.

CASSIO   Alas, poor rogue! I think, i'faith, she loves me.

OTHELLO   Now he denies it faintly and laughs it out.

IAGO   Do you hear, Cassio?

OTHELLO   Now he importunes him
To tell it o'er. Go to; well said, well said.

IAGO   She gives it out that you shall marry her.
Do you intend it?

CASSIO   Ha, ha, ha!

OTHELLO   Do you triumph, Roman? Do you triumph?

CASSIO   I marry her! What? A customer! I prithee, bear some charity
to my wit; do not think it so unwholesome. Ha, ha, ha!

OTHELLO   So, so, so, so! They laugh that win.

IAGO   Faith, the cry goes that you shall marry her.

CASSIO   Prithee, say true.

IAGO   I am a very villain else.

OTHELLO   Have you scored me? Well.

CASSIO   This is the monkey's own giving out. She is persuaded I will
marry her, out of her own love and flattery, not out of my promise.

OTHELLO   Iago beckons me; now he begins the story.

CASSIO   She was here even now; she haunts me in every place. I was
the other day talking on the sea bank with certain Venetians, and
thither comes the bauble, and, by this hand, she falls me thus
about my neck— [*He embraces Iago*]

OTHELLO   Crying, "O dear Cassio!" as it were; his gesture imports it.

CASSIO   So hangs and lolls and weeps upon me; so hales and pulls me. Ha, ha, ha!

OTHELLO   Now he tells how she plucked him to my chamber. O, I see that nose of yours, but not that dog I shall throw it to.

CASSIO   Well, I must leave her company.

IAGO   Before me! look where she comes.

Enter Bianca, with Desdemona's handkerchief

CASSIO   'Tis such another fitchew! marry, a perfumed one. What do you mean by this haunting of me?

BIANCA   Let the devil and his dam haunt you! What did you mean by that same handkerchief you gave me even now? I was a fine fool to take it. I must take out the work? A likely piece of work that you should find it in your chamber and not know who left it there! This is some minx's token, and I must take out the work? There, give it your hobbyhorse. Wheresoever you had it, I'll take out no work on't.

CASSIO   How now, my sweet Bianca! how now! how now!

OTHELLO   By heaven, that should be my handkerchief!

BIANCA   An you'll come to supper tonight, you may; an you will not, come when you are next prepared for.

Exit Bianca

IAGO   After her, after her.

CASSIO   Faith, I must; she'll rail i' the street else.

IAGO   Will you sup there?

CASSIO   Faith, I intend so.

IAGO   Well, I may chance to see you, for I would very fain speak with you.

CASSIO   Prithee, come; will you?

IAGO   Go to; say no more.

Exit Cassio

OTHELLO   [*advancing*] How shall I murder him, Iago?

IAGO   Did you perceive how he laughed at his vice?

OTHELLO   O Iago!

IAGO   And did you see the handkerchief?

OTHELLO   Was that mine?

IAGO   Yours, by this hand. And to see how he prizes the foolish woman your wife! She gave it him, and he hath given it his whore.

OTHELLO   I would have him nine years a-killing. A fine woman! a fair woman! a sweet woman!

IAGO   Nay, you must forget that.

OTHELLO   Ay, let her rot, and perish, and be damned tonight, for she shall not live. No, my heart is turned to stone; I strike it, and it hurts my hand. O, the world hath not a sweeter creature. She might lie by an emperor's side, and command him tasks.

IAGO   Nay, that's not your way.

OTHELLO   Hang her! I do but say what she is. So delicate with her needle, an admirable musician. O, she will sing the savageness out of a bear. Of so high and plenteous wit and invention—

IAGO   She's the worse for all this.

OTHELLO   O, a thousand, a thousand times. And then, of so gentle a condition!

IAGO   Ay, too gentle.

OTHELLO   Nay, that's certain. But yet the pity of it, Iago! O Iago, the pity of it, Iago!

IAGO   If you are so fond over her iniquity, give her patent to offend, for, if it touch not you, it comes near nobody.

OTHELLO   I will chop her into messes. Cuckold me!

IAGO   O, 'tis foul in her.

OTHELLO   With mine officer!

IAGO   That's fouler.

OTHELLO   Get me some poison, Iago, this night. I'll not expostulate with her, lest her body and beauty unprovide my mind again. This night, Iago.

IAGO   Do it not with poison, strangle her in her bed, even the bed she hath contaminated.

OTHELLO   Good, good, the justice of it pleases, very good.

IAGO   And for Cassio, let me be his undertaker. You shall hear more by midnight.

OTHELLO   Excellent good. [*A trumpet within*] What trumpet is that same?

IAGO   I warrant, something from Venice, sure.

    Enter Lodovico, Desdemona, and Attendants

    'Tis Lodovico. This comes from the Duke.

    See your wife is with him.

LODOVICO   God save you worthy General!

OTHELLO   With all my heart, Sir.

LODOVICO   The Duke and Senators of Venice greet you.

                    Gives him a letter

OTHELLO   I kiss the instrument of their pleasures.

Opens the letter, and reads

DESDEMONA   And what's the news, good cousin Lodovico?

IAGO   I am very glad to see you, signior.
   Welcome to Cyprus.

LODOVICO   I thank you. How does Lieutenant Cassio?

IAGO   Lives, Sir.

DESDEMONA   Cousin, there's fall'n between him and my lord
   An unkind breech; but you shall make all well.

OTHELLO   Are you sure of that?

DESDEMONA   My lord?

OTHELLO   [*Reads*] "This fail you not to do, as you will—"

LODOVICO   He did not call; he's busy in the paper.
   Is there division 'twixt my lord and Cassio?

DESDEMONA   A most unhappy one. I would do much
   To atone them, for the love I bear to Cassio.

OTHELLO   Fire and brimstone!

DESDEMONA   My lord?

OTHELLO   Are you wise?

DESDEMONA   What, is he angry?

LODOVICO   May be the letter moved him;
   For, as I think, they do command him home,
   Deputing Cassio in his government.

DESDEMONA   By my troth, I am glad on't.

OTHELLO   Indeed!

DESDEMONA   My lord?

OTHELLO   I am glad to see you mad.

DESDEMONA   Why, sweet Othello?

OTHELLO   [*He strikes her*] Devil!

DESDEMONA   I have not deserved this.

LODOVICO   My lord, this would not be believed in Venice,
   Though I should swear I saw't. 'Tis very much.
   Make her amends; she weeps.

OTHELLO   O devil, devil!
   If that the earth could teem with woman's tears,
   Each drop she falls would prove a crocodile.
   Out of my sight!

DESDEMONA   I will not stay to offend you. [*going*]

LODOVICO   Truly, an obedient lady.
   I do beseech your lordship, call her back.

OTHELLO   Mistress!

DESDEMONA   [*returning*] My lord?

OTHELLO   What would you with her, Sir?

LODOVICO   Who, I, my lord?

OTHELLO   Ay, you did wish that I would make her turn.
    Sir, she can turn and turn, and yet go on,
    And turn again; and she can weep, Sir, weep;
    And she's obedient, as you say, obedient,
    Very obedient. Proceed you in your tears.
    Concerning this, Sir—O well-painted passion!—
    I am commanded home. Get you away;
    I'll send for you anon. Sir, I obey the mandate,
    And will return to Venice. Hence, avaunt!   [*Exit Desdemona*]
    Cassio shall have my place. And, Sir, tonight,
    I do entreat that we may sup together.
    You are welcome, Sir, to Cyprus. Goats and monkeys!

                                                 Exit Othello

LODOVICO   Is this the noble Moor whom our full Senate
    Call all in all sufficient? This the nature
    Whom passion could not shake? whose solid virtue
    The shot of accident nor dart of chance
    Could neither graze nor pierce?

IAGO   He is much changed.

LODOVICO   Are his wits safe? Is he not light of brain?

IAGO   He's that he is. I may not breathe my censure
    What he might be: if what he might he is not,
    I would to heaven he were!

LODOVICO   What, strike his wife!

IAGO   Faith, that was not so well; yet would I knew
    That stroke would prove the worst!

LODOVICO   Is it his use?
    Or did the letters work upon his blood,
    And new create this fault?

IAGO   Alas, alas!
    It is not honesty in me to speak
    What I have seen and known. You shall observe him,
    And his own courses will denote him so
    That I may save my speech. Do but go after,
    And mark how he continues.

LODOVICO   I am sorry that I am deceived in him.

                                                 Exeunt

SCENE II—A room in the castle.

Enter Othello and Emilia

OTHELLO   You have seen nothing, then?

EMILIA   Nor ever heard, nor ever did suspect.

OTHELLO   Yes, you have seen Cassio and she together.

EMILIA   But then I saw no harm, and then I heard
Each syllable that breath made up between them.

OTHELLO   What, did they never whisper?

EMILIA   Never, my lord.

OTHELLO   Nor send you out o' the way?

EMILIA   Never.

OTHELLO   To fetch her fan, her gloves, her mask, nor nothing?

EMILIA   Never, my lord.

OTHELLO   That's strange.

EMILIA   I durst, my lord, to wager she is honest,
Lay down my soul at stake. If you think other,
Remove your thought; it doth abuse your bosom.
If any wretch have put this in your head,
Let heaven requite it with the serpent's curse!
For if she be not honest, chaste, and true,
There's no man happy; the purest of their wives
Is foul as slander.

OTHELLO   Bid her come hither; go.   [*Exit Emilia*]
She says enough; yet she's a simple bawd
That cannot say as much. This is a subtle whore,
A closet lock and key of villainous secrets.
And yet she'll kneel and pray; I have seen her do't.

Enter Desdemona and Emilia

DESDEMONA   My lord, what is your will?

OTHELLO   Pray you, chuck, come hither.

DESDEMONA   What is your pleasure?

OTHELLO   Let me see your eyes;
Look in my face.

DESDEMONA   What horrible fancy's this?

OTHELLO   [*to Emilia*] Some of your function, mistress,
Leave procreants alone and shut the door;
Cough, or cry "hem," if anybody come.
Your mystery, your mystery; nay, dispatch.

                                        Exit Emilia

DESDEMONA   Upon my knees, what doth your speech import?
    I understand a fury in your words,
    But not the words.
OTHELLO   Why, what art thou?
DESDEMONA   Your wife, my lord, your true
    And loyal wife.
OTHELLO   Come, swear it, damn thyself;
    Lest, being like one of heaven, the devils themselves
    Should fear to seize thee. Therefore be double-damn'd;
    Swear thou art honest.
DESDEMONA   Heaven doth truly know it.
OTHELLO   Heaven truly knows that thou art false as hell.
DESDEMONA   To whom, my lord? with whom? how am I false?
OTHELLO   O Desdemona! Away! away! away!
DESDEMONA   Alas the heavy day! Why do you weep?
    Am I the motive of these tears, my lord?
    If haply you my father do suspect
    An instrument of this your calling back,
    Lay not your blame on me. If you have lost him,
    Why, I have lost him too.
OTHELLO   Had it pleased heaven
    To try me with affliction, had they rain'd
    All kinds of sores and shames on my bare head,
    Steep'd me in poverty to the very lips,
    Given to captivity me and my utmost hopes,
    I should have found in some place of my soul
    A drop of patience; but, alas, to make me
    A fixed figure for the time of scorn
    To point his slow unmoving finger at!
    Yet could I bear that too, well, very well;
    But there, where I have garner'd up my heart,
    Where either I must live or bear no life;
    The fountain from the which my current runs,
    Or else dries up; to be discarded thence!
    Or keep it as a cistern for foul toads
    To knot and gender in! Turn thy complexion there,
    Patience, thou young and rose-lipp'd cherubin,
    Ay, there, look grim as hell!
DESDEMONA   I hope my noble lord esteems me honest.

OTHELLO   O, ay, as summer flies are in the shambles,
    That quicken even with blowing. O thou weed,
    Who art so lovely fair and smell'st so sweet
    That the sense aches at thee, would thou hadst ne'er been born!
DESDEMONA   Alas, what ignorant sin have I committed?
OTHELLO   Was this fair paper, this most goodly book,
    Made to write "whore" upon? What committed?
    Committed? O thou public commoner!
    I should make very forges of my cheeks,
    That would to cinders burn up modesty,
    Did I but speak thy deeds. What committed!
    Heaven stops the nose at it, and the moon winks;
    The bawdy wind, that kisses all it meets,
    Is hush'd within the hollow mine of earth,
    And will not hear it. What committed?
    Impudent strumpet!
DESDEMONA   By heaven, you do me wrong.
OTHELLO   Are not you a strumpet?
DESDEMONA   No, as I am a Christian.
    If to preserve this vessel for my lord
    From any other foul unlawful touch
    Be not to be a strumpet, I am none.
OTHELLO   What, not a whore?
DESDEMONA   No, as I shall be saved.
OTHELLO   Is't possible?
DESDEMONA   O, heaven forgive us!
OTHELLO   I cry you mercy then;
    I took you for that cunning whore of Venice
    That married with Othello. [*Raises his voice*] You, mistress,
    That have the office opposite to Saint Peter,
    And keep the gate of hell!
                    Enter Emilia
                You, you, ay, you!
    We have done our course; there's money for your pains.
                    He gives money
    I pray you, turn the key, and keep our counsel.
                                    Exit Othello
EMILIA   Alas, what does this gentleman conceive?
    How do you, madam? How do you, my good lady?
DESDEMONA   Faith, half asleep.

EMILIA   Good madam, what's the matter with my lord?
DESDEMONA   With who?
EMILIA   Why, with my lord, madam.
DESDEMONA   Who is thy lord?
EMILIA   He that is yours, sweet lady.
DESDEMONA   I have none. Do not talk to me, Emilia;
    I cannot weep, nor answer have I none
    But what should go by water. Prithee, tonight
    Lay on my bed my wedding sheets. Remember,
    And call thy husband hither.
EMILIA   Here's a change indeed!

Exit Emilia

DESDEMONA   'Tis meet I should be used so, very meet.
    How have I been behaved, that he might stick
    The small'st opinion on my least misuse?

Enter Emilia and Iago

IAGO   What is your pleasure, madam? How is't with you?
DESDEMONA   I cannot tell. Those that do teach young babes
    Do it with gentle means and easy tasks.
    He might have chid me so, for in good faith,
    I am a child to chiding.
IAGO   What's the matter, lady?
EMILIA   Alas, Iago, my lord hath so bewhored her,
    Thrown such despite and heavy terms upon her,
    As true hearts cannot bear.
DESDEMONA   Am I that name, Iago?
IAGO   What name, fair lady?
DESDEMONA   Such as she says my lord did say I was.
EMILIA   He call'd her whore; a beggar in his drink
    Could not have laid such terms upon his callet.
IAGO   Why did he so?
DESDEMONA   [*weeping*] I do not know; I am sure I am none such.
IAGO   Do not weep, do not weep. Alas the day!
EMILIA   Hath she forsook so many noble matches,
    Her father and her country and her friends,
    To be call'd whore? Would it not make one weep?
DESDEMONA   It is my wretched fortune.
IAGO   Beshrew him for't!
    How comes this trick upon him?
DESDEMONA   Nay, heaven doth know.

EMILIA   I will be hang'd, if some eternal villain,
    Some busy and insinuating rogue,
    Some cogging, cozening slave, to get some office,
    Have not devised this slander; I'll be hang'd else.
IAGO   Fie, there is no such man; it is impossible.
DESDEMONA   If any such there be, heaven pardon him!
EMILIA   A halter pardon him! And hell gnaw his bones!
    Why should he call her whore? Who keeps her company?
    What place? What time? What form? What likelihood?
    The Moor's abused by some most villainous knave,
    Some base notorious knave, some scurvy fellow.
    O heaven, that such companions thou'ldst unfold,
    And put in every honest hand a whip
    To lash the rascals naked through the world
    Even from the east to the west!
IAGO   Speak within door.
EMILIA   O, fie upon them! Some such squire he was
    That turn'd your wit the seamy side without,
    And made you to suspect me with the Moor.
IAGO   You are a fool; go to.
DESDEMONA   Alas Iago,
    What shall I do to win my lord again?
    Good friend, go to him, for by this light of heaven,
    I know not how I lost him. Here I kneel:
    If e'er my will did trespass 'gainst his love
    Either in discourse of thought or actual deed,
    Or that mine eyes, mine ears, or any sense,
    Delighted them in any other form,
    Or that I do not yet, and ever did,
    And ever will, though he do shake me off
    To beggarly divorcement, love him dearly,
    Comfort forswear me! Unkindness may do much,
    And his unkindness may defeat my life,
    But never taint my love. I cannot say "whore."
    It doth abhor me now I speak the word;
    To do the act that might the addition earn
    Not the world's mass of vanity could make me.]*She rises*]
IAGO   I pray you, be content; 'tis but his humor:
    The business of the state does him offense,
    And he does chide with you.

DESDEMONA   If 'twere no other—

IAGO   'Tis but so, I warrant. Trumpets within.
    Hark, how these instruments summon to supper!
    The messengers of Venice stay the meat.
    Go in, and weep not; all things shall be well.

Exit Desdemona and Emilia

Enter Roderigo

    How now, Roderigo!

RODERIGO   I do not find that thou dealest justly with me.

IAGO   What in the contrary?

RODERIGO   Every day thou daffest me with some device, Iago; and rather, as it seems to me now, keepest from me all conveniency than suppliest me with the least advantage of hope. I will indeed no longer endure it; nor am I yet persuaded to put up in peace what already I have foolishly suffered.

IAGO   Will you hear me, Roderigo?

RODERIGO   Faith, I have heard too much, for your words and performances are no kin together.

IAGO   You charge me most unjustly.

RODERIGO   With nought but truth. I have wasted myself out of my means. The jewels you have had from me to deliver to Desdemona would half have corrupted a votarist. You have told me she hath received them and returned me expectations and comforts of sudden respect and acquaintance; but I find none.

IAGO   Well, go to, very well.

RODERIGO   "Very well!" "go to!" I cannot go to, man; nor 'tis not very well. By this hand, I say 'tis very scurvy, and begin to find myself fopped in it.

IAGO   Very well.

RODERIGO   I tell you 'tis not very well. I will make myself known to Desdemona. If she will return me my jewels, I will give over my suit and repent my unlawful solicitation; if not, assure yourself I will seek satisfaction of you.

IAGO   You have said now.

RODERIGO   Ay, and said nothing but what I protest intendment of doing.

IAGO   Why, now I see there's mettle in thee; and even from this instant do build on thee a better opinion than ever before. Give me thy hand, Roderigo. Thou hast taken against me a most just exception; but yet, I protest, have dealt most directly in thy affair.

RODERIGO   It hath not appeared.

IAGO   I grant indeed it hath not appeared, and your suspicion is not without wit and judgement. But, Roderigo, if thou hast that in thee indeed, which I have greater reason to believe now than ever, I mean purpose, courage, and valor, this night show it; if thou the next night following enjoy not Desdemona, take me from this world with treachery and devise engines for my life.

RODERIGO   Well, what is it? Is it within reason and compass?

IAGO   Sir, there is especial commission come from Venice to depute Cassio in Othello's place.

RODERIGO   Is that true? Why then Othello and Desdemona return again to Venice.

IAGO   O, no; he goes into Mauritania, and takes away with him the fair Desdemona, unless his abode be lingered here by some accident; wherein none can be so determinate as the removing of Cassio.

RODERIGO   How do you mean, removing of him?

IAGO   Why, by making him uncapable of Othello's place; knocking out his brains.

RODERIGO   And that you would have me to do?

IAGO   Ay, if you dare do yourself a profit and a right. He sups tonight with a harlotry, and thither will I go to him. He knows not yet of his honorable fortune. If you will watch his going thence, which his will fashion to fall out between twelve and one, you may take him at your pleasure; I will be near to second your attempt, and he shall fall between us. Come, stand not amazed at it, but go along with me; I will show you such a necessity in his death that you shall think yourself bound to put it on him. It is now high supper-time, and the night grows to waste. About it.

RODERIGO   I will hear further reason for this.

IAGO   And you shall be satisfied.

Exeunt

SCENE III—Another room in the castle.

Enter Othello, Lodovico, Desdemona, Emilia, and Attendants

LODOVICO   I do beseech you, Sir, trouble yourself no further.

OTHELLO   O, pardon me; 'twill do me good to walk.

LODOVICO   Madam, good night; I humbly thank your ladyship.

DESDEMONA   Your honor is most welcome.

OTHELLO   Will you walk, Sir?
   O, Desdemona—
DESDEMONA   My lord?
OTHELLO   Get you to bed on the instant; I will be returned forth-
   with. Dismiss your attendant there; look it be done.
DESDEMONA   I will, my lord.
                Exit Othello, Lodovico, and Attendants
EMILIA   How goes it now? He looks gentler than he did.
DESDEMONA   He says he will return incontinent.
   He hath commanded me to go to bed,
   And bade me to dismiss you.
EMILIA   Dismiss me?
DESDEMONA   It was his bidding; therefore, good Emilia,
   Give me my nightly wearing, and adieu.
   We must not now displease him.
EMILIA   I would you had never seen him!
DESDEMONA   So would not I. My love doth so approve him,
   That even his stubbornness, his checks, his frowns—
   Prithee, unpin me—have grace and favor in them.
            Emilia prepares Desdemona for bed
EMILIA   I have laid those sheets you bade me on the bed.
DESDEMONA   All's one. Good faith, how foolish are our minds!
   If I do die before thee, prithee shroud me
   In one of those same sheets.
EMILIA   Come, come, you talk.
DESDEMONA   My mother had a maid call'd Barbary;
   She was in love, and he she loved proved mad
   And did forsake her. She had a song of "willow";
   An old thing 'twas, but it express'd her fortune,
   And she died singing it. That song tonight
   Will not go from my mind; I have much to do
   But to go hang my head all at one side
   And sing it like poor Barbary. Prithee, dispatch.
EMILIA   Shall I go fetch your nightgown?
DESDEMONA   No, unpin me here.
   This Lodovico is a proper man.
EMILIA   A very handsome man.
DESDEMONA   He speaks well.
EMILIA   I know a lady in Venice would have walked barefoot to Pales-
   tine for a touch of his nether lip.

DESDEMONA [*Sings*]

> The poor soul sat sighing by a sycamore tree,
>   Sing all a green willow;
> Her hand on her bosom, her head on her knee,
>   Sing willow, willow, willow.
> The fresh streams ran by her, and murmur'd her moans,
>   Sing willow, willow, willow;
> Her salt tears fell from her, and soften'd the stones—

Lay by these—

> Sing willow, willow, willow—

Prithee, hie thee; he'll come anon—

> Sing all a green willow must be my garland.
> Let nobody blame him; his scorn I approve—

Nay, that's not next. Hark, who is't that knocks?
EMILIA It's the wind.
DESDEMONA [*Sings*]

> I call'd my love false love; but what said he then?
>   Sing willow, willow, willow.
> If I court more women, you'll couch with more men—

So get thee gone; good night. Mine eyes do itch;
Doth that bode weeping?
EMILIA   'Tis neither here nor there.
DESDEMONA I have heard it said so. O, these men, these men!
Dost thou in conscience think—tell me, Emilia—
That there be women do abuse their husbands
In such gross kind?
EMILIA   There be some such, no question.
DESDEMONA Wouldst thou do such a deed for all the world?
EMILIA Why, would not you?
DESDEMONA   No, by this heavenly light!
EMILIA Nor I neither by this heavenly light! I might do't as well i' the
    dark.
DESDEMONA Wouldst thou do such a deed for all the world?
EMILIA The world's a huge thing; it is a great price for a small vice.
DESDEMONA In troth, I think thou wouldst not.
EMILIA In troth, I think I should, and undo't when I had done. Marry,
    I would not do such a thing for a joint-ring, nor for measures of

lawn, nor for gowns, petticoats, nor caps, nor any petty exhibition; but, for the whole world—why, who would not make her husband a cuckold to make him a monarch? I should venture purgatory for't.

DESDEMONA   Beshrew me, if I would do such a wrong
For the whole world.

EMILIA   Why, the wrong is but a wrong i' the world; and having the world for your labor, 'tis a wrong in your own world, and you might quickly make it right.

DESDEMONA   I do not think there is any such woman.

EMILIA   Yes, a dozen, and as many
To the vantage as would store the world they played for.
But I do think it is their husbands' faults
If wives do fall; say that they slack their duties,
And pour our treasures into foreign laps,
Or else break out in peevish jealousies,
Throwing restraint upon us, or say they strike us,
Or scant our former having in despite,
Why, we have galls, and though we have some grace,
Yet have we some revenge. Let husbands know
Their wives have sense like them; they see and smell
And have their palates both for sweet and sour,
As husbands have. What is it that they do
When they change us for others? Is it sport?
I think it is. And doth affection breed it?
I think it doth. Is't frailty that thus errs?
It is so too. And have not we affections,
Desires for sport, and frailty, as men have?
Then let them use us well; else let them know,
The ills we do, their ills instruct us so.

DESDEMONA   Good night, good night. Heaven me such uses send,
Not to pick bad from bad, but by bad mend!

Exeunt

ACT V

SCENE I—Cyprus. A street.

Enter Iago and Roderigo

IAGO   Here, stand behind this bulk; straight will he come.
Wear thy good rapier bare, and put it home.
Quick, quick; fear nothing; I'll be at thy elbow.
It makes us, or it mars us; think on that,
And fix most firm thy resolution.

RODERIGO   Be near at hand; I may miscarry in't.

IAGO   Here, at thy hand, be bold, and take thy stand.

Iago stands aside. Roderigo conceals himself

RODERIGO   I have no great devotion to the deed;
And yet he hath given me satisfying reasons.
'Tis but a man gone. Forth, my sword; he dies.

IAGO   I have rubb'd this young quat almost to the sense,
And he grows angry. Now, whether he kill Cassio,
Or Cassio him, or each do kill the other,
Every way makes my gain. Live Roderigo,
He calls me to a restitution large
Of gold and jewels that I bobb'd from him,
As gifts to Desdemona;
It must not be. If Cassio do remain,
He hath a daily beauty in his life
That makes me ugly; and besides, the Moor
May unfold me to him; there stand I in much peril.
No, he must die. Be't so. I hear him coming.

Enter Cassio

RODERIGO   [*coming forth*] I know his gait; 'tis he. Villain, thou diest!

Attacks Cassio.

CASSIO   That thrust had been mine enemy indeed,
But that my coat is better than thou know'st;
I will make proof of thine.

Cassio draws, and wounds Roderigo

RODERIGO   O, I am slain! [*He falls*]

Iago from behind wounds Cassio in the leg, then exits

CASSIO   I am maim'd forever. Help, ho! Murder! Murder! [*He falls*]

Enter Othello

OTHELLO   The voice of Cassio; Iago keeps his word.

RODERIGO   O, villain that I am!

OTHELLO   It is even so.

CASSIO   O, help, ho! Light! A surgeon!

OTHELLO   'Tis he. O brave Iago, honest and just,
    That hast such noble sense of thy friend's wrong!
    Thou teachest me. Minion, your dear lies dead,
    And your unblest fate hies. Strumpet, I come!
    Forth of my heart those charms, thine eyes, are blotted;
    Thy bed lust-stain'd shall with lust's blood be spotted.

Exit Othello

Enter Lodovico and Gratiano

CASSIO   What, ho! No watch? No passage? Murder! Murder!

GRATIANO   'Tis some mischance; the cry is very direful.

CASSIO   O, help!

LODOVICO   Hark!

RODERIGO   O wretched villain!

LODOVICO   Two or three groan; it is a heavy night.
    These may be counterfeits; let's think't unsafe
    To come in to the cry without more help.

They remain near the entrance

RODERIGO   Nobody come? Then shall I bleed to death.

Enter Iago, with a light

LODOVICO   Hark!

GRATIANO   Here's one comes in his shirt, with light and weapons.

IAGO   Who's there? Whose noise is this that cries on murder?

LODOVICO   We do not know.

IAGO   Did not you hear a cry?

CASSIO   Here, here! for heaven's sake, help me!

IAGO   What's the matter?

He moves toward Cassio

GRATIANO   [*to Lodovico*] This is Othello's ancient, as I take it.

LODOVICO   [*to Gratiano*] The same indeed; a very valiant fellow.

IAGO   [*to Cassio*] What are you here that cry so grievously?

CASSIO   Iago? O, I am spoil'd, undone by villains!

Give me some help.

IAGO   O me, Lieutenant! What villains have done this?

CASSIO   I think that one of them is hereabout,
And cannot make away.

IAGO   O treacherous villains!
[to Lodovico and Gratiano] What are you there? Come in and give
come help. [They advance]

RODERIGO   O, help me here!

CASSIO   That's one of them.

IAGO   O murderous slave! O villain!

Iago stabs Roderigo

RODERIGO   O damn'd Iago! O inhuman dog!

IAGO   Kill men i' the dark! Where be these bloody thieves?
How silent is this town! Ho! Murder! Murder!
[to Lodovico and Gratiano] What may you be? Are you of good or evil?

LODOVICO   As you shall prove us, praise us.

IAGO   Signior Lodovico?

LODOVICO   He, Sir.

IAGO   I cry you mercy. Here's Cassio hurt by villains.

GRATIANO   Cassio?

IAGO   How is't, brother?

CASSIO   My leg is cut in two.

IAGO   Marry, heaven forbid!
Light, gentlemen; I'll bind it with my shirt.
He hands them the light, and tends to Cassio's wound
Enter Bianca

BIANCA   What is the matter, ho? Who is't that cried?

IAGO   Who is't that cried?

BIANCA   O my dear Cassio,
My sweet Cassio! O Cassio, Cassio, Cassio!

IAGO   O notable strumpet! Cassio, may you suspect
Who they should be that have thus mangled you?

CASSIO   No.

GRATIANO   I am sorry to find you thus; I have been to seek you.

IAGO   Lend me a garter. [He applies a tourniquet] So. O, for a chair,
To bear him easily hence!

BIANCA   Alas, he faints! O Cassio, Cassio, Cassio!

IAGO   Gentlemen all, I do suspect this trash
To be a party in this injury.
Patience awhile, good Cassio. Come, come;

Lend me a light. Know we this face or no?
Alas, my friend and my dear countryman
Roderigo? No—yes, sure. O heaven! Roderigo.

GRATIANO   What, of Venice?

IAGO   Even he, Sir. Did you know him?

GRATIANO   Know him! ay.

IAGO   Signior Gratiano? I cry you gentle pardon;
These bloody accidents must excuse my manners,
That so neglected you.

GRATIANO   I am glad to see you.

IAGO   How do you, Cassio? O, a chair, a chair!

GRATIANO   Roderigo!

IAGO   He, he, 'tis he. [*A chair is brought in*] O, that's well said; the chair.
Some good man bear him carefully from hence;
I'll fetch the General's surgeon. [*to Bianca*] For you, mistress,
Save you your labor. He that lies slain here, Cassio,
Was my dear friend; what malice was between you?

CASSIO   None in the world; nor do I know the man.

IAGO   [*to Bianca*] What, look you pale? O, bear him out o' the air.

                  Cassio and Roderigo are borne off
Stay you, good gentlemen. Look you pale, mistress?
Do you perceive the gastness of her eye?
Nay, if you stare, we shall hear more anon.
Behold her well; I pray you, look upon her.
Do you see, gentlemen? Nay, guiltiness will speak,
Though tongues were out of use.

                  Enter Emilia

EMILIA   Alas, what's the matter? What's the matter, husband?

IAGO   Cassio hath here been set on in the dark
By Roderigo, and fellows that are scaped;
He's almost slain, and Roderigo dead.

EMILIA   Alas, good gentleman! alas, good Cassio!

IAGO   This is the fruit of whoring. Prithee, Emilia,
Go know of Cassio where he supp'd tonight.
[*To Bianca*] What, do you shake at that?

BIANCA   He supp'd at my house; but I therefore shake not.

IAGO   O, did he so? I charge you, go with me.

EMILIA   Fie, fie upon thee, strumpet!

BIANCA   I am no strumpet, but of life as honest

As you that thus abuse me.

EMILIA   As I! Foh! Fie upon thee!

IAGO   Kind gentlemen, let's go see poor Cassio dress'd.
Come, mistress, you must tell's another tale.
Emilia, run you to the citadel,
And tell my lord and lady what hath happ'd!
Will you go on? [aside] This is the night
That either makes me or fordoes me quite.

Exeunt

SCENE II—A bedchamber in the castle.
Enter Othello with a light. Desdemona in bed asleep

OTHELLO   It is the cause, it is the cause, my soul.
Let me not name it to you, you chaste stars!
It is the cause. Yet I'll not shed her blood,
Nor scar that whiter skin of hers than snow
And smooth as monumental alabaster.
Yet she must die, else she'll betray more men.
Put out the light, and then put out the light.
If I quench thee, thou flaming minister,
I can again thy former light restore,
Should I repent me; but once put out thy light,
Thou cunning'st pattern of excelling nature,
I know not where is that Promethean heat
That can thy light relume. When I have pluck'd the rose,
I cannot give it vital growth again,
It must needs wither; I'll smell it on the tree. [*He kisses her*]
O, balmy breath, that dost almost persuade
Justice to break her sword! One more, one more;
Be thus when thou art dead, and I will kill thee,
And love thee after. One more, and this the last;
So sweet was ne'er so fatal. I must weep,
But they are cruel tears; this sorrow's heavenly,
It strikes where it doth love. She wakes.

DESDEMONA   Who's there? Othello?

OTHELLO   Ay, Desdemona.

DESDEMONA   Will you come to bed, my lord?

OTHELLO   Have you pray'd tonight, Desdemona?

DESDEMONA   Ay, my lord.

OTHELLO   If you bethink yourself of any crime

Unreconciled as yet to heaven and grace,
Solicit for it straight.

DESDEMONA   Alas, my lord, what may you mean by that?

OTHELLO   Well, do it, and be brief; I will walk by.
I would not kill thy unprepared spirit.
No, heaven forfend! I would not kill thy soul.

DESDEMONA   Talk you of killing?

OTHELLO   Ay, I do.

DESDEMONA   Then heaven
Have mercy on me!

OTHELLO   Amen, with all my heart!

DESDEMONA   If you say so, I hope you will not kill me.

OTHELLO   Hum!

DESDEMONA   And yet I fear you, for you are fatal then
When your eyes roll so. Why I should fear I know not,
Since guiltiness I know not; but yet I feel I fear.

OTHELLO   Think on thy sins.

DESDEMONA   They are loves I bear to you.

OTHELLO   Ay, and for that thou diest.

DESDEMONA   That death's unnatural that kills for loving.
Alas, why gnaw you so your nether lip?
Some bloody passion shakes your very frame.
These are portents; but yet I hope, I hope,
They do not point on me.

OTHELLO   Peace, and be still!

DESDEMONA   I will so. What's the matter?

OTHELLO   That handkerchief which I so loved and gave thee
Thou gavest to Cassio.

DESDEMONA   No, by my life and soul!
Send for the man, and ask him.

OTHELLO   Sweet soul, take heed, take heed of perjury;
Thou are on thy deathbed.

DESDEMONA   Ay, but not yet to die.

OTHELLO   Yes, presently:
Therefore confess thee freely of thy sin,
For to deny each article with oath
Cannot remove nor choke the strong conception
That I do groan withal. Thou art to die.

DESDEMONA   Then Lord have mercy on me!

OTHELLO   I say, amen.

DESDEMONA   And have you mercy too! I never did
   Offend you in my life; never loved Cassio
   But with such General warranty of heaven
   As I might love. I never gave him token.
OTHELLO   By heaven, I saw my handkerchief in 's hand.
   O perjured woman! Thou dost stone my heart,
   And makest me call what I intend to do
   A murder, which I thought a sacrifice.
   I saw the handkerchief.
DESDEMONA   He found it then
   I never gave it him. Send for him hither;
   Let him confess a truth.
OTHELLO   He hath confess'd.
DESDEMONA   What, my lord?
OTHELLO   That he hath used thee.
DESDEMONA   How? Unlawfully?
OTHELLO   Ay.
DESDEMONA   He will not say so.
OTHELLO   No, his mouth is stopp'd;
   Honest Iago hath ta'en order for't.
DESDEMONA   O, my fear interprets! What, is he dead?
OTHELLO   Had all his hairs been lives, my great revenge
   Had stomach for them all.
DESDEMONA   Alas, he is betray'd, and I undone! [*She weeps*]
OTHELLO   Out, strumpet! Weep'st thou for him to my face?
DESDEMONA   O, banish me, my lord, but kill me not!
OTHELLO   [*attacking her*] Down, strumpet!
DESDEMONA   Kill me tomorrow; let me live tonight!
OTHELLO   Nay, if you strive—
DESDEMONA   But half an hour!
OTHELLO   Being done, there is no pause.
DESDEMONA   But while I say one prayer!
OTHELLO   It is too late. [*He smothers her*]
EMILIA   [*within*] My lord, my lord! What, ho! My lord, my lord!
OTHELLO   What noise is this? Not dead? not yet quite dead?
   I that am cruel am yet merciful;
   I would not have thee linger in thy pain.
   So, so.
EMILIA   [*within*] What, ho! My lord, my lord!
OTHELLO   Who's there?

EMILIA   [*within*] O, good my lord, I would speak a word with you!
OTHELLO   Yes, 'tis Emilia. By and by. She's dead.
   'Tis like she comes to speak of Cassio's death.
   The noise was here. Ha! no more moving?
   Still as the grave. Shall she come in? were't good?
   I think she stirs again. No. What's best to do?
   If she come in, she'll sure speak to my wife.
   My wife! My wife! What wife? I have no wife.
   O, insupportable! O heavy hour!
   Methinks it should be now a huge eclipse
   Of sun and moon, and that the affrighted globe
   Should yawn at alteration.
EMILIA   [*within*]   I do beseech you
   That I may speak with you, O, good my lord!
OTHELLO   I had forgot thee. O, come in, Emilia.
   Soft, by and by. Let me the curtains draw.
         He closes the bed-curtains and opens the door
   Where art thou? [*Enter Emilia*]
                     What's the matter with thee now?
EMILIA   O, my good lord, yonder's foul murders done!
OTHELLO   What, now?
EMILIA   But now, my lord.
OTHELLO   It is the very error of the moon;
   She comes more nearer earth than she was wont
   And makes men mad.
EMILIA   Cassio, my lord, hath kill'd a young Venetian
   Call'd Roderigo.
OTHELLO   Roderigo kill'd?
   And Cassio kill'd?
EMILIA   No, Cassio is not kill'd.
OTHELLO   Not Cassio kill'd! Then murder's out of tune,
   And sweet revenge grows harsh.
DESDEMONA   O, falsely, falsely murder'd!
EMILIA   Alas, what cry is that?
OTHELLO   That? What?
EMILIA   Out, and alas! That was my lady's voice.
               She opens the bed-curtains
   Help! help, ho! help! O lady, speak again!
   Sweet Desdemona! O sweet mistress, speak!
DESDEMONA   A guiltless death I die.

EMILIA   O, who hath done this deed?
DESDEMONA   Nobody; I myself. Farewell.
   Commend me to my kind lord. O, farewell! [*She dies*]
OTHELLO   Why, how should she be murder'd?
EMILIA   Alas, who knows?
OTHELLO   You heard her say herself, it was not I.
EMILIA   She said so; I must needs report the truth.
OTHELLO   She's like a liar gone to burning hell;
   'Twas I that kill'd her.
EMILIA   O, the more angel she,
   And you the blacker devil!
OTHELLO   She turn'd to folly, and she was a whore.
EMILIA   Thou dost belie her, and thou art a devil.
OTHELLO   She was false as water.
EMILIA   Thou art rash as fire, to say
   That she was false. O, she was heavenly true!
OTHELLO   Cassio did top her; ask thy husband else.
   O, I were damn'd beneath all depth in hell,
   But that I did proceed upon just grounds
   To this extremity. Thy husband knew it all.
EMILIA   My husband?
OTHELLO   Thy husband.
EMILIA   That she was false to wedlock?
OTHELLO   Ay, with Cassio. Nay, had she been true,
   If heaven would make me such another world
   Of one entire and perfect chrysolite,
   I'd not have sold her for it.
EMILIA   My husband?
OTHELLO   Ay, 'twas he that told me first.
   An honest man he is, and hates the slime
   That sticks on filthy deeds.
EMILIA   My husband?
OTHELLO   What needs this iteration, woman? I say thy husband.
EMILIA   O mistress, villainy hath made mocks with love!
   My husband say that she was false!
OTHELLO   He, woman;
   I say thy husband. Dost understand the word?
   My friend, thy husband, honest, honest Iago.
EMILIA   If he say so, may his pernicious soul
   Rot half a grain a day! He lies to the heart.

She was too fond of her most filthy bargain.
OTHELLO   Ha! [*He draws*]
EMILIA   Do thy worst;
    This deed of thine is no more worthy heaven
    Than thou wast worthy her.
OTHELLO   Peace, you were best.
EMILIA   Thou hast not half that power to do me harm
    As I have to be hurt. O gull! O dolt!
    As ignorant as dirt! Thou hast done a deed—
    I care not for thy sword; I'll make thee known,
    Though I lost twenty lives. Help! help, ho! help!
    The Moor hath kill'd my mistress! Murder, murder!
        Enter Montano, Gratiano, Iago, and others
MONTANO   What is the matter? How now, General?
EMILIA   O, are you come, Iago? You have done well,
    That men must lay their murders on your neck.
GRATIANO   What is the matter?
EMILIA   [*to Iago*] Disprove this villain, if thou be'st a man.
    He says thou told'st him that his wife was false;
    I know thou didst not, thou'rt not such a villain.
    Speak, for my heart is full.
IAGO   I told him what I thought, and told no more
    Than what he found himself was apt and true.
EMILIA   But did you ever tell him she was false?
IAGO   I did.
EMILIA   You told a lie, an odious, damned lie;
    Upon my soul, a lie, a wicked lie!
    She false with Cassio? Did you say with Cassio?
IAGO   With Cassio, mistress. Go to, charm your tongue.
EMILIA   I will not charm my tongue; I am bound to speak.
    My mistress here lies murder'd in her bed—
ALL   O heavens forfend!
EMILIA   And your reports have set the murder on.
OTHELLO   Nay, stare not, masters; it is true indeed.
GRATIANO   'Tis a strange truth.
MONTANO   O monstrous act!
EMILIIA   Villainy, villainy, villainy!
    I think upon't, I think, I smell't, O villainy!
    I thought so then. I'll kill myself for grief.
    O villainy, villainy!

IAGO   What, are you mad? I charge you, get you home.

EMILIA   Good gentlemen, let me have leave to speak;
　　　'Tis proper I obey him, but not now.
　　　Perchance, Iago, I will ne'er go home.

OTHELLO   O! O! O! [*He falls on the bed*]

EMILIA　　　　　　　Nay, lay thee down and roar;
　　　For thou hast kill'd the sweetest innocent
　　　That e'er did lift up eye.

OTHELLO   [*Rising*]　　　O, she was foul! [*To Gratiano*]
　　　I scarce did know you, uncle; there lies your niece,
　　　Whose breath indeed these hands have newly stopp'd.
　　　I know this act shows horrible and grim.

GRATIANO   Poor Desdemon! I am glad thy father's dead.
　　　Thy match was mortal to him, and pure grief
　　　Shore his old thread in twain; did he live now,
　　　This sight would make him do a desperate turn,
　　　Yea, curse his better angel from his side,
　　　And fall to reprobation.

OTHELLO   'Tis pitiful, but yet Iago knows
　　　That she with Cassio hath the act of shame
　　　A thousand times committed. Cassio confess'd it,
　　　And she did gratify his amorous works
　　　With that recognizance and pledge of love
　　　Which I first gave her. I saw it in his hand,
　　　It was a handkerchief, an antique token
　　　My father gave my mother.

EMILIA　　　　　　　O heaven! O heavenly powers!

IAGO   'Zounds! Hold your peace.

EMILIA　　　　　　　'Twill out, 'twill. I peace?
　　　No, I will speak as liberal as the north;
　　　Let heaven and men and devils, let them all,
　　　All, all, cry shame against me, yet I'll speak.

IAGO   Be wise, and get you home.

EMILIA　　　　　　　I will not. [*Iago tries to stab Emilia*]

GRATIANO　　　　　　　Fie!
　　　Your sword upon a woman?

EMILIA   O thou dull Moor! That handkerchief thou speak'st of
　　　I found by fortune and did give my husband,
　　　For often with a solemn earnestness,
　　　More than indeed belong'd to such a trifle,

He begg'd of me to steal it.
IAGO   Villainous whore!
EMILIA   She give it Cassio? No, alas, I found it,
    And I did give't my husband.
IAGO   Filth, thou liest!
EMILIA   By heaven, I do not, I do not, gentlemen.
    O murderous coxcomb! What should such a fool
    Do with so good a wife?
OTHELLO   Are there not stones in heaven
    But what serve for thunder? Precious villain!
    He runs at Iago, but Montano disarms him. Iago stabs Emilia
GRATIANO   The woman falls; sure, he hath kill'd his wife.
EMILIA   Ay, ay! O, lay me by my mistress' side.
                           Exit Iago

GRATIANO   He's gone, but his wife's kill'd.
MONTANO   'Tis a notorious villain. Take you this weapon,
    Which I have here recover'd from the Moor.
    Come, guard the door without; let him not pass,
    But kill him rather. I'll after that same villain,
    For 'tis a damned slave.
            Exit all but Othello and Emilia
        Emilia has been laid by Desdemona's side
OTHELLO   I am not valiant neither,
    But every puny whipster gets my sword.
    But why should honor outlive honesty?
    Let it go all.
EMILIA   What did thy song bode, lady?
    Hark, canst thou hear me? I will play the swan,
    And die in music. [*Sings*] "Willow, willow, willow."
    Moor, she was chaste; she loved thee, cruel Moor;
    So come my soul to bliss, as I speak true;
    So speaking as I think, I die, I die. [*She dies*]
OTHELLO   I have another weapon in this chamber;
    It is a sword of Spain, the ice-brook's temper—
    O, here it is. Uncle, I must come forth.
GRATIANO   [*within*] If thou attempt it, it will cost thee dear.
    Thou hast no weapon, and perforce must suffer.
OTHELLO   Look in upon me then, and speak with me,
    Or, naked as I am, I will assault thee.
                 Enter Gratiano

GRATIANO   What is the matter?
OTHELLO   Behold, I have a weapon;
A better never did itself sustain
Upon a soldier's thigh. I have seen the day
That with this little arm and this good sword
I have made my way through more impediments
Than twenty times your stop. But, O vain boast!
Who can control his fate? 'Tis not so now.
Be not afraid, though you do see me weapon'd;
Here is my journey's end, here is my butt
And very sea-mark of my utmost sail. [*Gratiano steps back*]
Do you go back dismay'd? 'Tis a lost fear.
Man but a rush against Othello's breast,
And he retires. Where should Othello go? [*He turns to Desdemona*]
Now, how dost thou look now? O ill-starr'd wench!
Pale as thy smock! When we shall meet at compt,
This look of thine will hurl my soul from heaven,
And fiends will snatch at it. Cold, cold, my girl?
Even like thy chastity. O cursed, cursed slave!
Whip me, ye devils,
From the possession of this heavenly sight!
Blow me about in winds! Roast me in sulphur!
Wash me in steep-down gulfs of liquid fire!
O Desdemon! dead, Desdemon! dead!
O! O! O!
>   *Enter Lodovico, Montano, Cassio; carried in a chair,*
>   *and Officers with Iago as prisoner*
LODOVICO   Where is this rash and most unfortunate man?
OTHELLO   That's he that was Othello. Here I am.
LODOVICO   Where is that viper? Bring the villain forth. [*Iago led forward*]
OTHELLO   I look down towards his feet; but that's a fable.
If that thou be'st a devil, I cannot kill thee. [*Wounds Iago*]
LODOVICO   Wrench his sword from him. [*Othello is disarmed*]
IAGO   I bleed, Sir, but not kill'd.
OTHELLO   I am not sorry neither. I'ld have thee live,
For, in my sense, 'tis happiness to die.
LODOVICO   O thou Othello, that wert once so good,
Fall'n in the practice of a damned slave,
What shall be said to thee?
OTHELLO   Why, anything;

An honorable murderer, if you will,
For nought did I in hate, but all in honor.

LODOVICO   This wretch hath part confess'd his villainy.
Did you and he consent in Cassio's death?

OTHELLO   Ay.

CASSIO   Dear General, I never gave you cause.

OTHELLO   I do believe it, and I ask your pardon.
Will you, I pray, demand that demi-devil
Why he hath thus ensnared my soul and body?

IAGO   Demand me nothing; what you know, you know.
From this time forth I never will speak word.

LODOVICO   What, not to pray?

GRATIANO   Torments will ope your lips.

OTHELLO   Well, thou dost best.

LODOVICO   Sir, you shall understand what hath befall'n,
Which, as I think, you know not. Here is a letter
Found in the pocket of the slain Roderigo,
And here another. The one of them imports
The death of Cassio to be undertook
By Roderigo.

OTHELLO   O villain!

CASSIO   Most heathenish and most gross!

LODOVICO   Now here's another discontented paper,
Found in his pocket too; and this, it seems,
Roderigo meant to have sent this damned villain;
But that, belike, Iago in the interim
Came in and satisfied him.

OTHELLO   O the pernicious caitiff!
How came you, Cassio, by that handkerchief
That was my wife's?

CASSIO   I found it in my chamber;
And he himself confess'd but even now
That there he dropp'd it for a special purpose
Which wrought to his desire.

OTHELLO   O fool! fool! fool!

CASSIO   There is besides in Roderigo's letter,
How he upbraids Iago, that he made him
Brave me upon the watch, whereon it came
That I was cast. And even but now he spake

After long seeming dead, Iago hurt him,
Iago set him on.

LODOVICO   [*to Othello*] You must forsake this room, and go with us.
Your power and your command is taken off,
And Cassio rules in Cyprus. For this slave,
If there be any cunning cruelty
That can torment him much and hold him long,
It shall be his. You shall close prisoner rest,
Till that the nature of your fault be known
To the Venetian state. Come, bring away.

OTHELLO   Soft you; a word or two before you go.
I have done the state some service, and they know't.
No more of that. I pray you, in your letters,
When you shall these unlucky deeds relate,
Speak of me as I am; nothing extenuate,
Nor set down aught in malice. Then must you speak
Of one that loved not wisely but too well;
Of one not easily jealous, but, being wrought,
Perplex'd in the extreme; of one whose hand,
Like the base Indian, threw a pearl away
Richer than all his tribe; of one whose subdued eyes,
Albeit unused to the melting mood,
Drop tears as fast as the Arabian trees
Their medicinal gum. Set you down this;
And say besides, that in Aleppo once,
Where a malignant and a turban'd Turk
Beat a Venetian and traduced the state,
I took by the throat the circumcised dog
And smote him, thus. [*He stabs himself*]

LODOVICO   O bloody period!

Gratiano   All that's spoke is marr'd.

OTHELLO   I kiss'd thee ere I kill'd thee. No way but this,
Killing myself, to die upon a kiss. [*He kisses Desdemona and dies*]

CASSIO   This did I fear, but thought he had no weapon;
For he was great of heart.

LODOVICO   [*to Iago*]   O Spartan dog,
More fell than anguish, hunger, or the sea!
Look on the tragic loading of this bed;
This is thy work. The object poisons sight;
Let it be hid. [*Bed-curtains are drawn*] Gratiano, keep the house,

And seize upon the fortunes of the Moor,
For they succeed on you. [*to Cassio*] To you, Lord Governor,
Remains the censure of this hellish villain,
The time, the place, the torture. O, enforce it!
Myself will straight aboard, and to the state
This heavy act with heavy heart relate.

Exeunt omnes

ANTONY AND CLEOPATRA

Dramatis Personae

MARK ANTONY, triumvir
OCTAVIUS CAESAR, triumvir
M. ÆMILIUS LEPIDUS, triumvir
SEXTUS POMPEIUS, triumvir
DOMITIUS ENOBARBUS,
   friend to Antony
VENTIDIUS, friend to Antony
EROS, friend to Antony
SCARUS, friend to Antony
DERCETAS, friend to Antony
DEMETRIUS, friend to Antony
PHILO, friend to Antony
MECÆNAS, friend to Caesar
AGRIPPA, friend to Caesar
DOLABELLA, friend to Caesar
PROCULEIUS, friend to Caesar
THYREUS, friend to Caesar
GALLUS, friend to Caesar
MENAS, friend to Pompey
MENECRATES, friend to Pompey
VARRIUS, friend to Pompey
TAURUS, Lieutenant-General to Caesar
CANIDIUS, Lieutenant-General to Antony
SILIUS, an Officer in Ventidius's army
EUPHRONIUS, an Ambassador from Antony to Caesar

CLEOPATRA, Queen of Egypt
OCTAVIA, sister to Caesar
   and wife to Antony
CHARMIAN, lady attending on
   Cleopatra
IRAS, lady attending on Cleopatra
ALEXAS, attendant on Cleopatra
MARDIAN, attendant on Cleopatra
SELEUCUS, attendant on Cleopatra
DIOMEDES, attendant on Cleopatra
A SOOTHSAYER
A CLOWN
OFFICERS
SOLDIERS
MESSENGERS
ATTENDANTS

ACT I

SCENE I—Alexandria. Cleopatra's palace
Enter Demetrius and Philo

PHILO   Nay, but this dotage of our general's
O'erflows the measure. Those his goodly eyes,
That o'er the files and musters of the war
Have glow'd like plated Mars, now bend, now turn
The office and devotion of their view
Upon a tawny front. His captain's heart,
Which in the scuffles of great fights hath burst
The buckles on his breast, reneges all temper,
And is become the bellows and the fan
To cool a gipsy's lust.

Flourish. Enter Antony, Cleopatra, her Ladies, the train,
with eunuchs fanning her

Look where they come!
Take but good note, and you shall see in him
The triple pillar of the world transform'd
Into a strumpet's fool. Behold and see.

CLEOPATRA   If it be love indeed, tell me how much.

ANTONY   There's beggary in the love that can be reckon'd.

CLEOPATRA   I'll set a bourn how far to be belov'd.

ANTONY   Then must thou needs find out new heaven, new earth.

Enter a Messenger

MESSENGER   News, my good lord, from Rome.

ANTONY   Grates me: the sum.

CLEOPATRA   Nay, hear them, Antony.
Fulvia perchance is angry; or who knows
If the scarce-bearded Caesar have not sent
His pow'rful mandate to you: "Do this or this;
Take in that kingdom and enfranchise that;
Perform't, or else we damn thee."

ANTONY   How, my love?

CLEOPATRA   Perchance? Nay, and most like,
You must not stay here longer; your dismission
Is come from Caesar; therefore hear it, Antony
Where's Fulvia's process? Caesar's I would say? Both?
Call in the messengers. As I am Egypt's Queen,
Thou blushest, Antony, and that blood of thine
Is Caesar's homager. Else so thy cheek pays shame
When shrill-tongu'd Fulvia scolds. The messengers!

ANTONY   Let Rome in Tiber melt, and the wide arch
Of the rang'd empire fall! Here is my space.
Kingdoms are clay; our dungy earth alike
Feeds beast as man. The nobleness of life
Is to do thus [*embracing*], when such a mutual pair
And such a twain can do't, in which I bind,
On pain of punishment, the world to weet
We stand up peerless.

CLEOPATRA   [*aside*] Excellent falsehood!
Why did he marry Fulvia, and not love her?
I'll seem the fool I am not. [*to Antony*] Antony
Will be himself.

ANTONY   But stirr'd by Cleopatra.
Now for the love of Love and her soft hours,
Let's not confound the time with conference harsh;
There's not a minute of our lives should stretch
Without some pleasure now. What sport tonight?

CLEOPATRA   Hear the ambassadors.

ANTONY   Fie, wrangling queen!
Whom everything becomes—to chide, to laugh,
To weep; whose every passion fully strives
To make itself in thee fair and admir'd.
No messenger but thine, and all alone
Tonight we'll wander through the streets and note
The qualities of people. Come, my queen;
Last night you did desire it. Speak not to us.

                    Exit Antony and Cleopatra, with the train

DEMETRIUS   Is Caesar with Antonius priz'd so slight?

PHILO   Sir, sometimes when he is not Antony,
He comes too short of that great property
Which still should go with Antony.

DEMETRIUS   I am full sorry
   That he approves the common liar, who
   Thus speaks of him at Rome; but I will hope
   Of better deeds tomorrow. Rest you happy!

                                              Exeunt

            SCENE II—Alexandria. Cleopatra's palace
     Enter Enobarbus, Lamprius, a Soothsayer, Rannius, Lucillius,
          Charmian, Iras, Mardian the eunuch, and Alexas
CHARMIAN   Lord Alexas, sweet Alexas, most anything Alexas, almost
   most absolute Alexas, where's the soothsayer that you prais'd so
   to th' Queen? O that I knew this husband, which you say must
   charge his horns with garlands!
ALEXAS   Soothsayer!
SOOTHSAYER   Your will?
CHARMIAN   Is this the man? Is't you, Sir, that know things?
SOOTHSAYER   In nature's infinite book of secrecy
   A little I can read.
ALEXAS   [*to Charmian*] Show him your hand.
                          Enter Enobarbus
ENOBARBUS   [*calling*] Bring in the banquet quickly; wine enough
   Cleopatra's health to drink.
CHARMIAN   [*to Soothsayer*] Good, Sir, give me good fortune.
SOOTHSAYER   I make not, but foresee.
CHARMIAN   Pray, then, foresee me one.
SOOTHSAYER   You shall be yet far fairer than you are.
CHARMIAN   He means in flesh.
IRAS   No, you shall paint when you are old.
CHARMIAN   Wrinkles forbid!
ALEXAS   Vex not his prescience; be attentive.
CHARMIAN   Hush!
SOOTHSAYER   You shall be more beloving than beloved.
CHARMIAN   I had rather heat my liver with drinking.
ALEXAS   Nay, hear him.
CHARMIAN   Good now, some excellent fortune! Let me be married to
   three kings in a forenoon, and widow them all. Let me have a
   child at fifty, to whom Herod of Jewry may do homage. Find me
   to marry me with Octavius Caesar, and companion me with my
   mistress.
SOOTHSAYER   You shall outlive the lady whom you serve.

CHARMIAN   O, excellent! I love long life better than figs.

SOOTHSAYER   You have seen and prov'd a fairer former fortune
Than that which is to approach.

CHARMIAN   Then belike my children shall have no names. Prithee,
how many boys and wenches must I have?

SOOTHSAYER   If every of your wishes had a womb,
And fertile every wish, a million.

CHARMIAN   Out, fool! I forgive thee for a witch.

ALEXAS   You think none but your sheets are privy to your wishes.

CHARMIAN   Nay, come, tell Iras hers.

ALEXAS   We'll know all our fortunes.

ENOBARBUS   Mine, and most of our fortunes, tonight, shall be drunk
to bed.

IRAS   [giving her hand to Soothsayer] There's a palm presages chastity, if
nothing else.

CHARMIAN   E'en as the o'erflowing Nilus presageth famine.

IRAS   Go, you wild bedfellow, you cannot soothsay.

CHARMIAN   Nay, if an oily palm be not a fruitful prognostication, I
cannot scratch mine ear. Prithee, tell her but a workaday fortune.

SOOTHSAYER   Your fortunes are alike.

IRAS   But how, but how? Give me particulars.

SOOTHSAYER   I have said.

IRAS   Am I not an inch of fortune better than she?

CHARMIAN   Well, if you were but an inch of fortune better than I,
where would you choose it?

IRAS   Not in my husband's nose.

CHARMIAN   Our worser thoughts heavens mend! Alexas—come, his
fortune, his fortune! O, let him marry a woman that cannot go,
sweet Isis, I beseech thee! And let her die too, and give him a
worse! And let worse follow worse, till the worst of all follow him
laughing to his grave, fiftyfold a cuckold! Good Isis, hear me this
prayer, though thou deny me a matter of more weight; good Isis, I
beseech thee!

IRAS   Amen. Dear goddess, hear that prayer of the people! For, as it is
a heartbreaking to see a handsome man loose-wiv'd, so it is a deadly
sorrow to behold a foul knave uncuckolded. Therefore, dear Isis,
keep decorum, and fortune him accordingly!

CHARMIAN   Amen.

ALEXAS   Lo now, if it lay in their hands to make me a cuckold, they
would make themselves whores but they'ld do't!

Enter Cleopatra

ENOBARBUS   Hush! Here comes Antony.

CHARMIAN   Not he; the Queen.

CLEOPATRA   Saw you my lord?

ENOBARBUS   No, lady.

CLEOPATRA   Was he not here?

CHARMIAN   No, madam.

CLEOPATRA   He was dispos'd to mirth; but on the sudden
A Roman thought hath struck him. Enobarbus!

ENOBARBUS   Madam?

CLEOPATRA   Seek him, and bring him hither. Where's Alexas?

ALEXAS   Here, at your service. My lord approaches.

Enter Antony, with First Messenger and Attendants

CLEOPATRA   We will not look upon him. Go with us.

Exit all but Antony, First Messenger, and Attendants

FIRST MESSENGER   Fulvia thy wife first came into the field.

ANTONY   Against my brother Lucius?

FIRST MESSENGER   Ay.
But soon that war had end, and the time's state
Made friends of them, jointing their force 'gainst Caesar,
Whose better issue in the war from Italy
Upon the first encounter drave them.

ANTONY   Well, what worst?

FIRST MESSENGER   The nature of bad news infects the teller.

ANTONY   When it concerns the fool or coward. On!
Things that are past are done with me. 'Tis thus:
Who tells me true, though in his tale lie death,
I hear him as he flatter'd.

FIRST MESSENGER   Labienus—
This is stiff news—hath with his Parthian force
Extended Asia from Euphrates,
His conquering banner shook from Syria
To Lydia and to Ionia,
Whilst—

ANTONY   Antony, thou wouldst say.

FIRST MESSENGER   O, my lord!

ANTONY   Speak to me home; mince not the general tongue;
Name Cleopatra as she is call'd in Rome.
Rail thou in Fulvia's phrase, and taunt my faults
With such full licence as both truth and malice

Have power to utter. O, then we bring forth weeds
When our quick minds lie still, and our ills told us
Is as our earing. Fare thee well awhile.

FIRST MESSENGER   At your noble pleasure. [*Exit First Messenger*]
                    Enter Second Messenger

ANTONY   From Sicyon, ho, the news! Speak there!

SECOND MESSENGER   The man from Sicyon—is there such an one?

ATTENDANT   [*at the door*] He stays upon your will.

ANTONY   Let him appear.
    These strong Egyptian fetters I must break,
    Or lose myself in dotage.
                Enter Third Messenger with a letter
                    What are you?

THIRD MESSENGER   Fulvia thy wife is dead.

ANTONY   Where died she?

THIRD MESSENGER   In Sicyon. [*gives a letter*]
    Her length of sickness, with what else more serious
    Importeth thee to know, this bears.

ANTONY   Forbear me. [*Exit Messengers*]
    There's a great spirit gone! Thus did I desire it.
    What our contempts doth often hurl from us
    We wish it ours again; the present pleasure,
    By revolution low'ring, does become
    The opposite of itself. She's good, being gone;
    The hand could pluck her back that shov'd her on.
    I must from this enchanting queen break off.
    Ten thousand harms, more than the ills I know,
    My idleness doth hatch. How now, Enobarbus!
                    Enter Enobarbus

ENOBARBUS   What's your pleasure, Sir?

ANTONY   I must with haste from hence.

ENOBARBUS   Why, then we kill all our women. We see how mortal an
    unkindness is to them; if they suffer our departure, death's the
    word.

ANTONY   I must be gone.

ENOBARBUS   Under a compelling occasion, let women die. It were
    pity to cast them away for nothing, though between them and a
    great cause they should be esteemed nothing. Cleopatra, catching
    but the least noise of this, dies instantly; I have seen her die twenty
    times upon far poorer moment. I do think there is mettle in death,

which commits some loving act upon her, she hath such a celerity in dying.

ANTONY   She is cunning past man's thought.

ENOBARBUS   Alack, Sir, no! Her passions are made of nothing but the finest part of pure love. We cannot call her winds and waters sighs and tears; they are greater storms and tempests than almanacs can report. This cannot be cunning in her; if it be, she makes a show'r of rain as well as Jove.

ANTONY   Would I had never seen her!

ENOBARBUS   O Sir, you had then left unseen a wonderful piece of work, which not to have been blest withal would have discredited your travel.

ANTONY   Fulvia is dead.

ENOBARBUS   Sir?

ANTONY   Fulvia is dead.

ENOBARBUS   Fulvia?

ANTONY   Dead.

ENOBARBUS   Why, Sir, give the gods a thankful sacrifice. When it pleaseth their deities to take the wife of a man from him, it shows to man the tailors of the earth; comforting therein that when old robes are worn out there are members to make new. If there were no more women but Fulvia, then had you indeed a cut, and the case to be lamented. This grief is crown'd with consolation: your old smock brings forth a new petticoat; and indeed the tears live in an onion that should water this sorrow.

ANTONY   The business she hath broached in the state
Cannot endure my absence.

ENOBARBUS   And the business you have broach'd here cannot be without you; especially that of Cleopatra's, which wholly depends on your abode.

ANTONY   No more light answers. Let our officers
Have notice what we purpose. I shall break
The cause of our expedience to the Queen,
And get her leave to part. For not alone
The death of Fulvia, with more urgent touches,
Do strongly speak to us; but the letters to
Of many our contriving friends in Rome
Petition us at home. Sextus Pompeius
Hath given the dare to Caesar, and commands
The empire of the sea; our slippery people,

Whose love is never link'd to the deserver
Till his deserts are past, begin to throw
Pompey the Great and all his dignities
Upon his son; who, high in name and power,
Higher than both in blood and life, stands up
For the main soldier; whose quality, going on,
The sides o' th' world may danger. Much is breeding
Which, like the courser's hair, hath yet but life
And not a serpent's poison. Say our pleasure,
To such whose place is under us, requires
Our quick remove from hence.

ENOBARBUS   I shall do't.

Exeunt separately

SCENE III–Alexandria. Cleopatra's palace
Enter Cleopatra, Charmian, Iras, and Alexas

CLEOPATRA   Where is he?

CHARMIAN   I did not see him since.

CLEOPATRA   [*to Alexas*] See where he is, who's with him, what he does.
I did not send you. If you find him sad,
Say I am dancing; if in mirth, report
That I am sudden sick. Quick, and return.

Exit Alexas

CHARMIAN   Madam, methinks, if you did love him dearly,
You do not hold the method to enforce
The like from him.

CLEOPATRA   What should I do I do not?

CHARMIAN   In each thing give him way; cross him in nothing.

CLEOPATRA   Thou teachest like a fool—the way to lose him.

CHARMIAN   Tempt him not so too far; I wish, forbear;
In time we hate that which we often fear.

Enter Antony

But here comes Antony.

CLEOPATRA   I am sick and sullen.

ANTONY   I am sorry to give breathing to my purpose—

CLEOPATRA   Help me away, dear Charmian; I shall fall.
It cannot be thus long; the sides of nature
Will not sustain it.

ANTONY   Now, my dearest queen—

CLEOPATRA   Pray you, stand farther from me.

ANTONY   What's the matter?

CLEOPATRA   I know by that same eye there's some good news.
　　What says the married woman? You may go.
　　Would she had never given you leave to come!
　　Let her not say 'tis I that keep you here—
　　I have no power upon you; hers you are.

ANTONY   The gods best know—

CLEOPATRA   O, never was there queen
　　So mightily betray'd! Yet at the first
　　I saw the treasons planted.

ANTONY   Cleopatra—

CLEOPATRA   Why should I think you can be mine and true,
　　Though you in swearing shake the throned gods,
　　Who have been false to Fulvia? Riotous madness,
　　To be entangled with those mouth-made vows,
　　Which break themselves in swearing!

ANTONY   Most sweet queen—

CLEOPATRA   Nay, pray you seek no colour for your going,
　　But bid farewell, and go. When you sued staying,
　　Then was the time for words. No going then!
　　Eternity was in our lips and eyes,
　　Bliss in our brows' bent, none our parts so poor
　　But was a race of heaven. They are so still,
　　Or thou, the greatest soldier of the world,
　　Art turn'd the greatest liar.

ANTONY   How now, lady!

CLEOPATRA   I would I had thy inches. Thou shouldst know
　　There were a heart in Egypt.

ANTONY   Hear me, queen:
　　The strong necessity of time commands
　　Our services awhile; but my full heart
　　Remains in use with you. Our Italy
　　Shines o'er with civil swords: Sextus Pompeius
　　Makes his approaches to the port of Rome;
　　Equality of two domestic powers
　　Breed scrupulous faction; the hated, grown to strength,
　　Are newly grown to love. The condemn'd Pompey,
　　Rich in his father's honour, creeps apace
　　Into the hearts of such as have not thrived
　　Upon the present state, whose numbers threaten;

And quietness, grown sick of rest, would purge
By any desperate change. My more particular,
And that which most with you should safe my going,
Is Fulvia's death.

CLEOPATRA   Though age from folly could not give me freedom,
It does from childishness. Can Fulvia die?

ANTONY   She's dead, my Queen. [*He offers letters*]
Look here, and at thy sovereign leisure read
The garboils she awak'd. At the last, best.
See when and where she died.

CLEOPATRA   O most false love!
Where be the sacred vials thou shouldst fill
With sorrowful water? Now I see, I see,
In Fulvia's death how mine receiv'd shall be.

ANTONY   Quarrel no more, but be prepar'd to know
The purposes I bear; which are, or cease,
As you shall give th' advice. By the fire
That quickens Nilus' slime, I go from hence
Thy soldier, servant, making peace or war
As thou affects.

CLEOPATRA   Cut my lace, Charmian, come!
But let it be; I am quickly ill and well—
So Antony loves.

ANTONY   My precious queen, forbear,
And give true evidence to his love, which stands
An honourable trial.

CLEOPATRA   So Fulvia told me.
I prithee turn aside and weep for her;
Then bid adieu to me, and say the tears
Belong to Egypt. Good now, play one scene
Of excellent dissembling, and let it look
Like perfect honour.

ANTONY   You'll heat my blood; no more.

CLEOPATRA   You can do better yet; but this is meetly.

ANTONY   Now, by my sword—

CLEOPATRA   And target. Still he mends;
But this is not the best. Look, prithee, Charmian,
How this Herculean Roman does become
The carriage of his chafe.

ANTONY   I'll leave you, lady.

CLEOPATRA   Courteous lord, one word.
  Sir, you and I must part—but that's not it.
  Sir, you and I have lov'd—but there's not it.
  That you know well. Something it is I would—
  O, my oblivion is a very Antony,
  And I am all forgotten!
ANTONY   But that your royalty
  Holds idleness your subject, I should take you
  For idleness itself.
CLEOPATRA   'Tis sweating labour
  To bear such idleness so near the heart
  As Cleopatra this. But, Sir, forgive me;
  Since my becomings kill me when they do not
  Eye well to you. Your honour calls you hence;
  Therefore be deaf to my unpitied folly,
  And all the gods go with you! Upon your sword
  Sit laurel victory, and smooth success
  Be strew'd before your feet!
ANTONY   Let us go. Come.
  Our separation so abides and flies
  That thou, residing here, goes yet with me,
  And I, hence fleeting, here remain with thee.
  Away!

                                              Exeunt

SCENE IV—Rome. Caesar's house
Enter Octavius Caesar, reading a letter, Lepidus, and their train
CAESAR   You may see, Lepidus, and henceforth know,
  It is not Caesar's natural vice to hate
  Our great competitor. From Alexandria
  This is the news: he fishes, drinks, and wastes
  The lamps of night in revel; is not more manlike
  Than Cleopatra, nor the queen of Ptolemy
  More womanly than he; hardly gave audience, or
  Vouchsaf'd to think he had partners. You shall find there
  A man who is the abstract of all faults
  That all men follow.
LEPIDUS   I must not think there are
  Evils enough to darken all his goodness.
  His faults, in him, seem as the spots of heaven,

More fiery by night's blackness; hereditary
Rather than purchas'd; what he cannot change
Than what he chooses.
CAESAR   You are too indulgent. Let's grant it is not
    Amiss to tumble on the bed of Ptolemy,
    To give a kingdom for a mirth, to sit
    And keep the turn of tippling with a slave,
    To reel the streets at noon, and stand the buffet
    With knaves that smell of sweat. Say this becomes him—
    As his composure must be rare indeed
    Whom these things cannot blemish—yet must Antony
    No way excuse his foils when we do bear
    So great weight in his lightness. If he fill'd
    His vacancy with his voluptuousness,
    Full surfeits and the dryness of his bones
    Call on him for't! But to confound such time
    That drums him from his sport and speaks as loud
    As his own state and ours—'tis to be chid
    As we rate boys who, being mature in knowledge,
    Pawn their experience to their present pleasure,
    And so rebel to judgment.
                    Enter First Messenger
LEPIDUS   Here's more news.
FIRST MESSENGER   Thy biddings have been done; and every hour,
    Most noble Caesar, shalt thou have report
    How 'tis abroad. Pompey is strong at sea,
    And it appears he is belov'd of those
    That only have fear'd Caesar. To the ports
    The discontents repair, and men's reports
    Give him much wrong'd.
CAESAR   I should have known no less.
    It hath been taught us from the primal state
    That he which is was wish'd until he were;
    And the ebb'd man, ne'er lov'd till ne'er worth love,
    Comes dear'd by being lack'd. This common body,
    Like to a vagabond flag upon the stream,
    Goes to and back, lackeying the varying tide,
    To rot itself with motion.
                    Enter Second Messenger
SECOND MESSENGER   Caesar, I bring thee word

Menecrates and Menas, famous pirates,
Make the sea serve them, which they ear and wound
With keels of every kind. Many hot inroads
They make in Italy; the borders maritime
Lack blood to think on't, and flush youth revolt.
No vessel can peep forth but 'tis as soon
Taken as seen; for Pompey's name strikes more
Than could his war resisted.

CAESAR   Antony,
Leave thy lascivious wassails. When thou once
Was beaten from Modena, where thou slew'st
Hirtius and Pansa, consuls, at thy heel
Did famine follow; whom thou fought'st against,
Though daintily brought up, with patience more
Than savages could suffer. Thou didst drink
The stale of horses and the gilded puddle
Which beasts would cough at. Thy palate then did deign
The roughest berry on the rudest hedge;
Yea, like the stag when snow the pasture sheets,
The barks of trees thou brows'd. On the Alps
It is reported thou didst eat strange flesh,
Which some did die to look on. And all this—
It wounds thine honour that I speak it now—
Was borne so like a soldier that thy cheek
So much as lank'd not.

LEPIDUS   'Tis pity of him.

CAESAR   Let his shames quickly
Drive him to Rome. 'Tis time we twain
Did show ourselves i' th' field; and to that end
Assemble we immediate council. Pompey
Thrives in our idleness.

LEPIDUS   Tomorrow, Caesar,
I shall be furnish'd to inform you rightly
Both what by sea and land I can be able
To front this present time.

CAESAR   Till which encounter
It is my business too. Farewell.

LEPIDUS   Farewell, my lord. What you shall know meantime
Of stirs abroad, I shall beseech you, Sir,
To let me be partaker.

CAESAR   Doubt not, Sir; I knew it for my bond.

Exeunt separately

SCENE V—Alexandria. Cleopatra's palace
Enter Cleopatra, Charmian, Iras, and Mardian

CLEOPATRA   Charmian!

CHARMIAN   Madam?

CLEOPATRA   Ha, ha! Give me to drink mandragora.

CHARMIAN   Why, madam?

CLEOPATRA   That I might sleep out this great gap of time
My Antony is away.

CHARMIAN   You think of him too much.

CLEOPATRA   O, 'tis treason!

CHARMIAN   Madam, I trust, not so.

CLEOPATRA   Thou, eunuch Mardian!

MARDIAN   What's your Highness' pleasure?

CLEOPATRA   Not now to hear thee sing; I take no pleasure
In aught an eunuch has. 'Tis well for thee
That, being unseminar'd, thy freer thoughts
May not fly forth of Egypt. Hast thou affections?

MARDIAN   Yes, gracious madam.

CLEOPATRA   Indeed?

MARDIAN   Not in deed, madam; for I can do nothing
But what indeed is honest to be done.
Yet have I fierce affections, and think
What Venus did with Mars.

CLEOPATRA   O Charmian,
Where think'st thou he is now? Stands he or sits he?
Or does he walk? or is he on his horse?
O happy horse, to bear the weight of Antony!
Do bravely, horse; for wot'st thou whom thou mov'st?
The demi-Atlas of this earth, the arm
And burgonet of men. He's speaking now,
Or murmuring "Where's my serpent of old Nile?"
For so he calls me. Now I feed myself
With most delicious poison. Think on me,
That am with Phoebus' amorous pinches black,
And wrinkled deep in time? Broad-fronted Caesar,
When thou wast here above the ground, I was
A morsel for a monarch; and great Pompey

Would stand and make his eyes grow in my brow;
There would he anchor his aspect and die
With looking on his life.

Enter Alexas

ALEXAS Sovereign of Egypt, hail!

CLEOPATRA How much unlike art thou Mark Antony!
Yet, coming from him, that great med'cine hath
With his tinct gilded thee.
How goes it with my brave Mark Antony?

ALEXAS Last thing he did, dear Queen,
He kiss'd—the last of many doubled kisses—
This orient pearl. His speech sticks in my heart.

CLEOPATRA Mine ear must pluck it thence.

ALEXAS   "Good friend," quoth he,
"Say the firm Roman to great Egypt sends
This treasure of an oyster; at whose foot,
To mend the petty present, I will piece
Her opulent throne with kingdoms. All the East,
Say thou, shall call her mistress." So he nodded,
And soberly did mount an arm-gaunt steed,
Who neigh'd so high that what I would have spoke
Was beastly dumb'd by him.

CLEOPATRA What, was he sad or merry?

ALEXAS Like to the time o' th' year between the extremes
Of hot and cold; he was nor sad nor merry.

CLEOPATRA O well-divided disposition! Note him,
Note him, good Charmian; 'tis the man; but note him!
He was not sad, for he would shine on those
That make their looks by his; he was not merry,
Which seem'd to tell them his remembrance lay
In Egypt with his joy; but between both.
O heavenly mingle! Be'st thou sad or merry,
The violence of either thee becomes,
So does it no man else. Met'st thou my posts?

ALEXAS Ay, madam, twenty several messengers.
Why do you send so thick?

CLEOPATRA   Who's born that day
When I forget to send to Antony
Shall die a beggar. Ink and paper, Charmian.

Welcome, my good Alexas. Did I, Charmian,
Ever love Caesar so?

CHARMIAN   O that brave Caesar!

CLEOPATRA   Be chok'd with such another emphasis!
Say "the brave Antony."

CHARMIAN   The valiant Caesar!

CLEOPATRA   By Isis, I will give thee bloody teeth
If thou with Caesar paragon again
My man of men.

CHARMIAN   By your most gracious pardon,
I sing but after you.

CLEOPATRA   My salad days,
When I was green in judgment, cold in blood,
To say as I said then. But come, away!
Get me ink and paper.
He shall have every day a several greeting,
Or I'll unpeople Egypt.

                                                Exeunt

ACT II

SCENE I—Messina. Pompey's house

Enter Pompey, Menecrates, and Menas, in warlike manner

POMPEY   If the great gods be just, they shall assist
   The deeds of justest men.

MENAS   Know, worthy Pompey,
   That what they do delay they not deny.

POMPEY   Whiles we are suitors to their throne, decays
   The thing we sue for.

MENAS   We, ignorant of ourselves,
   Beg often our own harms, which the wise pow'rs
   Deny us for our good; so find we profit
   By losing of our prayers.

POMPEY   I shall do well.
   The people love me, and the sea is mine;
   My powers are crescent, and my auguring hope
   Says it will come to th' full. Mark Antony
   In Egypt sits at dinner, and will make
   No wars without doors. Caesar gets money where
   He loses hearts. Lepidus flatters both,
   Of both is flatter'd; but he neither loves,
   Nor either cares for him.

MENAS   Caesar and Lepidus
   Are in the field. A mighty strength they carry.

POMPEY   Where have you this? 'Tis false.

MENAS   From Silvius, Sir.

POMPEY   He dreams. I know they are in Rome together,
   Looking for Antony. But all the charms of love,
   Salt Cleopatra, soften thy wan'd lip!
   Let witchcraft join with beauty, lust with both;
   Tie up the libertine in a field of feasts,
   Keep his brain fuming. Epicurean cooks

Sharpen with cloyless sauce his appetite,
That sleep and feeding may prorogue his honour
Even till a Lethe'd dullness—

Enter Varrius

                         How now, Varrius!

VARRIUS   This is most certain that I shall deliver:
Mark Antony is every hour in Rome
Expected. Since he went from Egypt 'tis
A space for farther travel.

POMPEY   I could have given less matter
A better ear. Menas, I did not think
This amorous surfeiter would have donn'd his helm
For such a petty war; his soldiership
Is twice the other twain. But let us rear
The higher our opinion, that our stirring
Can from the lap of Egypt's widow pluck
The ne'er-lust-wearied Antony.

MENAS   I cannot hope
Caesar and Antony shall well greet together.
His wife that's dead did trespasses to Caesar;
His brother warr'd upon him; although, I think,
Not mov'd by Antony.

POMPEY   I know not, Menas,
How lesser enmities may give way to greater.
Were't not that we stand up against them all,
'Twere pregnant they should square between themselves;
For they have entertained cause enough
To draw their swords. But how the fear of us
May cement their divisions, and bind up
The petty difference we yet not know.
Be't as our gods will have't! It only stands
Our lives upon to use our strongest hands.
Come, Menas.

Exeunt

SCENE II—Rome. The house of Lepidus
Enter Enobarbus and Lepidus

LEPIDUS   Good Enobarbus, 'tis a worthy deed,
And shall become you well, to entreat your captain
To soft and gentle speech.

ENOBARBUS   I shall entreat him
    To answer like himself. If Caesar move him,
    Let Antony look over Caesar's head
    And speak as loud as Mars. By Jupiter,
    Were I the wearer of Antonius' beard,
    I would not shave't today.
LEPIDUS   'Tis not a time
    For private stomaching.
ENOBARBUS   Every time
    Serves for the matter that is then born in't.
LEPIDUS   But small to greater matters must give way.
ENOBARBUS   Not if the small come first.
LEPIDUS   Your speech is passion;
    But pray you stir no embers up. Here comes
    The noble Antony.
                Enter Antony and Ventidius, in conversation
ENOBARBUS   And yonder, Caesar.
Enter Caesar, Mæcenas, and Agrippa, by another door, in conversation
ANTONY   If we compose well here, to Parthia.
    Hark, Ventidius. [*They confer apart*]
CAESAR   I do not know, Maecenas. Ask Agrippa.
LEPIDUS   Noble friends,
    That which combin'd us was most great, and let not
    A leaner action rend us. What's amiss,
    May it be gently heard. When we debate
    Our trivial difference loud, we do commit
    Murder in healing wounds. Then, noble partners,
    The rather for I earnestly beseech,
    Touch you the sourest points with sweetest terms,
    Nor curstness grow to th' matter.
ANTONY   'Tis spoken well.
    Were we before our armies, and to fight,
    I should do thus. [*Flourish*]
CAESAR   Welcome to Rome.
ANTONY   Thank you.
CAESAR   Sit.
ANTONY   Sit, Sir.
CAESAR   Nay, then. [*They sit*]
ANTONY   I learn you take things ill which are not so,
    Or being, concern you not.

CAESAR   I must be laugh'd at
    If, or for nothing or a little,
    Should say myself offended, and with you
    Chiefly i' the world; more laugh'd at that I should
    Once name you derogately when to sound your name
    It not concern'd me.
ANTONY   My being in Egypt, Caesar, what was't to you?
CAESAR   No more than my residing here at Rome
    Might be to you in Egypt. Yet, if you there
    Did practise on my state, your being in Egypt
    Might be my question.
ANTONY   How intend you "practis'd"?
CAESAR   You may be pleas'd to catch at mine intent
    By what did here befall me. Your wife and brother
    Made wars upon me, and their contestation
    Was theme for you; you were the word of war.
ANTONY   You do mistake your business; my brother never
    Did urge me in his act. I did inquire it,
    And have my learning from some true reports
    That drew their swords with you. Did he not rather
    Discredit my authority with yours,
    And make the wars alike against my stomach,
    Having alike your cause? Of this my letters
    Before did satisfy you. If you'll patch a quarrel,
    As matter whole you have not to make it with,
    It must not be with this.
CAESAR   You praise yourself
    By laying defects of judgment to me; but
    You patch'd up your excuses.
ANTONY   Not so, not so;
    I know you could not lack, I am certain on't,
    Very necessity of this thought, that I,
    Your partner in the cause 'gainst which he fought,
    Could not with graceful eyes attend those wars
    Which fronted mine own peace. As for my wife,
    I would you had her spirit in such another!
    The third o' th' world is yours, which with a snaffle
    You may pace easy, but not such a wife.
ENOBARBUS   Would we had all such wives, that the men might go to
  wars with the women!

ANTONY So much uncurbable, her garboils, Caesar,
    Made out of her impatience—which not wanted
    Shrewdness of policy too—I grieving grant
    Did you too much disquiet. For that you must
    But say I could not help it.

CAESAR   I wrote to you
    When rioting in Alexandria; you
    Did pocket up my letters, and with taunts
    Did gibe my missive out of audience.

ANTONY   Sir,
    He fell upon me ere admitted. Then
    Three kings I had newly feasted, and did want
    Of what I was i' th' morning; but next day
    I told him of myself, which was as much
    As to have ask'd him pardon. Let this fellow
    Be nothing of our strife; if we contend,
    Out of our question wipe him.

CAESAR   You have broken
    The article of your oath, which you shall never
    Have tongue to charge me with.

LEPIDUS Soft, Caesar!

ANTONY No; Lepidus, let him speak.
    The honour is sacred which he talks on now,
    Supposing that I lack'd it. But on, Caesar:
    The article of my oath—

CAESAR To lend me arms and aid when I requir'd them,
    The which you both denied.

ANTONY   Neglected, rather;
    And then when poisoned hours had bound me up
    From mine own knowledge. As nearly as I may,
    I'll play the penitent to you; but mine honesty
    Shall not make poor my greatness, nor my power
    Work without it. Truth is, that Fulvia,
    To have me out of Egypt, made wars here;
    For which myself, the ignorant motive, do
    So far ask pardon as befits mine honour
    To stoop in such a case.

LEPIDUS   'Tis noble spoken.

MÆCENAS If it might please you to enforce no further
    The griefs between ye—to forget them quite

Were to remember that the present need
Speaks to atone you.

LEPIDUS   Worthily spoken, Maecenas.

ENOBARBUS   Or, if you borrow one another's love for the instant, you
may, when you hear no more words of Pompey, return it again.
You shall have time to wrangle in when you have nothing else
to do.

ANTONY   Thou art a soldier only. Speak no more.

ENOBARBUS   That truth should be silent I had almost forgot.

ANTONY   You wrong this presence; therefore speak no more.

ENOBARBUS   Go to, then—your considerate stone!

CAESAR   I do not much dislike the matter, but
The manner of his speech; for't cannot be
We shall remain in friendship, our conditions
So diff'ring in their acts. Yet if I knew
What hoop should hold us stanch, from edge to edge
O' th' world, I would pursue it.

AGRIPPA   Give me leave, Caesar.

CAESAR   Speak, Agrippa.

AGRIPPA   Thou hast a sister by the mother's side,
Admir'd Octavia. Great Mark Antony
Is now a widower.

CAESAR   Say not so, Agrippa.
If Cleopatra heard you, your reproof
Were well deserv'd of rashness.

ANTONY   I am not married, Caesar. Let me hear
Agrippa further speak.

AGRIPPA   To hold you in perpetual amity,
To make you brothers, and to knit your hearts
With an unslipping knot, take Antony
Octavia to his wife; whose beauty claims
No worse a husband than the best of men;
Whose virtue and whose general graces speak
That which none else can utter. By this marriage
All little jealousies, which now seem great,
And all great fears, which now import their dangers,
Would then be nothing. Truths would be tales,
Where now half tales be truths. Her love to both
Would each to other, and all loves to both,
Draw after her. Pardon what I have spoke;

For 'tis a studied, not a present thought,
By duty ruminated.

ANTONY   Will Caesar speak?

CAESAR   Not till he hears how Antony is touch'd
With what is spoke already.

ANTONY   What power is in Agrippa,
If I would say "Agrippa, be it so,"
To make this good?

CAESAR   The power of Caesar, and
His power unto Octavia.

ANTONY   May I never
To this good purpose, that so fairly shows,
Dream of impediment! Let me have thy hand.
Further this act of grace; and from this hour
The heart of brothers govern in our loves
And sway our great designs!

CAESAR   There is my hand. [*They clasp hands*]
A sister I bequeath you, whom no brother
Did ever love so dearly. Let her live
To join our kingdoms and our hearts; and never
Fly off our loves again!

LEPIDUS   Happily, amen!

ANTONY   I did not think to draw my sword 'gainst Pompey;
For he hath laid strange courtesies and great
Of late upon me. I must thank him only,
Lest my remembrance suffer ill report;
At heel of that, defy him.

LEPIDUS   Time calls upon's.
Of us must Pompey presently be sought,
Or else he seeks out us.

ANTONY   Where lies he?

CAESAR   About the Mount Misenum.

ANTONY   What is his strength
By land?

CAESAR   Great and increasing; but by sea
He is an absolute master.

ANTONY   So is the fame.
Would we had spoke together! Haste we for it.
Yet, ere we put ourselves in arms, dispatch we
The business we have talk'd of.

CAESAR   With most gladness;
   And do invite you to my sister's view,
   Whither straight I'll lead you.
ANTONY   Let us, Lepidus, not lack your company.
LEPIDUS   Noble Antony, not sickness should detain me. [*Flourish*]
                Exit all but Enobarbus, Agrippa, Mæcenas
MÆCENAS   Welcome from Egypt, Sir.
ENOBARBUS   Half the heart of Caesar, worthy Mæcenas!
   My honourable friend, Agrippa!
AGRIPPA   Good Enobarbus!
MÆCENAS   We have cause to be glad that matters are so well digested.
   You stay'd well by't in Egypt.
ENOBARBUS   Ay, Sir; we did sleep day out of countenance and made
   the night light with drinking.
MÆCENAS   Eight wild boars roasted whole at a breakfast, and but twelve
   persons there. Is this true?
ENOBARBUS   This was but as a fly by an eagle. We had much more
   monstrous matter of feast, which worthily deserved noting.
MÆCENAS   She's a most triumphant lady, if report be square to her.
ENOBARBUS   When she first met Mark Antony she purs'd up his heart,
   upon the river of Cydnus.
AGRIPPA   There she appear'd indeed! Or my reporter devis'd well
   for her.
ENOBARBUS   I will tell you.
   The barge she sat in, like a burnish'd throne,
   Burn'd on the water. The poop was beaten gold;
   Purple the sails, and so perfumed that
   The winds were love-sick with them; the oars were silver,
   Which to the tune of flutes kept stroke, and made
   The water which they beat to follow faster,
   As amorous of their strokes. For her own person,
   It beggar'd all description. She did lie
   In her pavilion, cloth-of-gold, of tissue,
   O'erpicturing that Venus where we see
   The fancy out-work nature. On each side her
   Stood pretty dimpled boys, like smiling Cupids,
   With divers-colour'd fans, whose wind did seem
   To glow the delicate cheeks which they did cool,
   And what they undid did.
AGRIPPA   O, rare for Antony!

ENOBARBUS   Her gentlewomen, like the Nereides,
So many mermaids, tended her i' th' eyes,
And made their bends adornings. At the helm
A seeming mermaid steers. The silken tackle
Swell with the touches of those flower-soft hands
That yarely frame the office. From the barge
A strange invisible perfume hits the sense
Of the adjacent wharfs. The city cast
Her people out upon her; and Antony,
Enthron'd i' th' market-place, did sit alone,
Whistling to th' air; which, but for vacancy,
Had gone to gaze on Cleopatra too,
And made a gap in nature.
AGRIPPA   Rare Egyptian!
ENOBARBUS   Upon her landing, Antony sent to her,
Invited her to supper. She replied
It should be better he became her guest;
Which she entreated. Our courteous Antony,
Whom ne'er the word of "No" woman heard speak,
Being barber'd ten times o'er, goes to the feast,
And for his ordinary pays his heart
For what his eyes eat only.
AGRIPPA   Royal wench!
She made great Caesar lay his sword to bed.
He ploughed her, and she cropp'd.
ENOBARBUS   I saw her once
Hop forty paces through the public street;
And, having lost her breath, she spoke, and panted,
That she did make defect perfection,
And, breathless, pow'r breathe forth.
MÆCENAS   Now Antony must leave her utterly.
ENOBARBUS   Never! He will not.
Age cannot wither her, nor custom stale
Her infinite variety. Other women cloy
The appetites they feed, but she makes hungry
Where most she satisfies; for vilest things
Become themselves in her, that the holy priests
Bless her when she is riggish.
MÆCENAS   If beauty, wisdom, modesty, can settle

The heart of Antony, Octavia is
A blessed lottery to him.
AGRIPPA   Let us go.
Good Enobarbus, make yourself my guest
Whilst you abide here.
ENOBARBUS   Humbly, Sir, I thank you.

                                        Exeunt

                  SCENE III—Rome. Caesar's house
            Enter Antony, Caesar, Octavia between them
ANTONY   The world and my great office will sometimes
    Divide me from your bosom.
OCTAVIA   All which time
    Before the gods my knee shall bow my prayers
    To them for you.
ANTONY   Good night, Sir. My Octavia,
    Read not my blemishes in the world's report.
    I have not kept my square; but that to come
    Shall all be done by th' rule.
    Good night, dear lady.
OCTAVIA   Good night, Sir.
CAESAR   Good night.
                              Exit Caesar and Octavia
                        Enter Soothsayer
ANTONY   Now, sirrah, you do wish yourself in Egypt?
SOOTHSAYER   Would I had never come from thence, nor you thither!
ANTONY   If you can—your reason.
SOOTHSAYER   I see it in my motion, have it not in my tongue.
    But yet hie you to Egypt again.
ANTONY   Say to me, whose fortunes shall rise higher,
    Caesar's or mine?
SOOTHSAYER   Caesar's. Therefore, O Antony, stay not by his side.
    Thy daemon, that thy spirit which keeps thee, is
    Noble, courageous, high, unmatchable,
    Where Caesar's is not; but near him thy angel
    Becomes a fear, as being o'erpow'r'd. Therefore
    Make space enough between you.
ANTONY   Speak this no more.
SOOTHSAYER   To none but thee; no more but when to thee.
    If thou dost play with him at any game,

Thou art sure to lose; and of that natural luck
He beats thee 'gainst the odds. Thy lustre thickens
When he shines by. I say again, thy spirit
Is all afraid to govern thee near him;
But, he away, 'tis noble.
ANTONY   Get thee gone.
Say to Ventidius I would speak with him.   [*Exit Soothsayer*]
He shall to Parthia. Be it art or hap,
He hath spoken true. The very dice obey him;
And in our sports my better cunning faints
Under his chance. If we draw lots, he speeds;
His cocks do win the battle still of mine,
When it is all to nought, and his quails ever
Beat mine, inhoop'd, at odds. I will to Egypt;
And though I make this marriage for my peace,
I' th' East my pleasure lies.
                    Enter Ventidius
                    O, come, Ventidius,
You must to Parthia. Your commission's ready;
Follow me and receive't.

                                        Exeunt

                    SCENE IV—Rome. A street
            Enter Lepidus, Mæcenas, and Agrippa
LEPIDUS   Trouble yourselves no further. Pray you hasten
    Your generals after.
AGRIPPA   Sir, Mark Antony
    Will e'en but kiss Octavia, and we'll follow.
LEPIDUS   Till I shall see you in your soldier's dress,
    Which will become you both, farewell.
MÆCENAS   We shall,
    As I conceive the journey, be at th' Mount
    Before you, Lepidus.
LEPIDUS   Your way is shorter;
    My purposes do draw me much about.
    You'll win two days upon me.
MÆCENAS, AGRIPPA   Sir, good success!
LEPIDUS   Farewell.

                                        Exeunt

SCENE V—Alexandria. Cleopatra's palace
Enter Cleopatra, Charmian, Iras, and Alexas

CLEOPATRA   Give me some music—music, moody food
 Of us that trade in love.
ALL   The music, ho!
    Enter Mardian the eunuch
CLEOPATRA   Let it alone! Let's to billiards. Come, Charmian.
CHARMIAN   My arm is sore; best play with Mardian.
CLEOPATRA   As well a woman with an eunuch play'd
 As with a woman. Come, you'll play with me, Sir?
MARDIAN   As well as I can, madam.
CLEOPATRA   And when good will is show'd, though't come too short,
 The actor may plead pardon. I'll none now.
 Give me mine angle—we'll to th' river. There,
 My music playing far off, I will betray
 Tawny-finn'd fishes; my bended hook shall pierce
 Their slimy jaws; and as I draw them up
 I'll think them every one an Antony,
 And say "Ah ha! You're caught."
CHARMIAN   'Twas merry when
 You wager'd on your angling; when your diver
 Did hang a salt fish on his hook, which he
 With fervency drew up.
CLEOPATRA   That time? O times!—
 I laughed him out of patience; and that night
 I laugh'd him into patience; and next morn,
 Ere the ninth hour, I drunk him to his bed,
 Then put my tires and mantles on him, whilst
 I wore his sword Philippan.
    Enter a Messenger
     O! from Italy?
 Ram thou thy fruitful tidings in mine ears,
 That long time have been barren.
MESSENGER   Madam, madam—
CLEOPATRA   Antony's dead! If thou say so, villain,
 Thou kill'st thy mistress; but well and free,
 If thou so yield him, there is gold, and here
 My bluest veins to kiss—a hand that kings
 Have lipp'd, and trembled kissing.
MESSENGER   First, madam, he is well.

CLEOPATRA   Why, there's more gold. But, sirrah, mark, we use
  To say the dead are well. Bring it to that,
  The gold I give thee will I melt and pour
  Down thy ill-uttering throat.
MESSENGER   Good madam, hear me.
CLEOPATRA   Well, go to, I will.
  But there's no goodness in thy face. If Antony
  Be free and healthful—why so tart a favour
  To trumpet such good tidings? If not well,
  Thou shouldst come like a Fury crown'd with snakes,
  Not like a formal man.
MESSENGER   Will't please you hear me?
CLEOPATRA   I have a mind to strike thee ere thou speak'st.
  Yet, if thou say Antony lives, is well,
  Or friends with Caesar, or not captive to him,
  I'll set thee in a shower of gold, and hail
  Rich pearls upon thee.
MESSENGER   Madam, he's well.
CLEOPATRA   Well said.
MESSENGER   And friends with Caesar.
CLEOPATRA   Th'art an honest man.
MESSENGER   Caesar and he are greater friends than ever.
CLEOPATRA   Make thee a fortune from me.
MESSENGER   But yet, madam—
CLEOPATRA   I do not like "but yet." It does allay
  The good precedence; fie upon "but yet"!
  "But yet" is as a gaoler to bring forth
  Some monstrous malefactor. Prithee, friend,
  Pour out the pack of matter to mine ear,
  The good and bad together. He's friends with Caesar;
  In state of health, thou say'st; and, thou say'st, free.
MESSENGER   Free, madam! No; I made no such report.
  He's bound unto Octavia.
CLEOPATRA   For what good turn?
MESSENGER   For the best turn i' th' bed.
CLEOPATRA   I am pale, Charmian.
MESSENGER   Madam, he's married to Octavia.
CLEOPATRA   The most infectious pestilence upon thee! [Strikes him]
MESSENGER   Good madam, patience.
CLEOPATRA   What say you? [Strikes him]

Hence, horrible villain! or I'll spurn thine eyes
Like balls before me; I'll unhair thy head;
                    She hales him up and down
Thou shalt be whipp'd with wire and stew'd in brine,
Smarting in ling'ring pickle.
MESSENGER   Gracious madam,
    I that do bring the news made not the match.
CLEOPATRA   Say 'tis not so, a province I will give thee,
    And make thy fortunes proud. The blow thou hadst
    Shall make thy peace for moving me to rage;
    And I will boot thee with what gift beside
    Thy modesty can beg.
MESSENGER   He's married, madam.
CLEOPATRA   Rogue, thou hast liv'd too long. [*Draws a knife*]
MESSENGER   Nay, then I'll run.
    What mean you, madam? I have made no fault.
                                        Exit Messenger
CHARMIAN   Good madam, keep yourself within yourself:
    The man is innocent.
CLEOPATRA   Some innocents scape not the thunderbolt.
    Melt Egypt into Nile! and kindly creatures
    Turn all to serpents! Call the slave again.
    Though I am mad, I will not bite him. Call!
CHARMIAN   He is afear'd to come.
CLEOPATRA   I will not hurt him.
    These hands do lack nobility, that they strike
    A meaner than myself; since I myself
    Have given myself the cause.
                    Enter the Messenger again
                          Come hither, Sir.
    Though it be honest, it is never good
    To bring bad news. Give to a gracious message
    An host of tongues; but let ill tidings tell
    Themselves when they be felt.
MESSENGER   I have done my duty.
CLEOPATRA   Is he married?
    I cannot hate thee worser than I do
    If thou again say "Yes."
MESSENGER   He's married, madam.
CLEOPATRA   The gods confound thee! Dost thou hold there still?

MESSENGER   Should I lie, madam?
CLEOPATRA   O, I would thou didst,
    So half my Egypt were submerg'd and made
    A cistern for scal'd snakes! Go, get thee hence.
    Hadst thou Narcissus in thy face, to me
    Thou wouldst appear most ugly. He is married?
MESSENGER   I crave your Highness' pardon.
CLEOPATRA   He is married?
MESSENGER   Take no offence that I would not offend you;
    To punish me for what you make me do
    Seems much unequal. He's married to Octavia.
CLEOPATRA   O, that his fault should make a knave of thee
    That art not what th'art sure of! Get thee hence.
    The merchandise which thou hast brought from Rome
    Are all too dear for me. Lie they upon thy hand,
    And be undone by 'em!

Exit Messenger

CHARMIAN   Good your Highness, patience.
CLEOPATRA   In praising Antony I have disprais'd Caesar.
CHARMIAN   Many times, madam.
CLEOPATRA   I am paid for't now. Lead me from hence,
    I faint. O Iras, Charmian! 'Tis no matter.
    Go to the fellow, good Alexas; bid him
    Report the feature of Octavia, her years,
    Her inclination; let him not leave out
    The colour of her hair. Bring me word quickly.   [*Exit Alexas*]
    Let him for ever go—let him not, Charmian—
    Though he be painted one way like a Gorgon,
    The other way's a Mars. [*to Mardian*] Bid you Alexas
    Bring me word how tall she is. Pity me, Charmian,
    But do not speak to me. Lead me to my chamber.

Exeunt

SCENE VI—Near Misenum
Flourish. Enter Pompey and Menas at one door, with drum and trumpet; at another, Caesar, Antony, Lepidus, Enobarbus, Mæcenas, Agrippa, with soldiers marching
POMPEY   Your hostages I have, so have you mine;
    And we shall talk before we fight.
CAESAR   Most meet

That first we come to words; and therefore have we
Our written purposes before us sent;
Which if thou hast considered, let us know
If 'twill tie up thy discontented sword
And carry back to Sicily much tall youth
That else must perish here.

POMPEY   To you all three,
The senators alone of this great world,
Chief factors for the gods: I do not know
Wherefore my father should revengers want,
Having a son and friends, since Julius Caesar,
Who at Philippi the good Brutus ghosted,
There saw you labouring for him. What was't
That mov'd pale Cassius to conspire? and what
Made the all-honour'd honest Roman, Brutus,
With the arm'd rest, courtiers of beauteous freedom,
To drench the Capitol, but that they would
Have one man but a man? And that is it
Hath made me rig my navy, at whose burden
The anger'd ocean foams; with which I meant
To scourge th' ingratitude that despiteful Rome
Cast on my noble father.

CAESAR   Take your time.

ANTONY   Thou canst not fear us, Pompey, with thy sails;
We'll speak with thee at sea; at land thou know'st
How much we do o'er-count thee.

POMPEY   At land, indeed,
Thou dost o'er-count me of my father's house.
But since the cuckoo builds not for himself,
Remain in't as thou mayst.

LEPIDUS   Be pleas'd to tell us—
For this is from the present—how you take
The offers we have sent you.

CAESAR   There's the point.

ANTONY   Which do not be entreated to, but weigh
What it is worth embrac'd.

CAESAR   And what may follow,
To try a larger fortune.

POMPEY   You have made me offer
Of Sicily, Sardinia; and I must

Rid all the sea of pirates; then to send
Measures of wheat to Rome; this 'greed upon,
To part with unhack'd edges and bear back
Our targes undinted.

ALL   That's our offer.

POMPEY   Know, then,
I came before you here a man prepar'd
To take this offer; but Mark Antony
Put me to some impatience. Though I lose
The praise of it by telling, you must know,
When Caesar and your brother were at blows,
Your mother came to Sicily and did find
Her welcome friendly.

ANTONY   I have heard it, Pompey,
And am well studied for a liberal thanks
Which I do owe you.

POMPEY   Let me have your hand. [*They shake hands*]
I did not think, Sir, to have met you here.

ANTONY   The beds i' th' East are soft; and thanks to you,
That call'd me timelier than my purpose hither;
For I have gained by't.

CAESAR   Since I saw you last
There is a change upon you.

POMPEY   Well, I know not
What counts harsh fortune casts upon my face;
But in my bosom shall she never come
To make my heart her vassal.

LEPIDUS   Well met here.

POMPEY   I hope so, Lepidus. Thus we are agreed.
I crave our composition may be written,
And seal'd between us.

CAESAR   That's the next to do.

POMPEY   We'll feast each other ere we part, and let's
Draw lots who shall begin.

ANTONY   That will I, Pompey.

POMPEY   No, Antony, take the lot;
But, first or last, your fine Egyptian cookery
Shall have the fame. I have heard that Julius Caesar
Grew fat with feasting there.

ANTONY   You have heard much.

POMPEY   I have fair meanings, Sir.

ANTONY   And fair words to them.

POMPEY   Then so much have I heard;
    And I have heard Apollodorus carried—

ENOBARBUS   No more of that! He did so.

POMPEY   What, I pray you?

ENOBARBUS   A certain queen to Caesar in a mattress.

POMPEY   I know thee now. How far'st thou, soldier?

ENOBARBUS   Well;
    And well am like to do, for I perceive
    Four feasts are toward.

POMPEY   Let me shake thy hand. [*They shake hands*]
    I never hated thee; I have seen thee fight,
    When I have envied thy behaviour.

ENOBARBUS   Sir,
    I never lov'd you much; but I ha' prais'd ye
    When you have well deserv'd ten times as much
    As I have said you did.

POMPEY   Enjoy thy plainness;
    It nothing ill becomes thee.
    Aboard my galley I invite you all.
    Will you lead, lords?

ALL   Show's the way, Sir.

POMPEY   Come.

Exit all but Enobarbus and Menas

MENAS   [*aside*] Thy father, Pompey, would ne'er have made this treaty.—
    [*To Enobarbus*] You and I have known, Sir.

ENOBARBUS   At sea, I think.

MENAS   We have, Sir.

ENOBARBUS   You have done well by water.

MENAS   And you by land.

ENOBARBUS   I will praise any man that will praise me; though it can-
    not be denied what I have done by land.

MENAS   Nor what I have done by water.

ENOBARBUS   Yes, something you can deny for your own safety: you
    have been a great thief by sea.

MENAS   And you by land.

ENOBARBUS   There I deny my land service. But give me your hand,
    Menas; if our eyes had authority, here they might take two thieves
    kissing.

MENAS   All men's faces are true, whatsome'er their hands are.

ENOBARBUS   But there is never a fair woman has a true face.

MENAS   No slander: they steal hearts.

ENOBARBUS   We came hither to fight with you.

MENAS   For my part, I am sorry it is turn'd to a drinking. Pompey doth this day laugh away his fortune.

ENOBARBUS   If he do, sure he cannot weep't back again.

MENAS   Y'have said, Sir. We look'd not for Mark Antony here. Pray you, is he married to Cleopatra?

ENOBARBUS   Caesar' sister is call'd Octavia.

MENAS   True, Sir; she was the wife of Caius Marcellus.

ENOBARBUS   But she is now the wife of Marcus Antonius.

MENAS   Pray ye, Sir?

ENOBARBUS   'Tis true.

MENAS   Then is Caesar and he for ever knit together.

ENOBARBUS   If I were bound to divine of this unity, I would not prophesy so.

MENAS   I think the policy of that purpose made more in the marriage than the love of the parties.

ENOBARBUS   I think so too. But you shall find the band that seems to tie their friendship together will be the very strangler of their amity: Octavia is of a holy, cold, and still conversation.

MENAS   Who would not have his wife so?

ENOBARBUS   Not he that himself is not so; which is Mark Antony. He will to his Egyptian dish again; then shall the sighs of Octavia blow the fire up in Caesar, and, as I said before, that which is the strength of their amity shall prove the immediate author of their variance. Antony will use his affection where it is; he married but his occasion here.

MENAS   And thus it may be. Come, Sir, will you aboard? I have a health for you.

ENOBARBUS   I shall take it, Sir. We have us'd our throats in Egypt.

MENAS   Come, let's away.

                                                                Exeunt

SCENE VII—On board Pompey's galley, Misenum Music plays.
                Enter two or three Servants with a banquet

FIRST SERVANT   Here they'll be, man. Some o' their plants are ill-rooted already; the least wind i' th' world will blow them down.

SECOND SERVANT   Lepidus is high-colour'd.

FIRST SERVANT   They have made him drink alms-drink.

SECOND SERVANT   As they pinch one another by the disposition, he cries out "No more!"; reconciles them to his entreaty and himself to th' drink.

FIRST SERVANT   But it raises the greater war between him and his discretion.

SECOND SERVANT   Why, this it is to have a name in great men's fellowship. I had as lief have a reed that will do me no service as a partizan I could not heave.

FIRST SERVANT   To be call'd into a huge sphere, and not to be seen to move in't, are the holes where eyes should be, which pitifully disaster the cheeks. [*A sennet sounded*]

Enter Caesar, Antony, Lepidus, Pompey, Agrippa, Mæcenas, Enobarbus, Menas, with other Captains and a Boy

ANTONY   [*to Caesar*] Thus do they, Sir: they take the flow o' th' Nile
By certain scales i' th' pyramid; they know
By th' height, the lowness, or the mean, if dearth
Or foison follow. The higher Nilus swells
The more it promises; as it ebbs, the seedsman
Upon the slime and ooze scatters his grain,
And shortly comes to harvest.

LEPIDUS   Y'have strange serpents there.

ANTONY   Ay, Lepidus.

LEPIDUS   Your serpent of Egypt is bred now of your mud by the operation of your sun; so is your crocodile.

ANTONY   They are so.

POMPEY   Sit—and some wine! A health to Lepidus!

They sit and drink

LEPIDUS   I am not so well as I should be, but I'll ne'er out.

ENOBARBUS   Not till you have slept. I fear me you'll be in till then.

LEPIDUS   Nay, certainly, I have heard the Ptolemies' pyramises are very goodly things. Without contradiction I have heard that.

MENAS   [*aside to Pompey*] Pompey, a word.

POMPEY   [*aside to Menas*] Say in mine ear; what is't?

MENAS   [*aside to Pompey*] Forsake thy seat, I do beseech thee, Captain, And hear me speak a word.

POMPEY   [*to Menas*] Forbear me till anon—This wine for Lepidus!

LEPIDUS   What manner o' thing is your crocodile?

ANTONY   It is shap'd, Sir, like itself, and it is as broad as it hath breadth; it is just so high as it is, and moves with it own organs. It lives by that which nourisheth it, and the elements once out of it, it transmigrates.

LEPIDUS What colour is it of?

ANTONY Of it own colour too.

LEPIDUS 'Tis a strange serpent.

ANTONY 'Tis so. And the tears of it are wet.

CAESAR [*To Antony*] Will this description satisfy him?

ANTONY With the health that Pompey gives him, else he is a very epicure.

POMPEY [*aside to Menas*] Go, hang, Sir, hang! Tell me of that! Away! Do as I bid you.—Where's this cup I call'd for?

MENAS [*aside to Pompey*] If for the sake of merit thou wilt hear me, Rise from thy stool.

POMPEY [*aside to Menas*] I think th'art mad. The matter?

He rises and they walk aside

MENAS I have ever held my cap off to thy fortunes.

POMPEY Thou hast serv'd me with much faith. What's else to say?— Be jolly, lords.

ANTONY These quicksands, Lepidus, Keep off them, for you sink.

MENAS Wilt thou be lord of all the world?

POMPEY What say'st thou?

MENAS Wilt thou be lord of the whole world? That's twice.

POMPEY How should that be?

MENAS But entertain it, And though you think me poor, I am the man Will give thee all the world.

POMPEY Hast thou drunk well?

MENAS No, Pompey, I have kept me from the cup. Thou art, if thou dar'st be, the earthly Jove; Whate'er the ocean pales or sky inclips Is thine, if thou wilt ha't.

POMPEY Show me which way.

MENAS These three world-sharers, these competitors, Are in thy vessel. Let me cut the cable; And when we are put off, fall to their throats. All there is thine.

POMPEY Ah, this thou shouldst have done, And not have spoke on't. In me 'tis villainy: In thee't had been good service. Thou must know

'Tis not my profit that does lead mine honour:
Mine honour, it. Repent that e'er thy tongue
Hath so betray'd thine act. Being done unknown,
I should have found it afterwards well done,
But must condemn it now. Desist, and drink.

He returns to the feast

MENAS   [*aside*] For this, I'll never follow thy pall'd fortunes more.
Who seeks, and will not take when once 'tis offer'd,
Shall never find it more.

POMPEY   This health to Lepidus!

ANTONY   Bear him ashore. I'll pledge it for him, Pompey.

ENOBARBUS   Here's to thee, Menas! [*They drink*]

MENAS   Enobarbus, welcome!

POMPEY   Fill till the cup be hid.

ENOBARBUS   There's a strong fellow, Menas.

Pointing to the servant who carries off Lepidus

MENAS   Why?

ENOBARBUS   A bears the third part of the world, man; see'st not?

MENAS   The third part, then, is drunk. Would it were all,
That it might go on wheels!

ENOBARBUS   Drink thou; increase the reels.

MENAS   Come.

POMPEY   This is not yet an Alexandrian feast.

ANTONY   It ripens towards it. Strike the vessels, ho!
Here's to Caesar!

CAESAR   I could well forbear't.
It's monstrous labour when I wash my brain
An it grows fouler.

ANTONY   Be a child o' th' time.

CAESAR   Possess it, I'll make answer.
But I had rather fast from all four days
Than drink so much in one.

ENOBARBUS   [*to Antony*]   Ha, my brave emperor!
Shall we dance now the Egyptian bacchanals
And celebrate our drink?

POMPEY   Let's ha't, good soldier.

ANTONY   Come, let's all take hands,
Till that the conquering wine hath steep'd our sense
In soft and delicate Lethe.

ENOBARBUS   All take hands.
Make battery to our ears with the loud music,

The while I'll place you; then the boy shall sing;
The holding every man shall bear as loud
As his strong sides can volley.
            Music plays. Enobarbus places them hand in hand.
BOY   [*sings*]
                    Come, thou monarch of the vine,
                    Plumpy Bacchus with pink eyne!
                    In thy fats our cares be drown'd,
                    With thy grapes our hairs be crown'd.

ALL   [*Chorus*]   Cup us till the world go round,
                    Cup us till the world go round!

CAESAR   What would you more? Pompey, good night. Good brother,
      Let me request you off; our graver business
      Frowns at this levity. Gentle lords, let's part;
      You see we have burnt our cheeks. Strong Enobarb
      Is weaker than the wine, and mine own tongue
      Splits what it speaks. The wild disguise hath almost
      Antick'd us all. What needs more words? Good night.
      Good Antony, your hand.
POMPEY   I'll try you on the shore.
ANTONY   And shall, Sir. Give's your hand.
POMPEY   O Antony,
      You have my father's house—but what? We are friends.
      Come, down into the boat.
                            Exit all but Enobarbus and Menas
ENOBARBUS   Take heed you fall not.
      Menas, I'll not on shore.
MENAS   No, to my cabin.
      These drums! these trumpets, flutes! what!
      Let Neptune hear we bid a loud farewell
      To these great fellows. Sound and be hang'd, sound out!
                        Sound a flourish, with drums
ENOBARBUS   Hoo! says a. There's my cap. [*He flings it in the air*]
MENAS   Hoo! Noble Captain, come.
                                                Exeunt

ACT III

Scene I—A plain in Syria

Enter Ventidius, as it were in triumph, with Silius and other Romans, Officers and Soldiers; the dead body of Pacorus borne before him

VENTIDIUS Now, darting Parthia, art thou struck, and now
    Pleas'd fortune does of Marcus Crassus' death
    Make me revenger. Bear the King's son's body
    Before our army. Thy Pacorus, Orodes,
    Pays this for Marcus Crassus.

SILIUS   Noble Ventidius,
    Whilst yet with Parthian blood thy sword is warm
    The fugitive Parthians follow; spur through Media,
    Mesopotamia, and the shelters whither
    The routed fly. So thy grand captain, Antony,
    Shall set thee on triumphant chariots and
    Put garlands on thy head.

VENTIDIUS   O Silius, Silius,
    I have done enough. A lower place, note well,
    May make too great an act; for learn this, Silius:
    Better to leave undone than by our deed
    Acquire too high a fame when him we serve's away.
    Caesar and Antony have ever won
    More in their officer, than person. Sossius,
    One of my place in Syria, his lieutenant,
    For quick accumulation of renown,
    Which he achiev'd by th' minute, lost his favour.
    Who does i' th' wars more than his captain can
    Becomes his captain's captain; and ambition,
    The soldier's virtue, rather makes choice of loss
    Than gain which darkens him.
    I could do more to do Antonius good,
    But 'twould offend him; and in his offence

Should my performance perish.

SILIUS Thou hast, Ventidius, that
Without the which a soldier and his sword
Grants scarce distinction. Thou wilt write to Antony?

VENTIDIUS I'll humbly signify what in his name,
That magical word of war, we have effected;
How, with his banners, and his well-paid ranks,
The ne'er-yet-beaten horse of Parthia
We have jaded out o' th' field.

SILIUS   Where is he now?

VENTIDIUS He purposeth to Athens; whither, with what haste
The weight we must convey with's will permit,
We shall appear before him.—On, there; pass along.

Exeunt

SCENE II—Rome. Caesar's house
Enter Agrippa at one door, Enobarbus at another

AGRIPPA What, are the brothers parted?

ENOBARBUS They have dispatch'd with Pompey; he is gone;
The other three are sealing. Octavia weeps
To part from Rome; Caesar is sad; and Lepidus,
Since Pompey's feast, as Menas says, is troubled
With the green sickness.

AGRIPPA 'Tis a noble Lepidus.

ENOBARBUS A very fine one. O, how he loves Caesar!

AGRIPPA Nay, but how dearly he adores Mark Antony!

ENOBARBUS Caesar? Why he's the Jupiter of men.

AGRIPPA What's Antony? The god of Jupiter.

ENOBARBUS Spake you of Caesar? How! the nonpareil!

AGRIPPA O, Antony! O thou Arabian bird!

ENOBARBUS Would you praise Caesar, say "Caesar"—go no further.

AGRIPPA Indeed, he plied them both with excellent praises.

ENOBARBUS But he loves Caesar best. Yet he loves Antony
Hoo! hearts, tongues, figures, scribes, bards, poets, cannot
Think, speak, cast, write, sing, number—hoo!—
His love to Antony But as for Caesar,
Kneel down, kneel down, and wonder.

AGRIPPA   Both he loves.

ENOBARBUS They are his shards, and he their beetle. So—
Trumpets within

This is to horse. Adieu, noble Agrippa.

AGRIPPA   Good fortune, worthy soldier, and farewell.

Enter Caesar, Antony, Lepidus, and Octavia

ANTONY   No further, Sir.

CAESAR   You take from me a great part of myself;
Use me well in't. Sister, prove such a wife
As my thoughts make thee, and as my farthest band
Shall pass on thy approof. Most noble Antony,
Let not the piece of virtue which is set
Betwixt us as the cement of our love
To keep it builded be the ram to batter
The fortress of it; for better might we
Have lov'd without this mean, if on both parts
This be not cherish'd.

ANTONY   Make me not offended
In your distrust.

CAESAR   I have said.

ANTONY   You shall not find,
Though you be therein curious, the least cause
For what you seem to fear. So the gods keep you,
And make the hearts of Romans serve your ends!
We will here part.

CAESAR   Farewell, my dearest sister, fare thee well.
The elements be kind to thee and make
Thy spirits all of comfort! Fare thee well.

OCTAVIA   [weeping] My noble brother!

ANTONY   The April's in her eyes. It is love's spring,
And these the showers to bring it on. Be cheerful.

OCTAVIA   [to Caesar] Sir, look well to my husband's house; and—

CAESAR   What, Octavia?

OCTAVIA   I'll tell you in your ear.

She whispers to Caesar

ANTONY   Her tongue will not obey her heart, nor can
Her heart inform her tongue—the swan's down feather,
That stands upon the swell at the full of tide,
And neither way inclines.

ENOBARBUS   [aside to Agrippa] Will Caesar weep?

AGRIPPA   [aside to Enobarbus] He has a cloud in's face.

ENOBARBUS   [aside to Agrippa] He were the worse for that, were he a horse;
So is he, being a man.

AGRIPPA   [*aside to Enobarbus*] Why, Enobarbus,
        When Antony found Julius Caesar dead,
        He cried almost to roaring; and he wept
        When at Philippi he found Brutus slain.
ENOBARBUS   [*aside to Agrippa*] That year, indeed, he was troubled
            with a rheum;
        What willingly he did confound he wail'd,
        Believe't—till I weep too.
CAESAR   No, sweet Octavia,
        You shall hear from me still; the time shall not
        Out-go my thinking on you.
ANTONY   Come, Sir, come;
        I'll wrestle with you in my strength of love.
        Look, here I have you; thus I let you go,
        And give you to the gods.
CAESAR   Adieu; be happy!
LEPIDUS   Let all the number of the stars give light
        To thy fair way!
CAESAR   Farewell, farewell! [*He kisses Octavia*]
ANTONY   Farewell! [*Trumpets sound*]

                                        Exeunt

                SCENE III—Alexandria. Cleopatra's palace
                Enter Cleopatra, Charmian, Iras, and Alexas
CLEOPATRA   Where is the fellow?
ALEXAS   Half afeard to come.
CLEOPATRA   Go to, go to.
                    Enter the Messenger as before
                        Come hither, Sir.
ALEXAS   Good Majesty,
        Herod of Jewry dare not look upon you
        But when you are well pleas'd.
CLEOPATRA   That Herod's head
        I'll have. But how, when Antony is gone,
        Through whom I might command it? Come thou near.
MESSENGER   Most gracious Majesty!
CLEOPATRA   Didst thou behold Octavia?
MESSENGER   Ay, dread Queen.
CLEOPATRA   Where?
MESSENGER   Madam, in Rome

I look'd her in the face, and saw her led
Between her brother and Mark Antony
CLEOPATRA   Is she as tall as me?
MESSENGER   She is not, madam.
CLEOPATRA   Didst hear her speak? Is she shrill-tongu'd or low?
MESSENGER   Madam, I heard her speak. She is low-voic'd.
CLEOPATRA   That's not so good. He cannot like her long.
CHARMIAN   Like her? O Isis! 'tis impossible.
CLEOPATRA   I think so, Charmian. Dull of tongue and dwarfish!
    What majesty is in her gait? Remember,
    If e'er thou look'dst on majesty.
MESSENGER   She creeps.
    Her motion and her station are as one;
    She shows a body rather than a life,
    A statue than a breather.
CLEOPATRA   Is this certain?
MESSENGER   Or I have no observance.
CHARMIAN   Three in Egypt
    Cannot make better note.
CLEOPATRA   He's very knowing;
    I do perceive't. There's nothing in her yet.
    The fellow has good judgment.
CHARMIAN   Excellent.
CLEOPATRA   Guess at her years, I prithee.
MESSENGER   Madam,
    She was a widow—
CLEOPATRA   Widow? Charmian, hark!
MESSENGER   And I do think she's thirty.
CLEOPATRA   Bear'st thou her face in mind? Is't long or round?
MESSENGER   Round even to faultiness.
CLEOPATRA   For the most part, too, they are foolish that are so.
    Her hair, what colour?
MESSENGER   Brown, madam; and her forehead
    As low as she would wish it.
CLEOPATRA   [giving money] There's gold for thee.
    Thou must not take my former sharpness ill.
    I will employ thee back again; I find thee
    Most fit for business. Go make thee ready;
    Our letters are prepar'd.

Exit Messenger

CHARMIAN   A proper man.
CLEOPATRA   Indeed, he is so. I repent me much
    That so I harried him. Why, methinks, by him,
    This creature's no such thing.
CHARMIAN   Nothing, madam.
CLEOPATRA   The man hath seen some majesty, and should know.
CHARMIAN   Hath he seen majesty? Isis else defend,
    And serving you so long!
CLEOPATRA   I have one thing more to ask him yet, good Charmian.
    But 'tis no matter; thou shalt bring him to me
    Where I will write. All may be well enough.
CHARMIAN   I warrant you, madam.

                                                    Exeunt

            SCENE IV—Athens. Antony's house
                Enter Antony and Octavia
ANTONY   Nay, nay, Octavia, not only that—
    That were excusable, that and thousands more
    Of semblable import—but he hath wag'd
    New wars 'gainst Pompey; made his will, and read it
    To public ear; spoke scandy of me;
    When perforce he could not
    But pay me terms of honour, cold and sickly
    He vented them, most narrow measure lent me;
    When the best hint was given him, he not took't,
    Or did it from his teeth.
OCTAVIA   O my good lord,
    Believe not all; or if you must believe,
    Stomach not all. A more unhappy lady,
    If this division chance, ne'er stood between,
    Praying for both parts.
    The good gods will mock me presently
    When I shall pray "O, bless my lord and husband!"
    Undo that prayer by crying out as loud
    "O, bless my brother!" Husband win, win brother,
    Prays, and destroys the prayer; no mid-way
    'Twixt these extremes at all.
ANTONY   Gentle Octavia,
    Let your best love draw to that point which seeks
    Best to preserve it. If I lose mine honour,

I lose myself; better I were not yours
Than yours so branchless. But, as you requested,
Yourself shall go between's. The meantime, lady,
I'll raise the preparation of a war
Shall stain your brother. Make your soonest haste;
So your desires are yours.

OCTAVIA   Thanks to my lord.
The Jove of power make me, most weak, most weak,
Your reconciler! Wars 'twixt you twain would be
As if the world should cleave, and that slain men
Should solder up the rift.

ANTONY   When it appears to you where this begins,
Turn your displeasure that way, for our faults
Can never be so equal that your love
Can equally move with them. Provide your going;
Choose your own company, and command what cost
Your heart has mind to.

                                        Exeunt

SCENE V—Athens. Antony's house
Enter Enobarbus and Eros, meeting

ENOBARBUS   How now, friend Eros!

EROS   There's strange news come, Sir.

ENOBARBUS   What, man?

EROS   Caesar and Lepidus have made wars upon Pompey.

ENOBARBUS   This is old. What is the success?

EROS   Caesar, having made use of him in the wars 'gainst Pompey,
    presently denied him rivality, would not let him partake in the
    glory of the action; and not resting here, accuses him of letters he
    had formerly wrote to Pompey; upon his own appeal, seizes him.
    So the poor third is up, till death enlarge his confine.

ENOBARBUS   Then, world, thou hast a pair of chaps—no more;
And throw between them all the food thou hast,
They'll grind the one the other. Where's Antony?

EROS   He's walking in the garden—thus, and spurns
The rush that lies before him; cries "Fool Lepidus!"
And threats the throat of that his officer
That murd'red Pompey.

ENOBARBUS   Our great navy's rigg'd.

EROS   For Italy and Caesar. More, Domitius:
   My lord desires you presently; my news
   I might have told hereafter.
ENOBARBUS   'Twill be naught;
   But let it be. Bring me to Antony
EROS   Come, Sir.

Exeunt

SCENE VI—Rome. Caesar's house
Enter Caesar, Agrippa, and Mæcenas

CAESAR   Contemning Rome, he has done all this and more
   In Alexandria. Here's the manner of't:
   I' th' market-place, on a tribunal silver'd,
   Cleopatra and himself in chairs of gold
   Were publicly enthron'd; at the feet sat
   Caesarion, whom they call my father's son,
   And all the unlawful issue that their lust
   Since then hath made between them. Unto her
   He gave the stablishment of Egypt; made her
   Of lower Syria, Cyprus, Lydia,
   Absolute queen.
MÆCENAS   This in the public eye?
CAESAR   I' th' common show-place, where they exercise.
   His sons he there proclaim'd the kings of kings:
   Great Media, Parthia, and Armenia,
   He gave to Alexander; to Ptolemy he assign'd
   Syria, Cilicia, and Phoenicia. She
   In th' habiliments of the goddess Isis
   That day appear'd; and oft before gave audience,
   As 'tis reported, so.
MÆCENAS   Let Rome be thus inform'd.
AGRIPPA   Who, queasy with his insolence already,
   Will their good thoughts call from him.
CAESAR   The people knows it, and have now receiv'd
   His accusations.
AGRIPPA   Who does he accuse?
CAESAR   Caesar; and that, having in Sicily
   Sextus Pompeius spoil'd, we had not rated him
   His part o' th' isle. Then does he say he lent me
   Some shipping, unrestor'd. Lastly, he frets

That Lepidus of the triumvirate
Should be depos'd; and, being, that we detain
All his revenue.
AGRIPPA   Sir, this should be answer'd.
CAESAR   'Tis done already, and messenger gone.
I have told him Lepidus was grown too cruel,
That he his high authority abus'd,
And did deserve his change. For what I have conquer'd
I grant him part; but then, in his Armenia
And other of his conquer'd kingdoms,
Demand the like.
MÆCENAS   He'll never yield to that.
CAESAR   Nor must not then be yielded to in this.
                Enter Octavia, with her train
OCTAVIA   Hail, Caesar, and my lord! hail, most dear Caesar!
CAESAR   That ever I should call thee castaway!
OCTAVIA   You have not call'd me so, nor have you cause.
CAESAR   Why have you stol'n upon us thus? You come not
Like Caesar's sister. The wife of Antony
Should have an army for an usher, and
The neighs of horse to tell of her approach
Long ere she did appear. The trees by th' way
Should have borne men, and expectation fainted,
Longing for what it had not. Nay, the dust
Should have ascended to the roof of heaven,
Rais'd by your populous troops. But you are come
A market-maid to Rome, and have prevented
The ostentation of our love, which left unshown
Is often left unlov'd. We should have met you
By sea and land, supplying every stage
With an augmented greeting.
OCTAVIA   Good my lord,
To come thus was I not constrain'd, but did it
On my free will. My lord, Mark Antony,
Hearing that you prepar'd for war, acquainted
My grieved ear withal; whereon I begg'd
His pardon for return.
CAESAR   Which soon he granted,
Being an obstruct 'tween his lust and him.
OCTAVIA   Do not say so, my lord.

CAESAR   I have eyes upon him,
   And his affairs come to me on the wind.
   Where is he now?
OCTAVIA   My lord, in Athens.
CAESAR   No, my most wronged sister: Cleopatra
   Hath nodded him to her. He hath given his empire
   Up to a whore, who now are levying
   The kings o' th' earth for war. He hath assembled
   Bocchus, the king of Libya; Archelaus
   Of Cappadocia; Philadelphos, king
   Of Paphlagonia; the Thracian king, Adallas;
   King Malchus of Arabia; King of Pont;
   Herod of Jewry; Mithridates, king
   Of Comagene; Polemon and Amyntas,
   The Kings of Mede and Lycaonia,
   With more larger list of sceptres.
OCTAVIA   Ay me most wretched,
   That have my heart parted betwixt two friends,
   That does afflict each other!
CAESAR   Welcome hither.
   Your letters did withhold our breaking forth,
   Till we perceiv'd both how you were wrong led
   And we in negligent danger. Cheer your heart;
   Be you not troubled with the time, which drives
   O'er your content these strong necessities,
   But let determin'd things to destiny
   Hold unbewail'd their way. Welcome to Rome;
   Nothing more dear to me. You are abus'd
   Beyond the mark of thought, and the high gods,
   To do you justice, make their ministers
   Of us and those that love you. Best of comfort,
   And ever welcome to us.
AGRIPPA   Welcome, lady.
MÆCENAS   Welcome, dear madam.
   Each heart in Rome does love and pity you;
   Only th' adulterous Antony, most large
   In his abominations, turns you off,
   And gives his potent regiment to a trull
   That noises it against us.
OCTAVIA   Is it so, Sir?

CAESAR   Most certain. Sister, welcome. Pray you
    Be ever known to patience. My dear'st sister!

Exeunt

SCENE VII–Antony's camp near Actium
Enter Cleopatra and Enobarbus

CLEOPATRA   I will be even with thee, doubt it not.

ENOBARBUS   But why, why,

CLEOPATRA   Thou hast forspoke my being in these wars,
    And say'st it is not fit.

ENOBARBUS   Well, is it, is it?

CLEOPATRA   Is't not denounc'd against us? Why should not we
    Be there in person?

ENOBARBUS   [*aside*]   Well, I could reply:
    If we should serve with horse and mares together
    The horse were merely lost; the mares would bear
    A soldier and his horse.

CLEOPATRA   What is't you say?

ENOBARBUS   Your presence needs must puzzle Antony;
    Take from his heart, take from his brain, from's time,
    What should not then be spar'd. He is already
    Traduc'd for levity; and 'tis said in Rome
    That Photinus an eunuch and your maids
    Manage this war.

CLEOPATRA   Sink Rome, and their tongues rot
    That speak against us! A charge we bear i' th' war,
    And, as the president of my kingdom, will
    Appear there for a man. Speak not against it;
    I will not stay behind.

Enter Antony and Canidius

ENOBARBUS   Nay, I have done.
    Here comes the Emperor.

ANTONY   Is it not strange, Canidius,
    That from Tarentum and Brundusium
    He could so quickly cut the Ionian sea,
    And take in Toryne?–You have heard on't, sweet?

CLEOPATRA   Celerity is never more admir'd
    Than by the negligent.

ANTONY   A good rebuke,
    Which might have well becom'd the best of men

To taunt at slackness. Canidius, we
Will fight with him by sea.
CLEOPATRA   By sea! What else?
CANIDIUS   Why will my lord do so?
ANTONY   For that he dares us to't.
ENOBARBUS   So hath my lord dar'd him to single fight.
CANIDIUS   Ay, and to wage this battle at Pharsalia,
Where Caesar fought with Pompey. But these offers,
Which serve not for his vantage, he shakes off;
And so should you.
ENOBARBUS   Your ships are not well mann'd;
Your mariners are muleteers, reapers, people
Ingross'd by swift impress. In Caesar's fleet
Are those that often have 'gainst Pompey fought;
Their ships are yare; yours heavy. No disgrace
Shall fall you for refusing him at sea,
Being prepar'd for land.
ANTONY   By sea, by sea.
ENOBARBUS   Most worthy Sir, you therein throw away
The absolute soldiership you have by land;
Distract your army, which doth most consist
Of war-mark'd footmen; leave unexecuted
Your own renowned knowledge; quite forgo
The way which promises assurance; and
Give up yourself merely to chance and hazard
From firm security.
ANTONY   I'll fight at sea.
CLEOPATRA   I have sixty sails, Caesar none better.
ANTONY   Our overplus of shipping will we burn,
And, with the rest full-mann'd, from th' head of Actium
Beat th' approaching Caesar. But if we fail,
We then can do't at land.
                    Enter a Messenger
                    Thy business?
MESSENGER   The news is true, my lord: he is descried;
Caesar has taken Toryne.
ANTONY   Can he be there in person? 'Tis impossible—
Strange that his power should be. Canidius,
Our nineteen legions thou shalt hold by land,

And our twelve thousand horse. We'll to our ship.
Away, my Thetis!

Enter a Soldier

How now, worthy soldier?

SOLDIER   O noble Emperor, do not fight by sea;
    Trust not to rotten planks. Do you misdoubt
    This sword and these my wounds? Let th' Egyptians
    And the Phoenicians go a-ducking; we
    Have us'd to conquer standing on the earth
    And fighting foot to foot.

ANTONY   Well, well—away.

Exit Antony, Cleopatra, and Enobarbus

SOLDIER   By Hercules, I think I am i' th' right.

CANIDIUS   Soldier, thou art; but his whole action grows
    Not in the power on't. So our leader's led,
    And we are women's men.

SOLDIER   You keep by land
    The legions and the horse whole, do you not?

CANIDIUS   Marcus Octavius, Marcus Justeius,
    Publicola, and Caelius are for sea;
    But we keep whole by land. This speed of Caesar's
    Carries beyond belief.

SOLDIER   While he was yet in Rome,
    His power went out in such distractions as
    Beguil'd all spies.

CANIDIUS   Who's his lieutenant, hear you?

SOLDIER   They say one Taurus.

CANIDIUS   Well I know the man.

Enter a Messenger

MESSENGER   The Emperor calls Canidius.

CANIDIUS   With news the time's with labour and throes forth
    Each minute some.

                                      Exeunt

SCENE VIII—A plain near Actium

Enter Caesar, and Taurus, with his army, marching

CAESAR   Taurus!

TAURUS   My lord?

CAESAR   Strike not by land; keep whole; Provoke not battle
Till we have done at sea. Do not exceed

The prescript of this scroll. [*He gives a scroll*] Our fortune lies
Upon this jump.

Exeunt

SCENE IX—Another part of the plain
Enter Antony and Enobarbus

ANTONY   Set we our squadrons on yon side o' th' hill,
In eye of Caesar's battle; from which place
We may the number of the ships behold,
And so proceed accordingly.

Exeunt

SCENE X—Another part of the plain
*Canidius marcheth with his land army one way over the stage, and
Taurus, the Lieutenant of Caesar, the other way. After their going
in is heard the noise of a sea-fight
Alarum. Enter Enobarbus*

ENOBARBUS   Naught, naught, all naught! I can behold no longer.
Th' *Antoniad*, the Egyptian admiral,
With all their sixty, fly and turn the rudder.
To see't mine eyes are blasted.

Enter Scarus

SCARUS   Gods and goddesses,
All the whole synod of them!

ENOBARBUS   What's thy passion?

SCARUS   The greater cantle of the world is lost
With very ignorance; we have kiss'd away
Kingdoms and provinces.

ENOBARBUS   How appears the fight?

SCARUS   On our side like the token'd pestilence,
Where death is sure. Yon riband-red nag of Egypt—
Whom leprosy o'ertake!—i' th' midst o' th' fight,
When vantage like a pair of twins appear'd,
Both as the same, or rather ours the elder—
The breese upon her, like a cow in June—
Hoists sails and flies.

ENOBARBUS   That I beheld;
Mine eyes did sicken at the sight and could not
Endure a further view.

SCARUS   She once being luffed,

The noble ruin of her magic, Antony,
Claps on his sea-wing, and, like a doting mallard,
Leaving the fight in height, flies after her.
I never saw an action of such shame;
Experience, manhood, honour, ne'er before
Did violate so itself.

ENOBARBUS   Alack, alack!

Enter Canidius

CANIDIUS   Our fortune on the sea is out of breath,
And sinks most lamentably. Had our general
Been what he knew himself, it had gone well.
O, he has given example for our flight
Most grossly by his own!

ENOBARBUS   Ay, are you thereabouts? Why then, good night indeed.

CANIDIUS   Toward Peloponnesus are they fled.

SCARUS   'Tis easy to't; and there I will attend
What further comes.

CANIDIUS   To Caesar will I render
My legions and my horse; six kings already
Show me the way of yielding.

ENOBARBUS   I'll yet follow
The wounded chance of Antony, though my reason
Sits in the wind against me.

                                        Exeunt

SCENE XI—Alexandria. Cleopatra's palace
Enter Antony, with Attendants

ANTONY   Hark! the land bids me tread no more upon't;
It is asham'd to bear me. Friends, come hither.
I am so lated in the world that I
Have lost my way for ever. I have a ship
Laden with gold; take that; divide it. Fly,
And make your peace with Caesar.

ALL   Fly? Not we!

ANTONY   I have fled myself, and have instructed cowards
To run and show their shoulders. Friends, be gone;
I have myself resolv'd upon a course
Which has no need of you; be gone.
My treasure's in the harbour, take it. O,
I follow'd that I blush to look upon.

My very hairs do mutiny; for the white
Reprove the brown for rashness, and they them
For fear and doting. Friends, be gone; you shall
Have letters from me to some friends that will
Sweep your way for you. Pray you look not sad,
Nor make replies of loathness; take the hint
Which my despair proclaims. Let that be left
Which leaves itself. To the sea-side straight way.
I will possess you of that ship and treasure.
Leave me, I pray, a little; pray you now;
Nay, do so, for indeed I have lost command;
Therefore I pray you. I'll see you by and by. [*He sits down*]

Exit Attendants
Enter Cleopatra, led by Charmian and Iras, Eros following

EROS   Nay, gentle madam, to him! Comfort him.
IRAS   Do, most dear Queen.
CHARMIAN   Do? Why, what else?
CLEOPATRA   Let me sit down. O Juno!
ANTONY   No, no, no, no, no.
EROS   See you here, Sir?
ANTONY   O, fie, fie, fie!
CHARMIAN   Madam!
IRAS   Madam, O good Empress!
EROS   Sir, Sir!
ANTONY   Yes, my lord, yes. He at Philippi kept
His sword e'en like a dancer, while I struck
The lean and wrinkled Cassius; and 'twas I
That the mad Brutus ended; he alone
Dealt on lieutenantry, and no practice had
In the brave squares of war. Yet now—no matter.
CLEOPATRA   Ah, stand by!
EROS   The Queen, my lord, the Queen!
IRAS   Go to him, madam, speak to him.
He is unqualited with very shame.
CLEOPATRA   Well then, sustain me. O!
EROS   Most noble Sir, arise; the Queen approaches.
Her head's declin'd, and death will seize her but
Your comfort makes the rescue.
ANTONY   I have offended reputation—
A most unnoble swerving.

EROS   Sir, the Queen.
ANTONY   O, whither hast thou led me, Egypt? See
 How I convey my shame out of thine eyes
 By looking back what I have left behind
 'Stroy'd in dishonour.
CLEOPATRA   O my lord, my lord,
 Forgive my fearful sails! I little thought
 You would have followed.
ANTONY   Egypt, thou knew'st too well
 My heart was to thy rudder tied by th' strings,
 And thou shouldst tow me after. O'er my spirit
 Thy full supremacy thou knew'st, and that
 Thy beck might from the bidding of the gods
 Command me.
CLEOPATRA   O, my pardon!
ANTONY   Now I must
 To the young man send humble treaties, dodge
 And palter in the shifts of lowness, who
 With half the bulk o' th' world play'd as I pleas'd,
 Making and marring fortunes. You did know
 How much you were my conqueror, and that
 My sword, made weak by my affection, would
 Obey it on all cause.
CLEOPATRA   Pardon, pardon!
ANTONY   Fall not a tear, I say; one of them rates
 All that is won and lost. Give me a kiss; [*They kiss*]
 Even this repays me. [*to an Attendant*]
 We sent our schoolmaster; is a come back?
 Love, I am full of lead. Some wine,
 Within there, and our viands! Fortune knows
 We scorn her most when most she offers blows.

             Exeunt

    SCENE XII—Caesar's camp in Egypt
  Enter Caesar, Agrippa, Dolabella, Thyreus, with others
CAESAR   Let him appear that's come from Antony.
 Know you him?
DOLABELLA   Caesar, 'tis his schoolmaster:
 An argument that he is pluck'd, when hither

He sends so poor a pinion of his wing,
Which had superfluous kings for messengers
Not many moons gone by.

Enter Euphronius, Ambassador from Antony

CAESAR   Approach, and speak.

EUPHRONIUS   Such as I am, I come from Antony.
I was of late as petty to his ends
As is the morn-dew on the myrtle leaf
To his grand sea.

CAESAR   Be't so. Declare thine office.

EUPHRONIUS   Lord of his fortunes he salutes thee, and
Requires to live in Egypt; which not granted,
He lessens his requests and to thee sues
To let him breathe between the heavens and earth,
A private man in Athens. This for him.
Next, Cleopatra does confess thy greatness,
Submits her to thy might, and of thee craves
The circle of the Ptolemies for her heirs,
Now hazarded to thy grace.

CAESAR   For Antony,
I have no ears to his request. The Queen
Of audience nor desire shall fail, so she
From Egypt drive her all-disgraced friend,
Or take his life there. This if she perform,
She shall not sue unheard. So to them both.

EUPHRONIUS   Fortune pursue thee!

CAESAR   Bring him through the bands.

Exit Euphronius, attended

[*to Thyreus*] To try thy eloquence, now 'tis time. Dispatch;
From Antony win Cleopatra. Promise,
And in our name, what she requires; add more,
From thine invention, offers. Women are not
In their best fortunes strong; but want will perjure
The ne'er-touch'd vestal. Try thy cunning, Thyreus;
Make thine own edict for thy pains, which we
Will answer as a law.

THYREUS   Caesar, I go.

CAESAR   Observe how Antony becomes his flaw,
And what thou think'st his very action speaks
In every power that moves.

THYREUS   Caesar, I shall

                                             Exeunt

      SCENE XIII–Alexandria. Cleopatra's palace
       Enter Cleopatra, Enobarbus, Charmian, and Iras
CLEOPATRA   What shall we do, Enobarbus?
ENOBARBUS   Think, and die.
CLEOPATRA   Is Antony or we in fault for this?
ENOBARBUS   Antony only, that would make his will
   Lord of his reason. What though you fled
   From that great face of war, whose several ranges
   Frighted each other? Why should he follow?
   The itch of his affection should not then
   Have nick'd his captainship, at such a point,
   When half to half the world oppos'd, he being
   The mered question. 'Twas a shame no less
   Than was his loss, to course your flying flags
   And leave his navy gazing.
CLEOPATRA   Prithee, peace.
      Enter Euphronius, the Ambassador; with Antony
ANTONY   Is that his answer?
EUPHRONIUS   Ay, my lord.
ANTONY   The Queen shall then have courtesy, so she
   Will yield us up.
EUPHRONIUS   He says so.
ANTONY   Let her know't.
   To the boy Caesar send this grizzled head,
   And he will fill thy wishes to the brim
   With principalities.
CLEOPATRA   That head, my lord?
ANTONY   To him again. Tell him he wears the rose
   Of youth upon him; from which the world should note
   Something particular. His coin, ships, legions,
   May be a coward's whose ministers would prevail
   Under the service of a child as soon
   As i' th' command of Caesar. I dare him therefore
   To lay his gay comparisons apart,
   And answer me declin'd, sword against sword,
   Ourselves alone. I'll write it. Follow me.
                   Exit Antony and Euphronius

EUPHRONIUS   [aside] Yes, like enough high-battled Caesar will
    Unstate his happiness, and be stag'd to th' show
    Against a sworder! I see men's judgments are
    A parcel of their fortunes, and things outward
    Do draw the inward quality after them,
    To suffer all alike. That he should dream,
    Knowing all measures, the full Caesar will
    Answer his emptiness! Caesar, thou hast subdu'd
    His judgment too.

                    Enter a Servant
SERVANT   A messenger from Caesar.
CLEOPATRA   What, no more ceremony? See, my women!
    Against the blown rose may they stop their nose
    That kneel'd unto the buds. Admit him, Sir.   [*Exit Servant*]
ENOBARBUS   [aside] Mine honesty and I begin to square.
    The loyalty well held to fools does make
    Our faith mere folly. Yet he that can endure
    To follow with allegiance a fall'n lord
    Does conquer him that did his master conquer,
    And earns a place i' th' story.

                    Enter Thyreus
CLEOPATRA   Caesar's will?
THYREUS   Hear it apart.
CLEOPATRA   None but friends: say boldly.
THYREUS   So, haply, are they friends to Antony.
ENOBARBUS   He needs as many, Sir, as Caesar has,
    Or needs not us. If Caesar please, our master
    Will leap to be his friend. For us, you know
    Whose he is we are, and that is Caesar's.
THYREUS   So.
    Thus then, thou most renown'd: Caesar entreats
    Not to consider in what case thou stand'st
    Further than he is Caesar.
CLEOPATRA   Go on. Right royal!
THYREUS   He knows that you embrace not Antony
    As you did love, but as you fear'd him.
CLEOPATRA   O!
THYREUS   The scars upon your honour, therefore, he
    Does pity, as constrained blemishes,
    Not as deserv'd.

CLEOPATRA   He is a god, and knows
        What is most right. Mine honour was not yielded,
        But conquer'd merely.
ENOBARBUS   [aside]   To be sure of that,
        I will ask Antony. Sir, Sir, thou art so leaky
        That we must leave thee to thy sinking, for
        Thy dearest quit thee.

                                           Exit Enobarbus

THYREUS   Shall I say to Caesar
        What you require of him? For he partly begs
        To be desir'd to give. It much would please him
        That of his fortunes you should make a staff
        To lean upon. But it would warm his spirits
        To hear from me you had left Antony,
        And put yourself under his shroud,
        The universal landlord.
CLEOPATRA   What's your name?
THYREUS   My name is Thyreus.
CLEOPATRA   Most kind messenger,
        Say to great Caesar this: in deputation
        I kiss his conquring hand. Tell him I am prompt
        To lay my crown at 's feet, and there to kneel.
        Tell him from his all-obeying breath I hear
        The doom of Egypt.
THYREUS   'Tis your noblest course.
        Wisdom and fortune combating together,
        If that the former dare but what it can,
        No chance may shake it. Give me grace to lay
        My duty on your hand. [*He kisses her hand*]
CLEOPATRA   Your Caesar's father oft,
        When he hath mus'd of taking kingdoms in,
        Bestow'd his lips on that unworthy place,
        As it rain'd kisses.
                    Enter Antony and Enobarbus
ANTONY   Favours, by Jove that thunders!
        What art thou, fellow?
THYREUS   One that but performs
        The bidding of the fullest man, and worthiest
        To have command obey'd.
ENOBARBUS   [aside]   You will be whipt.

ANTONY Approach there.—Ah, you kite!—Now, gods and devils!
Authority melts from me. Of late, when I cried "Ho!"
Like boys unto a muss, kings would start forth
And cry "Your will?" Have you no ears? I am
Antony yet.

Enter Servants

Take hence this jack and whip him.
ENOBARBUS 'Tis better playing with a lion's whelp
Than with an old one dying.
ANTONY   Moon and stars!
Whip him. Were't twenty of the greatest tributaries
That do acknowledge Caesar, should I find them
So saucy with the hand of she here—what's her name
Since she was Cleopatra? Whip him, fellows,
Till like a boy you see him cringe his face,
And whine aloud for mercy. Take him hence.
THYMUS Mark Antony—
ANTONY   Tug him away. Being whipt,
Bring him again: the Jack of Caesar's shall
Bear us an errand to him.

Exit Servants with Thyreus

[*to Cleopatra*] You were half blasted ere I knew you. Ha!
Have I my pillow left unpress'd in Rome,
Forborne the getting of a lawful race,
And by a gem of women, to be abus'd
By one that looks on feeders?
CLEOPATRA Good my lord—
ANTONY You have been a boggler ever.
But when we in our viciousness grow hard—
O misery on't!—the wise gods seel our eyes,
In our own filth drop our clear judgments, make us
Adore our errors, laugh at's while we strut
To our confusion.
CLEOPATRA   O, is't come to this?
ANTONY I found you as a morsel cold upon
Dead Caesar's trencher. Nay, you were a fragment
Of Gnaeus Pompey's, besides what hotter hours,
Unregist'red in vulgar fame, you have
Luxuriously pick'd out; for I am sure,
Though you can guess what temperance should be,

You know not what it is.

CLEOPATRA Wherefore is this?

ANTONY To let a fellow that will take rewards,
And say "God quit you!" be familiar with
My playfellow, your hand, this kingly seal
And plighter of high hearts! O that I were
Upon the hill of Basan to outroar
The horned herd! For I have savage cause,
And to proclaim it civilly were like
A halter'd neck which does the hangman thank
For being yare about him.

Enter a Servant with Thyreus

Is he whipt?

SERVANT Soundly, my lord.

ANTONY Cried he? and begg'd a pardon?

SERVANT He did ask favour.

ANTONY [*to Thyreus*] If that thy father live, let him repent
Thou wast not made his daughter; and be thou sorry
To follow Caesar in his triumph, since
Thou hast been whipt for following him. Henceforth
The white hand of a lady fever thee!
Shake thou to look on't. Get thee back to Caesar;
Tell him thy entertainment; look thou say
He makes me angry with him; for he seems
Proud and disdainful, harping on what I am,
Not what he knew I was. He makes me angry;
And at this time most easy 'tis to do't,
When my good stars, that were my former guides,
Have empty left their orbs and shot their fires
Into th' abysm of hell. If he mislike
My speech and what is done, tell him he has
Hipparchus, my enfranched bondman, whom
He may at pleasure whip or hang or torture,
As he shall like, to quit me. Urge it thou.
Hence with thy stripes, be gone.

Exit Thyreus with Servant

CLEOPATRA Have you done yet?

ANTONY Alack, our terrene moon
Is now eclips'd, and it portends alone
The fall of Antony.

CLEOPATRA [*aside*] I must stay his time.
ANTONY To flatter Caesar, would you mingle eyes
　　With one that ties his points?
CLEOPATRA　　　　　　　　　　Not know me yet?
ANTONY Cold-hearted toward me?
CLEOPATRA　　　　　　　　　　Ah, dear, if I be so,
　　From my cold heart let heaven engender hail,
　　And poison it in the source, and the first stone
　　Drop in my neck; as it determines, so
　　Dissolve my life! The next Caesarion smite,
　　Till by degrees the memory of my womb,
　　Together with my brave Egyptians all,
　　By the discandying of this pelleted storm,
　　Lie graveless, till the flies and gnats of Nile
　　Have buried them for prey.
ANTONY　　　　　　　　　　I am satisfied.
　　Caesar sits down in Alexandria, where
　　I will oppose his fate. Our force by land
　　Hath nobly held; our sever'd navy to
　　Have knit again, and fleet, threat'ning most sea-like.
　　Where hast thou been, my heart? Dost thou hear, lady?
　　If from the field I shall return once more
　　To kiss these lips, I will appear in blood.
　　I and my sword will earn our chronicle.
　　There's hope in't yet.
CLEOPATRA That's my brave lord!
ANTONY I will be treble-sinew'd, hearted, breath'd,
　　And fight maliciously. For when mine hours
　　Were nice and lucky, men did ransom lives
　　Of me for jests; but now I'll set my teeth,
　　And send to darkness all that stop me. Come,
　　Let's have one other gaudy night. Call to me
　　All my sad captains; fill our bowls once more;
　　Let's mock the midnight bell.
CLEOPATRA　　　　　　　　　　It is my birthday.
　　I had thought t'have held it poor; but since my lord
　　Is Antony again, I will be Cleopatra.
ANTONY We will yet do well.
CLEOPATRA [*to attendants*] Call all his noble captains to my lord.
ANTONY Do so, we'll speak to them; and tonight I'll force

The wine peep through their scars. Come on, my queen,
There's sap in't yet. The next time I do fight
I'll make death love me; for I will contend
Even with his pestilent scythe.

Exit all but Enobarbus

ENOBARBUS   Now he'll outstare the lightning. To be furious
Is to be frighted out of fear, and in that mood
The dove will peck the estridge; and I see still
A diminution in our captain's brain
Restores his heart. When valour preys on reason,
It eats the sword it fights with. I will seek
Some way to leave him.

Exit

ACT IV

SCENE I–Caesar's camp before Alexandria
Enter Caesar, Agrippa, and Mæcenas, with his army;
Caesar reading a letter

CAESAR   He calls me boy, and chides as he had power
To beat me out of Egypt. My messenger
He hath whipt with rods; dares me to personal combat,
Caesar to Antony. Let the old ruffian know
I have many other ways to die; meantime
Laugh at his challenge.

MÆCENAS   Caesar must think
When one so great begins to rage, he's hunted
Even to falling. Give him no breath, but now
Make boot of his distraction. Never anger
Made good guard for itself.

CAESAR   Let our best heads
Know that tomorrow the last of many battles
We mean to fight. Within our files there are
Of those that serv'd Mark Antony but late
Enough to fetch him in. See it done;
And feast the army; we have store to do't,
And they have earn'd the waste. Poor Antony!

Exeunt

SCENE II–Alexandria. Cleopatra's palace
Enter Antony, Cleopatra, Enobarbus, Charmian, Iras,
Alexas, with others

ANTONY   He will not fight with me, Domitius?

ENOBARBUS   No.

ANTONY   Why should he not?

ENOBARBUS   He thinks, being twenty times of better fortune,
He is twenty men to one.

ANTONY   Tomorrow, soldier,
   By sea and land I'll fight. Or I will live,
   Or bathe my dying honour in the blood
   Shall make it live again. Woo't thou fight well?
ENOBARBUS   I'll strike, and cry "Take all!"
ANTONY   Well said; come on.
   Call forth my household servants; let's tonight
              Enter three or four servitors
   Be bounteous at our meal. Give me thy hand,
   Thou has been rightly honest. So hast thou;
   Thou, and thou, and thou. You have serv'd me well,
   And kings have been your fellows.
CLEOPATRA   [*aside to Enobarbus*]   What means this?
ENOBARBUS   [*aside to Cleopatra*] 'Tis one of those odd tricks which
     sorrow shoots
   Out of the mind.
ANTONY   And thou art honest too.
   I wish I could be made so many men,
   And all of you clapp'd up together in
   An Antony, that I might do you service
   So good as you have done.
SERVANT   The gods forbid!
ANTONY   Well, my good fellows, wait on me tonight.
   Scant not my cups, and make as much of me
   As when mine empire was your fellow too,
   And suffer'd my command.
CLEOPATRA   [*aside to Enobarbus*] What does he mean?
ENOBARBUS   [*aside to Cleopatra*] To make his followers weep.
ANTONY   Tend me tonight;
   May be it is the period of your duty.
   Haply you shall not see me more; or if,
   A mangled shadow. Perchance tomorrow
   You'll serve another master. I look on you
   As one that takes his leave. Mine honest friends,
   I turn you not away; but, like a master
   Married to your good service, stay till death.
   Tend me tonight two hours, I ask no more,
   And the gods yield you for't!
ENOBARBUS   What mean you, Sir,
   To give them this discomfort? Look, they weep;

And I, an ass, am onion-ey'd. For shame!
Transform us not to women.
ANTONY   Ho, ho, ho!
Now the witch take me if I meant it thus!
Grace grow where those drops fall! My hearty friends,
You take me in too dolorous a sense;
For I spake to you for your comfort, did desire you
To burn this night with torches. Know, my hearts,
I hope well of tomorrow, and will lead you
Where rather I'll expect victorious life
Than death and honour. Let's to supper, come,
And drown consideration.

Exeunt

SCENE III—Alexandria. Before Cleopatra's palace
Enter a company of soldiers
FIRST SOLDIER   Brother, good night. Tomorrow is the day.
SECOND SOLDIER   It will determine one way. Fare you well.
Heard you of nothing strange about the streets?
FIRST SOLDIER   Nothing. What news?
Second SOLDIER   Belike 'tis but a rumour. Good night to you.
FIRST SOLDIER   Well, Sir, good night. [*They meet other soldiers*]
SECOND SOLDIER   Soldiers, have careful watch.
First SOLDIER   And you. Good night, good night.
       The two companies separate and place themselves
             in every corner of the stage
SECOND SOLDIER   Here we. And if tomorrow
Our navy thrive, I have an absolute hope
Our landmen will stand up.
THIRD SOLDIER   'Tis a brave army, and full of purpose.
       Music of the hautboys is under the stage
SECOND SOLDIER   Peace, what noise?
THIRD SOLDIER   List, list!
SECOND SOLDIER   Hark!
THIRD SOLDIER   Music i' th' air.
FOURTH SOLDIER   Under the earth.
THIRD SOLDIER   It signs well, does it not?
FOURTH SOLDIER   No.
THIRD SOLDIER   Peace, I say! What should this mean?

SECOND SOLDIER   'Tis the god Hercules, whom Antony lov'd,
   Now leaves him.
THIRD SOLDIER   Walk; let's see if other watchmen
   Do hear what we do. [*The advance toward their fellow watchmen*]
SECOND SOLDIER   How now, masters!
SOLDIERS   [*speaking together*] How now! How now! Do you hear this?
FIRST SOLDIER   Ay; is't not strange?
THIRD SOLDIER   Do you hear, masters? Do you hear?
FIRST SOLDIER   Follow the noise so far as we have quarter;
   Let's see how it will give off.
SOLDIERS   [*speaking together*] Content. 'Tis strange.

                                       Exeunt

           SCENE IV–Alexandria. Cleopatra's palace
Enter Antony and Cleopatra, Charmian, Iras, with others attending
ANTONY   Eros! mine armour, Eros!
CLEOPATRA   Sleep a little.
ANTONY   No, my chuck. Eros! Come, mine armour, Eros!
             Enter Eros with armour
   Come, good fellow, put mine iron on.
   If fortune be not ours today, it is
   Because we brave her. Come.
CLEOPATRA   Nay, I'll help too.
   What's this for? [*She helps to arm him*]
ANTONY   Ah, let be, let be! Thou art
   The armourer of my heart. False, false; this, this.
CLEOPATRA   Sooth, la, I'll help. Thus it must be.
ANTONY   Well, well;
   We shall thrive now. Seest thou, my good fellow?
   Go put on thy defences.
EROS   Briefly, Sir.
CLEOPATRA   Is not this buckled well?
ANTONY   Rarely, rarely!
   He that unbuckles this, till we do please
   To daff't for our repose, shall hear a storm.
   Thou fumblest, Eros, and my queen's a squire
   More tight at this than thou. Dispatch. O love,
   That thou couldst see my wars today, and knew'st
   The royal occupation! Thou shouldst see
   A workman in't.

Enter an armed Soldier
Good-morrow to thee. Welcome.
Thou look'st like him that knows a warlike charge.
To business that we love we rise betime,
And go to't with delight.
SOLDIER   A thousand, Sir,
Early though't be, have on their riveted trim,
And at the port expect you. [*Shout. Flourish of trumpets within*]
Enter Captains and soldiers
CAPTAIN   The morn is fair. Good morrow, General.
ALL   Good morrow, General.
ANTONY   'Tis well blown, lads.
This morning, like the spirit of a youth
That means to be of note, begins betimes.
So, so. Come, give me that. This way. Well said.
Fare thee well, dame, whate'er becomes of me.
This is a soldier's kiss. Rebukeable,
And worthy shameful check it were, to stand
On more mechanic compliment; I'll leave thee
Now like a man of steel. You that will fight,
Follow me close; I'll bring you to't. Adieu.
Exit Antony, Eros, Captains and Soldiers
CHARMIAN   Please you retire to your chamber?
CLEOPATRA   Lead me.
He goes forth gallantly. That he and Caesar might
Determine this great war in single fight!
Then, Antony–but now. Well, on.
Exeunt

SCENE V–Alexandria. Antony's camp
Trumpets sound. Enter Antony and Eros, a Soldier meeting them
SOLDIER   The gods make this a happy day to Antony!
ANTONY   Would thou and those thy scars had once prevail'd
To make me fight at land!
SOLDIER   Hadst thou done so,
The kings that have revolted, and the soldier
That has this morning left thee, would have still
Followed thy heels.
ANTONY   Who's gone this morning?
SOLDIER   Who? One ever near thee. Call for Enobarbus,

He shall not hear thee; or from Caesar's camp
Say "I am none of thine."

ANTONY   What say'st thou?

SOLDIER   Sir, he is with Caesar.

EROS   Sir, his chests and treasure
He has not with him.

ANTONY   Is he gone?

SOLDIER   Most certain.

ANTONY   Go, Eros, send his treasure after; do it;
Detain no jot, I charge thee. Write to him—
I will subscribe—gentle adieus and greetings;
Say that I wish he never find more cause
To change a master. O, my fortunes have
Corrupted honest men! Dispatch. Enobarbus!

                                          Exeunt

SCENE VI—Alexandria. Caesar's camp
Flourish. Enter Agrippa, Caesar, with Dolabella and Enobarbus

CAESAR   Go forth, Agrippa, and begin the fight.
Our will is Antony be took alive;
Make it so known.

AGRIPPA   Caesar, I shall.

                                    Exit Agrippa

CAESAR   The time of universal peace is near.
Prove this a prosp'rous day, the three-nook'd world
Shall bear the olive freely.

                    Enter A Messenger

MESSENGER   Antony
Is come into the field.

CAESAR   Go charge Agrippa
Plant those that have revolted in the van,
That Antony may seem to spend his fury
Upon himself.

                          Exit all but Enobarbus

ENOBARBUS   Alexas did revolt and went to Jewry on
Affairs of Antony; there did dissuade
Great Herod to incline himself to Caesar
And leave his master Antony. For this pains
Casaer hath hang'd him. Canidius and the rest
That fell away have entertainment, but

No honourable trust. I have done ill,
Of which I do accuse myself so sorely
That I will joy no more.

Enter a Soldier of Caesar's

SOLDIER   Enobarbus, Antony
Hath after thee sent all thy treasure, with
His bounty overplus. The messenger
Came on my guard, and at thy tent is now
Unloading of his mules.
ENOBARBUS   I give it you.
SOLDIER   Mock not, Enobarbus.
I tell you true. Best you saf'd the bringer
Out of the host. I must attend mine office,
Or would have done't myself. Your emperor
Continues still a Jove.

Exit

ENOBARBUS   I am alone the villain of the earth,
And feel I am so most. O Antony,
Thou mine of bounty, how wouldst thou have paid
My better service, when my turpitude
Thou dost so crown with gold! This blows my heart.
If swift thought break it not, a swifter mean
Shall outstrike thought; but thought will do't, I feel.
I fight against thee? No! I will go seek
Some ditch wherein to die; the foul'st best fits
My latter part of life.

Exeunt

SCENE VII—Field of battle between the camps

Alarum. Drums and trumpets. Enter Agrippa and others

AGRIPPA   Retire. We have engag'd ourselves too far.
Caesar himself has work, and our oppression
Exceeds what we expected.

Exit Agrippa

Alarums. Enter Antony, and Scarus wounded

SCARUS   O my brave Emperor, this is fought indeed!
Had we done so at first, we had droven them home
With clouts about their heads.
ANTONY   Thou bleed'st apace.
SCARUS   I had a wound here that was like a T,

But now 'tis made an H. [*sound retreat, far off*]

ANTONY   They do retire.

SCARUS   We'll beat'em into bench-holes. I have yet
   Room for six scotches more.

Enter Eros

EROS   They are beaten, Sir, and our advantage serves
   For a fair victory.

SCARUS   Let us score their backs
   And snatch 'em up, as we take hares, behind.
   'Tis sport to maul a runner.

ANTONY   I will reward thee
   Once for thy sprightly comfort, and tenfold
   For thy good valour. Come thee on.

SCARUS   I'll halt after.

Exeunt

SCENE VIII—Under the walls of Alexandria
Alarum. Enter Antony again in a march; Scarus with others

ANTONY   We have beat him to his camp. Run one before
   And let the Queen know of our gests. [*Exit a Soldier*] Tomorrow,
   Before the sun shall see's, we'll spill the blood
   That has today escap'd. I thank you all;
   For doughty-handed are you, and have fought
   Not as you serv'd the cause, but as't had been
   Each man's like mine; you have shown all Hectors.
   Enter the city, clip your wives, your friends,
   Tell them your feats; whilst they with joyful tears
   Wash the congealment from your wounds and kiss
   The honour'd gashes whole.

Enter Cleopatra, attended
[*to Scarus*] Give me thy hand—

   To this great fairy I'll commend thy acts,
   Make her thanks bless thee. [*to Cleopatra*] O thou day o' th' world,
   Chain mine arm'd neck. Leap thou, attire and all,
   Through proof of harness to my heart, and there
   Ride on the pants triumphing. [*They embrace*]

CLEOPATRA   Lord of lords!
   O infinite virtue, com'st thou smiling from
   The world's great snare uncaught?

ANTONY   Mine nightingale,

We have beat them to their beds. What, girl! though grey
Do something mingle with our younger brown, yet ha' we
A brain that nourishes our nerves, and can
Get goal for goal of youth. Behold this man;
Commend unto his lips thy favouring hand—
Kiss it, my warrior—he hath fought today
As if a god in hate of mankind had
Destroyed in such a shape.

CLEOPATRA   I'll give thee, friend,
An armour all of gold; it was a king's.

ANTONY   He has deserv'd it, were it carbuncled
Like holy Phoebus' car. Give me thy hand.
Through Alexandria make a jolly march;
Bear our hack'd targets like the men that owe them.
Had our great palace the capacity
To camp this host, we all would sup together,
And drink carouses to the next day's fate,
Which promises royal peril. Trumpeters,
With brazen din blast you the city's ear;
Make mingle with our rattling tabourines,
That heaven and earth may strike their sounds together
Applauding our approach. [*Trumpets sound*]

Exeunt

SCENE IX—Caesar's camp
Enter a Centurion and his company; Enobarbus follows

CENTURION   If we be not reliev'd within this hour,
We must return to th' court of Guard. The night
Is shiny, and they say we shall embattle
By th' second hour i' th' morn.

FIRST WATCH   This last day was
A shrewd one to's.

ENOBARBUS   O, bear me witness, night—

SECOND WATCH   What man is this?

FIRST WATCH   Stand close and list him. [*They stand aside*]

ENOBARBUS   Be witness to me, O thou blessed moon,
When men revolted shall upon record
Bear hateful memory, poor Enobarbus did
Before thy face repent!

CENTURION   Enobarbus?
SECOND WATCH   Peace! Hark further.
ENOBARBUS   O sovereign mistress of true melancholy,
   The poisonous damp of night disponge upon me,
   That life, a very rebel to my will,
   May hang no longer on me. Throw my heart
   Against the flint and hardness of my fault,
   Which, being dried with grief, will break to powder,
   And finish all foul thoughts. O Antony,
   Nobler than my revolt is infamous,
   Forgive me in thine own particular,
   But let the world rank me in register
   A master-leaver and a fugitive!
   O Antony! O Antony! [He dies]
FIRST WATCH   Let's speak to him.
CENTURION   Let's hear him, for the things he speaks
   May concern Caesar.
SECOND WATCH   Let's do so. But he sleeps.
CENTURION   Swoons rather; for so bad a prayer as his
   Was never yet for sleep.
FIRST WATCH   Go we to him.
SECOND WATCH   Awake, Sir, awake; speak to us.
FIRST WATCH   Hear you, Sir?
CENTURION   The hand of death hath raught him. [Drums afar off]
   Hark! the drums demurely wake the sleepers.
   Let us bear him to th' court of guard;
   He is of note. Our hour Is fully out.
SECOND WATCH   Come on, then; he may recover yet.
                         Exeunt with the body

SCENE X—Between the two camps
Enter Antony and Scarus, with their army
ANTONY   Their preparation is today by sea;
   We please them not by land.
SCARUS   For both, my lord.
ANTONY   I would they'd fight i' th' fire or i' th' air;
   We'd fight there too. But this it is, our foot
   Upon the hills adjoining to the city
   Shall stay with us—Order for sea is given;
   They have put forth the haven—

Where their appointment we may best discover
And look on their endeavour.

Exeunt

SCENE XI—Between the camps
Enter Caesar and his army

CAESAR   But being charg'd, we will be still by land,
Which, as I take't, we shall; for his best force
Is forth to man his galleys. To the vales,
And hold our best advantage.

Exeunt

SCENE XII—A hill near Alexandria
Enter Antony and Scarus

ANTONY   Yet they are not join'd. Where yond pine does stand
I shall discover all. I'll bring thee word
Straight how 'tis like to go.

Exit Antony

Alarum afar off, as at a sea fight

SCARUS   Swallows have built
In Cleopatra's sails their nests. The augurers
Say they know not, they cannot tell; look grimly,
And dare not speak their knowledge. Antony
Is valiant and dejected; and by starts
His fretted fortunes give him hope and fear
Of what he has and has not.

Enter Antony

ANTONY   All is lost!
This foul Egyptian hath betrayed me.
My fleet hath yielded to the foe, and yonder
They cast their caps up and carouse together
Like friends long lost. Triple-turn'd whore! 'tis thou
Hast sold me to this novice; and my heart
Makes only wars on thee. Bid them all fly;
For when I am reveng'd upon my charm,
I have done all. Bid them all fly; begone.   [*Exit Scarus*]
O sun, thy uprise shall I see no more!
Fortune and Antony part here; even here
Do we shake hands. All come to this? The hearts
That spaniel'd me at heels, to whom I gave

Their wishes, do discandy, melt their sweets
On blossoming Caesar; and this pine is bark'd
That overtopp'd them all. Betray'd I am.
O this false soul of Egypt! this grave charm—
Whose eye beck'd forth my wars and call'd them home,
Whose bosom was my crownet, my chief end—
Like a right gypsy hath at fast and loose
Beguil'd me to the very heart of loss.
What, Eros, Eros!
                    Enter Cleopatra
                    Ah, thou spell! Avaunt!
CLEOPATRA   Why is my lord enrag'd against his love?
ANTONY   Vanish, or I shall give thee thy deserving
And blemish Caesar's triumph. Let him take thee
And hoist thee up to the shouting plebeians;
Follow his chariot, like the greatest spot
Of all thy sex; most monster-like, be shown
For poor'st diminutives, for doits, and let
Patient Octavia plough thy visage up
With her prepared nails. [*Exit Cleopatra*] 'Tis well th'art gone,
If it be well to live; but better 'twere
Thou fell'st into my fury, for one death
Might have prevented many. Eros, ho!
The shirt of Nessus is upon me; teach me,
Alcides, thou mine ancestor, thy rage;
Let me lodge Lichas on the horns o' th' moon,
And with those hands that grasp'd the heaviest club
Subdue my worthiest self. The witch shall die.
To the young Roman boy she hath sold me, and I fall
Under this plot. She dies for't. Eros, ho!
                                                    Exeunt

              SCENE XIII—Alexandria. Cleopatra's palace
              Enter Cleopatra, Charmian, Iras, and Mardian
CLEOPATRA   Help me, my women. O, he is more mad
Than Telamon for his shield; the boar of Thessaly
Was never so emboss'd.
CHARMIAN   To th'monument!
There lock yourself, and send him word you are dead.
The soul and body rive not more in parting

Than greatness going off.

CLEOPATRA   To th' monument!
Mardian, go tell him I have slain myself;
Say that the last I spoke was "Antony"
And word it, prithee, piteously. Hence, Mardian,
And bring me how he takes my death. To th' monument!

Exeunt

SCENE XIV—Cleopatra's palace
Enter Antony and Eros

ANTONY   Eros, thou yet behold'st me?
EROS   Ay, noble lord.
ANTONY   Sometime we see a cloud that's dragonish;
A vapour sometime like a bear or lion,
A tower'd citadel, a pendent rock,
A forked mountain, or blue promontory
With trees upon't that nod unto the world
And mock our eyes with air. Thou hast seen these signs;
They are black vesper's pageants.
EROS   Ay, my lord.
ANTONY   That which is now a horse, even with a thought
The rack dislimns, and makes it indistinct,
As water is in water.
EROS   It does, my lord.
ANTONY   My good knave Eros, now thy captain is
Even such a body. Here I am Antony;
Yet cannot hold this visible shape, my knave.
I made these wars for Egypt; and the Queen—
Whose heart I thought I had, for she had mine,
Which, whilst it was mine, had annex'd unto't
A million more, now lost—she, Eros, has
Pack'd cards with Caesar, and false-play'd my glory
Unto an enemy's triumph.
Nay, weep not, gentle Eros; there is left us
Ourselves to end ourselves.

Enter Mardian
                    O, thy vile lady!
She has robb'd me of my sword.
MARDIAN   No, Antony;
My mistress lov'd thee, and her fortunes mingled

    With thine entirely.

ANTONY   Hence, saucy eunuch; peace!
    She hath betray'd me, and shall die the death.

MARDIAN   Death of one person can be paid but once,
    And that she has discharg'd. What thou wouldst do
    Is done unto thy hand. The last she spake
    Was "Antony! most noble Antony!"
    Then in the midst a tearing groan did break
    The name of Antony; it was divided
    Between her heart and lips. She rend'red life,
    Thy name so buried in her.

ANTONY   Dead then?

MARDIAN   Dead.

ANTONY   Unarm, Eros; the long day's task is done,
    And we must sleep. That thou depart'st hence safe
    Does pay thy labour richly. Go.   [Exit Mardian]
                     Off, pluck off! [Eros unarms him]
    The sevenfold shield of Ajax cannot keep
    The battery from my heart. O, cleave, my sides!
    Heart, once be stronger than thy continent,
    Crack thy frail case. Apace, Eros, apace.—
    No more a soldier. Bruised pieces, go;
    You have been nobly borne.—From me awhile.   [Exit Eros]
    I will o'ertake thee, Cleopatra, and
    Weep for my pardon. So it must be, for now
    All length is torture. Since the torch is out,
    Lie down, and stray no farther. Now all labour
    Mars what it does; yea, very force entangles
    Itself with strength. Seal then, and all is done.
    Eros!—I come, my queen.—Eros!—Stay for me;
    Where souls do couch on flowers, we'll hand in hand,
    And with our sprightly port make the ghosts gaze.
    Dido and her Aeneas shall want troops,
    And all the haunt be ours.—Come, Eros, Eros!

                        Enter Eros

EROS   What would my lord?

ANTONY   Since Cleopatra died,
    I have liv'd in such dishonour that the gods
    Detest my baseness. I, that with my sword
    Quarter'd the world, and o'er green Neptune's back

With ships made cities, condemn myself to lack
The courage of a woman; less noble mind
Than she which by her death our Caesar tells
"I am conqueror of myself." Thou art sworn, Eros,
That, when the exigent should come—which now
Is come indeed—when I should see behind me
Th' inevitable prosecution of
Disgrace and horror, that, on my command,
Thou then wouldst kill me. Do't; the time is come.
Thou strik'st not me; 'tis Caesar thou defeat'st.
Put colour in thy cheek.
EROS   The gods withhold me!
Shall I do that which all the Parthian darts,
Though enemy, lost aim and could not?
ANTONY   Eros,
Wouldst thou be window'd in great Rome and see
Thy master thus with pleach'd arms, bending down
His corrigible neck, his face subdu'd
To penetrative shame, whilst the wheel'd seat
Of fortunate Caesar, drawn before him, branded
His baseness that ensued?
EROS   I would not see't.
ANTONY   Come, then; for with a wound I must be cur'd.
Draw that thy honest sword, which thou hast worn
Most useful for thy country.
EROS   O, Sir, pardon me!
ANTONY   When I did make thee free, swor'st thou not then
To do this when I bade thee? Do it at once,
Or thy precedent services are all
But accidents unpurpos'd. Draw, and come.
EROS   Turn from me then that noble countenance,
Wherein the worship of the whole world lies.
ANTONY   Lo thee! [He turns away]
EROS   My sword is drawn.
ANTONY   Then let it do at once
The thing why thou hast drawn it.
EROS   My dear master,
My captain and my emperor, let me say,
Before I strike this bloody stroke, farewell.
ANTONY   'Tis said, man; and farewell.

EROS   Farewell, great chief. Shall I strike now?
ANTONY   Now, Eros.
EROS   Why, there then! Thus do I escape the sorrow
    Of Antony's death. [*He kills himself*]
ANTONY   Thrice nobler than myself!
    Thou teachest me, O valiant Eros, what
    I should, and thou couldst not. My queen and Eros
    Have, by their brave instruction, got upon me
    A nobleness in record. But I will be
    A bridegroom in my death, and run into't
    As to a lover's bed. Come, then; and, Eros,
    Thy master dies thy scholar. To do thus
    I learn'd of thee. [*He falls on his sword*]
                        How? not dead? not dead?—
    The guard, ho! O, dispatch me!
                Enter Dercetas and others of a Guard
FIRST GUARD   What's the noise?
ANTONY   I have done my work ill, friends. O, make an end
    Of what I have begun.
SECOND GUARD   The star is fall'n.
FIRST GUARD   And time is at his period.
ALL   Alas, and woe!
ANTONY   Let him that loves me, strike me dead.
FIRST GUARD   Not I.
SECOND GUARD   Nor I.
THIRD GUARD   Nor any one.
                                        Exit Guard
DERCETAS   Thy death and fortunes bid thy followers fly.
    This sword but shown to Caesar, with this tidings,
    Shall enter me with him.
                    Enter Diomedes
DIOMEDES   Where's Antony?
DERCETAS   There, Diomed, there.
DIOMEDES   Lives he? Wilt thou not answer, man?   [*Exit Dercetas*]
ANTONY   Art thou there, Diomed? Draw thy sword and give me
    Sufficing strokes for death.
DIOMEDES   Most absolute lord,
    My mistress Cleopatra sent me to thee.
ANTONY   When did she send thee?
DIOMEDES   Now, my lord.

ANTONY   Where is she?

DIOMEDES   Lock'd in her monument. She had a prophesying fear
    Of what hath come to pass; for when she saw—
    Which never shall be found—you did suspect
    She had dispos'd with Caesar, and that your rage
    Would not be purg'd, she sent you word she was dead;
    But fearing since how it might work, hath sent
    Me to proclaim the truth; and I am come,
    I dread, too late.

ANTONY   Too late, good Diomed. Call my guard, I prithee.

DIOMEDES   What, ho! the Emperor's guard! The guard, what ho!
    Come, your lord calls!

Enter four or five of the guard of Antony

ANTONY   Bear me, good friends, where Cleopatra bides;
    'Tis the last service that I shall command you.

FIRST GUARD   Woe, woe are we, Sir, you may not live to wear
    All your true followers out.

ALL   Most heavy day!

ANTONY   Nay, good my fellows, do not please sharp fate
    To grace it with your sorrows. Bid that welcome
    Which comes to punish us, and we punish it,
    Seeming to bear it lightly. Take me up.
    I have led you oft; carry me now, good friends,
    And have my thanks for all.

Exeunt, hearing Antony and Eros

SCENE XV—Alexandria. A monument
Enter Cleopatra and her maids, aloft, with Charmian and Iras

CLEOPATRA   O Charmian, I will never go from hence!

CHARMIAN   Be comforted, dear madam.

CLEOPATRA   No, I will not.
    All strange and terrible events are welcome,
    But comforts we despise; our size of sorrow,
    Proportion'd to our cause, must be as great
    As that which makes it.

Enter Diomedes, below
           How now! Is he dead?

DIOMEDES   His death's upon him, but not dead.
    Look out o' th' other side your monument;
    His guard have brought him thither.

Enter, below, Antony, borne by the Guard

CLEOPATRA   O sun,
    Burn the great sphere thou mov'st in! Darkling stand
    The varying shore o' th' world. O Antony,
    Antony, Antony! Help, Charmian; help, Iras, help;
    Help, friends below! Let's draw him hither.

ANTONY   Peace!
    Not Caesar's valour hath o'erthrown Antony,
    But Antony's hath triumph'd on itself.

CLEOPATRA   So it should be, that none but Antony
    Should conquer Antony; but woe 'tis so!

ANTONY   I am dying, Egypt, dying; only
    I here importune death awhile, until
    Of many thousand kisses the poor last
    I lay upon thy lips.

CLEOPATRA   I dare not, dear.
    Dear my lord, pardon! I dare not,
    Lest I be taken. Not th' imperious show
    Of the full-fortun'd Caesar ever shall
    Be brooch'd with me. If knife, drugs, serpents, have
    Edge, sting, or operation, I am safe.
    Your wife Octavia, with her modest eyes
    And still conclusion, shall acquire no honour
    Demuring upon me. But come, come, Antony—
    Help me, my women—we must draw thee up;
    Assist, good friends.

ANTONY   O, quick, or I am gone.   [*They begin lifing*]

CLEOPATRA   Here's sport indeed! How heavy weighs my lord!
    Our strength is all gone into heaviness;
    That makes the weight. Had I great Juno's power,
    The strong-wing'd Mercury should fetch thee up,
    And set thee by Jove's side. Yet come a little.
    Wishers were ever fools. O come, come,
           They heave Antony aloft to Cleopatra
    And welcome, welcome! Die where thou hast liv'd.
    Quicken with kissing. Had my lips that power,
    Thus would I wear them out. [*She kisses him*]

ALL   A heavy sight!

ANTONY   I am dying, Egypt, dying.
    Give me some wine, and let me speak a little.

CLEOPATRA   No, let me speak; and let me rail so high
    That the false hussy Fortune break her wheel,
    Provok'd by my offence.
ANTONY   One word, sweet queen:
    Of Caesar seek your honour, with your safety. O!
CLEOPATRA   They do not go together.
ANTONY   Gentle, hear me:
    None about Caesar trust but Proculeius.
CLEOPATRA   My resolution and my hands I'll trust;
    None about Caesar
ANTONY   The miserable change now at my end
    Lament nor sorrow at; but please your thoughts
    In feeding them with those my former fortunes
    Wherein I liv'd the greatest prince o' th' world,
    The noblest; and do now not basely die,
    Not cowardly put off my helmet to
    My countryman—a Roman by a Roman
    Valiantly vanquish'd. Now my spirit is going
    I can no more.
CLEOPATRA   Noblest of men, woo't die?
    Hast thou no care of me? Shall I abide
    In this dull world, which in thy absence is
    No better than a sty? [*Antony dies*] O, see, my women,
    The crown o' th' earth doth melt. My lord!
    O, wither'd is the garland of the war,
    The soldier's pole is fall'n! Young boys and girls
    Are level now with men. The odds is gone,
    And there is nothing left remarkable
    Beneath the visiting moon. [*She faints*]
CHARMIAN   O, quietness, lady!
IRAS   She's dead too, our sovereign.
CHARMIAN   Lady!
IRAS   Madam!
CHARMIAN   O madam, madam, madam!
IRAS   Royal Egypt, Empress! [*Cleopatra stirs*]
CHARMIAN   Peace, peace, Iras!
CLEOPATRA   No more but e'en a woman, and commanded
    By such poor passion as the maid that milks
    And does the meanest chores. It were for me
    To throw my sceptre at the injurious gods;

To tell them that this world did equal theirs
Till they had stol'n our jewel. All's but nought;
Patience is sottish, and impatience does
Become a dog that's mad. Then is it sin
To rush into the secret house of death
Ere death dare come to us? How do you, women?
What, what! good cheer! Why, how now, Charmian!
My noble girls! Ah, women, women, look,
Our lamp is spent, it's out! Good sirs, take heart.
We'll bury him; and then, what's brave, what's noble,
Let's do it after the high Roman fashion,
And make death proud to take us. Come, away;
This case of that huge spirit now is cold.
Ah, women, women! Come; we have no friend
But resolution and the briefest end.

Exeunt; bearing off Antony's body

ACT V

SCENE I—Alexandria. Caesar's camp
Enter Caesar, Agrippa, Dolabella, Mæcenas, Gallus, Proculeius,
and others, with his Council of War

CAESAR   Go to him, Dolabella, bid him yield;
  Being so frustrate, tell him he mocks
  The pauses that he makes.

DOLABELLA   Caesar, I shall

                                                Exit Dolabella

        Enter Dercetas, with the sword of Antony

CAESAR   Wherefore is that? And what art thou that dar'st
  Appear thus to us?

DERCETAS   I am call'd Dercetas;
  Mark Antony I serv'd, who best was worthy
  Best to be serv'd. Whilst he stood up and spoke,
  He was my master, and I wore my life
  To spend upon his haters. If thou please
  To take me to thee, as I was to him
  I'll be to Caesar; if thou pleasest not,
  I yield thee up my life.

CAESAR   What is't thou say'st?

DERCETAS   I say, O Caesar, Antony is dead.

CAESAR   The breaking of so great a thing should make
  A greater crack. The rivèd world
  Should have shook lions into civil streets,
  And citizens to their dens. The death of Antony
  Is not a single doom; in the name lay
  A moiety of the world.

DERCETAS   He is dead, Caesar,
  Not by a public minister of justice,
  Nor by a hired knife; but that self hand
  Which writ his honour in the acts it did

Hath, with the courage which the heart did lend it,
Splitted the heart. This is his sword;
I robb'd his wound of it; behold it stain'd
With his most noble blood.

CAESAR   [*weeping*]   Look you, sad friends,
The gods rebuke me, but it is tidings
To wash the eyes of kings.

AGRIPPA   And strange it is
That nature must compel us to lament
Our most persisted deeds.

MÆCENAS   His taints and honours
Wag'd equal with him.

AGRIPPA   A rarer spirit never
Did steer humanity. But you gods will give us
Some faults to make us men. Caesar is touch'd.

MÆCENAS   When such a spacious mirror's set before him,
He needs must see himself.

CAESAR   O Antony,
I have follow'd thee to this! But we do lance
Diseases in our bodies. I must perforce
Have shown to thee such a declining day
Or look on thine; we could not stall together
In the whole world. But yet let me lament,
With tears as sovereign as the blood of hearts,
That thou, my brother, my competitor
In top of all design, my mate in empire,
Friend and companion in the front of war,
The arm of mine own body, and the heart
Where mine his thoughts did kindle—that our stars,
Unreconciliable, should divide
Our equalness to this. Hear me, good friends—
                    Enter an Egyptian
But I will tell you at some meeter season.
The business of this man looks out of him;
We'll hear him what he says. Whence are you?

EGYPTIAN   A poor Egyptian, yet the Queen, my mistress,
Confin'd in all she has, her monument,
Of thy intents desires instruction,
That she preparedly may frame herself
To th' way she's forc'd to.

CAESAR Bid her have good heart.
  She soon shall know of us, by some of ours,
  How honourable and how kindly we
  Determine for her; for Caesar cannot learn
  To be ungentle.
EGYPTIAN So the gods preserve thee!

Exit Egyptian

CAESAR Come hither, Proculeius. Go and say
  We purpose her no shame. Give her what comforts
  The quality of her passion shall require,
  Lest, in her greatness, by some mortal stroke
  She do defeat us; for her life in Rome
  Would be eternal in our triumph. Go,
  And with your speediest bring us what she says,
  And how you find her.
PROCULEIUS Caesar, I shall.

Exit Proculeius

CAESAR Gallus, go you along. [*Exit Gallus*] Where's Dolabella,
  To second Proculeius?
ALL Dolabella!
CAESAR Let him alone, for I remember now
  How he's employ'd; he shall in time be ready.
  Go with me to my tent, where you shall see
  How hardly I was drawn into this war,
  How calm and gentle I proceeded still
  In all my writings. Go with me, and see
  What I can show in this.

Exeunt

SCENE II—Alexandria. The monument
Enter Cleopatra, Charmian, Iras, and Mardian
CLEOPATRA My desolation does begin to make
  A better life. 'Tis paltry to be Caesar:
  Not being Fortune, he's but Fortune's knave,
  A minister of her will; and it is great
  To do that thing that ends all other deeds,
  Which shackles accidents and bolts up change,
  Which sleeps, and never palates more the dung,
  The beggar's nurse and Caesar's.
Enter, to the gates of the monument, Proculeius, Gallus, and Soldiers

PROCULEIUS   Caesar sends greetings to the Queen of Egypt,
   And bids thee study on what fair demands
   Thou mean'st to have him grant thee.
CLEOPATRA   What's thy name?
PROCULEIUS   My name is Proculeius.
CLEOPATRA   Antony
   Did tell me of you, bade me trust you; but
   I do not greatly care to be deceiv'd,
   That have no use for trusting. If your master
   Would have a queen his beggar, you must tell him
   That majesty, to keep decorum, must
   No less beg than a kingdom. If he please
   To give me conquer'd Egypt for my son,
   He gives me so much of mine own as I
   Will kneel to him with thanks.
PROCULEIUS   Be of good cheer;
   Y'are fall'n into a princely hand; fear nothing.
   Make your full reference freely to my lord,
   Who is so full of grace that it flows over
   On all that need. Let me report to him
   Your sweet dependency, and you shall find
   A conqueror that will pray in aid for kindness
   Where he for grace is kneel'd to.
CLEOPATRA   Pray you tell him
   I am his fortune's vassal and I send him
   The greatness he has got. I hourly learn
   A doctrine of obedience, and would gladly
   Look him i' th' face.
PROCULEIUS   This I'll report, dear lady.
   Have comfort, for I know your plight is pitied
   Of him that caus'd it.

   Proculeius, with Gallus and two of the guard ascend the monument
      by a ladder placed against a window, and come behind

Gallus   You see how easily she may be surpris'd.
      Some of the guard unbar and open the gates
   [*to the Soldiers*] Guard her till Caesar come.
IRAS   Royal Queen!
CHARMIAN   O Cleopatra! thou art taken, Queen!
CLEOPATRA   Quick, quick, good hands. [*Drawing a dagger*]
PROCULEIUS   [*He disarms her*] Hold, worthy lady, hold,

Do not yourself such wrong, who are in this
Reliev'd, but not betray'd.

CLEOPATRA   What, of death too,
That rids our dogs of languish?

PROCULEIUS   Cleopatra,
Do not abuse my master's bounty by
Th' undoing of yourself. Let the world see
His nobleness well acted, which your death
Will never let come forth.

CLEOPATRA   Where art thou, death?
Come hither, come! Come, come, and take a queen
Worth many babes and beggars!

PROCULEIUS   O, temperance, lady!

CLEOPATRA   Sir, I will eat no meat; I'll not drink, Sir;
If idle talk will once be necessary,
I'll not sleep neither. This mortal house I'll ruin,
Do Caesar what he can. Know, Sir, that I
Will not wait pinion'd at your master's court,
Nor once be chastis'd with the sober eye
Of dull Octavia. Shall they hoist me up,
And show me to the shouting varletry
Of censuring Rome? Rather a ditch in Egypt
Be gentle grave unto me! Rather on Nilus' mud
Lay me stark-nak'd, and let the water-flies
Blow me into abhorring! Rather make
My country's high pyramides my gibbet,
And hang me up in chains!

PROCULEIUS   You do extend
These thoughts of horror further than you shall
Find cause in Caesar.

Enter Dolabella

DOLABELLA   Proculeius,
What thou hast done thy master Caesar knows,
And he hath sent for thee. For the Queen,
I'll take her to my guard.

PROCULEIUS   So, Dolabella,
It shall content me best. Be gentle to her.
[*to Cleopatra*] To Caesar I will speak what you shall please,
If you'll employ me to him.

CLEOPATRA   Say I would die.

Exit Proculeius and Soldiers

DOLABELLA   Most noble Empress, you have heard of me?

CLEOPATRA   I cannot tell.

DOLABELLA   Assuredly you know me.

CLEOPATRA   No matter, Sir, what I have heard or known.
    You laugh when boys or women tell their dreams;
    Is't not your trick?

DOLABELLA   I understand not, madam.

CLEOPATRA   I dreamt there was an Emperor Antony—
    O, such another sleep, that I might see
    But such another man!

DOLABELLA   If it might please ye—

CLEOPATRA   His face was as the heav'ns, and therein stuck
    A sun and moon, which kept their course and lighted
    The little O, the earth.

DOLABELLA   Most sovereign creature—

CLEOPATRA   His legs bestrid the ocean; his rear'd arm
    Crested the world. His voice was propertied
    As all the tuned spheres, and that to friends;
    But when he meant to quail and shake the orb,
    He was as rattling thunder. For his bounty,
    There was no winter in't; an autumn 'twas
    That grew the more by reaping. His delights
    Were dolphin-like: they show'd his back above
    The element they liv'd in. In his livery
    Walk'd crowns and crownets; realms and islands were
    As plates dropp'd from his pocket.

DOLABELLA   Cleopatra—

CLEOPATRA   Think you there was or might be such a man
    As this I dreamt of?

DOLABELLA   Gentle madam, no.

CLEOPATRA   You lie, up to the hearing of the gods.
    But if there be nor ever were one such,
    It's past the size of dreaming. Nature wants stuff
    To vie strange forms with fancy; yet t' imagine
    An Antony were nature's piece 'gainst fancy,
    Condemning shadows quite.

DOLABELLA   Hear me, good madam.
    Your loss is, as yourself, great; and you bear it
    As answering to the weight. Would I might never

O'ertake pursu'd success, but I do feel,
By the rebound of yours, a grief that smites
My very heart at root.

CLEOPATRA   I thank you, Sir.
Know you what Caesar means to do with me?

DOLABELLA   I am loath to tell you what I would you knew.

CLEOPATRA   Nay, pray you, Sir.

DOLABELLA   Though he be honourable—

CLEOPATRA   He'll lead me, then, in triumph?

DOLABELLA   Madam, he will. I know't.

          Flourish. Within: "Make way there—Caesar!"
     Enter Caesar; Gallus, Proculeius, Mæcenas, Seleucus,
               and others of his train

CAESAR   Which is the Queen of Egypt?

DOLABELLA   It is the Emperor, madam. [*Cleopatra kneels*]

CAESAR   Arise, you shall not kneel. I pray you, rise; rise, Egypt.

CLEOPATRA   [*rising*] Sir, the gods will have it thus;
My master and my lord I must obey.

CAESAR   Take to you no hard thoughts.
The record of what injuries you did us,
Though written in our flesh, we shall remember
As things but done by chance.

CLEOPATRA   Sole Sir o' th' world,
I cannot project mine own cause so well
To make it clear, but do confess I have
Been laden with like frailties which before
Have often sham'd our sex.

CAESAR   Cleopatra, know
We will extenuate rather than enforce.
If you apply yourself to our intents—
Which towards you are most gentle—you shall find
A benefit in this change; but if you seek
To lay on me a cruelty by taking
Antony's course, you shall bereave yourself
Of my good purposes, and put your children
To that destruction which I'll guard them from,
If thereon you rely. I'll take my leave.

CLEOPATRA   And may, through all the world. 'Tis yours, and we,
Your scutcheons and your signs of conquest, shall
Hang in what place you please. Here, my good lord.

She gives him a scroll

CAESAR   You shall advise me in all for Cleopatra.

CLEOPATRA   This is the brief of money, plate, and jewels,
   I am possess'd of. 'Tis exactly valued,
   Not petty things admitted. Where's Seleucus?

Enter Seleucus

SELEUCUS   Here, madam.

CLEOPATRA   This is my treasurer; let him speak, my lord,
   Upon his peril, that I have reserv'd
   To myself nothing. Speak the truth, Seleucus.

SELEUCUS   Madam, I had rather seal my lips
   Than to my peril speak that which is not.

CLEOPATRA   What have I kept back?

SELEUCUS   Enough to purchase what you have made known.

CAESAR   Nay, blush not, Cleopatra; I approve
   Your wisdom in the deed.

CLEOPATRA   See, Caesar! O, behold,
   How pomp is followed! Mine will now be yours;
   And, should we shift estates, yours would be mine.
   The ingratitude of this Seleucus does
   Even make me wild. O slave, of no more trust

Seleucus retreats from her

   Than love that's hir'd! What, goest thou back? Thou shalt
   Go back, I warrant thee; but I'll catch thine eyes
   Though they had wings. Slave, soulless villain, dog!
   O rarely base!

CAESAR   Good Queen, let us entreat you.

CLEOPATRA   O Caesar, what a wounding shame is this,
   That thou vouchsafing here to visit me,
   Doing the honour of thy lordliness
   To one so meek, that mine own servant should
   Parcel the sum of my disgraces by
   Addition of his envy! Say, good Caesar,
   That I some lady trifles have reserv'd,
   Immoment toys, things of such dignity
   As we greet modern friends withal; and say
   Some nobler token I have kept apart
   For Livia and Octavia, to induce
   Their mediation—must I be unfolded
   With one that I have bred? The gods! It smites me

Beneath the fall I have. [*to Seleucus*] Prithee go hence;
Or I shall show the cinders of my spirits
Through th' ashes of my chance. Wert thou a man,
Thou wouldst have mercy on me.

CAESAR   Forbear, Seleucus.

Exit Seleucus

CLEOPATRA   Be it known that we, the greatest, are misthought
For things that others do; and when we fall
We answer others' merits in our name,
Are therefore to be pitied.

CAESAR   Cleopatra,
Not what you have reserv'd, nor what acknowledg'd,
Put we i' th' roll of conquest. Still be't yours,
Bestow it at your pleasure; and believe
Caesar's no merchant, to make prize with you
Of things that merchants sold. Therefore be cheer'd;
Make not your thoughts your prisons. No, dear Queen;
For we intend so to dispose you as
Yourself shall give us counsel. Feed and sleep.
Our care and pity is so much upon you
That we remain your friend; and so, adieu.

CLEOPATRA   My master and my lord!

CAESAR   Not so. Adieu.

Flourish. Exit Caesar and his train

CLEOPATRA   He words me, girls, he words me, that I should not
Be noble to myself. But hark thee, Charmian!

She whispers to Charmian

IRAS   Finish, good lady; the bright day is done,
And we are for the dark.

CLEOPATRA   [*to Charmian*] Hie thee again.
I have spoke already, and it is provided;
Go put it to the haste.

CHARMIAN   Madam, I will.

Enter Dolabella

DOLABELLA   Where's the Queen?

CHARMIAN   Behold, Sir. [*Exit Charmian*]

CLEOPATRA   Dolabella!

DOLABELLA   Madam, as thereto sworn by your command,
Which my love makes religion to obey,
I tell you this: Caesar through Syria

Intends his journey, and within three days
You with your children will he send before.
Make your best use of this; I have perform'd
Your pleasure and my promise.
CLEOPATRA   Dolabella,
    I shall remain your debtor.
DOLABELLA   I your servant.
    Adieu, good Queen; I must attend on Caesar.
CLEOPATRA   Farewell, and thanks.   [Exit Dolabella]
                              Now, Iras, what think'st thou?
    Thou an Egyptian puppet shall be shown
    In Rome as well as I. Mechanic slaves,
    With greasy aprons, rules, and hammers, shall
    Uplift us to the view; in their thick breaths,
    Rank of gross diet, shall we be enclouded,
    And forc'd to drink their vapour.
IRAS   The gods forbid!
CLEOPATRA   Nay, 'tis most certain, Iras. Saucy lictors
    Will catch at us like strumpets, and scald rhymers
    Ballad us out o' tune; the quick comedians
    Extemporally will stage us, and present
    Our Alexandrian revels; Antony
    Shall be brought drunken forth, and I shall see
    Some squeaking Cleopatra boy my greatness
    I' th' posture of a whore.
IRAS   O the good gods!
CLEOPATRA   Nay, that's certain.
IRAS   I'll never see't, for I am sure mine nails
    Are stronger than mine eyes.
CLEOPATRA   Why, that's the way
    To fool their preparation and to conquer
    Their most absurd intents.
                         Enter Charmian
                          Now, Charmian!
    Show me, my women, like a queen. Go fetch
    My best attires. I am again for Cydnus,
    To meet Mark Antony. Sirrah Iras, go.
    Now, noble Charmian, we'll dispatch indeed;
    And when thou hast done this chare, I'll give thee leave
    To play till doomsday. Bring our crown and all.   [Exit Iras]

A noise within; Enter a Guardsman

Wherefore's this noise?

GUARDSMAN   Here is a rural fellow
That will not be denied your Highness' presence.
He brings you figs.

CLEOPATRA   Let him come in.   [*Exit Guardsman*]
                              What poor an instrument
May do a noble deed! He brings me liberty.
My resolution's plac'd, and I have nothing
Of woman in me. Now from head to foot
I am marble-constant; now the fleeting moon
No planet is of mine.

          Enter Guardsman and Clown, with a basket

GUARDSMAN   This is the man.

CLEOPATRA   Avoid, and leave him.   [*Exit Guardsman*]
                              Hast thou the pretty worm of Nilus there
That kills and pains not?

CLOWN   Truly, I have him. But I would not be the party that should
desire you to touch him, for his biting is immortal; those that do
die of it do seldom or never recover.

CLEOPATRA   Remember'st thou any that have died on't?

CLOWN   Very many, men and women too. I heard of one of them no
longer than yesterday: a very honest woman, but something given
to lie, as a woman should not do but in the way of honesty; how
she died of the biting of it, what pain she felt—truly she makes a
very good report o' th' worm. But he that will believe all that they
say shall never be saved by half that they do. But this is most
falliable, the worm's an odd worm.

CLEOPATRA   Get thee hence; farewell.

CLOWN   I wish you all joy of the worm. [*Hw sets down the basket*]

CLEOPATRA   Farewell.

CLOWN   You must think this, look you, that the worm will do his
kind.

CLEOPATRA   Ay, ay; farewell.

CLOWN   Look you, the worm is not to be trusted but in the keeping
of wise people; for indeed there is no goodness in the worm.

CLEOPATRA   Take thou no care; it shall be heeded.

CLOWN   Very good. Give it nothing, I pray you, for it is not worth the
feeding.

CLEOPATRA   Will it eat me?

CLOWN   You must not think I am so simple but I know the devil himself will not eat a woman. I know that a woman is a dish for the gods, if the devil dress her not. But truly, these same whore-son devils do the gods great harm in their women, for in every ten that they make the devils mar five.

CLEOPATRA   Well, get thee gone; farewell.

CLOWN   Yes, forsooth. I wish you joy o' th' worm.

                                      Exit Clown

          Enter Iras, with a robe, crown, etc.

CLEOPATRA   Give me my robe, put on my crown; I have
Immortal longings in me. Now no more
The juice of Egypt's grape shall moist this lip. [*The women dress her*]
Yare, yare, good Iras; quick. Methinks I hear
Antony call. I see him rouse himself
To praise my noble act. I hear him mock
The luck of Caesar, which the gods give men
To excuse their after wrath. Husband, I come.
Now to that name my courage prove my title!
I am fire and air; my other elements
I give to baser life. So, have you done?
Come then, and take the last warmth of my lips.
Farewell, kind Charmian. Iras, long farewell.

          She kisses them. Iras falls and dies

Have I the aspic in my lips? Dost fall?
If thus thou and nature can so gently part,
The stroke of death is as a lover's pinch,
Which hurts and is desir'd. Dost thou lie still?
If thou vanishest, thou tell'st the world
It is not worth leave-taking.

CHARMIAN   Dissolve, thick cloud, and rain, that I may say
The gods themselves do weep.

CLEOPATRA   This proves me base.
If she first meet the curled Antony,
He'll make demand of her, and spend that kiss
Which is my heaven to have. Come, thou mortal wretch,

          Speaking to an asp, which she applied to her breast

With thy sharp teeth this knot intrinsicate
Of life at once untie. Poor venomous fool,
Be angry and dispatch. O couldst thou speak,

That I might hear thee call great Caesar ass
Unpolicied!
CHARMIAN   O Eastern star!
CLEOPATRA   Peace, peace!
Dost thou not see my baby at my breast
That sucks the nurse asleep?
CHARMIAN   O, break! O, break!
CLEOPATRA   As sweet as balm, as soft as air, as gentle—
O Antony! Nay, I will take thee too:
              She applys another asp to her arm
What should I stay— [*She dies*]
CHARMIAN   In this vile world? So, fare thee well.
Now boast thee, death, in thy possession lies
A lass unparallel'd. Downy windows, close;
And golden Phoebus never be beheld
Of eyes again so royal! Your crown's awry;
I'll mend it and then play—
              Enter the guard, rushing in
FIRST GUARD   Where's the Queen?
CHARMIAN   Speak softly, wake her not.
FIRST GUARD   Caesar hath sent—
CHARMIAN   Too slow a messenger.
              She applies an asp
O, come apace, dispatch. I partly feel thee.
FIRST GUARD   Approach, ho! All's not well: Caesar's beguil'd.
SECOND GUARD   There's Dolabella sent from Caesar; call him.
                              Exit a Guard
FIRST GUARD   What work is here! Charmian, is this well done?
CHARMIAN   It is well done, and fitting for a princess
Descended of so many royal kings.
Ah, soldier! [*She dies*]
              Enter Dolabella
DOLABELLA   How goes it here?
SECOND GUARD   All dead.
DOLABELLA   Caesar, thy thoughts
Touch their effects in this. Thyself art coming
To see perform'd the dreaded act which thou
So sought'st to hinder. [*within: "A way there, a way for Caesar!"*]
              Enter Caesar and all his train, marching
DOLABELLA   O Sir, you are too sure an augurer:

That you did fear is done.

CAESAR   Bravest at the last,
  She levell'd at our purposes, and being royal,
  Took her own way. The manner of their deaths?
  I do not see them bleed.

DOLABELLA   Who was last with them?

FIRST GUARD   A simple countryman that brought her figs.
  This was his basket.

CAESAR   Poison'd then.

FIRST GUARD   O Caesar,
  This Charmian liv'd but now; she stood and spake.
  I found her trimming up the diadem
  On her dead mistress. Tremblingly she stood,
  And on the sudden dropp'd.

CAESAR   O noble weakness!
  If they had swallow'd poison 'twould appear
  By external swelling; but she looks like sleep,
  As she would catch another Antony
  In her strong toil of grace.

DOLABELLA   Here on her breast
  There is a vent of blood, and something blown;
  The like is on her arm.

FIRST GUARD   This is an aspic's trail; and these fig-leaves
  Have slime upon them, such as th' aspic leaves
  Upon the caves of Nile.

CAESAR   Most probable
  That so she died; for her physician tells me
  She hath pursu'd conclusions infinite
  Of easy ways to die. Take up her bed,
  And bear her women from the monument.
  She shall be buried by her Antony;
  No grave upon the earth shall clip in it
  A pair so famous. High events as these
  Strike those that make them; and their story is
  No less in pity than his glory which
  Brought them to be lamented. Our army shall
  In solemn show attend this funeral,
  And then to Rome. Come, Dolabella, see
  High order in this great solemnity.

                    Exeunt omnes, bearing the dead bodies

Keeping with our family tradition of book publishing and manufacturing excellence, The Ann Arbor Media Group and Edwards Brothers, Inc. are proud to bring you this extraordinary classic edition.

Established in 1893, Edwards Brothers, Inc. is a well-respected leader in book manufacturing, recognized the world over for quality and unsurpassed attention to detail.

This edition has been crafted using archival quality natural stock for the interior.

The text font is 11 point Goudy Old Style, designed by United States printer and topographer, Frederic W. Goudy (1865-1947). This serif font was chosen for its strength, beautiful characteristics, and readability.

The finished volume is an outstanding reflection of fine craftsmanship and contemporary technique that this classic work, and your library, deserves.